The cobwebs fluttered over the tops of her boots.

Her nose worked frantically at the air and now the scent drew her eyes up the paneling, into the geometry of pipes and beams. There, suspended from the ceiling, were three oblong-shaped objects larger than she was.

Cocoons, three huge cocoons, Jesus God, it can't be.

The lighter burned her fingers and went out as she leaped back.

Suddenly, somewhere upstairs, a door slammed.

They're here. In the house. Upstairs.

She jumped up, looking around wildly for someplace to hide. She tore blindly toward the walk-in closet and pressed back into Dani's clothes. Something was wrong with the door, it wouldn't close all the way. So she hunkered down and scooted back as far into the closet as she could, covering her knees and legs with a coat that nearly brushed the floor.

And then she waited, the floorboards above her head creaking, the smell moving closer.

Closer.

Also by Alison Drake
Published by Ballantine Books:

TANGO KEY
FEVERED
BLACK MOON

LAGOON

Alison Drake

BALLANTINE BOOKS • NEW YORK

Library of Congress Catalog Card Number: 90-93028

ISBN 0-345-35778-7

Manufactured in the United States of America

First Edition: August 1990

For my husband, Rob,
with love and thanks
for copiloting the story

Special thanks, again,
to my agent, Diane Cleaver,
and my editor, Chris Cox,
for their invaluable suggestions

Part I

PRESENCE

"Today I felt pass over me a breath of wind from the wings of madness."

—CHARLES BAUDELAIRE

"It is possible that we do, after all, live in an amnesic world that is governed by eternal laws. But it is also possible that memory is inherent in nature; and if we find that we are indeed living in such a world, we shall have to give up many of our old habits of thought and adopt new ones; habits that are better adapted to life in a world that is living in the presence of the past—and is also living in the presence of the future, and open to continuing creation."

—RUPERT SHELDRAKE

1

The Blue Inn

A disturbing scent rode the evening breeze and lingered in the air like spice or perfume or some last remnant of summer. And yet it was none of these things. Katie Suffield couldn't figure out exactly what it was or where it was coming from. But it made her uneasy in the same way that the smell of smoke in a dark and crowded theater would.

"What's wrong?" asked Hank, glancing up from his menu.

"I thought I smelled something weird."

"Only thing I smell is food. So what's it going to be, kiddo? Are we health freaks tonight or cholesterolmongers?"

"Mongers." She laughed.

Her stepfather's question and her response were always the same when they were eating out together at the Blue Inn. It was integral to their being alone, as much a part of the ritual as sitting at this particular table at the back corner of the deck, where it jutted out over the lagoon, a tongue of pine and redwood suspended magically above the water on pilings Katie couldn't see. If Hank's girlfriend, Jo, had been along, they would have been sitting close to the sliding glass doors at the front. Jo was afraid of being over the water because she couldn't swim—and suppose the deck crumbled while they were on it? Suppose the railing gave way and she fell·in?

The breeze skipped through the potted plants that separated the tables. Katie caught the strange scent again, then it flitted away, a quick, elusive butterfly escaping the rapidly cooling air. She rubbed her hands over her arms, wishing she'd brought a sweater. But as Hank was forever telling her, the major drawback of being sixteen was that you never planned ahead. The way he usually said this implied that his own memories of being sixteen were as clear as yesterday, which she doubted.

3

His memories, she was sure, went back only as far as the sixties. In some ways, he still lived in that time: his dark hair was long and pulled back into a ponytail; jeans and a work shirt were his favorite clothes; he preferred grass to booze; and he wasn't fond of the so-called "establishment," even though he was part of it.

If biology had never become his passion, they would probably be trying to live off the land in a shack in the sticks somewhere. Hank would be growing his own hybrid strain of pot, something that got you zonked in under five seconds, and he'd be teaching new tricks to the animals he adopted, and she would . . . Well, she didn't know what she would be doing. She supposed that was another drawback of being sixteen. She didn't have the faintest idea what she wanted to do with her life.

Whenever she tried to imagine herself at twenty-one or at thirty, nothing came to mind. Oh, she saw herself as taller than her present five-foot-five, ten pounds thinner than her chunky one-twenty, with eyes that were a deeper blue. Sometimes her long blond hair was short and fluffy, other times it was a mass of electric curls or maybe even a different color. But that had nothing to do with a *profession*. According to Hank, her future was limitless; she could be anything. But what?

"Want my jacket, Kate?" he asked.

"Yeah, thanks. It's kind of chilly for August, don't you think?"

Hank nodded and gazed out at the lagoon, as if the chill had originated in the center of it. "Weather everywhere seems to be going through changes." He passed her the jacket and she shrugged it on.

"Hey, look at that." He stood and leaned on the railing, pointing directly below. Katie got up to take a look. A long, thin snake twisted across the surface of the water, its glossy back gleaming in the last of the light.

"Gross," she muttered. "What kind of snake is it?"

"I don't know. It looks more like an eel, but there aren't any in the lagoon."

As they bent closer for a better look, the snake suddenly coiled and sprang at them. It lifted four or five inches out of the water, needle-thin, eyes glistening like wet rubies. They both leaped back from the railing. "Jesus," Hank whispered.

He glanced at the water again but didn't touch the railing. Katie, her heart still careening in her chest, tugged on Hank's shirt.

"C'mon, don't get so close."

"No way in hell it could jump this high, Kate. Don't worry." They watched it twist through the wheat-colored weeds toward shore. When it vanished, Hank sat down, checked the time, and jotted something in the notepad he removed from his pocket. "I don't want you swimming in here for a while."

She hated the way her laughter sounded, nervous and afraid, the laugh of a kid. "Like you need to tell me." She took one last look at the water, the shoreline, the dwindling light tipping the weeds. "What're you writing?"

"Date, time, what we saw."

"Why?"

His dark eyes crinkled with amusement—and a secret pleasure that she'd asked. He gave her his full attention, something that hadn't happened much since Jo had moved in with them six months ago. "It might be important. What good is a biologist if he doesn't remember the things he observes?"

"But what's the snake going to tell you?"

Hank's brows furrowed as he laced his long fingers together: his studious look. "Patterns. Everything is part of a pattern. What happened with the snake might be part of an emerging pattern, something new."

"Like cold weather in August."

"Yeah, exactly." He snapped the notepad shut. "When we get home, remind me to show you something Ike and Tina have learned that could be part of a pattern. Maybe the same pattern, I don't know yet."

Ike and Tina were the canaries Hank had rescued from the Hartwell lab, where he worked as a research biologist. "The only trick I've ever seen them do is take a dump in Jo's coffee cup."

Hank chuckled. "Better than that. You'll see."

She was about to ask him to give her a hint, but the breeze shifted just then and she found the scent again. Stronger, darker, menacing. It *nudged* at her. It *tickled*. She looked around, trying to follow it, and saw Ben, the inn owner, on the other side of the sliding glass door, which was open a foot or so.

Katie lifted her hand to wave him over and suddenly realized the dark odor came from him. As he opened the door all the way, the smell rushed toward her, a black wave that stank of closed cellars, cemeteries, of death. Then it crashed over her, stealing her breath, paralyzing her, filling her head with pictures, and she understood what it meant. She wrenched free of it and leaped up, shouting, *"No, Ben, no!"*

Heads snapped their way.

She heard Hank mutter, "C'mon, Katie, what the hell's wrong with you?" But her eyes were on Ben, who hesitated, his mouth moving soundlessly, his eyes blinking fast, as though he were trying to clear his vision. For just a second, their gazes locked, and he frowned, as if he were trying to remember who she was. Then his lips drew away from his teeth in a grin that glowed like an early moon, a white, hideous grin, barely human, a grin she would remember the rest of her life. He whipped something out of his jacket, spun away from them, to the left, and sprayed bullets across the deck, cutting a path of blood and death through the crowd.

The chatter of the machine gun echoed out across the water, startling birds from trees, nearly drowning out the screams that tore the air as people ran, stumbled, twitched, fell. Time screeched into slow motion; visions of carnage filled Katie's head, thick as a poisonous gas. Blood splattered everywhere. She couldn't move, couldn't pull air into her lungs, couldn't take her eyes off Ben, Ben and the gun, Ben as he continued to turn, a deadly soldier on a lazy Susan.

Seconds before they would have been in the direct line of fire, Hank yanked her back, lifted her like she weighed nothing at all, and hurled her and himself over the railing into the lagoon where the snake had been swimming minutes ago.

She screamed. She dropped like a stone through the dark waters, weighted by her clothes, her shoes. She swallowed a ton of water—it had to be a ton; she felt it filling her lungs, inflating them, and knew she was going to die.

Her sneakers sank into the muck on the bottom, weeds tangled around her ankles, the screams on deck echoed with utter clarity. Katie swam frantically toward the surface, her lungs threatening to burst. When her head popped free, she coughed and sputtered and gulped at the air. Gunfire, more gunfire, echoed across the lagoon, covering it like an invisible mist.

She dived, tore off her sneakers, and swam madly toward the area under the deck, where she would be safer. Hank found her, clutched her hand, pulled her into the air again and back under the deck as far as they could go. They pressed against weeds, rocks, moss. Katie clung to him, her eyes squeezed shut against the screams and another burst of gunfire that swallowed every other sound.

Things moved and splashed in the water around them. Something slithered past her leg. People struck the deck overhead. She opened her eyes and, through the spaces between the deck's planks, saw the dark shapes of fallen bodies. Blood oozed between slats several feet in front of her. Waves of dark smells rippled through the air. She buried her face against Hank's chest, seeking the comforting scent of his shirt, a scent she could follow, a scent that would sweep her away from the blackness. Chilled and terrified, she trembled against him, certain that in the next second or the next Ben would spray bullets through the floor of the deck, the snake would find them, they would die as they were meant to die before they'd leaped.

But there were no snakes and no more shots. The screaming stopped.

The only sound was the steady *ping ping ping* of blood as it dripped between the planks and struck the water.

2

Fay

As the county mobile medical unit trundled out of the hills, Lagoon appeared way below, varnished in twilight. It looked as lovely and serene as a town on a postcard, thought Fay. Brick and pine buildings, gabled roofs, neat squares of greenery that were parks. And there, three miles east of downtown, the body of water it was named after, just a few miles from South Carolina.

The town was wedged in a narrow funnel of land between two foothills in northeast Georgia. With a population of just under three thousand—which rose to five during the tourist season—it was the largest hamlet in the district and the county seat. The main employer in the region was Hartwell Research, a pharmaceutical company on the South Carolina side of the lagoon. Almost everyone else in town either worked for the county, like Fay, or owned businesses that catered to the tourist industry. Thirty-three miles lay between Lagoon and its nearest neighbor, a separation that was due as much to the terrain as to attitudes. Change did not happen quickly here.

"What was the final count on the eczema cases today?" asked Mona Stawson, who was driving.

Fay glanced down at the clipboard on her lap. They'd seen thirty-two people today, most of them backwoods folks whose ailments ranged from colds to cancer. Out of those, there were five new cases of eczema, which brought the grand total in the last two months to twenty-two. She said as much and Mona let out a soft whistle.

"Maybe it's not eczema."

"Then what is it?"

"Hey, I'm just a nurse, Fay. You're the doc. You tell me." She tapped a pack of Camels against the steering wheel and a cigarette shot halfway out. She put it between her lips and lit it with a kitchen match. "It looks like discoid eczema, it responds to the cortisone cream . . . I don't know. If it isn't eczema, then it's a damn good imitation."

"I'm going to send those scrapings I took today to a friend of mine at the CDC and have him run tests on them."

Mona tapped her bright red nails against the steering wheel; her numerous rings caught the last of the twilight. None of the stones was real, but on Mona's long, delicate hands they could have been sapphires, rubies, diamonds.

She was a striking blonde in her mid-thirties, slender and flashy, the local "bad girl" and proud of it. She'd been born and raised just over the state line, but her voice held no trace of a southern drawl. She'd lost it during the eight years of her marriage, when she'd lived in New York and gone to nursing school. Like Fay, she was divorced, and now lived at the edge of town with a local bush pilot. They had worked together since Fay had taken the Lagoon County physician and coroner's job more than two years ago. If she had any complaint about Mona at all, as a coworker or as a friend, it was her chain-smoking.

Fay rolled her window down halfway to let out the smoke. The van filled with an unseasonal coolness which promised an early fall, but that still smelled of summer. Freshly mown grass, fields flourishing with wildflowers, rivers that ran through the red Georgia clay toward the dark bruise of the hills in the distance. In another month, Labor Day would mark the end of the tourist season, she thought, and then maybe she'd have time to take a couple of weeks off. She needed it. She hadn't had a real vacation since she'd moved here from Atlanta.

"Suppose this eczema business is the beginning of a new epidemic or something?" asked Mona, the alarmist.

Fay laughed and lifted her stockinged feet onto the dash. "I bet you were the worst hypochondriac in your nursing-school class."

"Second-worst." Mona stabbed her cigarette out in the ashtray and downshifted as they rounded the last curve toward town. "My roommate was the worst. When we were studying blood diseases, she was convinced she had leukemia. When we got to the brain, she just knew she had a brain tumor." She scratched at her elbow. "And now I feel like I've got this mutant eczema."

"It's not contagious, Mona."

"Then how come we've seen twenty-two cases of it in eight weeks?"

"I don't know."

Fay suddenly thought of Ben, of the rash she'd noticed on his back four or five months ago. He'd said it was poison ivy he had probably picked up while working around the inn. But it had looked, she realized, like those dry, crusted patches of eczema they'd been seeing.

So what, Fay? What's it prove?

Nothing.

Their affair hadn't fallen apart because she'd commented on a rash, for God's sakes. It had ended because . . . Well, she didn't know why.

For a few minutes, she was back inside his bedroom on that warm evening in mid-March. She could see the curtains billowing in his bedroom, blue sails filling with wind, the ceiling fan turning slowly, the smell of water from the lagoon mixing with the scent of sweat, of sex. She could see her own hands against his back and feel the patch of dry skin under her fingers.

Four months, two weeks, and six days ago: one of the last times they had made love. *But who's counting, Fay? You haven't even seen him in weeks.* There was no event she could pinpoint, no conversation she could recall in which they had discussed the end of the affair. They'd simply seen each other less and less frequently and eventually stopped seeing each other at all. Her pride had prevented her from asking what had happened, but she spent more evenings than she cared to remember speculating about why. Another woman. Business problems. A resurgence of the old grief over the death of his wife three years earlier. In the end, she was left with her questions and long evenings in which she drank too much.

Men. She would never understand them, and Ben least of all.

The van's phone rang as Mona pulled up to a stoplight. It had taken Fay weeks to get used to it when it was first installed. The county commissioners had insisted on it and on the computer hookup when they'd proposed the idea of a county medical van, and the voters had approved it. Now, she couldn't imagine getting along without either of them.

"Mobile unit," she said as she picked up the receiver. "Dr. Donovan speaking."

"Ma'am, this is Sergeant Moses. Ah'm calling for Captain Oliver. He says you're needed at the Blue Inn pronto. We've got a medical emergency. How long will it take you to get here?"

Dread beat a frantic rhythm at her temple when he said *Blue Inn.* "What sort of emergency situation, Sergeant?" She glanced at Mona, who was already looking at her, and mouthed, *Blue Inn*. The van shot through the light, siren screeching.

"We've got dead and wounded, ma'am. The ambulance from Franklin General is on the way, but it'll take a while to get here. We need help immediately."

"We'll be there in less than five minutes."

The only thought in her mind as she hung up was that the Blue Inn was Ben's place.

The inn stood on the north side of the lagoon, set back among the pines, dogwood, and hickory, with a wide deck that jutted out over the water. It was three stories of pine and cypress, with thirty-three rooms, high open-beam ceilings and one of the best restaurants in the area. Ben and his wife had bought it five years ago, and every summer since it had been filled to capacity.

Right now, all of the guests seemed to be clustered around outside, a mass that parted like the Red Sea to admit the van. Inside the circle were three police cars, a paramedic truck, and cops keeping the crowd back. Fay's dread now reached so deep inside her, she could feel its roots worming their way through her intestines.

As she and Mona leaped out, Lew Oliver raced down the steps toward them. He wasn't in uniform, and in his navy-blue pressed slacks and impeccable shirt he could have passed for a local businessman. Until he opened his mouth. Then he became what he was: a local yokel with a cheek stuffed with tobacco. "Got ten dead and nineteen wounded." He ran a hand over his thinning blond hair. "Some seriously. The ambulance from Franklin should be here in another ten minutes tops, but Jesus, you can't never tell. We set up a temporary clinic in the lobby that—"

"What happened?" Fay interrupted.

"Bastard freaked. Came out onto the deck with a goddamn Uzi and just mowed people down. Then he turned the gun on himself."

"Who?" Fay asked. But Oliver was already gone.

The lobby was strewn with bodies, and the floor streaked with blood. Heaps of bloody towels were everywhere. Two paramedics were doing what they could, but it wasn't enough. Fay had never been in a battle zone, but she knew it couldn't look much different than this. People moaning, sobbing, bleeding; people in agony. She assessed their immediate general needs and ticked off a list of things for Mona to fetch from the van.

Then she did what she'd been trained to do, tried to alleviate suffering and save lives. But it was apparent from the moment she examined her first patient, a woman who'd been nearly cut in half by a spray of bullets, that she wasn't going to be able to do either very well. The injuries were too serious for what was available in the van. This woman alone needed a team of surgeons, life-support systems, blood, plasma—sweet Christ, the list was endless.

Fay did what she could for the woman, then sent her off in the ambulance to Franklin General, more than thirty miles away, certain she would die en route, and went to work on the next person.

It was a long time later, she didn't know how long, four hours, maybe five. Her eyes were closed. She was kneading away an ache in her right temple. The chair in which she sat molded itself to her body as though it had been made specifically for the shape of her hips, her buttocks, her legs, and spine. It caught the back of her head like a pair of hands, cupping it. She kept sliding down toward a soft, cushioned blackness, but the drone of voices jerked her back.

Whose voices?

Cops, she thought. Mona. The last of the guests checking out of the inn.

I should leave. Go home. Feed Samson. Take a sleeping pill.

But she couldn't muster the strength to open her eyes, rise from the chair, speak to anyone; she was listening to the tape in her head. The tape that played on and on, the sound of Lew Oliver's voice when he'd said, *Ben did this, Fay. He went berserk. We don't know why. No one knows why.*

A forty-two-year-old man whose wife died of cancer three years ago gunned down twenty-nine people while they were having supper on the deck of *his* inn and no one knew why.

Do I know why? Do I?

She attempted a laugh, but it rolled into the air as a sob. Her eyes snapped open as she pressed the back of her hand to her mouth, and there was Mona in her wrinkled white lab jacket, gazing down at her, holding out a cup of coffee.

"Drink this."

"Thanks." The coffee was thick and strong, and the taste, achingly familiar. It was the Cuban stuff Ben had favored. "Have all of the guests vacated?"

"Most of them, I think." Mona plopped into the chair next to Fay's and kicked off her shoes with a sigh. She moved her stockinged feet over the polished pine floor, up over the faded Persian throw rug.

Which Ben's dead wife bought in Hong Kong the year he made a killing on that computer program.

Fay's eyes skipped around the lobby, seeking other details of Ben's life, stories connected to objects, stories shared in that room of his at the top of the stairs. The Ming vase over the fireplace: *My wife had a thing about the Orient.* The crystal ball that rested on tiny brass legs: *She collected them the way other people collect art. Her sister has the rest of them.* Everywhere her eyes paused, a memory leaped out at her, whispered to her, beckoned.

"Where is he?" she asked finally, sensing that was what Mona had intended to tell her all along.

"At the morgue."

"Did anyone call his brother?"

"Lew's trying to track him down."

Fay rubbed her eyes. It was suddenly an effort to speak, to even form the words, to get them rolling down her tongue. "I can't do the autopsy, Mona. Not tonight." *Not ever.*

Mona sat forward, a soft urgency in her voice when she spoke. "I think you'd better take a look at him, though, Fay. Just a look. There was something strange about his skin."

"You saw him?"

"Briefly. The sleeve of his shirt was pushed up to the elbow. It . . ." She bit at the inside of her cheek and shook her head; she didn't know how to describe it.

The morgue. I don't want to go to the morgue. Not tonight. Not now.

The morgue was cold, cavernous, impersonal, with gleaming aluminum counters and cabinets and shelves. Memories haunted it, danced through it with the quickness of light, the brightness of mercury. A specific memory. It pulsed in the upper right-hand corner of her eye, an image as clear as a photograph of her and Ben making love on the aluminum table where corpses had lain. An affirmation of life on the table of death. Ben had always been big on symbolism.

"Will you go with me?"

A corner of Mona's mouth dimpled. "Do you really have to ask?"

"Let me go wash up first."

The bathroom off the lobby was the one Ben had called his Art Deco showcase: black and pink tiles that climbed halfway up the walls, pink sinks, black toilets, a mirror with a curved top and beveled corners.

She had to crouch a little to peer into the mirror, because she stood five foot eleven in her bare feet and the mirror was positioned much lower on the wall.

"You look like shit," she said to her reflection.

The thirty-seven-year-old woman in the mirror grimaced. It deepened the creases in her face and added five years to her appearance.

She drew a brush through her curly auburn hair, remembering how it had felt when Ben had done it. The memory was enough to make her hazel eyes go soft and dreamy. A peculiar knot formed in her stomach, the one Ben used to untie with his mouth, his hands, the one she'd concentrated on when they made love so she wouldn't float out of her skin with the pleasure of it all. And just like that, she was crying, great, heaving sobs she tried to stifle, to swallow, but which kept slapping the air, as dark and ugly as bats.

Control yourself.

Fay grabbed paper towels from the dispenser, wet them, and pressed them against her face, riding the wave of her grief until it had exhausted itself. Then she returned to the lobby, wondering what would fill the gaping hole in her heart.

At twilight, Lagoon had been struck through with charm, with magic. But darkness transformed the town. It swallowed the surrounding hills, stripped away the vibrant red of the bricks, smoothed the sharp corners of buildings where edges met. Light glowing in windows became a source of wonder in much the same way Fay imagined fire had been for Neanderthals. It kept the darkness manageable.

The streets were almost empty; it was after midnight. But Route 16, the main road through town, the artery that connected Lagoon to the rest of the world, had its usual share of trucks speeding toward dawn.

Mona parked the van behind the clinic, where she and Fay had left their cars this morning, lifetimes ago. The building would eventually be enlarged and become the emergency room for the desperately needed Lagoon County Hospital. *And if it were already built . . .* No, best not to think like that.

As she got out of the van, she rubbed her arms against the chill and hurried toward the back door of the clinic. She and Mona descended the rear stairs to the basement. The silence was tense, eerie, as if the building possessed a rudimentary consciousness and was aware of their intrusion. The air was cool but stale, and their footsteps echoed in the stillness. Mona whispered that the place always gave her the creeps at night; Fay didn't bother replying. She was about to leap out of her skin as it was.

Into the morgue. Lights on. The body bag was on an aluminum gurney, where the paramedics had left it. Fay stared at it, her hands sliding down her arms in a slow, distracted motion, tears building at the back of her eyes.

He turned the gun on himself. This isn't going to be a pretty sight.

Control, whispered an inner voice, echoes of her father. *You've undoubtedly seen worse.* She felt the soft click of her consciousness shifting gears and summoned whatever professional detachment she possessed as she pulled on a pair of latex gloves. She opened the bag and peeled it away from his body. Her detachment slipped.

He had shot himself in the chest at point-blank range, and his blood-soaked shirt told her how fast he had died. *Why, Ben? Why?*

"Look," said Mona, and pushed up the sleeve of Ben's shirt with gloved hands.

"My God." Fay turned up the brightness of the overhead light and shone it directly on him.

His arm was covered with what looked like a growth of some kind, a fungus that had gone wild—impetigo, maybe pityriasis rosea or shingles. But she knew it wasn't any of those things. She had never seen anything like this, anything so hideous, so alien.

"What is it?" Mona whispered.

"I don't know. Can you get me some scissors?"

Fay cut open his shirt, wincing at the torn flesh in his chest, the ruined muscles, the chips of bone. She snipped on down to the hems of his jeans and examined him closely. The stuff was the worst on his back and upper thighs, where it was thick, discolored, almost spongy to the touch.

She took samples of it, scraping from the worst areas, and decided to take Polaroids as well before she autopsied him. She asked Mona if she could be here by nine tomorrow morning.

"You sure you feel up to it?"

Can I cut on him?

Fay touched Ben's face, turning it toward her, and wiped

away the blood on his cheeks and forehead with a damp towel. When she was a kid, she'd thought a dead person would look as though he were asleep. But it wasn't like that at all. Death created an absence in the features, a vagueness, an incompleteness, as if the face were an artist's sketch where details would be filled in later. She had loved this man and lost him, and now, after shooting down twenty-nine people for no apparent reason, he was dead.

She wanted to know why.

3

New Tricks

". . . and in the state news this morning, the town of Lagoon is still reeling from the incident at the Blue Inn two days ago that resulted in ten people dead and nineteen wounded. So far, police have been unable to discover an explanation for why Ben Nash, owner of the inn, fired an automatic weapon into the crowd dining on the inn's deck. He . . . ''

Katie turned down the volume on the little TV in the kitchen but continued to stare at the screen as the camera panned the back deck of the inn. Sorrow filled her chest like phlegm; tears stung the corners of her eyes. She could still hear the echo of gunfire in her head.

She remembered the numerous Saturdays when Ben had tutored her in math, making a wonderful game out of it that she could understand. Sometimes the two of them had spent hours in front of one of his computers as he worked out algebra and geometry problems for her, explaining the steps in a way that none of her teachers ever could. Under Ben's tutelage, even computers had become comprehensible to her. But making the difficult simple had been his special gift. She remembered, and it hurt.

Jo stuck her head out of the adjoining breakfast nook, where she was setting the table. "What happened to the TV? I was listening to it. Turn it back up."

"They're not saying anything different than they did on the national news last night. I'm sick of hearing about it."

"Thank God you and Hank were sitting where you were." Jo shuffled into the kitchen and stood in front of the TV, gazing at the images on the screen, a hand on her slender denimed hip. "I always knew there was something strange about Ben. You could see it in his face."

Jo had an opinion about everything, even about people she barely knew. She'd only met Ben once or twice; Katie had known him since he'd moved here. "*What* could you see in his face, Jo?"

She combed her fingers through her short red hair, which was still damp from the shower, and thought about it. Her face was a perfect oval, like a family locket, and when she concentrated, as she was doing now, her mouth slipped into a sexy pout. "You know what I mean," she said finally. "It was this sort of . . . vacancy in Ben's face, like he wasn't all there."

A vacancy. Yeah, sure. "Ted Bundy's face was vacant, Jo. Ben's wasn't."

"Well, maybe *vacant* isn't the right word." She walked over to the stove to stir the oatmeal. "But there was something just not right."

You're the one who's not right, Katie thought, but kept her mouth shut and filled the glasses with juice. She couldn't stop thinking about the strange, dark odor that had emanated from Ben, of the pictures it had created in her head of what he was about to do.

For the past few months, something weird had been happening to her sense of smell. She couldn't remember when it had started; she'd just gradually become aware of a subtle change in how she perceived odors. Sometimes, like the other night, she saw pictures in her head. Other times, a scent elicited a particular feeling or a sense of mood or color. It frightened her a little, but she hadn't mentioned it to anyone. What would she say, anyway? *You smell like blue? You smell happy? Your relationship with so-and-so smells bad?*

"Hey, Kate, could you get started on the canary cage?" Jo asked. "They're fussing."

They weren't fussing. They were singing up a storm, as if to remind everyone that the cage hadn't been cleaned, that the water was yesterday's, and that new feed would be greatly appreciated. Their smooth little throats throbbed and they hopped along their perch as Katie unlatched the door.

Tina, the plumpest of the two, flitted out of the cage and landed on the edge of the open oatmeal box to Jo's left. "I really wish you wouldn't let them out, Katie."

"I didn't. She got out."

"They crap all over everything."

"They're hungry."

Tina tipped forward to sample the contents of the box, and it toppled, spewing dry oatmeal across the counter. The bird fluttered up before Jo could catch her and darted into the hall.

"Look at this mess," Jo fumed. "I'm telling you, someday it's going to come down to the birds leaving or me leaving."

Good, because I know who'll win.

"I mean, if it isn't the pot Hank smokes, it's his stupid birds making a mess all over the house or all the overtime he works. . . ."

Katie tuned her out as Ike flew from the cage a moment later and fluttered down the hall after Tina. When the birds reappeared, one was riding on Hank's head and the other clung to his shoulder.

"Voilà," boomed Hank, throwing his arms out at his sides, a joint in one hand as he did a soft-shoe shuffle. The birds clung to their respective spots on his anatomy and Katie burst out laughing.

But Jo wasn't amused. No surprise there, Katie thought. The woman had been born without a sense of humor. "You oughta be on Letterman's stupid pet tricks," she snapped. "And do you *have* to smoke a joint before breakfast and in the house? What kind of example is that for Katie?"

Like I'm not even here. "I'm a little old for him to be setting examples, Jo. Besides, I don't like grass. I don't care if he smokes it."

"That's not the point. It just isn't done."

"It is here." Hank's voice had that hard, *Don't-give-me-any-shit* edge to it, so Jo changed the subject and asked him to *please* put the canaries back in the cage while they ate.

"Yesterday, they crapped in my coffee cup."

"Only because you wouldn't let Ike sample the strawberry jam." Hank returned them to the cage. "I keep telling you that if you humor them, they behave."

"Ha. For *you* they behave."

"They behave for Kate, don't they, Button."

"Sure."

"There. See?"

Jo sighed heavily as if to say they were all impossible and she didn't know why she put up with them, anyway. But Katie knew why. Jo wanted to marry Hank. She believed he was her ticket out of a dead-end secretarial job at the post office, where she'd worked since her first marriage had gone on the rocks six years ago. So she performed all the functions of a good little wifey, hoping to make herself indispensable. Now here they sat, settled at the round glass table in the breakfast nook like a normal family. *Pass the jam, please. Here's the butter. More biscuits? More grits?*

Katie tried to absent herself from the room, just as she did most mornings, and wished they were eating in the living room. It faced the lagoon, while the nook was at the side of the house. From where she sat, she could just make out the glimmer of water through trees that sloped gradually down to the lagoon. She imagined herself outside, maybe down by the dock where the canoe was tethered. She was swinging her legs over the edge of the dock, her bare feet skimming the water, the sun warm against her cheeks, her head. A peaceful silence surrounded her that was unbroken by the irritating sound of Jo's voice which, even now, even in the middle of her stupid fantasy, intruded, poking at her.

What time did Katie's math tutorial start today? Jo asked. The same time it always did, Katie replied. Would Hank be working late again tonight? No? He was staying home to work on the book? How was it coming along? Couldn't Hartwell give him a leave of absence or something while he finished it?

Hank was something of a celebrity in certain circles because of the four books he'd published, and Hartwell paid him a lot of money as a result. As one of his buddies had put it, Hank's theories could be to biology what relativity was to physics, if others were able to verify his findings.

In scientific circles, his ideas were alternately referred to as "heretical" or "brilliant." Nothing in between. Which was exactly the point. His theories struck at fundamental truths that ran throughout all facets of science, and if they were proven, they would change the face of science forever. Unfortunately, Katie didn't understand the theories; Hank lacked Ben's gift of making the difficult mundane. To her, his passion for biology was simply one of his many quirks and the main reason he'd met her mother eight years ago.

She'd been a science teacher in Atlanta when Hank had come to town to sign autographs at a local bookstore for his first book. She'd gone to the session and asked him to speak to her high-school science classes. He had, and by the next fall, they were married and the three of them were living just across the lagoon, in South Carolina. But when Katie's mother had been killed in a car accident four years ago, Hank had sold the house there and bought this one.

No one would ever mistake her and Hank for daughter and

father. He had brown hair and eyes; she was blond and blue-eyed. He was tall, lean, and small-boned, while she took after her mother—a little plump, with large bones, high cheeks, a full mouth.

Katie couldn't remember her real father. The only thing she knew about him was that he taught P.E. at some school in New York state where her mom had been teaching at the time. They were married a couple of years before he just up and left one day. So when Katie thought of *Dad*, she thought of Hank, and there was just no way that she would ever think of Jo as *Mom*.

"You never showed me Ike and Tina's new tricks," Katie said.

"Oh, God," Jo moaned. "Not now. Not while we're eating."

"We're finished eating. Clear the dishes, Button, and get ready for something absolutely staggering."

Hank pushed away from the table. He moved the way people sometimes did in her dreams, quickly, urgently, like he was flying toward a future he couldn't reach fast enough to suit him. He talked to the birds while Katie cleared the table and Jo refilled her mug with coffee, resigned to the show.

The birds stopped singing and cocked their heads, listening to Hank as though they could actually understand him. He coaxed Ike onto his index finger and latched the door again so that Tina couldn't get out. Then he covered the cage and carried Ike to the table. He was darker than Tina, yellow-streaked orange like a Popsicle. Hank set him on the edge of his coffee cup, and Jo groaned.

"God, I can see it now. We're going to contract some foul disease that comes from bird droppings."

Hank ignored her. "I only taught Tina this trick, but Ike's going to know how to do it." He dropped a couple of sugar cubes into a mason jar and fixed a piece of clear plastic over it, sealing it. Then he stepped back from the table, waiting. For the first few moments, Ike just picked at his feathers and pooped on the saucer. Katie giggled.

Jo rolled her eyes. "Terrific trick, Hank. He took a dump on the saucer. We already knew he could do that."

"Just watch."

Ike fluttered his orange-streaked wings and lifted up onto the mason jar. His claws tapped against the plastic. He pecked at it. He puffed out his chest, sang a few notes, then went back to his pecking until he'd poked several holes in the thin plastic. Katie didn't realize the holes formed a pattern until Ike carefully fit his claws into them. He jerked one foot up, then the other, over and over again until the holes enlarged, tore, and finally shredded the plastic. He tipped back, toppling the jar, and as it rolled across the table, Ike hovered just above it, fussing, his feet touching it now and then to keep it rolling. The sugar cubes moved around inside, getting closer and closer to the opening until they tumbled out. Ike landed on the table, pecking at the cubes, pausing to sing, peck again, sing, obviously delighted with himself. "Neat," said Katie.

"There's nothing *neat* about it," Jo muttered, and turned back to the sink, filling it with water.

Hank's cheeks flushed with excitement. "Don't you understand? Ike learned the trick *on his own*, without ever having seen Tina do it."

Jo shrugged. "So Tina told him about it. Big deal."

"Told Ike how, Jo?" He spoke to her back. "How the hell can a canary with a brain half the size of a pea learn a complex procedure like this and then communicate it to another canary whose brain capacity is no greater? Tell me that, Jo. I'm really interested in your theory on this."

Katie heard the anger in Hank's voice and so did Jo. She turned, flustered now, and drew her fingers quickly through her hair. Her mouth twitched with annoyance; she hated being put on the spot. "Well, I guess canaries must have some kind of language, like we do. We just don't understand it."

"Like dolphins," said Katie.

"Exactly," chimed Jo.

"*All* animals have a language. But explain this. Last week, I went into a pet shop over in Franklin. That's a little over thirty miles from here."

Jo emitted one of her practiced sighs. "We *know* how far Franklin is, Hank."

"I had a mason jar like this one and chose a canary at random and it was able to do the same trick. A couple weeks ago, when I was in Atlanta, I visited *two* canary breeders and hey, guess what? Their birds can do the same trick. *Thirty* birds, Jo, that I'd never seen before in my life. So who taught them?"

"Maybe the breeders did."

Hank laughed. It was a strange, tight sound. "I'd never met the breeders and no one knew about this experiment but Tina and me. I taught her the trick three months ago. So in twelve weeks, Jo, more than thirty canaries that haven't had any contact with Ike or Tina have learned the trick. How?''

"You're the biologist."

"But you're the one who thinks it's no big deal. So c'mon, let's hear your theory.''

She glared at him, her pale eyes the green of old celery. "I don't have any goddamn theories and you're trying to provoke me into an argument. Just forget I said anything. I've got to get ready for work." She marched out of the room, arms swinging, and slammed the bedroom door.

"I think she's pissed."

Hank shrugged. "Nothing new." He watched Ike finishing off one of the sugar cubes, then plucked the cover from the cage and unlatched the door so that Tina could fly around, too. "C'mon, let's get the kitchen cleaned up. Then I need to get cracking on the book.''

Jo came out before they were finished, her hair now framing her face in soft curls, her slender figure pressed into black slacks and a crimson sweater, makeup perfect. Her perfume filled the entire kitchen and mixed with another fragrance, faint yet familiar, a scent that was layered, complex, neither pleasant nor unpleasant, light nor dark. Katie knew if she followed it, as she had a few times, she would find herself in some memory from Jo's childhood rather than a more recent memory. It was almost as if everything that had happened to Jo since she'd grown up didn't matter as much as the experiences she'd had as a kid. Katie distanced herself from the scent.

"Since you're going to be home all day, would you mind putting the roast in the oven around four?''

"I may go into work later this afternoon," Hank replied.

She gave an exasperated sigh. "Then what time should dinner be ready?''

"I'll try to be home by eight.''

She was fiddling with the band of her watch, not looking at Hank. "If you can't, I'd appreciate a call.''

"What'd you do to your wrist?" Hank touched her hand, holding it so the underside of her wrist showed. An angry patch of red flamed against it.

"I must've burned it." She reclaimed her arm, scratched at the patch, slipped on her sunglasses, and left without another word.

Ike and Tina swooped low over Hank's head, serenading him in the silence.

* * *

Katie pedaled her bike along the shoulder of Hawthorne Lane, where the dirt was packed hard and covered in pine needles. Birds sang from unseen branches. Shadows eddied across the road, puddled under trees, and rippled down the gentle slope toward the lagoon.

The pines through here were so thick and lustrous that sunlight barely penetrated the overhead branches; the air was five or six degrees cooler than it would have been otherwise. Katie zipped up her jacket and wished she'd thought to ask Hank if she could drive his Mustang to summer school for her math tutorial.

The bike whispered past homes and cabins half hidden in trees, most of them empty until Friday evening when the weekenders arrived. Once Labor Day rolled around, the majority of the places would be sealed up until spring. Of the fourteen homes on the lagoon, eight were winterized and lived in year-round. The rest were used periodically throughout the winter. The inn, of course, had always stayed open even though business was slow during the winter. She wondered what would happen to it now.

As Katie swung into the turn that would take her away from the lagoon and out toward the main road, the tendrils of a faint, musty odor tickled her nose. It smelled like a dead animal and was coming from her right. As she kept pedaling, it got stronger and seemed to change, to darken. It reminded her of the odor that had come from Ben shortly before he'd opened fire on the crowd. But it was different somehow, thicker, stickier, not at all like a dead animal now. It didn't trigger any pictures in her head, either.

She stopped, slid off the seat, straddled her bike. She sniffed at the air, tracking the scent as far as the pines just ahead of her, hoping for a picture that would tell her what it was. But the inside of her head remained as blank and white as a screen at the drive-in at high noon. She was suddenly afraid, unreasonably afraid, to pedal past the spot.

It's nothing. Just a dead animal. Move or you'll be late for class.

But she stayed where she was, her nose working at the air, fighting the *tickle* in her gut and the sound of Ben's voice in her head. *You ever get nudges about things, Katie?*

Nudges?

Yeah. A feeling something isn't right, but you don't know what it is. A nudge. A tickle.

Oh, that. Sure. Sometimes.

What do you do when it happens?

Try to ignore it.

Christ almighty, don't ever do that. Pay attention to it. Go with it.

Like she had two nights ago at the inn.

Like she was going to do now.

She mounted her bike and moved to the left shoulder. The odor wafted across the road in waves that threatened to choke her, and she pedaled faster, faster.

Go with it.

Despite the chilly air, sweat erupted on her forehead. Her fingers tightened over the handlebars. Her eyes burned. Her temple ached. Why had the birds stopped singing? Where was that rustling noise coming from? Behind her? To her right where the smell was?

Panic burst like a boil inside her. She flew past the odor, body hunched forward over the handlebars, ears ringing, eyes tearing. She could barely see the road. The front wheel hit something—a log, a rock, she couldn't tell—and the bike bucked, throwing her off.

She landed hard on her side, the air knocked out of her. Red dust fluttered up around her, swirling into her nostrils, her mouth. She coughed and coughed as the bike's wheels spun. Her head snapped around. She scrambled to her feet. The smell was thicker, blacker, uglier, closing in on her. She grabbed the handlebars, jerked the bike upright, leaped onto the seat. She tore down the road, pedaling fast and hard, the green of the trees blurring, melting into the red clay.

She didn't glance back and didn't stop until she reached the outskirts of town.

4

Around Town

1.

Captain Lew Oliver heard the rolling mop bucket echoing in the station's hallway and thought, *Aw shit*. He leaped up from his desk chair to close the door before Harness and the bucket reached his office. But it was too late. Harness's mop swished through the doorway, stopped, and the man's weird, idiot eyes met Oliver's. His mouth swung into that terrible half-smile that made his plump face go lopsided and crooked, the smile that announced: *I'm slow, but don't hold it against me.*

"What's up, mate?"

Ever since Harness's mother had rented *Crocodile Dundee*, he'd been calling Oliver and every other officer in the department *mate*. "It's down, Harness."

Blink, blink went his stupid eyes as he frowned, mulling over what it meant. "Down?"

"Yeah. As in up." Oliver pointed at the ceiling. "And down." His index finger stabbed toward the floor. "Today it's down."

Harness grinned and shook his finger at Oliver, a parent scolding a kid. "Mustn't be sad, mate."

"Right. Well. You have a good day, Harness." He started to close the door, but the man held out his massive arm and his huge hand pressed up against the wood, a brick masquerading as flesh and bone.

"Wait, mate."

Christ. "What is it, Harness?"

"About Ben." His hand dropped away from the door and clung to the mop handle again.

"Ben Nash, you mean?"

His index finger shot out, imitating a gun. "Got it, mate."

"What about him?"

26

Harness clutched himself at the waist and his face seemed to cave in like a squashed grapefruit. "Pain." The word hissed out through clenched teeth.

"Ben was in pain?"

The question released him from his stance and he grinned, flashing his crooked white teeth. His index finger flicked out again. "Bad pain."

Stories about Harness had been circulating for years, and Oliver had heard damn near all of them. They were part of Lagoon's village lore, embellished in gossip traded on porch swings at night, over beers at the local saloons, in old-lady sewing circles. Some people claimed that the brain damage that had left Harness only marginally functional had blessed him with second sight. Oliver knew it was bullshit, but Harness did get around. He heard things. People talked openly around him because they thought he was too stupid to understand or remember, and for that reason he was sometimes worth listening to. "What kind of pain was Ben in?"

"Badmadbadmadbadmad." He flung his mop back and forth across the floor again, shaking his head, saying badmad over and over in the same dull voice.

"Do you know what Ben did, Harness?"

He lifted the mop from the floor and aimed the handle at Oliver. Then he slid it through the air, making chattering noises like gunfire. "People dead. Harness knows." His head bobbed. "Harness knows."

"And the pain made him do it?"

"Pain and hunger, pain and fear." He dropped the mop to the floor again and moved away, swishing the mop back and forth, rolling the bucket along in front of him.

"Hey, Harness," called Oliver. "What caused Ben's pain?"

"Change."

"Change? What do you mean? What kind of change?"

But Harness was already lost in his own world once more, humming to himself, the bucket clattering along in front of him as he swished the mop back and forth across the hall.

Fucking fruitcake.

Oliver shut his door and sat down again, his head tipped back against the dark leather chair as he watched sunlight eddy across the pale yellow ceiling. It made him dizzy and he swiveled around, gazing into the street two floors below.

His office was a perfect isosceles triangle, with the window at the widest side. From here he could see Four Corners, the heart of Lagoon's downtown: the library and city park to the northwest; a clutch of tourist shops to the southwest; a small shopping center with a Kroger's grocery store, a couple of restaurants, and Castleton's Army/Navy to the northeast. The police station was catty-corner to the library and the park, at the end of a row of businesses that included a feed shop and the Nameless Café. Hardly good city planning.

The cooler weather and clear skies had brought people out in droves for the lunch hour. The breeze flapped at skirts, tousled hair, and swirled dry leaves along the sidewalks in front of the park. To an outsider, he thought, Lagoon probably looked like a prosperous, thriving town cashing in on the last month of the tourist season. Shops bustled with business, trucks hauled produce in from outlying farms, restaurants were jammed to capacity, construction was booming.

But Oliver sensed the wrongness that skulked beneath the surface of it all, as though some terrible darkness were hidden in the alleys, the side streets, waiting to disrupt the serenity. Today he didn't feel like Clint Eastwood in *Dirty Harry*, protector of Lagoon's integrity. Today he felt like shit. He could almost taste the wrongness and knew it was part of the same darkness that had existed in Ben Nash.

He picked through his files for the one on Nash and pushed the others—a couple of robberies, a slew of burglaries around the lagoon—to the side. He read through the information on Nash, seeking something that would tell him why a forty-two-year-old *good citizen* would suddenly go berserk. When good citizens broke, it usually happened in less dramatic ways. Drugs. Booze. Beating up on wives. Fucking a hooker. Good citizens didn't crack up and suddenly cut down twenty-nine people with an Uzi.

The information in the file told him little about Ben Nash that he didn't already know. He was a computer whiz who'd spent seven years with IBM and another four in Silicon Valley before designing a sophisticated program that destroyed computer viruses. It had made him a bundle of money and enabled him and his wife to ''retire'' here five years ago, when they'd bought the Blue Inn.

According to county records, he'd paid cash for the inn, and his recent bank statements indicated he had close to half a million in savings, money markets, investments, and whatnot. So money sure as hell wasn't a problem.

Love life? Oliver knew Ben and the doc hadn't been seeing

each other in a while and maybe that, coupled with a lingering depression over his wife's death, had snapped him in half. *Pain*, the fruitcake had said. Pain caused from some sort of change. It would fit. But for a good citizen, it would have to be more than that.

Oliver knew Nash had done occasional consulting for Hartwell Research and Pharmaceuticals, but it seemed unlikely that a problem there had been responsible for what had happened. How could it? He didn't need the work.

Maybe a health problem? That would show up in the autopsy, and he doubted the doc had done one since Ben's death was clearly a suicide. But with the city-father pricks breathing down his neck for answers, he needed to know what was what. The doc would just have to cut on Nash.

He called the clinic. Fay's secretary said she'd just stepped out, could she take a message? Stepped out where? Oliver asked. Over to the Nameless for coffee. Perfect, he thought. The man who owned the Nameless Café had been a close friend of Ben's. Surely if he'd been suffering from a physical or emotional problem, Andy Horn would know about it. He could talk to him and Fay at the same time.

Oliver shrugged on his black leather jacket and glanced at his reflection in the window. He smoothed his hands over his thinning sandy hair, ran a finger under his thick mustache, flicked at a speck of lint on his jeans. If he'd known he was going to see the doc today, he would have worn his gray slacks and gotten a haircut. But he was as good-looking as Ben Nash even without the gray slacks and a haircut, wasn't he?

Five-ten, lean, with wide shoulders (not as wide as Clint's, but what the hell) and a roguish quality about his face most women seemed to find attractive. His deeply set gray eyes were, by his own assessment, his best quality, capable of seducing or pulverizing in a single glance. So how come the doc was immune?

With Ben gone, maybe she would pay some attention to him and accept an invitation for dinner. If she gave him half a chance, he could make her forget Ben in a flash, and once he got her into the sack, the rest would be easy. He knew how to please a woman, all right, and in bed a lady doctor was the same as a dime-store clerk. He felt a stirring in his groin just thinking about it.

Oliver flipped up the collar of his jacket and headed for the streets.

2.

The Nameless Café reminded Fay of something you'd find in New Orleans. It was located on Route 16 and was built around a brick courtyard with a fountain, a proliferation of plants, and half a dozen tables with chips of colorful tiles on the surfaces that Horn had laid himself. Inside, tables lined two of the sliding glass doors.

In all, she guessed the café's capacity stood at around fifty. The place was jammed from five A.M., when it opened, to eight P.M., when it closed. Locals, truckers, tourists were all looking for the same thing: good food that was cheap, which Andy Horn provided in abundance.

Horn's family had lived in these parts since the turn of the century. He was a bear of a man in his sixties, with skin the color of bitter chocolate, a laugh so deep it rumbled, and hair that had gone absolutely white. Fay had met him when Horn had galvanized the blacks in the county to vote for the medical unit. It hadn't endeared him to the people who'd wanted the van to be used as a county bookmobile, many of whom were racists from way back, and Horn had paid dearly for it.

For several months after the vote, he was plagued by "bad luck": vandalism to the café, the theft of his car, a "clerical error" that resulted in the loss of his restaurant license for a few weeks. It was at that point that Fay had intervened. She went to the mayor's office and demanded an investigation. When they started to give her the usual runaround, she threatened to go to the Atlanta newspapers with the story. Horn's license was reinstated two days later and the vandalism stopped as quickly as it had begun.

". . . haven't been able to get it off my mind since it happened," Horn was saying, referring to Ben.

She nodded, thinking of the autopsy. She'd done it yesterday and hadn't felt right since. "Same here."

They were sitting outside in the courtyard under a hazelnut tree. Its soft, velvet leaves stirred in the cool breeze. Fay's half-eaten sandwich was in front of her; Horn was picking at a piece of French bread.

"I've been remembering a few things, Fay."

"Like what?"

"Well, how Ben dressed, for instance. Here it was, the hottest June and July on record, and he was wearing long-sleeve shirts buttoned at the cuffs. Light hurt his eyes something fierce, too. We were out fishing one day and the sun was real bright, and even though he was wearing shades, real dark shades, his eyes started watering bad and we had to go in. I told him he oughta see a doctor about his eyes and he said he'd gone to someone over in Franklin and the guy gave him some drops to use.''

"That's all he said?''

"Near as I recall.''

Light-sensitive eyes: How's that fit?

She wasn't sure yet.

A number of things she'd discovered during the autopsy puzzled her, like some of the changes in Ben's organs. His lungs were larger than they should have been for a man his size, and his liver and spleen were smaller. A normal spleen weighed about six ounces; his had weighed four. The smaller liver and spleen meant a diminished storage capacity for red blood cells, which was part of what had made him severely anemic.

Other changes were even more puzzling. His brain, for instance, was different. The hypothalamus was usually the size of a lump of sugar; Ben's was about four times larger. The hypothalamus controlled blood sugar levels and body temperature, as well as metabolism, appetite, digestion, sexual desire, and reproduction. It was also the "emotional brain,'' which meant that changes in it, combined with hormonal fluctuations and other factors, could conceivably cause violent behavior.

Then there was the mysterious rash that had covered at least seventy-five percent of his body. She hoped the Center for Disease Control would be able to give her an answer within a week on the slides she'd sent. But the real question was: What had caused these massive changes to begin with?

"Does his brother know yet?'' Horn asked.

"Supposedly, Lew got in touch with him.''

Horn shook his head. "Jesus, he's a hell of a nice guy and he and Ben were real close. This is going to hit him hard. You ever meet him?''

"No. But Ben talked about him so much, I feel like I know him.''

"I met him when Ben and his wife first moved here. Last time I saw him was about a year and a half ago. He was on his way someplace to do a story for some magazine and he spent a couple of weeks at the inn.'' His eyes flicked over Fay's shoulder. "Shee-it. Here comes trouble. And his name's Lew.''

"Gawd.'' She groaned.

Horn grinned. "He still hittin' on you?"

"He hasn't stopped since he heard Ben and I weren't seeing each other anymore."

Oliver stopped at the table, smiling pleasantly, his hands lost in the pockets of his leather jacket. For a clotheshorse, he was definitely casual today. But his jeans were neatly pressed—dry-cleaned, she thought—and his pin-striped cotton shirt looked like it had been starched. "Afternoon, Fay, Andy. Mind if I join you?"

We mind plenty, Lew.

"Pull up a chair," Horn said. "How about some coffee?"

"Yeah, thanks." His dove-gray eyes followed Horn as he strolled across the courtyard to the coffeepot, then slipped back to Fay. "I was just wondering if you were planning on doing an autopsy on Ben."

"I already did it. Yesterday."

His bushy brows lifted, giving him a slightly simian look. "Did you find anything that would explain why he went nuts?"

"It'll all be in my report, Lew. You'll have it tomorrow. But I'm afraid it raises more questions than it answers."

"How so?"

She explained briefly, and knew from the lack of expression on Oliver's face that it wasn't specific enough for him. He wanted something he could hand to his bosses in a neat package that would tell them, in ten words or less, why Ben Nash had killed or wounded twenty-nine people. *He lost it, Lew, is that specific enough?*

As Horn returned with the coffee, Oliver asked, "You know the janitor over at the station?"

"Harness?" Fay nodded. "Sure. Everyone knows him. He used to do work for Ben at the inn from time to time."

"You think he's got this . . ." Oliver gestured with his hand, as if to pull the right word or phrase from the air, and kept his eyes on his mug of coffee. ". . . this, you know . . . second sight?"

"He's got something," Horn said. "That much is for sure."

Oliver rubbed his jaw, looking uneasy. "Yeah? How do you know?"

"I've known him and his ma for a lotta years and seen too many things, that's how. Don't think I'd call it second sight, exactly. It's more like dreams. He sees things in dreams and he doesn't have to be sleeping to do it." Horn sat forward. "He say something to you about Ben?"

"Yeah." Oliver laughed as if to show them he didn't take any of it seriously. Then he related what Harness had said.

Horn nodded. "Might be something to it."

"Could be that Ben talked to him sometimes," Oliver said. "I figure that when his brother, Scott, gets here in a couple days, he'll probably have some answers. They were pretty close from what I hear."

"Then you got in touch with him?" Fay asked.

"Yeah. Late last night. He was in the South Pole doing a travel story. Don't that beat all? They had to patch me through on a radio." He guffawed, then added: "He didn't think he'd be able to get a plane out for two, three days. You know how it is in those places."

Like you're a seasoned traveler, huh, Lew. Fay dropped a five on the table to cover her barely touched lunch and said she had to get back to the clinic. She'd had enough of Oliver for the day, thank you very much.

Outside again, away from him, she breathed more easily. The sun was playing hide-and-seek with the clouds and the air seemed cooler than it had an hour ago. She buttoned up her tweed jacket and took the long way back to the clinic, Harness's cryptic remarks running through her head, as inscrutable as mantras. *Pain and change, pain and hunger.*

What kind of pain? What kind of change? And what did Harness mean by hunger?

If Ben had told her, come to her, if he'd confided in her . . .

But he hadn't. And nothing was going to change that or bring him back.

5

Scott Nash and the Others

1.

He'd flown from the Antarctic to Punta Arenas in southern Chile to Santiago, Miami, and Atlanta. The cold in the Antarctic and later, in Chile, had been wet, penetrating, bone-deep. Even though a continent, nearly forty hours of traveling, and summer in Atlanta now separated him from it, Nash still felt that cold. It had taken up residence inside him, huddled like a tumor against his heart.

During the three-hour drive from Atlanta to Lagoon, the cold kept him company. It spoke to him from the passenger seat of the rented Subaru, separate from him yet a part of him, like a figure in a dream. It reminded him of the past, the past with Ben, and conjured up vivid visions of how it had been. Childhood. Adolescence. Later. Ben, older by two years, the family eccentric, the high-strung computer genius, the brother with the mind like quicksilver and a heart of gold.

Who gunned down twenty-nine people and turned the fucking gun on himself.

End of story.

Except for why.

It got progressively cooler as he drove north, but fifteen miles out of Lagoon the air plunged from summer to deep autumn in a single breath, as if someone had turned down the thermostat. Nash swung the car to the shoulder and parked in a lookout spot. He unpacked a sweater from his bag in the trunk and pulled it on as he walked back along the side of the road for about three hundred yards, looking for the place where he thought he'd first felt the dramatic drop in temperature. He wasn't sure he'd found it until the air suddenly turned at least fifteen or twenty degrees warmer. He crossed the invisible line several times, making sure he wasn't imagining it.

34

He wasn't.

The cool air smelled sweetly of autumn, of smoke, of change. The warm air was summer, black earth, richness. He returned to the car and backed up to the exact point where the air changed. A bridge. He was on a small bridge, he thought.

He dug a flashlight out of his bag and walked the invisible line, seeking something that would explain the phenomenon.

Like what, Nash? Hidden wires? A portable heater? Dry ice?

He didn't know. Something, that was all.

He leaned over the wooden railing and shone the flashlight below and then out. A creek ran under the bridge, but that alone wouldn't account for it. There didn't seem to be any physical explanation, at least not one he could determine.

Years ago, on assignment for a tabloid, he'd investigated a house in northern Florida that was supposedly haunted and had discovered something similar to this, a cold spot in one of the rooms that had no apparent cause. Since the tabloid was footing the bill, he'd called in experts—a geologist, an architect, a builder, a psychic, a historian. The only answer—and Nash wasn't so sure how *reasonable* an answer it was—came from the historian, who claimed that the man who'd built the house had been murdered in the exact site where the cold was.

But this was hardly the same thing.

He stood there a few minutes longer, debating about whether he should climb over the railing to see how far the cold extended into the trees. But it was dark and late and he knew he was only postponing his inevitable arrival at the Blue Inn, where memories of Ben would be hard to shake off. He'd managed not to think about it for much of the forty hours he'd been traveling. But during the eleven-hour flight from Chile to Miami, while frantically trying to complete his story on the Antarctic, he'd suddenly thought of his life without Ben in it and everything inside him had crumbled.

Back in the Subaru. Forward. Speeding over the bridge to where it connected with Route 16. Lagoon was just over the next hill. Faster. Faster.

Moonlight struck the dark shapes of the foothills in the distance and tipped the trees—oak and hickory, dogwood, birch, pine, hazelnut. He smelled water, smoke, the sharp cleanness of the chilly air. And then, at the crest of the hill, there it was, the town where Ben had died. It winked in the dark, a mirage, a promise, a place of secrets.

He gunned the accelerator and sped down the hill, caught up

in the momentum of his grief again, the invisible line behind him that marked the cold, the warm, now forgotten.

Hawthorne Lane swung around the east side of the fifteen-acre lagoon. It ended at the Blue Inn to the north and emptied into a cabin driveway at the south. It was a dirt road cushioned by seasons of fallen leaves and pine needles. The trees converged overhead, blocking out moonlight, but the moon's reflection against the water was bright as aluminum. Spanish moss hung from some of the branches like dark lace or cobwebs. He passed half a dozen camps and bungalows, most of them summer places and all of them occupied.

As he approached the north shore of the lagoon, something in his gut constricted and expanded several times in rapid succession, like the pupil of an eye that didn't know whether it was in sunlight or in darkness. He considered staying someplace in town and coming out here first thing in the morning. But he was bushed, and besides, a part of him needed to be here, where Ben had lived the last five years of his life.

The only light on in the place came from the porch lamp. It glowed yellow, a solitary beacon that illuminated the steps, strewn with leaves, and a slice of driveway. He parked the Subaru in front and got out.

The trees seemed to sing as a breeze kicked up off the lagoon. An owl hooted. Nash's eyes climbed from the ground to the second and third floors, where all the windows were black. The utter emptiness of the place both saddened and spooked him.

He got his bags, camera equipment, and laptop computer from the car and found his key to the place. A yellow band across the front door said that the inn was off limits to everyone, by order of the Lagoon County Sheriff's Department. Nash tore it off and unlocked the door.

It creaked when it swung inward and a rush of strange air flooded over him. He knew that smell, had known it ever since he'd covered the fall of Saigon for UPI. But even so, when he turned on the lobby lights, he wasn't prepared for the sight of blood that stained the pine floors, the furniture, the outside deck. Until now, the magnitude of what happened here had existed mostly as an abstract, a headline. *Man goes berserk in small Georgia town.*

He stood there, muscles tightening, loosening, tightening again, and tried to imagine Ben doing what the cop had described. It just didn't connect with what he knew of his brother.

His first impulse was to start scrubbing the place down, tossing out the ruined furniture, the rugs. But his body, suspended between continents and states for days, yearned desperately for food—and sleep.

Nash set his things on the stairs and wandered through the rooms on the first floor, making a cursory check of windows and doors. Except for the lobby, the place was just as he remembered it from his trip here over a year ago. The dining room, with its open-beam ceilings and fireplace, looked expectant, as though it were holding its breath, waiting for someone to set its tables. In the kitchen, the butcher-block counters were lined with glass jars of spices and herbs and Ben's Cuban coffee. The pantry and walk-in freezer were jammed with food. Even the fridge was loaded.

He slapped together a baloney and Swiss cheese sandwich, popped open a beer, and followed a set of raccoon tracks from the kitchen to the back porch. The lower part of the screen door had been chewed and torn and the outer door was ajar. He shut it, saw the dead bolt was broken, and fastened the chain. It was rusted enough to be practically useless and he added it to a mental list of things that needed to be done around here.

Upstairs. Second floor. Third. Ben's room.

Emotion balled in his throat. It was a moment before he could step inside.

Two computers and a printer stood on a desk against the far wall, with a stack of paper and disks, pencils and pens arranged neatly to one side. There was a small color TV on a shelf halfway up the wall at the foot of the bed, a CD player on top of a shelf that was crowded with books grouped by subject and alphabetized by author. And there, on the bureau, were a brush and comb, loose change, and a family photograph.

Nash picked up the framed picture, remembering the day it had been taken eight or nine years ago. They were on the deck of a sloop owned by an Aussie Scott had met in Panama. He and Ben were standing next to each other, with their wives on either side of them.

It struck him how little they resembled each other. Ben's hair was straight and blond; Scott's was dark and curly. At just under six feet, Ben was a good three inches shorter. He sported a mustache and Scott had a beard. Ben's eyes were a mesmerizing blue, the color of the Aegean; Scott's were the black of Greek olives. Their wives, he thought, had looked more like sisters than they had looked like brothers.

He kept staring at the picture, as if to divine some clue as to why his brother had done what he had, then went downstairs.

He fetched linens from the second-floor closet and made up the king-size bed in the room where he'd slept during his last visit. It was large and comfortable, with an exposed-beam ceiling, pine walls, a rolltop desk at the wide window that overlooked the lagoon, and a bathroom with a tub large enough for a party. Nash finished his beer in the tub and fell into bed at half-past three, the mattress a cushion of air that fit his bones as snugly as a pair of kid gloves.

A while later, he bolted awake, alert, tense, listening for whatever it was that had jerked him from a sound sleep. The window was partially open; he could hear a dog barking in the distance. The wind prowled through the eaves. Leaves blew across the deck below. Then he heard something else, a scraping sound that seemed to be coming from inside the house.

The raccoon. He pulled on jeans and a sweater, picked up the flashlight, and hurried quietly down the hall to the back staircase, which was closer to the kitchen. In the utility room, he grabbed hold of the broom and advanced through the hall toward the kitchen doorway with it in front of him like a sword. He felt ridiculous. But if the raccoon was rabid or felt cornered, it would become aggressive, and he wanted an edge, however slight.

He paused to the left of the doorway, listening. He didn't hear anything so he reached around, patting the wall for the light switch. He flicked it on and gaped at the mess on the floor.

The fridge door was open and the floor was strewn with its contents: tomatoes and heads of lettuce, jars that leaked strawberry jam, slices of bread, Tupperware containers that had been torn open, rivulets of milk from the overturned gallon container, broken eggs whose yolks gleamed and quivered like jaundiced eyeballs.

In the middle of it all was a garbage bag, the edges folded back so he could see what was inside. Frozen chickens, turkeys, steaks, and ribs from the freezer. It was a neat, deliberate little package, hardly the work of any raccoon.

The chilly air licking at his feet meant the door of the back porch was open. He'd apparently scared off whoever it was when he'd come down the rear stairs.

He checked, and sure enough, the door stood ajar, the chain snapped in two. He stepped outside, toes curling against the pine needles and dry leaves, and shone the flashlight over the ground, looking for footprints. By the time he heard something behind him and glanced back, it was too late. Someone slammed into him, knocking him off his feet, and raced toward the trees.

Nash scrambled up and charged after him, his arms pumping at his sides, the cold air stinging his eyes, his cheeks. He glimpsed the man cutting right, toward the road. He was carrying something, a bag. Nash ran faster. Seconds later, he tackled the bastard and they both flew forward, smacked the ground, rolled.

The man punched Nash in the gut, struggled to get free, but Nash clung to his leg and he went down again. Nash scrambled onto his back and sank his fist into the man's ribs. He yelped and bucked, throwing Nash off, then leaped up and scooped his garbage bag from the ground. He spun, anticipating that Nash would tackle him again, and kicked out his right foot. Nash grabbed it, jerked, and the man hopped around on one foot, trying to maintain his balance, arms pinwheeling, garbage bag swinging wildly through the air.

For a split second, moonlight washed across him, exposing a face with cheeks that were raised and porous, like volcanic rock, small eyes that were the deep smooth black of eight balls, a nose that was little more than a pair of nostrils, a mouth that had been practically squeezed into nothingness by the suppurating mass of his skin.

The face was grotesque, utterly unlike anything he'd ever seen before, and shocked him so deeply, he leaped back, releasing the man's foot. His opponent swung the garbage bag, and the load of frozen meat, hard as rocks, caught Nash on the chin, leveling him. Stars exploded behind his eyes. He tasted blood in his mouth. He heard the man charging through the trees, knew that he was headed for Hawthorne Lane and that he would lose him if he didn't get up.

But when Nash rocked onto the balls of his feet, he promptly fell forward onto his hands, too dizzy to stand. He spat out blood. He remained where he was, on all fours, the smell of earth and trees and blood swirling in his nostrils, that face a blaze in his head.

The slam of a car door reverberated with the clarity of underwater sound. Then a car shrieked as it tore away from the lagoon.

2.

"What *happened*?" she hissed, swerving the old VW bus from one side of Hawthorne Lane to the other, as though she'd just learned to drive. "What took you so goddamn long, Bud?"

"The inn wasn't empty. I had to leave one of the bags behind, but there's plenty of food in this one.'' He dug into the garbage bag and held up a steak. ''See?''

Betty grabbed at it, then dropped it quickly, as though it had burned her. ''It's frozen, for Christ's sakes.''

''So it'll thaw.''

''But I'm hungry now,'' she whimpered, and started to cry. The bus careened from one side of the road to the other, seeming to float in the clouds of red dust the tires kicked up. Bud was afraid she was going to kill them unless she slowed down, so he suggested she stop and let him drive for a while.

''I'm fine. I can drive.'' She caught her breath, wiped a hand across her eyes, then swung out onto the highway again, headed toward the room they'd rented at the north end of the county. ''I'm just hungry, and pretty soon it's going to be light and we won't be able to go out for anything and the meat won't be thawed by then and . . .''

Bud stopped listening to her. For the last three weeks, since they'd left Dade City, Florida, she'd done nothing but whimper and complain about how hungry and uncomfortable she was, and he was sick of it. Hell, he was hungry, too. He'd done the best he could, but oh, no, that just wasn't good enough for Betty, now, was it?

''Look, it's just frozen, it's not spoiled. You gotta develop a taste for it, that's all.'' He bit off the end of the raw steak, peeled away the wrapper, nibbled at it. It was hard, not very juicy, but once he got the hang of chewing it, the taste wasn't bad. ''Here, try it.''

''No.'' Stubborn.

Bud, disgusted with her, threw the steak back in the garbage bag. ''Then get your own food from now on.''

He anxiously scanned the sky to the east, hoping they made it back to the motel before the sun rose. Light hurt his eyes something fierce now and even the dark sunglasses no longer helped. It wasn't quite as bad for Betty yet. In fact, everything had been slower with her. Except for the hunger. And that had accelerated alarmingly in the last few days, since they'd gotten to Georgia.

''We need gas,'' she said. ''The needle's on empty.''

''There's nothing open along this road.''

''Yeah, there is. That Chevron station.''

''You'll have to go in.''

She sighed. ''I'd just like to know what the hell we're going to do, lambchops, when I look like you.''

He wished she wouldn't say things like that. It hurt. And she knew it. Besides, under her clothes she looked just like he did. Only her face, hands, and a few other spots hadn't changed yet.

"How much money do we have left?" she asked.

"Enough."

"Enough for what, Bud? For another week in a hotel? For tickets to Australia, what?"

He rubbed his aching temple with the heel of his hand. "Eight thousand and change." Half of what he'd socked away for his retirement; he'd left the other half in the bank for his wife.

And here you are, retired, buddy boy.

"Fine. Then we can afford gas."

She turned into the Chevron station, stopped at a self-service pump. Before she went in to pay, she applied fresh lipstick and drew a comb through her hair. That, Bud knew, was for the benefit of the young stud inside.

He watched her as she strolled toward the building. Small, petite Betty, ex–Avon lady, still moved like an angel, those hips swiveling, swaying, that soft blond hair swinging as she moved, arms loose at her sides.

Now he could see her through the station window, flirting with the young attendant, laughing, tossing her head. Now she pranced back out to the car to pump the gas, humming to herself, pleased by the stud's attention.

In their other lives in Dade City, when they were happily married to other people, they were next-door neighbors and good friends. The four of them. Barbecues on Sundays, camping on long holiday weekends, even a trip up the California coast to Alaska on one of those fancy cruise ships. Not a bad life, he thought.

Until the change.

It had started with a rash, that was all, just a stupid rash. But it had escalated quickly to include a sensitivity to light, the strange, desperate hunger, the dreams. He didn't realize anyone else was even afflicted until he ran into Betty one afternoon at the doctor's office. And that was when things between them began to change.

Part of it was that their mutual condition bonded them. But there was also something else, an ineffable attraction that had never existed before, an odd chemistry that, even now, he couldn't really define. It wasn't long before they were meeting on the sly, stealing time from their lives to be with each other. Bud started taking more "business trips" and Betty attended more "workshops" and "conventions."

The affair intensified in direct proportion to their worsening conditions. There was a terrible urgency about it all. Their need to be together—and it *was* a need, he thought, like a physical dependency on a drug—overpowered discretion and common sense. It made them careless. When their spouses found out, neither of them even considered ending the affair. They just left together, as though other options didn't exist.

For several weeks, they drove aimlessly through Florida, traveling at night. They rarely stayed in one place longer than a day or two. It was as if, on some level, they were searching for a particular location that felt right, and they'd found it here. In Georgia. In this county. He understood the presence here.

Yeah? And what kind of presence is that, buddy boy?

He pressed the heels of his hands against his eyes and laughed. *I'm tired. I'm hungry. I need . . .*

What? Just what the hell did he need? His old life? His wife? His job selling insurance?

His hands dropped into his lap. Betty was hurrying back toward the station. Hadn't she already paid? Had she forgotten something? He glanced east, where faint, pale light teased the sky. *Hurry up,* he thought, seeking her through the window again.

She was laughing with the man behind the register. He offered her a cigarette. She accepted. He lit it for her. She leaned close to him, her hair shining in the harsh fluorescent lights, and asked him something. He tilted his head to the side. She walked down a hall, probably to the ladies' room. Bud wished she'd just hurry up. But a moment or two later, when the stud fiddled with his register then followed her, Bud smelled trouble.

When she wasn't hungry, she was horny, and either way it meant trouble. So now she was going to hump the stud in a storage room or the hallway or wherever, and when he saw or felt what was under her clothes, he was going to freak.

Freak in a big way.

He waited. Three minutes. Five. Seven. She didn't come back out. The sky kept lightening. Bud reached under the seat for the gun. There was nothing subtle about the weapon, nothing sleek. It was a .45 that had belonged to Betty's husband, a trucker who'd carried it to protect himself against "road pirates." Bud had never heard the term before but didn't doubt that such beings existed. If someone told him that Mickey Mouse and Donald Duck came alive after Disney World closed down at night, he would at least believe that such a thing was entirely possible. How could he believe otherwise? After all, he was a middle-aged man, an ex-insurance salesman, who had changed into something that seemed less human to him every day.

He slid behind the steering wheel, started the car, drove closer to the front door. He pulled off his gloves and stared at his dreadful hands, turning them over slowly, spreading the fingers, curling them up again. The skin was tougher than it looked, almost like a hide, and he was afraid his index finger would be too thick to fit inside the hole where the trigger was. But it fit and fit well. He got out, the gun tucked inside his waistband and covered by his parka, and went inside.

"Hey, anyone here?"

His voice echoed in the stillness. The refrigerators along the wall hummed. In the east, the sky continued to lighten. Bud imagined he could feel the weight of the light against his spine. "Hello?"

A sound from the back. From the hallway. Where Betty and the stud had disappeared. Bud pulled out the gun, keeping it parallel to his body. His temple drummed. His hands sweated. *Stupid bitch. Stupid, horny bitch.*

The absence of sound worried him.

Now he was rounding the Coke machine, stepping into the darkened hall. His shoes crunched over some Fritos. The hallway was empty, but he had five doors to choose from. A freezer, a storage room, restrooms, an exit. His fear collapsed suddenly into an anger that rushed hotly through his blood, and he jerked the doors open in quick succession, hating Betty for getting him into this situation, hating the stud for having what he did not.

He found them in the walk-in freezer, and several things about them would later stand out in his mind with absolute clarity: the way the toes of the young stud's loafers pointed in opposite directions; the curve of Betty's back as she leaned over him, her head blocking Bud's view of the young stud from the neck up; and the look on her face when he whispered, "Sweet Christ," and she turned her head toward him.

Her dreamy eyes didn't recognize him and blinked slowly, languidly, as if she were surfacing from a deep sleep. Her skin was the color of stale bread, except around the mouth, where it was stained cranberry with the man's blood.

Bud stared at the stud's neck. "Aw, Christ."

"Hi, lambchops." The words fluttered out in a plume of white air and took wing, solitary doves. She wiped her hand across her mouth, looked down at the man, then back up at Bud as if she couldn't quite decide whether to finish eating, use the john, or return to the car. She let out a soft, almost delicate burp, covered her bloody mouth with her fingers, and giggled. Then she rocked toward the stud again and Bud lurched forward.

He grabbed her arm, yanked her up. "We're getting the fuck outta here."

She struggled, but not very hard. The change had endowed him with a strength that was almost obscene for a man his age, and he knew that if he exerted a fraction more pressure on her forearm, it would snap like a chicken bone.

"You're hurting me," she said hoarsely.

He shoved her into the nearest bathroom, forced her head low over the sink, and roughly washed the blood from her mouth.

"Cut it out, Bud," she spat, finding her voice again, trying to pull free of him. "You're hurting me. I mean it. Now just cut it out. I was hungry. I told you I was hungry. If we'd just gotten that girl the other morning, this wouldn't have happened. But oh, no, you were afraid to, so it's your fault. . . ."

He grabbed a handful of her hair, jerked her head back, and slammed his open hand across her face. It felt so good, he did it again, then let go of her, and she stumbled back against the toilet.

Blood bloomed in a corner of her mouth. The imprint of his palm stood out against her white skin, as if she'd been branded. Her blue eyes bulged in her face as she stumbled into the toilet, as she pressed the back of her hand to her mouth. Then she squeezed her eyes shut and began to cry.

"I . . . I was so hungry. God, I couldn't help it, he . . . it . . . tasted so good."

Bud's fingers closed around her upper arm, squeezing, jerking her forward. In the hallway, he grabbed her hand, barely resisting the urge to crush the bones in her fingers, and slammed her against the wall. He jammed the .45 into her mouth.

"Now listen real good, Betty. I'm only going to say this once. I don't give a shit how hungry you get. We're still civilized. What you did is not civilized. If you do it again, I'll blow your fucking head off. Got it?"

Her eyes were wide and terrified. She grunted.

"*Got it?*" he repeated.

Her head bobbed. He pulled the gun out of her mouth and shoved her down the hall, out the door, toward the dust-covered VW bus. For days afterward, her skin and the inside of the bus smelled of the young stud's blood.

6

Introductions

1.

Hypochondria, thought Fay, was a professional hazard for a physician. It was especially true for one whose specialty was pathology, tracing the history of the dead.

The twitch in a hip joint, for instance, could signal the beginning of rheumatoid arthritis. The rumble in the chest might be the onset of pneumonia—or lung cancer. An eye sensitive to light might portend the early stage of iritis or glaucoma. The list was endless, and the possible diseases and ailments were always dire, terrible, and often, terminal.

This morning's little complaints—a calf muscle that wouldn't loosen up, a curious lack of hunger, a stubborn itch between her thumb and index finger—might be the onset of multiple sclerosis. But more than likely they were due to the three miles she was running in air that hovered just under forty degrees.

Her time was actually better than usual. Six and a half minutes for the first mile and, at this rate, maybe six-twenty for the second, and six-forty-five for the third. As she started to swing into a turn for the mile-and-a-half run back to her house, the trees opened up and there was the Blue Inn, a vision of tranquillity at the north end of the lagoon.

Fay ducked through the trees to the edge of the water where she had a better view of it. The blues and greens of the lagoon melted across the glass deck doors; morning light winked in the tall windows. Her gaze paused on the corner window of the third floor, Ben's room. She wondered if Oliver and his men had searched it. Probably. But she doubted that they'd found the cache of weapons inside the phony panel in the closet wall, ten guns, including the Uzi, which he'd collected over the years for God knew what reason. She hadn't mentioned it to Oliver and didn't intend to. The guns wouldn't tell them anything about

Ben's motives, and legally they belonged to his heir. As did the inn, his boat, his Jeep, all of it.

The glass doors slid open and a man appeared on the deck. From this distance, Fay couldn't see who he was. But there shouldn't have been anyone up there at all; the inn had been sealed off by the sheriff's department.

She sprinted the distance and stopped in the driveway, where a navy-blue Subaru was parked. An etheric, celestial sound drifted from the open lobby doors, a piece she recognized by Kitaro. "The Silk Road." Fay trotted up the steps and went into the lobby.

The music came from a stereo system next to the fireplace. The air smelled vaguely like a hospital, of disinfectants that were also intended to mask unpleasant odors. All of the furniture had been moved to one side of the room, the rugs were rolled up against the wall, the floor was wet. The man on the deck was swabbing it down, and she realized that Oliver must have hired a cleaning service to get the place in shape before Scott Nash arrived. How considerate, she thought wryly. She didn't know he had it in him.

But if this was a cleaning service, where was everyone else?

She came up behind him, amused that he was dressed for summer in shorts, a T-shirt, windbreaker, and bare feet, while she was bundled in a warm-up suit. "Morning."

He glanced around. Despite the bruise on his cheek that his beard didn't hide, she immediately recognized him from photographs Ben had shown her. Scott Nash wasn't as handsome as Ben, but his face possessed an openness Ben's had lacked. His eyes were larger, expressive, the darkest eyes she'd ever seen, set deeply in his face. His leanness, the tight contours of his legs, the muscular calves, all said he was a runner. His beard and mustache were flecked with gray and neatly trimmed. Overall, her impression was of a man comfortable with himself.

His smile was quick, mercurial. "Hi." He set the mop in the bucket, wiped his palms on his shorts, extended his hand. "Scott Nash."

"Fay Donovan."

His expression told her he recognized her name. "I live just down the road," she went on. "I was out running and saw someone on the deck. I was afraid it might be vandals or something. When did you get in?"

"Late last night."

"Aren't you cold?"

He looked down at himself, as if he'd forgotten how he was dressed, and chuckled. "Not too bad. It was a lot colder where I was. Weird weather around here for August."

"Very."

A brief, awkward silence ensued, which Nash broke. "You're the coroner Ben was so crazy about."

It wasn't a question. "Yes to the coroner bit, but I'm not so sure about the second part. We stopped seeing each other about four months ago."

"Oh." Nash didn't seem to know what to say to that; he looked embarrassed. "Were you here when it happened?"

"No. Only afterward."

"Was he, uh, autopsied?"

She nodded. "I found some irregularities that might explain why it happened, Mr. Nash, but which also raise some other questions."

"Scott. Call me Scott."

No, she didn't want to call him Scott. She didn't want that sort of familiarity with him. But he spoiled it by asking if she had some time, would she like some coffee, maybe breakfast? "It'll take me three years to eat the stuff stocked in the kitchen."

She laughed. "I can imagine. Ben always tended to overdo it." Even though she wasn't in the mood to discuss the results of the autopsy, she wasn't due on the medical van until noon and it was obvious he needed answers as desperately as she had the night it had happened. "And coffee sounds great."

They settled at the butcher-block counter under the kitchen window that overlooked the lagoon. He made espresso. It was from Ben's Cuban stash, she knew, and it was strong, thick, with milk frothing on the top, just the way she liked it. When she commented on the taste, Nash eagerly shared a story about how he used to bring the coffee back from South America by the dozens of pounds until a customs agent told him the best brand could be bought right in his neighborhood in Coconut Grove.

"Once I sent Ben some of it, he was after me every month."

Fay smiled and jerked a thumb toward the pantry. "On the top shelf in there, hidden behind some other things, you'll probably find about thirty pounds of it."

"I ran across it this morning. Ever since he was a kid, Ben hoarded things he liked."

Fay thought of the guns hidden in the closet on the third floor. Another stash. But she didn't mention it. They fell into a strained silence, each alone with private memories, until she changed the subject. "How much did Lew Oliver tell you when you talked to him?"

"Not much. Just that Ben had shot twenty-nine people, then turned the gun on himself, and no one knew yet why it had happened." His voice didn't betray any emotion, but his eyes did. "Then he wanted to know when I could get here."

Good going, Oliver. "Lew's not known for his subtlety, especially when the big boys are riding him for answers."

Nash shrugged it off.

"Nothing like this has ever happened in Lagoon before, and I think people are afraid that all the publicity is going to hurt the tourist business. Folks here can be a little odd sometimes. You may find yourself in some uncomfortable situations just because you're Ben's brother."

"I'm sort of expecting it. I guess that's why I haven't been in any great hurry to contact the cop. Or Ben's attorney. Or anyone."

"Don't get me wrong. Ben had some good friends here and they'll do anything they can for you. It's the people who didn't know him who may react strangely to you."

His smile bore a trace of sadness. "How come I get the feeling that you're trying to prepare me for something totally bizarre?"

His insight was unexpected, and for a second or two, she felt completely transparent to him. It was as though the ninety percent of her that was water had suddenly risen like an errant tide and now she was fluid, amorphous, awaiting the shape of the vessel into which she would be poured. But the feeling passed quickly, and once again he was just a man she didn't know, Ben's brother, who was waiting for her to tell him what secrets the autopsy had uncovered.

As she talked, his black eyes seemed to change in shade and intensity, a barometer of his emotions. But it wasn't until she described Ben's skin that his expression changed sharply. "Was it puffy? Porous? Discolored?"

"Yes." She wondered how he knew. "I took some Polaroids that're included in the report and sent copies of everything, plus scrapings, to the Center for Disease Control in Atlanta."

"You think a disease made him psychotic?"

"I didn't say he *had* a disease, just a skin condition of some sort. How'd you know about his skin?"

He sipped from his mug and gazed out the window, where a

hawk circled lazily over the trees on the other side of the lagoon. He told her how someone had broken into the inn last night. "I chased him, tackled him, and he did a number on me and got away." He looked back at her. "His face was porous, the way volcanic rock is, and it was swollen or puffy or something so his features had just kind of disappeared. This morning, I was trying to remember everything about it and realized he smelled weird."

"Weird how?"

Nash rubbed his jaw. "I don't know. Not *like* anything I've ever smelled before. Maybe a combination of singed hair, swamp, sweat. . . . I can't describe it."

"And he only took meat?"

"Meat, chickens, turkeys."

Anemia? Like Ben? she wondered.

Her beeper, snuggled inside the pocket of her jacket, sounded just then, a soft, muted noise she wanted very much to ignore. But if her answering service was bothering her this early, it was probably important. Served her right for carrying the damn thing when she ran.

She used the phone in the kitchen. One of Oliver's boys answered at the number her service had given her. When she identified herself, he told her Captain Oliver needed her out at the Chevron station on Hypoluxo right away. They'd found a dead man in a freezer. He said it in a hushed voice that was tight and hot with excitement, as if this were the most riveting thing that had happened to him today or ever. That meant it wasn't just a dead man in a freezer, but something a bit strange, off color, something twisted that didn't fit where it was supposed to in Oliver's tidy categories of crimes.

"I'll be there in about thirty minutes."

Nash, after changing into jeans and a sweater, gave her a lift back to her place. But when they pulled up behind her Jetta, she saw that the right rear tire was flat, something she hadn't noticed when she'd left for her run. They checked the spare, which was as flat as a dime, so Nash offered to drive her out to the Chevron station.

Twenty minutes later, they were speeding north in the Subaru, through sunlight and shadow, the chilly morning air whistling past the windows and through the open sunroof. Moisture sparkled from the pines, the hickories. White blooms from the dogwoods were strewn on the ground. Despite the absolute brilliance of the light, a kind of gloom skulked beneath the surface.

She sensed a wrongness in the air that might have been due to any number of things—the unusual weather, being in a car with Ben's brother, the lingering effects of his story about the intruder, the puzzle of Ben's afflictions, or simply where they were headed.

Nash didn't say much during the ten-minute drive. Unlike Ben, he apparently didn't feel the need to fill in silence with idle chatter. She liked that. Sometimes Ben had talked too much and said nothing, revealed nothing, almost as if he'd used words as a buffer between himself and the world.

Stop comparing them. It isn't fair.

But she couldn't help it. Comparisons were as inevitable as breakfast. "I owe you a home-cooked meal for imposing like this."

"It's not an imposition. Besides, it gives me an excuse to let Captain Oliver know I'm in town." He glanced at her, his black eyes smiling. "But I'd love a home-cooked meal."

"Great. I'll talk to Andy Horn and find out when he's free. I know he'd like to see you again. What night would be good for you?"

"My social calendar's wide open." He said it, she thought, as though it were also true of his life.

A police car, a station wagon, and an old junker were parked in front of the station. Oliver was standing in the doorway with Bill Quickson, the reverend from the Protestant church in Lagoon. He was tall, very thin, an Ichabod Crane with white hair and thick spectacles that rode low on his nose.

Oliver hurried over as Fay and Nash got out. "Thanks for coming, Doc."

His gray eyes darted toward Nash, questioning, and before Fay could introduce them, Nash introduced himself. "Nice to meet you, Captain." He extended his hand.

Fay took a perverse delight in Oliver's surprise, despite his admirable recovery. "Well, uh, Mr. Nash. I hope you can stick around until we finish here. I've got a million questions to ask you." Then he turned his attention to Fay. "The reverend stopped in here for gas and found the attendant dead in the freezer. He's—"

"It's the most godawful thing I've ever seen." Quickson butted in as he joined them. His voice was breathless. He was extremely nearsighted, and behind his thick glasses his eyes seemed small, intensely blue. "I stopped here on my way back from Franklin to buy a cup of coffee and to fill the tank and there was no one around. I found Joe in the meat freezer.''

"Joe?'' asked Fay.

"Joe Fenuzo. The family attends my church. You know them?''

"Just through the clinic. Has the family been notified?''

"No, not yet,'' Oliver said quickly. "I want to get things tied up around here first, then I'll go by the house.''

"I'd be glad to go with you, Lew.'' The reverend was looking at Nash as he said it, and once again Nash took the initiative before Fay could make the introductions. It was as if Nash were testing what she'd told him earlier about people's possible reactions to him as Ben's brother. She wondered what he was looking for. A twitch of the mouth? A tic under the eye? A sudden inhalation of air? Or maybe it was something as small as the way Quickson's body seemed to tilt back a little, as though the good reverend thought Nash might infect him somehow.

"Ah. Right.'' Quickson's smiled strained his spare features. "The photojournalist.''

"More or less,'' Nash replied.

The reverend gave a quick nod and walked into the building, as eager as a tour guide to show them the way. She and Oliver followed, with Nash bringing up the rear.

2.

Nash had carried a camera for so many years that even when he didn't have it, his eyes seemed to perceive things as though he were peering through a lens. It was a focused perception that had more to do with details than with the brightness or the quality of light or the way a particular object or person was framed in the lens.

The first thing he noticed about Joe Fenuzo, for example, was that his fly was unzipped. It seemed rather odd, considering that he was flat on his back in a walk-in freezer. But it was no stranger than the smear of lipstick on the back of the kid's hand. He didn't think the others had noticed; they were too involved in the wound Fay was examining.

"Got any ideas what killed him?'' Oliver asked.

"I won't know for sure until I autopsy him, but it looks like he bled to death from the neck wound.''

"But his neck looks . . .'' Quickson faltered.

"Chewed,'' Fay finished for him.

"Yeah."

No one seemed to know what to say to that.

It was too cold to stand around in the freezer, so Nash stepped back into the hall. He poked around, puzzling over the kid's open fly, the lipstick smear, looking for nothing in particular. The camera in his brain whirred, snapping pictures of the stained tiles, the dirty bathroom sink in the men's room, the empty hanger on the back of the ladies'-room door, the floating butt in the toilet bowl.

There was lipstick on the filter.

He fished out the butt with the hanger. A Winston. Well, fine, that didn't tell him much. He dropped it on a paper towel, folded it, and walked into the front of the station, which doubled as a convenience store. A pack of cigarettes next to the register caught his eye. Winstons. A possible scenario began to take shape in his head, forming the way an idea for a photograph often did.

He unfolded the towel and looked at the soggy butt. He carried it into the freezer and held it out to Oliver, an offering.

"I found this in the john in the ladies' room. If the lipstick on it matches the smear of lipstick on the back of his hand, the chances are good he was killed by a woman."

Oliver looked at him, at the butt. He crouched next to the body, turned Fenuzo's hand so he could see the lipstick smear, then glanced at the unzipped fly when Nash pointed it out. It was obvious to everyone in the freezer that Oliver hadn't noticed either of these things and that he knew they knew. The back of his neck flamed with color and Nash suddenly realized that his attempt to help had backfired. Rule one in this neck of the woods was: *Do not fuck with a small-town cop's turf.*

Oliver's eyes snapped at Nash; anger had brightened them like metal. "I got news for you, Mr. Nash." His clipped voice was as brittle as the air in the freezer. "Statistics say women don't usually commit crimes like this."

"All I'm saying is that if the lipsticks match, it's possible a woman killed him. She stopped for gas. She came inside to pay. She and Joe got to talking. He offered her one of his cigarettes, which she smoked on her way to the ladies' room. She tossed it in the john when she'd finished it and they ended up in here."

Oliver exploded with laughter. "Screwing in the freezer and she nailed him. Yeah. Sure."

Fay snapped her bag shut; it rang out with a kind of finality, the voice of a referee shouting, *Time out.* Quickson cleared his throat, and he and Fay looked at Nash. Their eyes appraised but didn't judge. Not yet. Nash leaned over the corpse and jerked Fenuzo's jeans down over his hips, freeing his flaccid cock and exposing the spots of semen that had dried on the inside of his jeans.

"Now he was either in here jerking off, Captain, or he was getting a blow job. If you're lucky, there might still be traces of the woman's saliva on him." With that, he stood and left the freezer.

Outside, the chill slipped over him, around him, and he blew into his hands, wishing he'd brought gloves. He was waiting for Fay to finish up, waiting for the paramedics to cart Fenuzo's body to the Lagoon County morgue. Waiting.

Oliver had asked him a dozen questions about Ben, then split. Stupid questions. When had Nash last talked to his brother? Three months ago, before he'd left for the Antarctic. Did he seem depressed? No. Was he ill? Not that Nash knew of. Was he having financial problems? No. What kind of consulting did he do for Hartwell Research? Computer programming. Could he possibly have been despondent over the death of his wife? Doubtful, it had happened three years ago.

But now that he thought about that last part, Nash admitted that yes, it was possible. Three years was nothing when you mourned someone you loved.

He counted the cars that whizzed past on Hypoluxo. People on their way to work. Women with kids. A schoolbus. Ordinary life, ordinary people with families, mortgages, dreams. *If Melissa had lived, she'd be nearly sixteen now,* he thought. A princess with her mother's gold hair and sensuous mouth, his dark eyes and nose. The best of each of them.

Eight years ago, in their neighborhood in Coconut Grove, Melissa had fallen off her bicycle and ruptured her spleen. She'd died en route to the hospital. His life had bottomed out not long afterward—his marriage fell apart, he lost his job at the *Miami Herald*, his wife got the house. Nash had lived on his sloop for a while at a marina in Coconut Grove, drinking too much, baking in the hot sun, doing nothing at all.

Ben was still out in Silicon Valley then, but he had flown home and spent more than a month with him on the boat. He hadn't lectured, hadn't gotten on his back, hadn't done anything except offer his support. And when Scott's money had started running low, Ben had lent him eight grand to tide him over until he found a job.

Through a journalist friend, he'd gotten a lead on a free-lance job for *National Geographic*. Less than a month later, he found himself in Morocco, in the city of Fez. And he'd been free-lancing ever since.

A death had sent him away and now another death had brought him back. Full circle.

It had taken him two years to repay Ben, and by then he didn't need the money. His Virus Kill program had just been snatched up by IBM for four million. A paltry sum, considering how widely the program was used now. But it had enabled Ben to retire.

A '64 Chrysler chugged into the station, exhaust shooting from the tailpipe, engine coughing. It pulled up at the self-service pump, a woman with gray hair at the wheel. Nash recognized the man who got out, but couldn't immediately place his face. He started up to the station, counting bills as he pulled them from his wallet, then stopped, frowned, looked around.

Nash suddenly remembered who he was and walked over. "Hi, Harness."

His drowsy eyes blinked and drew away from the police cars, the van, to Nash. He blinked again. "I know you." He grinned, his stained, crooked teeth lining up in his mouth. "I know you. You know me. Scott. Big Ben's little brother." His soft, fleshy hand pumped Nash's arm up and down, up and down. "Sure. Scott." His head bobbed and Nash reclaimed his hand.

"Nice to see you again, Harness. You on your way to work?"

"Work. Yes." His head bobbed and he thumbed the air over his shoulder, indicating the Chrysler. "Mother drives."

"You still working at the police station?"

"Sure." He shrugged. "Maybe for always."

"Would you like to do some work for me out at the inn? Like you did for Ben?"

"Ben?" The name curled into the air, sweet and soft.

"C'mon, Harness," called his mother, sticking her head out the window. "We're going to be late."

Harness didn't seem to hear her. He touched Nash's arm. "Ben. Pain to blame. Hunger to blame. Pain and hunger, bad bad." He stopped, his fingers tightening on Nash's arm, his mushroom-colored eyes glazing over, sliding back and forth through the station lot, faster and faster until his eyes were blurs in his face. "Oh, oh. Poor Joe. He didn't know. Lady in the car. Oh, oh. Poor Joe." His pace picked up, the words rushing together, his fingers digging into the underside of Nash's wrist.

"Lady craves, lady hurting, poor Joe didn't know, didn't know . . ."

"Harness!" his mother shouted as she got out of the car and slammed the door. "We're going to be late!" Her voice silenced him, but he still clutched Nash's wrist. The short, plump woman waddled toward them as fast as her little legs would carry her. "There's obviously something wrong here, son, what with these police cars and all, so let's just mosey on down the road and buy gas elsewhere, huh?"

Her pygmy eyes flitted to Nash, then widened with alarm. "I know you." She grabbed Harness's hand, tearing it off Nash's wrist, and gripped it tightly, stepping back and pulling Harness with her. "He was evil," she whispered. "Your brother was an evil man. All those people. You stay away from my son, you understand? You just stay away from him." Then she spun around, yanking Harness along behind her.

He glanced back once before he and his mother reached the car, flashed Nash a lopsided grin, and aimed his finger like a gun. "Catch you later, 'gator," he called.

7

Anomalies

1.

". . . so he's, like, just *standing* there in front of me, with one hand resting against the wall and the other against the edge of my locker, blocking me in, and I say, 'You mind, Ray? I've got to get to my math tutorial,' and he gives me that smile. . . . You know that smile I mean, Katie?"

"Yeah." Katie giggled. "The one that makes his mouth look so sexy."

"Exactly." Dani Menninger's dark head moved up and down several times as she cracked her gum. They were hurrying through the hall of Lagoon High School, en route to the cafeteria after a very boring two-hour math tutorial that they'd been trapped in four days a week since June.

"And what'd you do?"

"Melted." She lowered her voice to a conspiratorial whisper. "If he'd asked me to go back to his place, Katie, I would've gone in a minute and screwed him the rest of the afternoon."

"Yeah, and your dad would've disinherited you if he'd found out."

Dani rolled her soft blue eyes. "*Only* because Ray's old man owns a garage and isn't a lawyer or something. It doesn't have anything to do with Ray. Daddy's only met him twice; how the hell could he possibly know what he's like?"

Katie wasn't sure the first part was true but kept her mouth shut. It never paid to argue with Dani, especially about guys. And there'd been a lot of them since Katie had met Dani four years ago, when she'd swept into Lagoon, the New Yorker who had every guy in school drooling before the end of her first week.

She had everything: looks, body, clothes, money, and smarts, except in math. Her father was the president of Hartwell, and

56

Hank's boss. Her mother was a hotshot clothes designer who worked out of their home on the lagoon, but who had offices in Atlanta, New York, and Paris. Big bucks, as Hank said. Which was, of course, why Dani had driven a snappy red MG since her sixteenth birthday last January.

They were best friends, a fact that still astonished Katie since they had practically nothing in common except terrible math grades and the Hartwell Connection, as they called it. Dani lived fast and loose and wild; Katie liked things slow and safe. Dani had lost her virginity when she was thirteen years old and had already had one abortion; Katie figured she would die a virgin. Dani drank, smoked, and snorted anything she was given; alcohol made Katie sick, grass made her sleepy, and she had no desire to try cocaine. Dani had read maybe two books in her entire life; Katie read a book a week. Dani loved the spotlight; Katie shunned it. Differences like that. But on some level, their friendship worked and had found its own peculiar balance.

"Ray said he saw you at the Blue Inn the night Ben Nash freaked out. He and some of his buddies were in the bar." Dani dropped her books on the table and looked over at Katie, her blue eyes as wide as dinner plates. "*Were* you there? Did you see what happened?"

"Yeah, Hank and I were there." *We spent half an hour in the water under the deck and I really don't feel like talking about it.* "C'mon, let's go through the line." She turned away, and Dani caught up with her.

"That's it? You're not going to tell me what went down that night?"

The old ache filled Katie's chest. "He flipped out and shot a bunch of people and then he shot himself."

"Weren't you two friends?"

"He helped me with math and showed me how to work his computers. He was a neat man."

"Neat and crazy," Dani scoffed with a toss of her dark hair. "I mean, how fucking *bizarre* and even more bizarre because it happened here in *boring* Lagoon."

Katie thought of the dark smell which Ben had exuded that night and the vivid image that had burned through her of Ben shooting at the crowd seconds before he'd done it. Until that night, the pictures that had come with the smells were of moods, of old things that had already happened. She had never seen something that was *about* to happen.

Well, so what? The other day on Hawthorne, she didn't see

any pictures in her head at all. She ran from a *smell*, a lousy smell, and that was what she should have been thinking about. It was a *weird* thing to do, an *abnormal* thing. It meant something. But what?

"Where were you and Hank sitting when he started shooting?" Dani scooped some pasta onto her plate, unwilling to let it go until she'd heard the gruesome details. "Did you see it?"

"No," Katie lied. If she told the truth, Dani would hound her until she'd spilled everything: the smell, the picture, the dive over the railing. "We were inside."

They started through the lunch line. "Daddy says he was one of these genius types. Brilliant with computers but real unstable."

As though Daddy's word on the topic of Ben was The Truth. Katie let the remark pass.

They settled at their table with plates heaped high with salad and pasta. Dani chatted away about her mother's line of fall clothes, which would hit the stores in early September, and suggested they swing by the house to look at them. "She's got all these leftovers, see, the originals for each design, and I think some of them would fit you."

Katie laughed. "I can't afford your mom's designs, Dani."

Another roll of those baby-blue eyes. "She doesn't sell these, silly. She gives them away. To friends. To me. To whoever they fit. We'll try some on."

Just then, three guys in black leather jackets, jeans, and boots strolled into the cafeteria. "Guess who just walked in," Katie whispered.

Dani's eyes leaped from her plate to Katie's face. "Ray?"

"Uh-huh."

"Oh, shit." A hand slipped under her dark, curly hair, flicking it off her shoulders. "Do I look okay?"

It was like Snow White asking one of the dwarfs if she was presentable for the prince. "You look great."

"What's he doing now?"

"Coming over here."

"Remind me that we're going to my house to look at clothes."

"We're going to your house to look at clothes, Dani."

"Right. Okay. Got it."

Ray Bosque was tall and thin, with sharp, predatory features, a full mouth, dark eyes. A gold post glittered in his left earlobe. His dark hair was longish, loose, shiny. He reminded Katie of a nineties version of James Dean, a rebel who'd graduated in June and now worked at his father's garage. He strutted over to their table and stopped.

"My favorite ladies. How was math toot this morning?"

"*Boring,*" drawled Dani, looking as cool as whipped cream. "Like it always is."

He pulled out the chair between them, turned it around, straddled it, and rested his elbows on the back. "You two hear about Reverend Quickson finding Fenuzo's body out at the Chevron station?"

Dani made a face. "Who *hasn't* heard? It's been all over the papers for the last four days. I mean, his neck was chewed. Is that gross or what?"

"Animal got him, if you ask me," said Ray. "So. What's on the agenda for the rest of the day, ladies?"

"Clothes," said Dani.

"Clothes," he repeated, nodding. "Uh-huh. Like you need more clothes, Dani."

"Clothes for Katie."

Those dark, insolent eyes slid toward Katie. "Looks to me like she's doing just fine in the clothes department, too. I was thinking maybe you ladies would like to ride down to the border."

"What border?" Dani asked.

"Ah." He grinned; his white teeth were absolutely perfect. "You'll have to come along to see."

"There's not room for three of us on your bike," Dani pointed out.

"Got my car."

Dani glanced at Katie, her lifted brows asking, *You game? If you are,* said her shrug.

Dani wanted to know how far the border was.

"Twelve or fifteen miles south," Ray replied, "just outside town. No big deal. A short ride."

"Okay," said Dani. "Where're you parked?"

"Back lot."

"We'll meet you out there as soon as we finish lunch."

"Righto." He knocked his knuckles against the table and left.

"You sure you want to go?" Dani asked.

"Sure, why not. But the only reason he included me was because I was sitting here. You ought to just go alone."

"No way. I don't want him to think I'm too interested."

The art of playing hard to get was one that Dani had mastered and which Katie hadn't learned. Although she'd been dating for a year, there had never been anyone special. Dani blamed it on Katie's aloofness, told her she had to loosen up, party down, stop being so bookish. So she decided to tag along and see how the pros got loose and wild. She didn't have anything else to do today.

And what the hell. Maybe she'd learn something.

2.

Fay was alone in the clinic lunchroom, updating her notes on the patients she'd seen this morning, poking at a tossed salad she'd brought with her from home. But her thoughts were on Fenuzo's autopsy, which she'd completed yesterday afternoon.

She'd found two bite marks on his neck that were most certainly human and had severed his jugular. The flesh around the area had definitely been chewed. She'd taken tissue and blood samples from his neck and a sperm sample in hopes that the lab would be able to detect something from the spittle the killer had left behind. But the only thing the lab had told her was that the spittle belonged to a female with O-positive blood that had a high white cell count and was anemic. Hardly the stuff with which murders were solved.

"Fay?" Paul Sumoto strolled into the room.

"Hi, Sumo. Sit down and I'll share my salad with you."

He wrinkled his nose with distaste. "Thanks, but I brought my lunch." He plucked a paper bag from the fridge and joined her at the table. He was a short, slender GP from Franklin General who worked two days a week at the Lagoon clinic. He was half-Oriental and possessed that serene countenance that seemed to be the birthright of most Orientals, as though he lived perpetually in a state of grace.

"Question." His lunch bag rustled as he opened it.

"Shoot."

"These eczema cases. I saw three this morning. How many did you see?"

"Two."

"Both new?"

"Yes. Yours?"

"New." He removed his glasses, held them up to the light, cleaned them with a handkerchief. "You don't think it's eczema, do you, Fay?"

"No. Do you?"

Sumoto's dark eyes seemed large and grave behind his glasses. "No. It looks and acts like eczema, but it's behaving like a contagious virus."

"Contagious how, though? In most instances, one family member will have it and the rest are free of it. So how's it transmitted?"

"Good questions for the CDC. When do you expect an answer from them on the scrapings you sent?"

She shrugged. "Who knows."

Sumoto worked away at his sushi; just the sight of it turned Fay's stomach. What she really had a yearning for, she thought, was a rare steak. Thick, juicy, and tender. She had several in the freezer that she was saving for the end of the week, when Horn and Nash were supposed to come over for dinner, and maybe she'd have one of them tonight. A high-cholesterol treat.

The thought of seeing Nash again left her with a pleasant flush that spelled trouble. One Nash in her life had been enough. But then again, wasn't that the attraction? As though he represented a second chance to rectify what had gone wrong with Ben?

Nice try, Fay. But that rationalization just doesn't cut it.

The phone in the lunchroom buzzed and the receptionist at the front told Fay there was a call for her on line one from Lance Blair at the CDC. Did she want to take it in there or her office?

"My office," she replied, and hung up. "Hey, Paul. The CDC's on the line. Maybe we'll get some answers."

"Or more questions."

A sage reply, she thought, and left.

Fay had known Blair since her residency in Atlanta. Although they were both in their late thirties, he had always seemed older, almost as if medical research had depleted his personal reserves. He was as crisp and professional over the phone as he was in person, prefacing the call with a few perfunctory questions about how she was doing and so on, then getting right to the point.

"I've got a few things on those slides you sent me. I can tell you what the stuff isn't, but I can't tell you yet what it is."

"Then it's not eczema?"

"Nope. It has some of the same characteristics, but it definitely isn't eczema. We've also ruled out psoriasis, lichen planus, skin cancer, shingles, and purpura. It's not any of the common skin disorders, Fay. And it's not a fungus. We don't know what the hell it is. Thing is, in the last four or five months, we've gotten identical samples from small towns in central Florida, Massachusetts, south Texas, Arizona, Louisiana, and Hawaii.''

"Identical?" She swiveled her chair and lifted her feet onto the edge of the windowsill. ''You're sure?''

''Absolutely. Now, maybe it's just a coincidence that those are some of the places that are experiencing unusual weather for this time of year. But it's the sort of coincidence we're obligated to check out because it might be part of a pattern.''

He's building up to something. ''I agree.''

''If you've got a few minutes, I've got a list of questions I need to ask you, which are, I hope, going to help us define the parameters of this thing.''

''Sure. Hold on, let me get my stats on this.'' She swiveled again and faced the computer terminal. She booted up, keyed in ECZEMA. A moment later, she was in the file.

Blair's questions were the sort she expected. Total number of cases to date, the breakdown between genders, the range of ages, preliminary symptoms, the time span for the spread of the rash, other factors.

''Just how contagious is this thing, Lance?'' she interrupted before he finished.

''At this point, we really don't know.''

We. He keeps talking about we, us, our. ''Cut the shit, will you? Just lay it out.''

Silence.

''Lance?''

''I can't.''

''Then I can't cooperate with you any further on this.''

''Aw, c'mon, don't do this to me, Fay. I'm being honest with you. I can't say anything right now. We just don't know enough.''

''You're being a goddamn bureaucrat. This is between you and me. I have a right to know. I need answers, just like you do.''

Another silence. She could almost see Blair in his comfortable office, papers stacked in neat, orderly piles across his desk, his palm moving over his balding head. Now he was turning in his chair to gaze through the picture window behind him, at downtown Atlanta.

''On one condition. We never had this conversation.''

''I understand.''

''Right now, we're leaning toward the virus theory. We don't know yet how it's transmitted, but it's certainly infectious. The first report the CDC received was last February. It came from a backwater town called Edgard, not far from New Orleans. Population four hundred. During a routine autopsy, the county coroner found that sixty percent of the man's body was covered with red, flaky patches of skin. Some of the patches were raised and filled with pus. He took samples and sent them to the CDC.''

The red, flaky patches of skin fit Ben, she thought, but his skin hadn't been pus-filled.

"The next report came from a town in Massachusetts. Then from Dade City, Florida . . . '' Fay jotted down the states and towns as he spoke, seven names in all, her mind already seeking a pattern in geography, topography, something. She stopped when he said, "In all, we've got over two thousand identical samples, Fay.''

Two thousand. Statistically, it wasn't a huge number. But it alarmed her nonetheless.

"So far, the breakdown runs from fourteen years of age to sixty-six. It's pretty evenly divided between men and women and among races. The only symptoms are those usually found in eczema—some itching and a tightening of the skin before the patches appear.''

She looked down at her thumb and forefinger and scratched. *Allergies. You're being a hypochondriac.*

"What about other physiological changes?'' She was thinking of the irregularities in Ben's organs. His brain.

"Well, in the fellow autopsied in Louisiana, his spleen and liver were considerably smaller than normal.''

She shut her eyes and rubbed her temple. "What about his brain?''

"Can't say. The coroner didn't look at his brain. Why?''

"Just wondering.''

"Once the first patch appears, the rate at which it spreads seems to vary among individuals.''

"Give me an example.''

She heard the tap of computer keys. "Okay, let's see. A fifteen-year-old boy in Massachusetts saw his family doctor when the rash showed up on his hands. A mild cortisone cream was prescribed. Three weeks later, he was covered with the rash. A fifty-two-year-old woman in one of the towns north of Honolulu claims her rash appeared almost two years ago. We have no way of verifying it because she didn't see her dermatologist until it had spread to her face.''

"And now?''

"She disappeared three weeks ago."

"What do you mean 'disappeared'?"

"Disappeared. Didn't come home one day. Her husband says the only parts of her body that weren't afflicted were her eyelids, hands, and nails. Cortisone seems to retard the spreading somewhat in certain people."

"Does this woman's husband have it?"

"No. No one else in the family contracted it. But we've found some rather alarming things about the areas in which this rash appears."

"The weather, you mean."

"Yeah, extreme heat or cold that's unusual for that time of year. Like I said, we don't know yet if that's related. But the crime rates have shot up in these areas. There are more incidents of violence, often unprovoked."

Like a man shooting down twenty-nine people, Lance? That kind of unprovoked? She spun in her chair again, gazing out the window, suddenly grateful that she hadn't included names in her samples, that she'd numbered them. "What else?"

"A lot of people in these areas have just vanished. Like the woman in Hawaii. They walk out the door, supposedly on their way to school, or work or whatever, and that's it. They're never seen again." He barely paused, barely gave her time to mull this over before he went on. "There're also some unusual plant and animal mutations, which have led us to believe it might be related to something in the water, soil, or air. Maybe a chemical pollutant. Or some side effect of the thinning ozone. We just don't know yet."

"You're grasping, you mean."

Softly: "Yes."

"What kind of mutations?"

"Well, the one that comes to mind immediately is oranges."

"Oranges." She almost laughed. "An orange becomes a pear? An orange becomes a banana? What kind of mutation could possibly occur in an orange?"

"The town in Florida. Some of the groves there are producing oranges that are fuzzy, almost like peaches. But more so. It's like they've grown fur or something."

"Fur." Oh, yeah, swell. Fur.

"I told you it was nuts."

"What else?"

"The . . . Oh, excuse me for a second." He covered the receiver with his hand, and she heard him speaking to someone who'd just come into his office. "Fay, I'll have to get back to you. I've got an overseas call on the other line."

"Wait, Lance. One more question. What's the fatality rate on this?"

"No known fatalities yet."

"*All* two thousand are still alive?"

"As far as we know. The mysterious thing is the disappearances. The count stands at around two hundred now, and those are only the ones that have been reported. We think the actual figure could be twice that."

Ten to twenty percent, vanished. To where? And why? "What else? What aren't you telling me."

He sighed. "Look, let me call you back and—"

"Tell me." A command.

"I've got to run, Fay. Talk to you in a few days." He hung up, the click sharp, almost hurtful. The dead line sounded hollow, as though she were in a huge, cavernous room that had no furniture in it. If she breathed too loudly, if she sneezed, if she blinked, that slight noise would fill her office. She quietly replaced the receiver. *What're you hiding, Blair? What?*

3.

The red Firebird flew down Route 16, sunroof open to the clear blue sky, a tune by Bon Jovi blaring from the tape deck.

Katie leaned forward from the backseat and glanced at the speedometer. The needle leaped toward eighty. A strange, wild scent radiated from the pores of Ray's skin, an intoxicating smell that drew her in quickly and completely, and held on even after she'd moved away from it, from him. Tendrils of it curled around her, through her, luring, taunting, *Follow me, follow.*

She closed her eyes and seized a tendril, it didn't matter which it was, any would do. Then she let herself go, burrowing into the scent, tracking it in much the same way a cat might, seeking its history, its story, its secrets.

Fragmented images. Momentary. Coming too fast to tell what they were. She dug deeper, deeper, twisting where the scent twisted, pausing where it paused, rushing forward when it rushed. She found the rhythm, the flow, the pulse, and lost herself in it.

"Stop it! You're killing her!" Ray shouts.

But his old man is drunk and keeps punching her in the stomach, the hips, the kidneys, the face, over and over again.

Ray lunges for him, grabs his old man's arm, jerks him away from his mother, slams his fist into his father's jaw. He stumbles back and crashes into the kitchen table. Plates and glasses and bowls slide to the floor. His old man struggles to his feet, but Ray kicks him hard in the ribs and he topples sideways and lays still, blood leaking from his mouth and a gash in his forehead.

For long seconds, Ray stands there, staring at him, hating him. Then he spins around and gently lifts his mother from the floor and carries her into the living room. She's bleeding all over him. Her right eye is swollen shut. A chip of enamel from a broken tooth is stuck to her lower lip. Her nose is lopsided. Her soft, painful cries beat the air. He holds her, whispering, "Don't die, Ma, don't die. C'mon, please, don't die . . ."

Katie wrenched herself free and flopped forward at the waist, face pressed against her thighs, blood rushing into her head. She sucked in her own familiar scents. Denim. Shalimar. Pears soap. Images kept pulsing behind her lids, hard, hot, insistent. But gradually they dimmed like old photographs the sun had bleached.

You imagined it all. None of it was real.

When she lifted her head, the Firebird was slowing, pulling in under the bridge that crossed Meadow Creek. The air was like summer again and she *wasn't* imagining that.

They shrugged off their jackets and left them in the car. Ray had a pair of binoculars around his neck. Dani stood with her fingers tucked in the waistband of her slacks and bit at her lower lip as she looked around. Katie's eyes followed a monarch butterfly. A warm August breeze lifted strands of her hair. The creek gurgled like an infant. The air smelled sweet, of grass and water and wildflowers.

"I don't get it," Dani said, fixing her hands to her hips. "It must be seventy-five here."

"At least." Ray fingered the binoculars around his neck. "Follow me, ladies."

They strolled single file along the creek, none of them speaking. The meadow the creek was named after fell away on either side of them, gradually giving way to hills covered with trees. Off to Katie's right, the trees were still green and full, the way they were supposed to be in August. Wildflowers burst from the green. Bees and butterflies flitted through the sunlight. But on their left, where it was colder, branches were thin of leaves, there were hardly any flowers, the grass had turned brown.

Ray waded through the creek where it was shallow, where

the water wasn't any deeper than his ankles, and Katie and Dani followed. On the other side, the air was fifteen or twenty degrees cooler.

"The creek's a border," Ray said.

Dani laughed and hugged her arms against her. "Weird."

"Impossible," Katie said.

Ray nodded. "Impossible, yeah, but here it is. Now I've got a couple of other things to show you."

They crossed the creek again to where it was warmer and walked for twenty or thirty minutes, veering into the trees, climbing one of the hills. The air was humid and still, and every now and then Katie caught a faint whiff of something that seemed out of place. But she couldn't focus on it, couldn't track it.

At the top of the hill, they stopped behind a line of pines and crouched down. Below them was a clearing that was perfectly hidden between this hill and one about half a mile away. Two semis were parked in the grass, engines idling. Their rear doors were down, and to the right of the semi closest to them was a Jeep.

"Take a look." Ray passed Katie the binoculars. She lifted them to her eyes and focused. The two men inside the jeep were in uniform; the driver held a microphone to his mouth.

"Are they army?" she asked.

"I don't know. Military of some sort."

"Lemme take a look." Dani reached for the binoculars.

"I've never seen more than four guys in uniform," Ray went on. "And there're three or four dudes who're here sometimes. They cross the creek in these cars that look like glass bubbles with long metal arms on the front. They take samples of everything. Weirdest shit I've ever seen."

"Far out," Dani breathed. "How'd you find this place?"

Ray shrugged and sat back, working a toothpick between his teeth. "Me and some of the guys were down here a couple days ago fishing in the creek. I kept hearing these sounds, so I went to investigate. That's when I saw these little bubble cars."

"Have you told anyone?" Katie wanted to know.

"Nope. Just you two. I figure it's got something to do with the border. Seeing how your fathers work out at Hartwell, maybe they know something about it."

"Hartwell doesn't do research on weather," Dani said. "It's a pharmaceutical company. They do research on plants and stuff."

"And those dudes are taking samples of plants."

"I still think Daddy would've said something about it."

"How about your old man?" Ray asked Katie.

"I'll ask him, but he hasn't mentioned it."

Ray flicked the toothpick away from him. "C'mon, I'll show you one more thing."

They trekked back down the hill and crossed the creek to the cold side. Ray moved quickly through the tall, brown grass, his eyes on the ground, looking for something. Then he kneeled and spread the grass with his hands. "Take a look."

The cluster of flowers resembled roses. But they were at least three feet tall, prospered in the cold, smelled like basil, and had suction roots that were attached to rock, not to soil. Ray plucked one and held it up. Sunlight struck the delicate petals and spilled over onto the pale green leaves, creating a thing of exquisite beauty.

"The night we were fishing," Ray said, "I caught a trout with an extra set of eyes on top of its head. So there're two examples of what these guys have probably collected. I'm sure there's more."

"But what's it mean?" Katie's question was directed to no one in particular. "Why's this happening?"

The words echoed in the still, chilly air, an empty sound that begged to be filled. Dani filled it, but not with an answer. "I'm cold. Let's get out of here."

As they left, Katie scooped up the fallen flower.

8

Obie's Place

Lew Oliver sped north through the twilight in his bright silver truck, shadows shifting and sliding like liquid or wet sand across the windshield. His headlights grazed the trees on either side, illuminating the trunks, creating ghosts of the thinning leaves. Patches of bruised sky bled through the branches, and he kept watching it, uneasy at the thought of impending darkness. He felt as if it symbolized something over which he had no control, something he couldn't penetrate or understand.

Damn fool. He was letting the weirdness around here get to him.

Like the murder of the Fenuzo kid. And the autopsy report on Ben Nash. Just what the hell was he supposed to make of it? *A rash . . . an enlarged hypothalamus . . .* Yeah, fine. But what the fuck did it mean? He'd turned it over to the mayor. Let *him* figure it out.

As he reached the rise in the hill the truck had been climbing, he adjusted the rearview mirror and watched Lagoon sliding away from him. Always before, there had been something magical about this particular spot where the village melted into twilight and vanished. It had made him feel that Lagoon was his personal secret, as though he'd discovered it and he alone knew the way back. But tonight it troubled him at a level too deep for words. He was almost afraid that if he pulled over to the side of the road and got out to look, Lagoon simply wouldn't be there.

The thought was as foolish as his newfound fear of the dark, but there you had it. He couldn't help it. Some men were possessive of their wives, of their lovers; Oliver felt that way about Lagoon. It was home. Roots. It was his personal history. He couldn't imagine himself existing separate from it.

As the truck started down the other side of the hill, Oliver turned on the radio. He tuned in the country station over in Asheville. At night, the reception was always better, and there was nothing like Tanya Tucker to chase away the blues and the dark. He rolled down his window and the cold, fresh air swept through the truck, energizing him.

The notions he'd had just a few minutes ago now seemed laughable. Hell, the only unusual things going on in town were due to Ben Nash and the nasty business at the inn and to the murder of Joe Fenuzo. Everyone was jumpy.

Fenuzo reminded him of Scott Nash, of how that stupid bastard had shown him up in front of Fay. He was just like his brother. Ben had thought he was better than everyone else in town, too, what with his movie-star looks and his brains with computers, but a lot of good it had done him in the end.

Yeah, so much for fancy educations and good looks.

He spat the wad of tobacco in his cheek out the window. For some reason, he thought of a remark Fay had made to him once about chewing tobacco, about how it would rot his tongue or the back of his throat or some goddamn thing. But what she'd really been saying, he knew, was that a man who chewed tobacco turned her off. Well, he'd show her different one of these days. He'd take her down a peg or two and give her what she really wanted, what neither Nash could give her. Yeah, he would.

Smiling now, feeling a hundred percent better than he had earlier, he slowed as he approached the sign ahead that said OBIE'S ANTIQUES. Harry Oberman was a cantankerous hillbilly who owned a shop full of junk that he sold as antiques. He lived with four cats in a shack adjacent to his shop, guzzled a quart of vodka a day, and guarded his property with a twelve-gauge shotgun he handled like Wyatt Earp.

Oliver didn't like him much, not really. But from time to time Obie would call him up and invite him out to the shack for a drink. That usually meant he had some bit of information to pass on in return for a favor. The favors were no big deal; mostly they involved things like fixing parking or speeding tickets for Obie's wild-ass daughter, Polly, who worked in a saloon in town. Oliver always did what the old man asked. But that had more to do with his daughter—with whom Oliver enjoyed periodic romps in the sack—than with the old man's tips, which rarely panned out.

Oliver hung a right onto the dirt road just beyond the sign. Pebbles pinged against the sides of the truck. Dust flew through his window and settled on the dash. It was pitch-black in here and the truck's lights flickered across the trees, creating weird ghost shapes that seemed to loom, float, then vanish. But somehow it wasn't quite as disturbing as the sight of Lagoon vanishing in the twilight.

He pulled up in front of the shop, where the porch light was on. Its dim yellow glow washed across the junk that littered the porch: brass and copper spittoons, woven baskets, an old radio shaped like Napoleon's hat, tires, the hood of a 1957 Thunderbird as red as a strawberry, pots and pans, bumpers, washtubs. It was like trying to make his way through a mine field. One step in the wrong direction might upset the delicate balance and bring down everything.

As he knocked, he heard the drone of the TV inside.

"Yeah? Who is it?"

"Lew."

"Well, shit, boy, since when do you gotta knock? Door's open."

A bell tinkled as Oliver stepped into the shop. The *things* were everywhere in here, too, more things than were on the porch. A dozen stained-glass lamps burned from various spots in the room, tinging everything the color of nicotine. Obie was stretched out on a worn red velvet couch watching the tube. A cat was curled at his feet, a second sprawled on the armrest at his head. The place smelled faintly of cat piss.

Obie aimed the remote-control device at the TV, lowering the volume, and made space for Oliver on the couch. "Now there's the kinda woman you need, Lew." He pointed at Loni Anderson on the screen. "Ain't she just the prettiest woman you done seen?"

"She married Burt Reynolds, Obe."

His frown threw his forehead into a chaos of wrinkles. He was a lean old coot with skin that looked like well-worn leather, thinning white hair, a pointed chin. His prissy mouth rolled syllables and consonants around before spitting them out. "Yeah? Now what'd she go do a fool thing like that for? You'd be better for her than Burt, for Christ's sakes." He swung his skinny legs over the side of the couch and splashed vodka into a couple of glasses from the bottle on the coffee table. "But there's always Polly, boy."

Oliver gave a noncommittal nod and Obie exploded with laughter. "My daughter not good enough for you or what?"

She's interested in screwing, Obe, not marriage. "I don't think I'm her type."

"Shee-it. She's no one's type." He passed Oliver a glass of straight vodka. "Cheers, boy." Obie clicked his glass against Oliver's and knocked back half the vodka. Then he wiped his arm across his mouth, belched, set the glass down. "I heard about the Fenuzo boy, but no one's saying much about what happened. So's how about you telling me, Lew? Seeing that I'm less than a mile from that Chevron station and it's just me out here, I'd like to know what's what."

As Oliver related what had happened, he pulled out his pouch of tobacco, squeezed some between his thumb and index finger, and stuck it inside his mouth, against a cheek. "As long as you've got the twelve-gauge and aren't afraid to use it, Obe, you've got nothing to worry about."

"Yeah? You think so, huh?" He finished the rest of his drink and stood. "Well, there's some things that even a twelve-gauge got no power against, Lew. Lemme show you something out back."

Obie plucked a large flashlight from some junk on the table, grabbed his jacket, then they went outside. The cold air smelled sweet and clean, of pine and that smoky scent that seemed to ride tandem with autumn. Except this was August, not autumn, Oliver thought.

"Weather's weirded out," he said, turning his head to spit.

Obie guffawed. "Ayup. And the weather ain't the half of it."

They followed the dirt road for a quarter of a mile or so past Obie's shack. Even the beam of the flashlight seemed frail against the darkness out here. The moon hadn't risen yet and trees cut off most of the starlight. Oliver heard soft, muted sounds to his left, noises that might have been rodents scurrying through pine needles or the breeze whispering through branches . . . or something else. He zipped his jacket to his throat and walked a little faster.

They reached a pen where Obie kept chickens and a couple of pigs. "I wanted you to see this before I get rid of it, Lew. This here's part of the weirdness, I think, and I'd be real interested in hearing your opinion." Obie lifted the lid of the aluminum garbage can near the pen, tipped it over, and a baby pig slid out. With the toe of his dusty boot, he rolled it over, exposing its belly.

Oliver crouched down; a chill sped along his spine. "Goddamn."

The pig had been slit down the middle, skin and fat and ribs peeled back, exposing its insides. Most of the organs—including the heart—had been torn out. It hadn't been dead long—there wasn't much of a stench. The cold weather had probably kept it from decomposing as quickly as it would have if it had been any other August. But there was something grotesque about the deliberateness of the act, about the almost surgical precision of the wound.

"Where'd you find it?"

"Back in the trees a piece late this afternoon." The flashlight's beam followed the slit from the pig's throat to its tail. "That wasn't made by no animal, Lew. Critters don't give a shit about being so tidy."

He handed Oliver the flashlight, pulled gardening gloves from his back pocket, slipped them on. Then he lifted the little pig back into the garbage and righted the can. The lid clattered as he replaced it; the sound echoed in the quiet.

"I can see why a man would kill a pig for food. But I got no idea why he'd kill a pig and only take the insides. You got any notions on that, Lew?"

Oliver shook his head and spat out another stream of tobacco juice. "I'm still trying to figure why a woman killed Joey Fenuzo and chewed his neck to shit, Obe. Or why a good citizen like Ben Nash cut down twenty-nine people with an Uzi."

The words seemed to weight the air, then rolled along between them like lead balls as they walked back toward the shack in silence. One of Obie's cats pranced along in front of them, fascinated by the flashlight's beam skipping over the dirt.

"Tell you one goddamn thing," Obie said after a bit. "I've lived in these parts all my life. Seen plenty of strange things, been through plenty of bad seasons. But they never felt nothing like this. There's something real wrong, Lew. Don't know what the hell it is or where it's coming from, but I feel it."

The flashlight dimmed, then winked out. The assault of darkness was so sudden, so total, that Oliver froze in place, his breath caught in his throat, a wave of sweat leaping across his back. He was dimly aware of Obie hitting the flashlight with his hand and cursing the batteries. But the dark dwarfed his presence. It was a demon, this darkness, and it tightened like a hot hand around Oliver's eyes, licked obscenely at his cheeks, slithered up the legs of his jeans. He barely repressed an urge to scream, to slap at his jeans, to claw at his face, his arms.

Clint Eastwood wouldn't be scared of the dark, Lew ole buddy. Clint's not afraid of shit.

But he heard something in the brush, in the trees. A crackle of leaves, a soft, lewd laugh. He heard it, he did; he wasn't imagining it. He pulled his gun, spun, and fired four shots into the brush, but he could still hear the laughing, the crackles. He tore loose from the ground where his feet had rooted and ran toward his truck, the shack, light, his shoes pounding the dirt, fear thickening inside his mouth.

Move, legs, move.

Oliver flew into the shack, and a second later, Obie lumbered in after him and slammed the door behind them. He bolted it. He leaped to the windows, locking them, peering out, jerking the blinds down. Then he turned, and he and Oliver looked at each other. They both exploded with laughter, wild, nervous laughter. Obie weaved like a drunk toward the bottle of vodka on the coffee table. He gulped a swig from the bottle before he filled their glasses. Oliver downed his like water.

Gradually, the warmth seeped through him. His knees turned solid again. He walked over to the window and raised the blind.

Nothing out there, you goddamn fool.

But Oliver knew he was lying to himself. Deep inside where light didn't reach, his fear coiled like a spring, waiting.

9

At the Lagoon

1.

The Menningers' house was the largest on the lagoon, a tri-level with several decks and a wide, private beach. In the moon-light, looming in the pines like it did, Katie thought it looked like an elaborate treehouse.

The party was in full swing, with lights blazing from the downstairs windows and people spilling out onto the first two decks. The doors were thrown open to the chilly night air and music pumped into the dark, following Katie as she made her way down the sloped yard to the beach.

She didn't know most of the people Dani had invited. They were friends she'd met in the private school she'd attended in Atlanta before her parents had moved to Lagoon. They were older than Katie, already in college, and had driven here in their own cars. Their primary interests in life seemed to be drugs, music, and fun. Which was fine, except those weren't *her* inter-ests, and she wished she hadn't come.

The worst of it was that she couldn't leave. She'd driven over in Hank's Mustang and it was blocked by two BMWs and a Mercedes whose drivers Katie couldn't find. So she was stuck until the party ended, unless she walked home. But just the idea of braving Hawthorne on foot at night made her throat go tight and hot.

She'd hoped to find a spot out here where she could sit for a while. But the dock and the beach were occupied by couples huddled together against the cold, drinking and smoking grass. She walked past them toward the end of the beach, where it turned into rocks and curved into the lagoon's south shore.

From here, she could see straight across the moonlit waters to the Blue Inn. Lights glimmered in a couple of the first-floor windows, but otherwise the place was dark. Ben's brother was probably just living in the downstairs rooms. She felt sorry for him, knocking around in that huge place with just his memories for company.

Only yesterday she'd seen him in the army/navy store when she stopped by there on her way home from school. Although she'd met him when he'd last visited Ben and should have gone up to him yesterday and at least said hi, she hadn't. She not only didn't know what to say to him, but his scent was a thick cloud weighted with grief that she'd found oppressive even from a distance. So she'd avoided him and left the store before he'd seen her.

Maybe she'd drop by the inn this weekend, though. Considering what was being said in town about Ben, Scott probably needed to hear from someone that his brother wasn't the monster people were making him out to be. She didn't have any idea why he'd done what he had, but the Ben she had known wasn't like that.

"Hey, Katie-o."

She glanced back to see Ray Bosque stepping carefully over the rocks. "Hi."

Hi? That's all you can think of to say? C'mon, crack a joke, laugh, say something clever. But her tongue had already twisted in on itself, proving once again that when it came to guys, she was socially retarded. She wished the sand would just open up and swallow her.

"I saw you earlier." He stopped beside her, twisting the gold post in his ear. "But you got away before I could come over."

"Too noisy inside."

"And boring. If you can believe even half of what you hear in there, then just about everyone has had a nose or a boob job."

Katie laughed. "Probably."

He tilted his head to the left. "C'mon, let's walk farther down here."

The strains of music and laughter from Dani's house echoed across the water, rising and falling like an erratic tide as they made their way over the rocks. They followed the shore's curve to the next stretch of beach. There were a few scattered cabins through here that usually weren't vacated until after Labor Day. But with the onslaught of cold weather, most of them had already been closed up for the winter. It had left the air strangely empty and hollow, as though there were a hole in the very dark that begged to be filled by something.

Now and then, she noticed a vague scent that seemed at odds with the fragrance of pine and water. It was too faint to track, but it bothered her. It didn't fit. It was like seeing a green cloud drifting across a purple sky: that kind of wrongness.

As they neared the end of the beach, where the trees started again, rising like dark shoots toward the sky, the scent strengthened. It wasn't exactly like what she'd smelled that one morning on her bike, but it was close enough. She stopped, and Ray glanced at her.

"What's wrong?"

"Do you smell something?"

Ray sniffed at the air like a dog. "Just smoke. From the fireplace. Why?"

Keep your mouth shut. He can't smell it. She shrugged. "I thought I smelled something else."

"Maybe you did. I'm just getting over a cold, so I can't smell much of anything. Let's sit over here." They settled on a log, and he pulled a flask out of his pocket and spun the lid. He held it out. "Here, this will take off the chill. Vodka and OJ."

She tipped the flask to her mouth. The fumes swirled into her nostrils, burned a path down her throat, and she started to cough. Ray patted her on the back. "Hey, take it easy."

She wiped her hand across her mouth. "It's kind of strong."

He smiled, and she knew she hadn't fooled him for a minute. She might as well have come out and said this was her first taste of vodka ever. If there'd been any doubt in his mind that she was straight and uptight, as Dani was always telling her, there wasn't now. He drank from the flask, capped it again, and slipped it back inside his jacket.

"Your buddy Dani guzzles this stuff straight like it's water," he remarked. "You know that day the three of us went to the meadow?"

Like she could possibly forget, she thought, and nodded.

"Well, after we'd dropped you off, Dani brings out this pint, right? And she starts putting the stuff away like nothing I've ever seen. By the time I drove her back to school to pick up her car, she was pretty blasted. I followed her home just to make sure she didn't kill herself."

As he talked, his scent reached out and touched her. It was playful and light, a cool green like peppermint, and easy to follow, to slide into. Within moments, she was inside his memory of that afternoon seeing it as he had, like a movie.

He and Dani are in the Firebird. She is sitting with her back against the door, legs drawn up against her, the open pint resting on her knees as she laughs and chatters and gets progressively drunker. Once, when Ray stops at a light, Dani leans toward him, nibbles at his earlobe, then giggles and works the pint down between his thighs.

"Your turn," she says.

"Can't. I'm driving." He passes the pint back to her.

Another time, Dani presses up close to Ray on the seat and lets her fingers glide lazily along his arm as her tongue darts for his earlobe again.

"Cut it out. I can't drive when you do that."

"Then let's stop somewhere."

"I'll take you back to your car."

"I don't want to go back to my car. I thought we were going to have some fun."

"I need to get to the garage."

The image skipped ahead, to the school parking lot, where Dani weaved to her own car and was too loaded to unlock the door. Ray had to help her, then drove her home in her car and walked back into town to get his Firebird.

It was a slightly different version from what he'd told Katie, and she wondered if it was just her imagination running wild and hopeful. Maybe the truth was that he'd kissed Dani, that they'd gone back to her house and . . .

She burrowed to the surface of the dark again, annoyed with herself. The other scent found her immediately, as if it had been waiting for her. It was much closer now. The hair on the back of her neck stood up. Goose bumps rose on her arms. Ray must have sensed something, too, because he suddenly stopped talking and peered at the trees.

The music from the house had stopped. Even though Katie could still hear voices and laughter skipping across the water, these sounds seemed distant, unconnected to her and Ray, to this slice of beach they were on. She felt as if they were trapped inside a transparent box, unable to move, unable to flee from whatever was watching them.

You're imagining it. Nothing's out there.

But she felt the *tickle*. The *nudge*. And now Ray was standing, reaching out a hand to help her to her feet. "It's getting cold." His eyes were still glued to the trees. "Let's go back."

Katie grabbed hold of his hand, and they moved down the beach and over the rocks again, both of them silent, quick, tense.

2.

Fay's home was midway between the inn and the southern tip of the lagoon, a distance of about three miles. Nash could have walked the distance, but Ben's Jeep, Delilah, needed to be driven worse than he needed exercise.

He rolled open her sunroof and cranked her up. She sputtered and spewed exhaust when he backed her out of the garage and stalled twice before he reached the end of the driveway. But once he got her going, she hummed along, a sign—as Ben would have said—of her extreme pleasure at being driven again.

The mystical bent to Ben's personality had endowed everything with awareness. To him, a frying pan was as cognizant as a plant or an animal or a human being; the difference was merely of degree. It was even true for Ben on microscopic levels. He believed that a cell, for example, communicated with other cells, with tissues and blood and the body that contained it. A cell possessed memory. It wasn't like man's memory, but that didn't diminish its capacity or strength within the framework it existed.

Nash suspected the belief was rooted in a time before he was born, when Ben was an only child. According to his parents, who had loved telling and retelling childhood anecdotes, Ben had ridden their father's shoulders at bedtime, stopping at each object in the house to say good night to it and to wish it pleasant dreams. Nash recalled his own journeys on those same shoulders and wondered why he'd never thought of it as anything more than a marvelous game, while for Ben it had become the foundation, really, of who and what he was. Even his computers had been alive to him; perhaps that had been part of his genius.

And his life ended when he shot down twenty-nine people.

It didn't make sense. It never would, even though Fay had given him medical explanations that could possibly shed light on that final, terrible act of violence.

He downshifted as he approached her driveway and swung in behind a pink and black Caddy that looked to be thirty years old. Horn's wheels. He picked up the bottle of wine from the passenger seat and got out. His breath congealed in the still air. The moon, standing on end like a banana, peeked up over the roof of Fay's house.

Her place, like most of those along the lagoon, was sequestered among trees that provided ample privacy. It was constructed of pine and cedar, with a wide porch at the front and windows that ran from floor to ceiling.

As Nash climbed the porch steps, a St. Bernard the size of a small horse galloped toward him, teeth bared. Its huge paws pounded the ground, but otherwise it didn't make a sound. Before he even reacted, the dog leaped onto the porch. It was airborne, flying toward him, then those tremendous paws struck his chest, knocking him back against the railing. He slipped to the floor of the porch and the dog was all over him, licking his cheeks and neck and eyes, whimpering and whining as though Nash were a long-lost friend.

He struggled to avoid the long, wet tongue and kept trying to push the monster off, telling it over and over again that it was a good boy, a good friend, sit back, please. A wedge of light fell over them as the door opened.

"Okay, that's enough, Samson." Fay grabbed hold of the monster's collar and pulled him away from Nash. "God, I'm really sorry, Scott. He gets so excited whenever there's company."

"Excited," Nash repeated, and laughed. "I thought he was going to make chopped liver out of me." He sat up. Now he was eye to eye with the St. Bernard, who was panting and whimpering. "How come he didn't bark?"

"He can't. His vocal cords are defective."

The animal's topaz eyes blinked as Nash stood, then he broke away from Fay and lumbered into the house, paws hitting the wooden floors like hooves. "Ben saved him from the pound and gave him to me a year ago," she was saying as they stepped inside. "About six weeks after I got him, he contracted a virus that settled in his vocal cords, and that was it." She shrugged. "On top of it, he loves everyone. So much for my watchdog. What can I get you to drink?"

"A glass of this would be fine." He held out the bottle of wine.

"Coming up."

As she rummaged in a drawer for a corkscrew, Nash watched her, liking what he saw, the camera in his head clicking away, composing photographs of her. She was nearly six feet tall, willowy, graceful, wearing jeans tight enough to set off her curves. Her red wool turtleneck complemented her soft, creamy complexion. Her hair was the color of walnuts or chestnuts or maybe hazelnuts. Some kind of nut. It depended on how the light struck it. She'd brushed it away from her face and it fell to her shoulders in waves. He had a sudden urge to slide his fingers through it: that sort of hair.

This was the woman Ben had been crazy about, whose name Nash had heard at least half a dozen times during any one phone call. *If I were ever going to get married again, bro, she would be it.* So who had dumped who and why?

"Here you go." Fay handed him the glass of wine, then shooed him out of the kitchen with a platter of steaks that he was to deliver to Horn, who was on the porch tending the grill. She needed to check the sweet potatoes, the rolls, the works.

Sent on his way, Nash wandered into the spacious front room. High-beam ceilings. A thick throw rug in front of the fire. Furniture that looked as if it had been collected from antique stores, then stripped down and refinished. Rustic but comfortable and rather solitary, he thought, the room of someone who didn't mind her own company.

The far wall was entirely glass and offered a magnificent view of the moonlit lagoon and the wide deck that extended over it. Horn was at the grill, fiddling with the coals, while Samson hovered nearby, waiting for the handouts he was sure would come.

"Hey, Andy."

Horn glanced around, all six foot six of him straightening as he did so. He was only two inches taller than Nash, but it was a vital two inches; Nash felt like he was watching a giant unfold. Horn broke into a wide grin that creased his eyes at the corners and bracketed his mouth with a pair of identical lines. He looked exactly as he had more than a year ago when Nash had last seen him—lean, with the musculature of a man half his age, curly hair completely white.

"Well, if it ain't my favorite globe-trotter." He crushed Nash in a bear hug that communicated everything he wanted to say about Ben but didn't. "So's you were at the South Pole, huh?" He held Nash at arm's length as if he were a kid, patted him once on either shoulder, and stepped back. "See any penguins? Polar bears?"

"Penguins." Horn was the only person who ever asked what animals he saw in the places he traveled.

"They got bad politics down there?"

"Only the kind you don't see."

"Good. Then we don't got to worry 'bout any irate dictators coming to look for you 'cause you pissed them off, taking pictures of stuff you weren't s'posed to know about, huh. Let's get these steaks on, Scotty, I'm starved." He nodded toward Samson, who peered up at him hopefully. "And so's my good buddy here." In response, Samson wiggled his rear end and whimpered, and both men laughed.

They caught up on news, neither of them mentioning Ben. It was as if Nash's presence here were unrelated to those events at the Blue Inn. He might have been someone who'd just dropped into town to visit old friends and would soon be on his way again.

When Horn put the steaks on the grill, smoke billowed up, an ethereal white lace against the moonlight. It smelled good enough to make Nash's mouth water. "How do you want yours done, Scotty?"

"Medium, no blood."

"Make mine rare," Fay said, stepping through the sliding glass doors with a cold beer for Horn and a refill on Nash's wine. "The thermometer outside the kitchen window says it's thirty-five."

"And it's s'posed to freeze by morning," Horn remarked. "Last time we had a summer like this, you know what happened that winter?"

Fay chuckled. "Andy, the local historian."

"I'm not talking local, though. I'm talking global. 1941. Six months to the day the cold spell started that summer, the Japs bombed Pearl Harbor."

"Oh, c'mon, Andy. No doom and gloom."

He shrugged. "Just stating a fact. The weather's got stories to tell us if we listen."

"And what's the story this time?" Nash asked.

"A warning about something, I reckon." He flipped the steaks, sliced off a corner of one, and fed the piece to Samson. "It's tied in with all this business. Ben, the Fenuzo kid, what the CDC found, the—"

"What'd the CDC find?" Nash interrupted, glancing at Fay.

She told him about her conversation with Lance Blair. As she spoke, her fingers worked at the buttons on her suede jacket, fastening them, and he imagined those fingers, those hands, cutting on Ben, prodding at his organs, his brain, ferreting out the secrets of whatever had afflicted him. Superimposed over this image was another one, of these same hands and fingers stroking and caressing Ben, making love to him. The vision created a deep ache in his chest, but he couldn't tell if it was an ache of pain or of desire.

"Have they gone to these areas?" Nash asked. "Seen the

people? Taken soil and water samples? Tested the foods for contaminants?''

"I don't know. He didn't say."

Nash thought of the cold line he'd discovered the night he'd arrived in Lagoon and made a mental note to return there. "Did he say anything at all about what they were going to do in Lagoon, if anything?"

"No. We got interrupted. There's something he wasn't telling me, though."

"No surprise there," said Horn. "Your buddy's CDC. That means his first obligation is to the government."

She smiled and leaned back against the railing, one arm folded at her waist, the elbow of the other resting against it as she sipped her wine. In the moonlight, it stained her upper lip pale pink. "You're making it sound awfully dire."

"Honey, I got news for you. Anytime the government's involved in something they want to keep secret, you're talking nasty dealings of one kind or another."

"If this thing is contagious, they can't afford to keep it secret."

"And they would've done something by now," added Nash.

"Like what, Scotty? You think they would've released a statement to the media about two thousand weirdo cases? About folks disappearing? About folks getting crazed? Shee-it, boy. You been outta the country too long if you believe that. The government tells you just what they want you to know and not a word more. Look at AIDS."

Fay's sigh was testimony that she and Horn had had this conversation before. He smiled. "Fay's got no patience for me when I get going like this. She still believes in the system."

"You're impossible." She looked at Nash. "Andy thinks there's this conspiracy of silence about AIDS, that they haven't told us everything about the disease because if they did, there'd be mass hysteria. People would stop eating in restaurants for fear of catching it through saliva; we'd have a critical shortage of hospital personnel; we'd see more incidents of kids who're carriers being barred from public schools; there'd be an escalation in violence against high-risk groups. Like that. The beginning of anarchy."

Horn shrugged. "But you just got finished telling us your buddy's hiding something."

"He is. But I don't think it's anything as bleak as what you're suggesting."

"Maybe, maybe not." He cut into the rarest steak. "This the way you like it, hon?"

She checked it and nodded. "Perfect."

"Why don't you keep it warm till these two are done?"

"Good idea." She started toward the sliding doors, then stopped. "And Scott, don't believe a word he says about how I've been brainwashed by the so-called system, okay?"

Horn laughed. "She always suspects me of the worst."

"With good reason." She winked at him when she said it, then went inside.

"She's been brainwashed by the so-called system," Horn said. He and Nash laughed.

They ate in the front room near the fire, Samson begging for handouts, logs crackling and spitting in the fireplace. Maybe it was the wine or the fact that he hadn't been in the company of a woman longer than he cared to remember, or maybe it was nothing more than Fay's connection to Ben. But Nash was completely taken with her. She was bright, funny, and quick, and seemed to be, at different moments throughout the evening, not one woman but several.

Fay the physician was cool, opinionated, controlled, as inscrutable as a fortune cookie. Fay the woman was looser, warmer, quick to laugh, with a repertoire of expressions to rival any actress's. Then there were the other women: the flirt with smoldering eyes, the bookworm who was quiet and somewhat remote, the country lady who was as self-sufficient as a pioneer.

It wouldn't take much to fall hard for a woman like this, if he were so inclined, which he wasn't. Once he uncovered the full truth about Ben and tied up his legal affairs, he was gone. But he understood now why his brother had been so smitten with her.

During dessert, Samson started scratching at the porch and whimpering. Nash opened it for him and the dog tore outside.

"Reckon he's smelled a coon," Horn said.

"The last time he tangled with a raccoon, it cost him fourteen stitches in the right flank. I'd better check." Fay picked up a poker from the stand beside the fireplace and a flashlight from the mantel, shrugged on her jacket, and turned on the porch light. "Be back in a jiffy, guys."

But Nash and Horn were already on their feet, following her. She plucked the leash from a hook on the outside wall, then they descended the deck steps at the left side of the house. They came out on a dirt path that led down to the edge of the lagoon. Before they reached the end of it, Fay veered left into the brush. She whistled for Samson, fell silent to listen for his whimpers, then whistled again and called his name. Nash heard a rustling in the bed of dry leaves, and a second later, the beam of the flashlight struck Samson, hunched over something on the ground.

He let out a soft, dry wheeze as they approached. "What've you got, boy?" Fay whispered, going over to him, snapping the leash on his collar.

Nash took the flashlight from her and shone it over the ground in front of the dog. A short, dark snake was coiled less than a foot from the end of Samson's nose. "How'd you pick up this scent inside the house, boy?"

"He was probably chasing something else," Fay replied. "What kind of snake is it?"

"I don't know."

As Nash crouched to get a closer look, the damn thing uncoiled and sprang at the light, its tiny eyes glowing red, its mouth falling open, that primitive snout like something in a nightmare.

He scrambled back, stumbled, and the flashlight flew out of his hand and rolled. The snake struck the lens once, twice, a third time. It drove Samson into a near frenzy as he struggled to break free of Fay's hold.

Nash leaped forward to kick the flashlight out of the way, but Horn was faster. He hooked the end of the poker under the flashlight and pulled it through the leaves. "We need a box or something to get this critter in."

"I'll get it." Fay handed Nash the leash and took off for the house.

"Never seen a snake pull shit like this." Horn spoke softly, reaching carefully for the flashlight. "They never strike 'less they're cornered, and this critter wasn't cornered. He just didn't like the light." He fixed the beam on the reptile, which was coiled again, head hidden under the leaves, and kept the poker trained on him, a sword, a saber. "Just don't get no ideas, snake."

Samson whimpered and tugged on the leash; Nash pulled him back. He emitted a soft wheeze of defeat and plunked down, resigned to his role as a spectator.

"Here he goes, Scotty, wiggling again. Watch out. Don't get too close."

The snake dug deeper under the leaves until only its tail was visible, twitching back and forth. But Nash sensed the heat of its eyes, burning through the leaves like X rays, watching them. Waiting.

Horn glanced around, mumbling something about how long Fay was taking. Nash reached for the poker, and just then the snake sprang out from under the leaves, a thin, black torpedo that literally lifted up from the ground. He saw it in a kind of surreal slow motion—the snake, the pale light, those red eyes— and slammed the poker into it. Samson wrenched free of the leash, Horn spun around stammering, "What . . . . what . . . ."

The snake clung to the poker like a caterpillar and inched its way toward Nash's hand.

He dropped it.

The reptile kept working its way up the metal, the light fixed on its head, those eyes still glowing. Samson raced around it, wheezing, panting, but was too smart to attack it.

"Don't like you much, snake," Horn mumbled, and threw the flashlight at the reptile's head, crushing it.

A moment later, Fay reached them. "I wish you hadn't killed it." She set a box on the ground. "It might've been easier for Hank to identify if the head weren't crushed."

Horn snorted. "Taking no chances. Besides, I got a feeling Hank wouldn't know even if we had ourselves a perfect snake." He scooped the reptile into the box.

The utility room. Door closed to keep Samson out. Newspaper spread open on the washing machine. Bright light overhead. Safe, Nash thought.

But then Horn dumped the dead snake out of the box and he had never felt less safe in his life. Its skin gleamed like a wet street. It was black and dark gray, maybe two feet in length, with a head that—even crushed—seemed too large for its body. He had no idea what sort of snake it was, whether it was poisonous, young or old or middle-aged. But it had definitely been aggressive.

Something oozed from the head wound. Fay, wearing thick gardening gloves, cleaned the head with a corner of an old towel, then turned it over. Growing from its belly were four nubs. "They look like keloids," she said softly.

"What're keloids?" asked Nash.

"Scar tissue that on humans never stops growing. They might be caused by something as insignificant as piercing an ear. But these aren't keloids; they're too precisely situated, too exact, too damn similar."

Under a magnifying glass, the nub resembled a tiny bud that was about to open, Nash thought. When Fay touched the edge of a spoon against the nub, it triggered a reflex of some sort. The thing curled outward at the edges, a Venus flytrap opening to lure an insect, an infant's fingers reaching for something, a . . . "It's a foot. A webbed foot," he said suddenly.

"You got that right," Horn agreed.

"But what the hell are four webbed feet doing on a snake?" Fay glanced up, her hazel eyes meeting Nash's, then Horn's, but not as if she really expected an answer.

She folded the edges of the newspaper over the snake and dropped it back into the box.

Horn left around eleven with apologies for scooting out early, but he had to open the Nameless by five tomorrow morning. Nash and Fay did the dishes, their talk smooth and effortless, a flow like water that brushed distant shores, connecting present to past. Her medical training in Atlanta, his free-lancing and travels, the demise of her marriage and his, the death of his daughter.

But neither of them mentioned Ben or the snake. Their mutual silence on these two topics fastened them together in Nash's mind, as if one had somehow grown out of the other, given birth to it, a tumor popping out of diseased flesh. He knew it was clearly ridiculous. There couldn't be any link between Ben and the snake. But he felt a sudden need to get out of the house, to move around, and suggested they take a walk.

Samson, busy with a bowl of leftovers, heard the magic word *walk* and immediately trotted over to the door, where his leash hung from a hook. He pulled it down and set it in front of Nash, his tail wagging.

"He's rarely subtle." Fay laughed.

Outside, the sky was a sheet of black aluminum that shimmered with luminous stars, and the dark was alive with animal sounds. The cold revived him. "Do you run every morning?" he asked.

"Usually, unless I've got to be at the clinic early, then I try to run at night."

"Mind if I join you tomorrow?"

As she turned her head, moonlight slipped down the curve of her nose and spilled onto her cheeks. The skin glowed like electrified stone. "I have a feeling I'd never be able to keep up with you. Most mornings, I'm lucky if I can do a seven-minute mile."

"That's two minutes faster than I'll be able to do. There's not anywhere to run in the South Pole."

She chuckled. "What time do you want to go?"

"Whenever's good for you. You're the one with the job."

"Eight?"

"Perfect."

"You always so agreeable?"

"Is that what I am?"

She kicked at a pebble in the road and it flew off into the trees to their right. "More so than Ben was."

There was no rancor in her voice, only a restrained sadness that hinted at unsettled issues in her relationship with Ben. "Sometimes," said Nash, "he was too stubborn for his own good. He was like that even as a kid. He just wasn't one of those people who could learn anything vicariously. He had to experience something to understand it." He paused, uncertain of the parameters, of what he could or could not ask. "What happened between the two of you, anyway?"

She shrugged. "I don't know. It just sort of ran out of steam or something." He felt her shiver. "You mind if we start back? It's really chilly out here. I should've put on a heavier jacket."

Nash tugged on Samson's leash and steered him around in the other direction. As they walked back, neither of them said much. He could sense her withdrawal into some dark, gloomy memory that the talk of Ben had stirred up.

"Look, I'm sorry, I didn't mean to pry."

"You weren't. Really. My God, you're his brother, you have a right to ask whatever you want."

Samson stopped to sniff at a bush and Nash unwound some of the leash from his hand, giving him some freedom. Nash and Fay stood where they were, watching Samson because neither of them could think of anything to say. Then they looked at each other, and she laughed and so did he. It dispelled the gloom, warming him inside, and he reached out, brushing the back of his hand against her cheek. It was the first time he'd touched her; he'd never felt skin so soft. He cupped her chin in his hand and kissed her lightly on the mouth, tasting a trace of coffee. Her hand found the back of his neck, sliding across it.

Samson tugged on the leash, ending the moment. But the cool imprint of her mouth lingered against his long after he'd left her place and driven back to the inn. His last thought before he fell asleep was that it was only seven hours until he would see her again.

10

Bud and Betty

The alluring voice of the dark soothed him, moved around him like water, guided him through its inky depths. But Bud could see perfectly at night, better than he ever had in daylight.

It wasn't just a matter of being able to see the *shapes* of things, but details like the texture of bark on a tree from six feet away and the delicate network of veins in its leaves. He could even see the flickering ears of a jackrabbit, motionless near the edge of the water. He watched it, just as he had watched a young couple earlier at the south end of the lagoon, and felt the same thing he had then: the deep, gnawing hunger in his gut that never went away.

Even though he was downwind from the rabbit, it didn't seem to smell him. He guessed it had something to do with his changing skin. But the little creature definitely sensed him nearby. Its ears twitched, its nose worked furiously at the air, but it hadn't budged since he'd spotted it.

He was crouched about two yards away, his bare toes curled against the pine needles, the muscles in his legs begging to spring. He could almost taste the rabbit's warm, sweet blood, the succulence of its tiny heart, the tenderness of its liver. It wouldn't fill their bellies like the organs of the young pig out at the junkman's place had, but it would be more satisfying.

The rabbit suddenly unfroze and Bud leaped toward it, missing it by a fraction of an inch. Now it scampered away from the water, up the slope through the trees, darting this way and that, its breath pluming in the gelid air. Bud moved as it moved, picking up speed, his lips drawn away from his teeth in a hungry grin. His new skin insulated him against the cold, his new and improved eyes made tracking a cinch, and since he was wearing just shorts, a T-shirt, and no shoes, he felt light, free, faster than the wind that whistled past his ears.

He let the rabbit lead him for a few minutes, tiring it out. When he lost it momentarily in the underbrush, his improved sense of smell homed in on it like a radar and Bud pounced. He caught the rabbit with his bare hands. It squealed and squirmed, but he held it fast, drunk with the odor of its panic. Then he snapped its neck and sank his teeth into its throat, tearing back fur, skin, muscle. Blood poured into his mouth, hot, sweet, and copper-tasting, with a faint tinge of salt. It relieved the worst of the hunger, and although he was tempted to rip the rabbit open right there and scoop out the delectable organs, he wanted to share his first live kill with Betty.

He wiped the back of his hand across his mouth, smearing blood from one cheek to the other, and lumbered through the trees toward the cabin, the rabbit tight in his hand. Every couple of seconds his tongue darted out, licking the excess blood from his lips, the corner of his mouth.

Human blood would have been better. But then he thought of Betty crouched over the kid in the freezer at the gas station, sucking from his neck, and he shook the image away and walked faster.

The cabin was on the west side of the lagoon, the undeveloped side, deep in the woods where Hawthorne Lane didn't reach. Whoever had lived there had already closed the place for the summer. There was no electricity, but they'd found lanterns and kerosene in the garage, linen in the closets, and a full cellar. All the comforts of home and, most important, it was safe. He didn't know why he was so sure of this, but he was.

It took him thirty minutes at a steady lope to reach the cabin. He burst through the front door and hurried into the kitchen, where Betty was. She was filling empty plastic bottles with water, which she would later store in the cellar for when the others arrived. He didn't know who these others were or when they would get here, but he didn't question the fact that they would arrive. There were many things he simply knew now and no longer questioned.

As usual, Betty was naked. Her new skin was so thick, she could barely get into any of her clothes now, and it was simply more comfortable for her to go around without anything on. Bud found clothes uncomfortable as well, but they represented one of the few vestiges of his humanity, so he continued to wear them.

He dropped the rabbit on the butcher-block counter and Betty stared at it, then looked up at him. Her smile elongated her mouth, stretching the new skin at the corners and making her nostrils flare. She was almost completely changed now, with patches of her old skin showing through only on her neck, a cheek, her throat. Her hair, like his, was beginning to thin and recede as the new skin claimed more and more of her forehead and skull. Her brows were nearly gone. The skin on her lids had weighted them, giving them a hooded, shifty look. She smelled different, too, and that scent, mixed with the odor of blood, excited him, drawing his hand to one of her new breasts. He stroked it, streaking it with the rabbit's blood, then leaned over and licked the blood off.

She giggled and turned, picking up the rabbit. "I get the heart," she said, and sliced it open from head to tail, then peeled back the flesh, the ribs. She bowed her head and lapped at the blood.

When she was finished, when she smacked her lips and whispered, "Good," Bud scooped out the organs. The skin had made his fingers less dexterous for most things, but not for this. For this, they were perfect. They functioned like sharp-edged spoons, slicing through sinew, scooping, slicing again.

They stood at the counter, feeding themselves and each other, the aroma of blood and fresh meat thickening in the air, intoxicating them. When the organs were gone, they scraped the inside of the skin clean with their fingers and mouths. Then they fell on each other, grunting, groaning, biting, their coupling frenzied and heated.

When it was over, Betty curled on her side on the kitchen floor and fell asleep, blood drying on her mouth, her hands. Bud tried to wake her, but her sleep was too deep, so he left her there and followed the seductive voice of the dark into the woods again.

11

Trails

1.

The loud, rhythmic squeaking on the other side of Katie's bedroom wall was punctuated by low, soft moans that she found a little embarrassing. She turned her head toward the nightstand. The hands of the clock stood at 7:02. That was about right.

Nearly every morning for the last six months, it had been the same: the squeaking at seven, the moans starting at two or three minutes after and continuing for six to ten minutes—she knew, she'd timed them, she'd watched the hands of the clock moving, moving—and then, between 7:20 and 7:25, there would be a muffled cry and it was over. Occasionally, like this morning, it went on longer, which meant Hank would be staying home today to work on his book.

Katie pulled the edges of the pillow over her ears, trying to block out the noises. But it didn't help. She finally just lay there and listened, alternately embarrassed and fascinated. Dani, of course, had told her what happened when you did it. Who did what to whom, what it felt like, how sometimes it was great and other times it was not so great. But hearing it from someone else wasn't the same thing as having it happen to you. It left too many questions. And since Dani had never loved any of the guys she'd slept with, Katie wasn't so sure how accurate her descriptions were. Loving the guy *had* to make a difference, didn't it?

"That hurts, Hank." Jo's voice. Katie heard it so clearly, it was as if Jo were right in the room with her. "Don't."

"What hurts?"

Aw, shit, I don't need this. Katie threw off the covers and padded across the room. She switched on the radio and turned it up loud enough to drown out their voices. Then she puttered around, washing her face, brushing her teeth, making her bed, imagining what it would be like to sleep with Ray.

But since he'd never even kissed her, it was stupid to think about it, now, wasn't it? *You're a jerk, plumpo,* she thought, looking at herself in the bedroom mirror. Her gaze fell on the roselike flower in the glass vase that she'd taken from the place near the meadow nearly two weeks ago.

It looked as fresh as when Ray had picked it. The fragrance was no longer like basil, but sweeter, deeper, like clove. She'd snipped off most of the three-foot stem and now, poking up out of the vase like it was, it looked like a particularly lovely rose, that was all. It had even fooled Hank, who'd commented on how pretty it was.

She leaned closer, inhaling its fragrance, wondering if she could track it. She closed her eyes and breathed deeply, sucking the scent up into her nose and then deeper, deeper, into her lungs. Pictures of grass, trees, and sunlight flashed through her head. Birds flitted across the inside of her eyes. Insects darted above fields. Caterpillars spun cocoons. Bees hovered over flowers like miniature helicopters.

Then summer suddenly collapsed into winter and sagging gray skies. The creek froze. Drifts blew across the meadow. The world went dark and cold. She couldn't see, but she heard the wind howling and sensed she was enclosed in something, that she couldn't get out. An acute sense of claustrophobia started to engulf her, but a warm, sleepy sensation overcame it and. . . .

"Kate?"

Her eyes flew open, and she spun around, blinking to clear them. Her arms seemed strangely heavy; it was an effort to swallow, to pull air in through her nose. She felt drugged.

What was *all that?*

"Button? You all right?"

Hank. Standing in the doorway. Okay, it was okay now. She was in her bedroom and Hank was in the doorway asking her a question and her head bobbed up, down, yes, she was fine.

"Would you mind getting breakfast this morning? Jo's sleeping in. She doesn't feel well."

Circles ringed his dark eyes. His hair hung loose and looked funny; she was used to seeing it pulled back in a ponytail. His scent was worried, fretful, scattered, not at all like the smell of the rose. She glanced at it, then at Hank again, then stepped away from the flower. Her legs felt weak, hollow, as though she'd been disembodied and had floated back into her bones the wrong way.

"Breakfast. Sure." *You're losing it, kid.* Her arms dropped to her sides. "What's wrong with Jo?"

He shrugged. "The usual."

That meant it was just another one of Jo's ailments—like the cramps, allergies, and the migraines—which she used to get attention when she thought she was being ignored or not appreciated. "Cold cereal okay?"

"Sure. Fine. Whatever. I'll be working on the book today, so if you want to take the car to math, go ahead."

"Great. Thanks."

She showered quickly, dressed quickly, made breakfast quickly, anxious to get out of the house before Hank changed his mind about the car.

In the kitchen, signs of Jo's illness were everywhere: last night's breakfast dishes soaking in the sink, bits of food on the floor where she hadn't swept, the dishwasher stacked with clean dishes that hadn't been put away, the trash can overflowing. Jo on strike. Jo saying, *You two do my chores. I'm tired. I don't feel good. You aren't grateful for everything I do around here.*

She'd pulled this same shit last week, when Katie and Hank were about to leave for Ben's memorial service. Then, she'd whined that she had a fever, she ached all over, and how could they both go off and desert her like this? Suppose she needed something from the pharmacy? Suppose she needed a doctor? Just look at the mess in the kitchen, how could she clean it up all by herself? In the end, Hank had stayed with her and Katie had gone alone.

She put on her jacket, jerked the trash bag from the can, took it outside for garbage pickup. The sky was leaden with clouds. Frost blanketed the grass and sparkled from the hood of Jo's battered Pinto. Her breath formed clouds in the chilly air.

Just south of the cold line, it was probably like summer.

The garbage cans were jammed with trash, and she practically had to climb inside one of them to get the bag inside. Another bag had been ripped open, probably by a raccoon or a stray cat, and bits of supper three nights ago littered the driveway. Meatballs. Pasta. A crust of garlic bread. A slice of tomato. *Shitfuckdamn.* She hated picking up garbage with her bare hands. It smelled so—

That smell's not garbage.

Her head snapped up. Jerked right, left. Her nose worked frantically at the air, seeking the source of the odor, a stronger trail, something she could follow. There. To her right. Leading toward the lagoon.

The lid clattered against the driveway as she dropped it and moved forward, sniffing, tracking. Her limbs felt rubbery, not fully connected to her body. Her arms swung; her feet lifted, fell, lifted, fell. The scent grew stronger. Water, moss, mud, and something else. It was similar to the dark odor that had radiated from Ben that night, similar to what had stalked her on Hawthorne when she was on her bike—*Stalk? Can a scent stalk?*—and yet it was also different.

She stopped at the edge of the water. It purled against the sand, pulling dry pine needles and leaves back into itself, then depositing them on shore again. An endless rhythm. Like the smell.

There was a weird rhythm to this odor. Reggae mixed up with punk, punk mixed with blues, blues mixed with something else, as if the smell couldn't quite make up its mind what it was, what it wanted to be. She turned to the left, where the smell seemed strongest. She kept hoping for a tendril she could seize, burrow into, for a thread that would offer up a picture. But the scent remained whole, unified, pulsing to its own strange beat. Then, about three hundred yards from the house, it just ended.

Katie turned slowly in a circle, trying to pick it up again. She crouched and sniffed at the ground. There were so many odors tangled up with the pine needles, leaves, and dirt, it was hard to separate them from the smell she was looking for. She caught a faint whiff of something that seemed similar, but not quite right. It was like the difference between gray and silver or between shades of blue. She tracked it to the edge of the water, where it stopped.

Katie stretched out on her stomach, nose to the ground, fingers clawing through leaves and needles, digging into the cold dirt, unearthing the odor. It was faint, but she scooted forward on her belly, twisting right, left, right again. The odor leaped a fallen tree, weaved around bushes, climbed the dock, and went all the way to the end. So it—*what?*—either arrived or left via the lagoon after pillaging the garbage. Then why did the scent loop around and end just under Jo and Hank's bedroom window? She even detected the scent on the sill.

A shadow loomed in the glass, the window flew upward, and Jo snapped, "Just what the *hell* do you think you're doing, young lady?"

Jo's red hair was mussed; bright pink splotches bloomed in

her cheeks; and her pale green eyes looked hot, feverish. She held her robe closed against her throat.

"I, uh, saw this yellow bird and I thought Tina had gotten out."

"I think you'd better get in here and fix breakfast because I sure can't do it."

She sneezed as if to make her point. For a second, Katie thought the scent that flew away from her skin was the one she'd been tracking. But it conjured pictures in her head, the usual ones of Jo as a kid who whined and complained and was always sick with one thing or another. Katie realized it was only the odor of sickness that was similar.

"You listening to me, young lady?"

Katie turned around without replying.

"*Don't* you walk away from me like that," Jo called after her. "Katie, do you hear me?"

Yeah, yeah, Jo, I hear you, she thought, and kept on walking. The window slammed shut and Katie smiled. *One point for me, shithead.*

"Fay, it's Hank. . . . Fine, thanks. Do you have a minute? . . . I just wanted to let you know what our snake expert had to say about the reptile you dropped by a couple weeks ago. . . ."

Katie stood in the doorway of Hank's den with a mug of coffee for him in one hand and the keys to the Mustang in the other.

"He said it was a genetic mutation of a black snake. The growths on its belly are like suction cups. Anomalies. It was young, female, and pregnant. He wasn't able to salvage any of the eggs. . . . What? . . . Oh, yeah, I was just getting to that. He can't explain the aggressive behavior. Black snakes are usually terrified of people, and the only time they'll strike is if they're cornered. . . . Sure thing, Fay. I'll be in touch."

"Have you ever seen a brook trout with an extra set of eyes on top of its head?" Katie asked when he'd hung up.

Hank spun in his chair, smiling at the question. "Nope. Have you?"

"Yeah."

"C'mon."

"Really. This guy I know caught one in Meadow Creek."

"And you saw it? A trout with an extra set of eyes?"

"Uh-huh." After math tutorial three days ago, she and Ray

had ridden down to Meadow Creek on his bike to go fishing. "I was there when he caught it."

Hank looked interested now. "What'd he do with it?"

"Tossed it back in."

"But you got a good look at it?"

"Yes."

"And it was definitely a trout?"

"Yeah."

He thought a moment, then hurried over to the bookcase that covered the entire far wall, ran his finger along one row and another until he found what he was looking for. He flipped through the book and showed her a picture. "It looked like this?"

"I *know* what a trout looks like, Hank, and yeah, that was it. Except for the extra eyes."

"Jesus." He snapped the book shut. "How big was it?"

"I don't know, maybe half a pound."

"Where in Meadow Creek?"

"It's kind of hard to explain. I'd have to show you. But you know that flower in my room?"

"The rose?"

"I don't think it's a rose, Hank." She described where it had been growing and what it had looked and smelled like before they'd picked it. "And there's something else." Out came the story about the cold line, the semis, the jeeps. Hank's dark, serious eyes drew together as he frowned and glanced at his watch.

"How about if you and I take a drive down to this place, kiddo?"

"What about Jo?"

"What about her?"

"Aren't you staying home to keep an eye on her?"

He laughed and ruffled her hair just like the old Hank used to do before Jo moved in. In a soft, conspiratorial voice, he said, "I think it'd be more accurate to say that Jo is staying home because I am. Now why don't you go back the car out of the garage while I throw on some other clothes? I'll be out in a jiffy."

"I've got math tutorial."

"Oh."

"But I can cut," she added quickly. "I haven't missed all summer."

He grinned. "Once won't hurt. See you outside."

The day had suddenly taken on a whole new meaning.

2.

Nash's favorite camera for fieldwork was the Nikon F4. He'd used it in temperatures hot enough to sizzle bacon and cold enough to freeze the balls off a bull. It was hardy, durable, high quality, and would be his choice of equipment if he ever photographed Fay.

Its best feature was something called focus tracking. When an object was moving at a constant rate of speed, the F4's eight-bit microcomputer calculated the position of the object at the precise instant the shutter fired and prefocused the lens to that position. Even though he didn't think he'd need this particular feature at the creek, his years on the move had taught him that photography was founded on the same principle he'd learned as a kid in Boy Scouts: *Be Prepared.* Good photographs didn't wait around for you to get your act together.

He didn't have any trouble finding the cold spot again; he'd clocked it on the odometer that night. It lay exactly 15.2 miles from Lagoon. The moment he crossed it, the air was considerably warmer. High-fifties, he guessed, instead of low thirties, and it probably got progressively warmer the farther south you went. Even though the sky was still gray, with pockets of clouds hanging down like sacks of old flour, it didn't look like the same sky. He couldn't have said exactly what the difference was, but the camera would tell him.

He pulled off onto the shoulder, the tires kicking up red dust, and turned sharply down a dirt road that led under the bridge on the warm side. When he parked Delilah and got out, he realized it was too warm for the parka. He stripped it off, tied it at his waist, slung his camera bag over one shoulder and his knapsack over the other. He unzipped one of the half-dozen compartments and brought out two weather thermometers. He left one in the shade on the warm side of the creek and the second in the shade on the cold side. Then he shot photos of the sky from both sides, recording the time, shutter speed, and aperture for each. Before he continued on, he checked the thermometers. They read forty-eight and thirty-one degrees, respectively.

In the tropics, he thought, he had seen it rain on one side of the street and not on the other.

In Germany four years ago, he happened to be walking through a neighborhood in Munich where a sudden hailstorm devastated cars, roofs, storefront windows, causing millions in damage. The hail lasted less than fifteen minutes and fell only in a two-block-square area.

Ten years ago, when he and his wife were living in an apartment in Coconut Grove, he'd seen a shower of frogs over the building directly across the street from theirs. Hundreds of frogs. Some had struck windows or sills and died. Others landed on the roof or on cars. Most ended up on the sidewalk and hopped off, a quivering, croaking green mass.

But this was invisible and that made it unlike the other phenomena. It was more difficult to measure in ways that would convince other people. *Like who, Nash ole buddy? Just who're you going to convince? And why? What difference does it really make?*

It mattered, he knew it did. He sensed that the cold was part of a larger pattern that would explain what had happened to Ben and everything else he'd seen here since his arrival. He intended to document it in any way he could and piece it together to find his answers. When the riddle of his brother's final act was solved, he would go back to his own life. But only then.

He waded across the creek to the cold side, put on his parka, and strolled along it for a mile or more. He snapped photos of the tall, wheat-colored grass, stones, trees, birds, everything. He wanted pictures of the most ordinary things on both sides of the creek.

As Nash moved upstream, the land began to rise into a series of gentle slopes that would eventually roll into hills. He cut through the grass and weeds, which reached nearly to his waist now and rustled as he passed through. The blades became more slender, sharper, snagging on his jeans, scratching his hands. He realized the grass was more like sawgrass now, the stuff that proliferated in the Everglades, with sharp, tiny teeth on the sides that cut like daggers.

He started back down toward the creek, where the grass was kinder, and nearly stumbled into a strange growth that jutted up from the ground like a tumor. It resembled the termite hives he'd seen in the Venezuelan interior except that it was roughly conical, a sorcerer's hat made of mud and grass and pebbles that was at least two feet tall.

Nash photographed it from every side, then sat back and watched the hive. No insects swarmed over it or even nearby.

He poked a long stick through the top of the thing, knocking off the peak of the cone, and stepped back to see what would happen. For a beat or two, nothing did.

Then bits of dust swirled up from the hole and a butterfly struggled through it. Its turquoise and silver wings shimmered damply in the gray light, and for a few moments, it simply rested on the top, drying off. Its beauty was breathtaking. Pale yellow swirled inside the turquoise, streaks of black coiled in the silver. As the wings dried, Nash saw they were paper-thin and layered. Three, four, maybe as many as five layers on both wings, each a slightly different shade of turquoise and silver. He snapped seven pictures of it, three with a red filter, then used the focus tracking as it lifted into the chilly air.

A few minutes later, a second butterfly emerged, rested on the top of the cone until it was dry, then flew off.

During the next forty minutes, eleven more butterflies left the cone. When Nash was sure the thing was empty, he lopped off the upper third of it and peered inside. The floor of the cone was padded with dried flower petals and grass. The walls were tiered and looked like miniature balconies in an opera house—seven on one side and six on the other. Strands of silk trailed from each, presumably from the cocoons the butterflies had been in.

He took half a dozen pictures of the interior, some with the red filter again, then walked around the hive and realized he'd missed something important. The broad sides of the hive faced north and south and the narrow sides faced east and west, thus exposing a minimum surface area to sunlight during the hottest part of the day. An architect couldn't have designed a more energy-efficient home.

He followed the creek uphill, where the trees were more numerous. When he reached the top, he stopped and stared at three odd vehicles moving silently through the meadow below. They looked like electric cars with glass dome bubbles covering the tops. *Moon buggies,* he thought. They had two long metal arms that protruded from the front and cameras mounted on the glass domes—video cameras, he guessed.

Nash dropped to his knees, quickly fished out the zoom lens, attached it to the camera, and stretched out on his stomach, focusing on the car closest to him. The two men inside swam into view—one was bald, the other younger, with bright red hair. The older guy's lips were moving, but Nash couldn't read them. He scanned the side of the buggy, looking for writing, an insignia, any identifying mark. But the buggy's exterior was as smooth and blank as an egg.

He finished off the roll of film, popped in another roll, and followed the progress of the buggies through the meadow, snapping pictures of them every five or ten seconds. As they swung around and headed back toward him, he got close-ups of Baldy and Red.

Then the vehicles continued down through the meadow, stopping here, there, those metal arms snipping, lifting, probing for samples of dirt and flora. They paused as they were crossing the creek and the arms dug down, sifting through pebbles and mud. They finally vanished around another hill. Nash leaped up and went after them.

On the warm side again, he shucked his parka, his sweater, and sprinted up another hill. He stopped just short of the trees, where a man and a woman were hunkered down, binoculars glued to their eyes. Before he could decide what to do, the woman glanced around.

It was Katie Suffield, who he'd seen for the first time since his arrival at Ben's memorial service. She seemed as surprised to see him as he was to see her, and nudged the man next to her. They both got up and hurried over.

She introduced him to Hank, her stepfather, a thin, spacy-looking man with a dark ponytail who was obviously uneasy standing out in the open. "We'd better talk elsewhere." He spoke softly and gestured at Nash's camera. "You got pictures of them? Of the buggies?"

"And a few other things."

"Then I think you'd better get some photos of this." He motioned for Nash to follow.

They threaded through brush and trees to a vantage point above a narrow culvert. Two semis were parked in the shade of an exuberant oak, and the moon buggies were lined up behind one of them. A ramp was being lowered, sticking out from the back like a giant silver tongue. As it touched the ground, the first moon buggy slipped silently forward and disappeared inside, quickly followed by the second and the third.

Nash's camera got it all.

The semis, like the buggies, had no identifying marks, no license plates. When the vehicles were inside, both cranked up and moved forward, chugging through the meadow, beneath an overcast sky.

A long time later, after the three of them had shared their

various discoveries, they made their way downhill on the cold side toward the bridge. The stillness of the air seemed unnatural, expectant and ominous. The sky was thicker, darker, lower. Nash felt a sudden urgency to get out of the meadow and into an enclosed place—a car, the inn, it wouldn't matter. He walked faster, and the other two also picked up their paces.

"What do you make of all this?" Nash glanced at Suffield.

"It's fascinating, disturbing, alarming. Beyond that, I don't know."

"But what's it mean?" Katie exclaimed. "What's causing it?"

Suffield shook his head and shoved his hands deeper into his parka pockets. "I'm not sure, kiddo. Nature seems to playing some tricks on us, and there might be a lot of factors contributing to it. Pollution, the greenhouse effect, Chernobyl, chemical contaminants—any of those things or none of them. It's impossible to say for sure at this point. But the fact that the weather is going wild is a pretty good indication that nature's fed up with the whole thing."

As if nature possessed consciousness, Nash thought. Suffield sounded like Ben.

In the past decade, Suffield went on, the United States had seen three of the coldest winters and four of the warmest average years ever recorded. These extremes would occur by chance less than once in a millenium. In other parts of the world, it had been much the same. Snow in Venice, the French Riviera, South Africa, and even subtropical Brazil.

In the late eighties, summer heat waves shriveled crops from the east to the west and left the Mississippi so dry in parts that dredges had to open a channel for barges. The heat closed Harvard University, and in Detroit, auto workers walked off the lines when some job stations reached temperatures of over a hundred. In September of 1988, the fiercest hurricane of the century roared into the Caribbean.

"And the last two years have been even worse. In early March of this year, for instance, record highs were recorded across the northeast, tornados devastated towns in the midwest, and Florida had its worst drought ever. The earth's average temperature has already risen one degree in this century. And there're some scientists who're predicting that even if we don't pollute our atmosphere another iota, the heat that's already trapped will raise temperatures another one to five degrees in the next century. It seems low until you realize that it was a rise like this that ended the last ice age a hundred thousand years ago.''

"Meaning what?" asked Nash.

"That depends on who you listen to. On the one hand," Suffield told them, "the droughts and terrible heat waves could become routine. As rainfall diminishes by as much as forty percent, droughts would become more common. Summer would bring plagues of insects, more forest fires, stronger hurricanes hitting farther north and during more months of the year. Then, of course, polar ice caps would melt and ocean levels would rise up to four feet during the next century. Florida would be underwater. New York City would look like Venice, with canals instead of streets. Water supplies would be contaminated, and wildlife habitats would be destroyed. The entire ecological balance of the world goes to shit.''

"Unless nature compensates somehow," said Nash.

"Or tries like hell to compensate." Suffield's gesture encompassed the meadow and everything beyond it. "Which is what I think is going on here and probably in other places, too. The real question is whether Nature is succeeding. These mutations we've seen—the black snake you all found at Fay's, everything here in the meadow—makes me think that maybe she's given up trying to compensate and has something else in mind.''

"Like what?"

"I don't know."

"What about the boys in the buggies?" Nash asked.

Suffield shrugged. "No telling."

"Are they maybe connected to Hartwell somehow?" Katie asked.

"I can't speak for the entire company, but they sure aren't connected to the biology division.''

"Would Karl Granger know anything?" Nash asked.

"If Hartwell's involved, then yeah, he might. You know him?"

"I've met him a few times." Granger was Ben's boss at Hartwell. Nash had called him last week, but his wife had said he was out of town and not due back until mid-September. "He seems pretty straightforward.''

"Yeah, he is. But he's got his share of enemies within the company." Suffield shrugged. "Local power struggles and all that. He's on a sabbatical in the Galápagos right now. I doubt he even knows about Ben, unless he's spoken to his wife. But when he gets back, he'd be the man to ask.''

Katie changed the subject by asking Suffield what he thought was causing the cold line. He shook his head. "I don't know. But whatever's going on seems to be focused on Lagoon south to here and maybe north to another line. It's like the cold line defines the parameters of this thing. We've never had weather this cold in this part of Georgia in August, and I think whatever is involved is a lot more complicated than we can even imagine."

Suffield held out his palm, and the three of them looked up. It had started to snow.

Part II

THE TOWN

"There is nothing permanent except change."
—HERACLITUS

1.

"Snow in early September. If that don't beat all," said Charlie.

Luanne Castleton glanced up from the box of canned goods she was unpacking. Her husband stood at the front of their store, gazing up at the army/navy sign outside, then into the street, his hands in the pockets of his favorite navy-blue cardigan. He'd bought it during a ski trip to Aspen eighteen years ago. As they'd come out of the shop, their youngest son—who was eight at the time—had slipped on a patch of ice and broken his arm. Ever since, she'd thought of the sweater as bad luck.

Charlie, of course, considered it just one of her silly superstitions. But she couldn't help it. Whenever he wore the damn thing, she felt uneasy, as though the sweater were a sign that she should brace herself for something.

"You think the snow will effect business today?" she asked.

"Bound to." He smoothed his palm over his balding head as he turned away from the window. "Want me to help you with that?"

"No, thanks. I can do it. I could use some coffee, though."

His smile deepened the web of lines at the corners of his eyes, eyes the color of plums that had charmed and loved her for forty years. "Coming up."

But the first sip of coffee pooled like acid in her stomach, stirring the vague nausea she'd felt since she'd awakened this morning. By her second sip, she knew she was going to get sick. She told Charlie she'd left something in the apartment upstairs and beat a hasty retreat. She made it to the bathroom before she vomited. She was so dizzy afterward, she couldn't stand. She pulled a towel from the rack, wet it under the faucet, pressed it to her face. The cold helped, but not enough. Her head still swirled and her stomach felt like giant hands were squeezing it.

Only one thing that makes you feel this sick so early in the morning, Lu.

She started to laugh, quick, almost hysterical sounds that rapidly collapsed into sobs she muffled with the towel. *I'm sixty-one years old. It's impossible.* Maybe it was the onset of the flu or something she'd eaten that had disagreed with her.

But even as she thought it, she knew it wasn't true. She'd had three sons in her forty years of marriage, and although each pregnancy had been different, she'd always known before the doctor that she was pregnant.

Just as she knew now.

2.

Business at Kroger's grocery store that morning was really slow; Sammy Loman blamed it on the snow. It was funny what weather could do to people's buying habits, he thought. In June, one of their slowest times had been a Sunday and a Monday when the thermometer hit 96, even though those two days were normally their busiest. And yet, in July when the temp peaked at 101, they'd been swamped with people and had to call in some part-time cashiers.

He made his way down the meat aisle, straightening packages, glancing at the expiration dates. Loman considered himself an astute observer of human behavior and some of the things he'd been observing recently bothered him. It wasn't just how weather influenced people's shopping routines, either. Buying habits seemed to be undergoing drastic changes.

A couple of his vegetarian customers, for instance, had started to buy meat—not just fish and fowl, but *red* meat. Even those customers who for years had eaten meat in moderation were now buying in tremendous quantities, as though they were stocking their freezers in anticipation of some imminent shortage. In fact, he was having trouble keeping steak, roast, and liver in stock. During the fifteen years he'd been the assistant manager here, he'd ordered red meats once a week even during the tourist season. Now he ordered every other day.

"Morning, Sam."

Reverend Quickson had stopped a few feet away. Despite his pea coat, he looked thin and undernourished. Dark circles ringed his eyes. "Hi, Reverend. Glad to see someone dared the snow."

Quickson smiled. "I figured everyone else would stay indoors and I'd whiz through here in nothing flat. I was right." His long fingers picked at the packages of steak and liver. He tossed three of each into his cart and added a roast on top of it. Loman wondered who else the reverend was feeding besides himself. He couldn't remember him having ever bought this much meat just for a week.

"They're predicting another couple inches by tonight. That'd give us a total of five since yesterday. That's got to be a record for Lagoon, huh, Sammy."

"I reckon. And probably by tomorrow it'll have all melted."

Quickson's bushy white brows fanned together as he frowned and shook his head. "I don't think so. I think we've been cheated out of an autumn, maybe as punishment for what Ben Nash did."

Loman always felt uncomfortable when Quickson started in on his hellfire-and-damnation shit. It was the main reason he'd stayed away from the reverend's Sunday services, even though his wife and kids attended. But he couldn't help putting in his two cents. "With all due respect, Bill, it doesn't make sense that any god would punish other people for something Ben did."

Quickson's smile could have frozen the lagoon. "Think again. We're all still paying for Adam sampling that apple. We're born tainted."

"Says who?" Loman laughed, wondering where this sanctimonious prick got off talking like that.

Quickson's face seized up with anger and he leaned toward Loman, violating his personal space. His breath was faintly sour, a little stale, as though he'd been sick or hadn't brushed his teeth this morning. "If you value your immortal soul, Sammy, then you'd best get down on your knees right here and now and ask for Christ's forgiveness. It's not too late. It's never too late for sinners like you. It's—"

"Excuse me, Bill." Loman stepped back quickly. "I've got a delivery I need to check on."

But as he started away, Quickson grabbed his hand with surprising strength. "Listen to me, boy," he hissed. His tiny blue eyes possessed a wild, feverish sheen that his thick spectacles exaggerated. His grip tightened until Loman winced in pain. "You repent and you'll be saved. Believe me. I know. I know what's loose in this town. I've seen it. It's come for the sinners, Sammy. It knows who we are. It knows, sweet Christ, it knows. . . ."

Loman jerked his hand free and hurried off. "You can't run away from it, Sammy," Quickson called after him. "You can't. . . ." The words struck Loman's back like hot, burning stones.

3.

Six-year-old Bobby Peters hated doctors.

They always poked him, stuck him with needles, hurt him until he cried, then they tried to make up for it with a lollipop or candy. He explained this to his mom as they drove across town to the clinic, but she didn't want to hear about it. She was cross and grumpy today, like she was whenever she wore her dark sunglasses, and she kept snapping at him. *Don't do that, Bobby. . . . Stop fiddling with that, Bobby. . . . Can't you be a good boy, Bobby? . . . No, Bobby.* He sometimes wondered if his name was really No Bobby.

"I already had my shots for school," he said as they swung into the clinic parking lot.

She sighed. "That was for school last year."

"Was not."

His mom grabbed him by the hair and jerked his head back. Tears swam in his eyes. "Don't sass me like that, young man. You hear me?"

"But it's true! I had my shots two weeks ago when we came down here to get medicine for Dad's sore throat."

Her eyes went soft and funny, like she was trying to peer back in time, trying to remember. Then she let go of his hair. "No, you're wrong. That was last year. C'mon, zip up your jacket. We're going to be late."

"You never used to be this mean," he said softly.

But she didn't hear him. She was already outside, moving quickly toward the clinic, her jacket flapping in the cold breeze, snow falling in her hair. She looked like his real mom just then, her hair soft and dark and sparkling with snow. But his real mom would've waited for him, she wouldn't have just zoomed ahead like that, leaving him back here by himself. She would've taken his hand and chatted gaily about this or that, making a game out of visiting the doctor. But his real mom had gotten sick a few weeks ago and had turned into this mean lady. He kept hoping she would come back, but he was beginning to think she wouldn't because her sickness was worse.

Bobby didn't know what her sickness was or if there was even a name for it. But the skin on her shoulders and back was red and puffy, the light hurt her eyes, she was mean all the time, and sometimes at night, when his dad was out of town traveling, Bobby heard her in the bedroom talking to herself. Her sickness seemed to get better when his dad was home, but even then she was never really well.

"Would you hurry up?" She stood on the clinic steps, holding the door open for him, and he hurried inside before she could swat him.

It was hot in the waiting room, but there weren't many people. The nurse at the desk took their names and came back over a few minutes later. "Mrs. Peters, my records indicate that Bobby was here about two and a half weeks ago for his shots."

"He was?"

"Yes, ma'am. Shots, his physical, the works. If there's some other problem, Dr. Donovan could see him, of course, but—"

"No, that's all right. I feel so silly about this. I could've sworn . . . Oh, well."

Just then Bobby saw Dr. Fay come out into the lobby. She waved at him, left some papers on the front desk, and walked over. He decided she was okay, for a doctor. And she was awful pretty. You could tell just by looking at her that no mean lady lived inside her.

"Hi, Bobby." She was tall and had to lean down to talk to him, her hands against her thighs. "I thought I just saw you a couple of weeks ago."

"Mommy made a mistake," he said.

Dr. Fay smiled and patted his shoulder. "Moms do that sometimes." She greeted his mom, and Bobby wondered if Dr. Fay could tell she was the mean lady and not his real mom. Probably not. Even his dad couldn't tell. Maybe no one could tell but him.

A few minutes later, they were on their way outside again. This time his mom took his hand and even said she was sorry about getting so mad before. "I don't know what's wrong with me lately. I feel so . . . Oh, I don't know." She glanced down at him, smiling almost like his real mom did. "I guess Mommy just needs a break or something, honey, you know what I mean?"

"A break from me?"

She laughed. "Of course not. Just a little vacation. Listen, I have an idea. Why don't we go over to the Nameless and you get one of those *big* ice cream shakes you like so much? While you're working on that, I'm going to dash over to the library to check out some books for your dad, okay?''

He loved the shakes Mr. Horn whipped up in his magical blender, and suddenly broke loose from his mom and ran to the car, shouting, "Hurry, Mommy, hurry!"

4.

Horn and Sammy Loman were sitting at a front table having a spot of coffee and playing a quick game of backgammon when Catherine Peters and her boy came in. He rushed over to the table, his cheeks pink from the cold, his wheat-colored hair damp with snow and tousled by the wind.

"Mom says I can have one of those special shakes, Mr. Horn."

"Is that so." Horn laughed and glanced at Catherine. She was a mighty fine-looking woman, all right, with that dark hair, those high cheekbones, and a kind of dignified countenance you didn't see much of anymore. She was a teacher over at the high school and her husband worked for Hartwell as a salesman. Traveled a lot. Damn fool, Horn thought, leaving a woman like that alone so much.

"So we've got Mom's permission for the shake?"

"Absolutely, Andy." She smiled, but he got the feeling she was a little uptight, like maybe she had a lot on her mind. "Would you mind if I leave Bobby here for a few minutes while I run over to the library?"

"No problem. He'll be just fine."

"Thanks, Andy, I appreciate it." Her black eyes darted to Loman. "Nice to see you, Sammy," she said, and then she was gone.

"Why don't you fix me up one of those shakes, too, Andy," Loman said.

"Sure thing."

"Can I see the magic blender, Mr. Horn?"

"What magic blender?" asked Loman.

The boy's eyes glinted with excitement. "Can I show him the blender, Mr. Horn?"

"You bet. And while you're back there, get out all the flavors you want. You know where the ice cream is. I've got to make a quick call."

The boy shucked his jacket, and he and Loman retreated to the kitchen. Horn called his wholesaler to give him the week's order. While he was waiting to be put through, he watched Catherine's black Volvo driving slowly through the snow, the taillights like red eyes glowing in all the white. Instead of turning left at the corner, toward the library, she kept on going straight, out of town.

Odd, he thought, that she would lie about where she was going.

Then his wholesaler got on the line and he forgot about Catherine Peters.

5.

She needed to get out, to escape the closed, claustrophobic feel of the town, the people, her husband, her son, all of them, everything. And she knew the way. It was as if a map were spread out across the insides of her eyes, the route marked in red. *Go straight for eight miles. Turn right onto Barlow Road and follow it into South Carolina, to the state park.*

After that, she wasn't sure which way to go; it wasn't on the map. But she felt confident she would know what to do when she got there. The voice would tell her. The voice had been with her for weeks now.

It had started as the barest of whispers about the same time she had noticed the rash and had grown steadily louder, more insistent, tugging at her, courting her, seducing her. Sometimes at night, she thought she could feel hands touching her, exciting her. Just the thought of those hands made her skin burn and her breath hitch in her chest. They knew what her husband did not; they understood the secrets of her body, of its strange, erotic changes, of its needs.

Catherine suddenly couldn't stand the constriction of her clothes. She tore off her jacket, jerked her blouse from her slacks, unbuckled her belt, kicked off her shoes. Much better. She could breathe now and feel the cold seeping through her thin silk blouse, stroking her skin. Her nipples hardened, and when she moved, the fabric of the bra rubbed up against them, creating an excruciating pleasure that flashed through her like heat, like lightning, wrenching an involuntary gasp from her lips.

The Volvo swerved on the slippery road and she tightened her hands on the wheel, trying to pay attention to the road, to where she was going. But the heat swept through her again and again and the voice whispered to her. It seemed she could feel the invisible hands right now, trailing lightly across her burning skin. She pressed her thighs together to stem the hot throb of her need, but it only made it worse.

She was breathing so hard the windshield had fogged inside. She had to rub it with her hand to see the road and her breasts brushed up against the steering wheel. The top buttons on her blouse popped off as she groped inside the silk, pushed the bra inside, and tried to satisfy the need. But it only made it worse, and she cried out in frustration, in pain.

Turn here, whispered the voice.

She swung the wheel violently to the right. The Volvo slid off the road and bounced onto a narrow path blanketed in white. Catherine slammed her foot against the accelerator and sped past snow-covered pines and denuded hickories and oaks that crowded around her, laughing. The heat kept pounding at her. The voice grew more insistent, louder, closer.

About a mile in, she jammed on the brakes, leaped out of the car, and started ripping at her clothes, desperate to feel the snow and cold against her skin. She needed to feel it. She would die if she didn't.

She flung her blouse into the trees. She hurled her slacks into the nearby bushes. She wadded up her bra and panties and threw them into the car. And then, laughing madly, she ran into the woods and rolled in the snow like a dog.

Blisters erupted in the rash on her shoulders. Patches of the rash sprouted on her cheeks, her arms and legs, her belly. She bolted upright and stared at herself, watching as the rash sped up and down and across her body, as it blistered and oozed, darkened and thickened.

She felt a quick, intense hunger that drove her to her feet and consumed her just as completely as the need for sex. She ran, she galloped, she flew through the woods on legs so powerful that at times she felt as if she had lifted from the ground and was airborne. The voice guided her. The web would provide.

Not once did she think of the life or the son she had left behind.

Part III

IMPOSSIBLE THINGS

"Sometimes I've believed as many as six impossible things before breakfast."

—LEWIS CARROLL

12

Visits

1.

The cavernous silence in the clinic seemed to deepen in direct proportion to the diminishing light outside Fay's office window. She found it vaguely unsettling.

She was accustomed to working in a familiar backdrop of sounds: the blare of the P.A. system, kids whining in the waiting room, the echo of voices and footsteps in the corridors. But everyone had left with the last patient at four, when it had started to snow. She'd stayed on to finish some paperwork and now wished she hadn't. The quiet in here was the sort that tricked the imagination into believing all kinds of impossible things: that the dead were dancing downstairs in the morgue, that the terrible itching on her hand was the incipience of eczema, that she wasn't alone inside the clinic.

It was ridiculous, she knew it was. Mona had been the last to leave this afternoon, and Fay had locked the front door after her, then secured the back door as well. But for the last half hour or so, she'd been hearing small, scratching noises from somewhere in the clinic. Squirrels had probably gotten into the rafters. But her imagination had created something else of the sounds, something threatening. That was happening a lot lately. It was as if she'd fallen prey to the same psychic malaise that had slowly and insidiously afflicted the rest of the town since Ben's suicide.

Catherine Peters abandoning her son at the Nameless, the murder of the Fenuzo kid, and the break-in at the inn . . . Her mind faithfully ticked off a growing list of incidents, of casualties. *Leave it alone, Fay.*

She knuckled her eyes, pushed away from her desk, and stood at the window, watching the snow fall. Light from the street lamps tinged it a pale yellow, like dirty teeth. It wasn't coming down hard, but it was steady and the gusting wind hurled it against the window. The weather forecast was for two to three inches by morning. There was already an accumulation of five inches on the ground because it had been snowing off and on for most of the Labor Day weekend.

In cities like Minneapolis, seven or eight inches was what you got in a spring storm. But in Lagoon, where it had snowed perhaps half a dozen times this century (and never at the tail end of summer), five inches could create major problems. No snowplows existed in the county. If Route 16 became impassable, the town would be effectively cut off from everything, unless plows were brought in from somewhere else. So far, though, the steady flow of traffic on Route 16 had kept the snow packed down, manageable. But as a result of all this, Lagoon was making the headlines usually reserved for places like North Dakota at this time of year.

Her stomach fussed with hunger, and she debated about stopping by the Nameless on her way home for a bite to eat. She wasn't up to cooking for herself tonight. For that matter, she wasn't particularly enthused about a long evening at home alone. What she really wanted to do was drop by the Blue Inn to see Nash. But she hadn't heard a word from him since Ben's memorial service.

They had gone out for something to eat afterward and had spent much of the evening talking about Ben, as if to compensate for the many times they had avoided discussing him. It had been a purging for her, but it had created a barrier between the two of them. By the time he'd dropped her at home, he'd been moody and quiet, as withdrawn as a monk in seclusion. When she'd suggested running the next morning, as they'd done for almost two weeks straight before the snow had first fallen, he said he'd strained a calf muscle and was going to lay off for a while. Since then, she'd been running alone in the evenings and keeping her distance from the inn.

It was probably just as well. One Nash as a lover in her life was enough. Besides, the source of their mutual attraction was Ben, and what basis was that for anything?

She heard the scratching noise again, louder this time, and walked out into the corridor. It was coming from the rear entrance and sounded like the wind rattling the door. Her shoes clicked in the quiet as she walked back through the hall. Only the night lights were on; shadows puddled in corners and streamed across the polished floors.

Fay stopped in front of the door, staring at it, waiting for the noise again. The wind whistled through the cracks and crevices, but that wasn't what she'd heard earlier. She pressed her ear to the wood, listening, her hands moving over her arms to ward off a sudden chill. She felt as spooked as an eight-year-old kid at home alone in the dark.

Just open the goddamn door and take a look outside.

But as she reached for the knob, it started to turn. Her heart leaped into her throat and she jerked her hand away. Blood rushed into her head. "Who's out there?" she demanded.

"Fay? Is that you, Fay? It's Bill Quickson."

He rapped sharply, and Fay, giddy with relief, laughed aloud and unlatched the dead bolt. The wind grabbed the knob out of her hand and hurled the door against the wall. Snow swirled into the clinic as Quickson darted inside and shut the door behind him, stomping his feet and blowing into his hands.

Drops of melting snow speckled his glasses, puddled at his feet, and glistened against his white hair and pea coat. Its collar was up and made him look a bit sinister.

"Were you out there earlier?" she asked.

"I was at the front door first." He shrugged off his pea coat and draped it over his arm. "I guess you couldn't hear me because of the wind."

"When was that?"

"Five minutes ago."

"What about twenty or thirty minutes ago?"

"No. But when I drove up, I saw someone at the front door. He was wearing a long coat with a hood; I couldn't see his face. But he took off when he saw me."

"Took off?"

"Yes. On foot."

"That's odd." They walked down to her office. "What brings you out in this ugly weather?"

"I, uh, need some medical advice." Quickson eased himself into the chair across from her desk, as though the movement hurt him. She hadn't seen him since that morning out at the Chevron station and thought he looked thinner. His features were pinched, strained. He worked his gloves off his fingers, then rolled the right sleeve of his sweater up to his elbow.

"I was hoping you could recommend something for this." He turned his arm, showing her the back of it. Just beneath his elbow was a patch of angry red skin. "You have any idea what this is?"

It looked exactly like the dozens of other eczema cases she'd diagnosed since early summer. But she examined it under the bright desk lamp just to make sure and was careful not to touch it. "Do you have it anywhere else?"

Softly: "Yes." He hooked his fingers at the throat of his sweater and pulled it down to below his collarbone. Here, the stuff was thick, discolored, and had begun to suppurate. The sweater popped back up as he let go of it. He touched his fingers lightly to his chest. "And across most of my chest and back." His hands fell to his thighs. "And some on my legs. I was going to stop by here a couple weeks ago, but the . . . the stuff I was using seemed to be working. And it wasn't as bad then, just a rash, you know?" He poked his glasses farther up onto the bridge of his nose. "I thought I'd gotten into poison oak or poison ivy. And then I thought maybe it was eczema. Now I don't know."

"What kind of ointment did you use?"

"Calamine lotion." He sniffled and ran his finger across his upper lip. "I, uh, also got some holy water from the Catholic church over in Franklin." The admission seemed to embarrass him. "I thought it was working, too, for a while."

Holy water. Wonderful.

"But in the last week or so, it's gotten much worse. Do you know what it is?" he asked again.

No. She worded her response carefully. "It's an eczemalike condition, Bill, and seems to respond fairly well to cortisone in the early stages. It's so new, we don't know much about it yet." She wrote out a prescription for cortisone cream, tore it off the pad, and slipped it across the desk. Before she could draw her hand back, Quickson covered it with his own, trapping it like a small bird he hoped to suffocate. "Tell me the truth, Fay."

She moved her arm back, freeing her hand, but not before she'd felt the damp heat of his palm seeping into her skin and seen the wild, almost desperate look in his dark eyes. "The truth about what?"

We're alone in the clinic.

"This is what Ben had, isn't it?"

Get him out of here.

"What're you talking about, Bill? Ben killed himself. Now take this prescription and have—"

"You think I don't know what's going on in town?" The words shot out at her, a sibilant hiss. "You think I don't know about all the other people in the county who've gotten this thing? Some of them are members of my congregation. I hear stories.

People confide in me. Three people up at the north end of the
county who had this just . . . just vanished about a week ago,
Fay. Walked out on their lives.

"Another man hanged himself, and you know why his body
never passed through the morgue, Fay? Because his family was
so terrified by what had happened to him that they just buried
him in the backyard and left. Migrants. They just packed up
their truck and split. And I heard about Ben, too. I heard. He
was covered with this thing. He was a sinner and God punished
him with this . . . this plague." He stopped, blinked like a man
coming out of a deep sleep, and looked down at his arm.
"Plague," he repeated more softly, and suddenly raked his nails
through the ugly, discolored skin. "Plague. Punishment."

Blood oozed from the claw marks. Quickson kept scratching
at the rash, murmuring, "Plague, punishment, I heard, I know,
plague, punishment . . ."

Fay stood. It was an effort to keep her voice soothing and
calm. "The cortisone cream will help, Bill, but not if you keep
irritating the skin. It'll get infected."

"Infected." He spat the word as his head snapped up. Behind
his glasses, his eyes blazed with fury, terror, madness. "I *am*
infected, don't you understand?" He pushed himself to his feet;
blood ran down his arm as he leaned over her desk, his mouth
puckering. "The whole goddamn town is *infected*." He stabbed
at the air with his long index finger.

"Out there, Fay. People like me. They're hungry. They're
changing. They're scared. A lot of them. All coming to Lagoon." He stabbed at his own chest, and the blood on his fingers
smeared against the wool of his sweater. "I hear them, you
know. They talk to me. They whisper things to me. I don't want
to listen, but I can't help it." He rubbed his cheek against his
shoulder, quick, jerky motions, as though he were afflicted with
a nervous disorder, and moved toward her, around the corner
of her desk. "I just can't help it. That's how it is. . . ."

Fay had been around enough mental patients in med school
to know that Quickson had lost it. Her own mind split in half
like a chromosome, an atom. Part of her was aware of what he
was saying, of how he was moving slowly but inexorably toward
her, and the other part was quickly assessing her options.

She was cornered against the wall between her desk and the
window. If she waited until he came around the side of the desk,
she could scramble over it and make it into the hall and out the
back door. But she would have only one chance and if she blew

it, she might be worse off than she was now. On the other hand, if she could knock him out. . . . Her fingers closed over the phone and worked loose the wire that connected it to the wall. She was ready to hurl it at him if she had to.

". . . God's fed up with us, Fay. He's tired of how we sin all the time and how we don't listen to Him and how we fuck other men's wives and husbands and steal and foul the earth, and so He's created this plague. . . ." His head kept twitching against his shoulder. His eyes blinked. He was now less than four feet from her. ". . . and He infected Ben first to punish him for all the lust in his heart . . . and Ben . . . Ben transmitted it to others who were weak in the same way. I know you're infected, too, Fay, I can smell it on you. . . . I smell better than before and I can see better in the dark . . . that's because the dark is Satan's world, Fay. . . . And right now Satan's whispering to me, he's telling me to fuck you. . . ."

Quickson's lips drew back from his teeth and his hand dropped to his groin. He rubbed himself. His fingers worked at his zipper. His head kept twitching, his eyes kept blinking, he kept moving toward her, groaning, grinning. Three feet away now. Two and a half. His fly was open. She could no longer hear what he was saying. Her fingers tightened on the phone, her eyes were glued to his face, her right foot was ready to shoot out and slam her chair into him.

Two feet.

A strange, cloying sweetness leaped from the pores of his skin as he fondled himself. Suddenly, he groaned, a deep, rumbling sound of pain, of pleasure, and his eyes rolled back in his head. Her right leg flew out and her foot rammed the chair. It flew toward him and hit him in the knees a second or two before the phone struck him in the temple.

He fell back, his hands jerking to his head, and Fay leaped onto her desk, scrambling over it so fast she knocked files and papers to the floor. She lurched into the hall and raced toward the rear door, Quickson right behind her, shouting obscenities. She burst through the double doors, and the cold wind exploded against her unprotected body.

As she stumbled down the porch steps, she lost her balance on a patch of ice and landed hard on her left side in the parking lot. Her breath spun out of her. A white pain flashed through her elbow. And then Quickson charged out the doors, a human torpedo, a blur of speed. Fay scrambled up and raced toward the entrance of the parking lot—and the road.

Just then headlights swung into the lot. Fay waved her arms and opened her mouth to scream, but nothing came out. The cold had frozen her breath in her throat. The driver slammed on the brakes, and for a split second, the headlights impaled Quickson, paralyzing him, stripping his face of everything except panic. Then he whirled around, a puppet in a pirouette, and vanished through the rear door into the clinic.

The driver reached Fay before she reached the vehicle. It was Nash. He threw his parka around her shoulders and held it in place with his arm as he guided her quickly toward the Jeep. She assured him she was okay, really, but it wasn't until they were inside the Jeep, where he could see her, that he seemed convinced. He rubbed her hands with his own, warming them, as she quickly told him what had happened.

Nash backed the Jeep out into the street and sped around to the front of the clinic. Quickson's car was nowhere in sight; the door of the clinic stood wide open.

"The bastard split fast enough." Nash pulled over to the curb.

"All my things are inside."

"I'll get them. Wait here."

"No way." She let out a nervous, clipped laugh and climbed out of the Jeep behind him.

2.

It was obvious *something* had happened in here, Oliver thought, surveying the mess in Fay's office. But he had a tough time believing it was Quickson.

Oliver had known the reverend for fifteen years and the idea of Quickson doing what Fay had described was about as plausible as his ma rising from the dead. But she wanted to file charges, so he called Sergeant Moses at the station and told him to get a warrant for Quickson's arrest and to meet him at the church.

"*Reverend* Quickson?"

"You know any other Quickson, Mo?"

"Well, no, sir, but what—"

"Assault and attempted rape."

"*Rape?* The reverend? Who'd he try to rape?"

"Dr. Donovan."

Moses let out a long, soft whistle. "Jesus Christ. Okay."

"Then meet me at the church. Don't do nothing until I get there, unless he tries to split, then arrest him."

"Yes, sir."

Oliver hung up. "If we bring him in tonight, he'll be arraigned tomorrow morning, Fay."

"And suppose he gets out on bond and comes after her again?" Nash asked.

"He's not going to do that."

Nash folded his arms and leaned against Fay's desk, his eyes as black as the night swimming in the office window now. "You going to guarantee that?"

"Look, all I'm saying is that the reverend's going to know what's what, Nash."

Oliver caught the glance Nash and Fay exchanged and felt like punching the asshole in the mouth. Just being around this turkey made his blood seethe. His brother had started all the weirdness in Lagoon and Nash's presence only reminded people of that. They'd all be better off if he'd just pack up and mosey on back to Florida.

"The reverend," said Fay, "is beyond knowing what's what, Lew. That's what I've been trying to tell you. He's dangerous."

"The only thing I can do is bring him in." He snapped his notebook shut and slipped it back into his shirt pocket. "I'll call you tomorrow."

Nash followed him into the corridor. "If you don't find him tonight, let us know."

Us. Like they were married or something. "I'll call *Fay* later." He emphasized her name just to let Nash know that none of this concerned him, then left.

Outside, the wind had diminished, but the snow was coming down harder. The cruiser's wipers whipped back and forth across the windshield, and now and then the tires spun for purchase on the slippery road. Oliver barely noticed; he was still back there in the clinic with Fay and Nash. If the bastard hadn't put the moves on her yet, he would probably take advantage of the situation and do it tonight. It wasn't hard to imagine what would happen; he'd already seen it a thousand times in his head. But in these fantasies he was always doing the seducing, not Nash, and it rankled him that he couldn't mold the images the way he wanted to.

No matter how hard he tried, he saw Nash's fingers, not his own, unfastening the buttons on her blouse. He saw Nash's hands sliding over the smooth curves of her body, Nash's mouth at a shoulder, a breast, Nash pumping away inside her. But, even worse, his own body responded to the fantasy just as faithfully as it did when *he* was doing these things to Fay, and that made him even angrier.

The cruiser skidded as he swung around a corner, startling him. His hands spun the steering wheel in the same direction as the skid, the tires leaped the curb, and the car stalled. He got it started again, but after that he kept his thoughts on the road.

In the falling snow, the church looked strangely serene, almost magical, an enchanted church in a fairy tale. It was tucked under the folds of a towering oak that still had some of its summer leaves. The front lawn was blanketed in white. Light from a nearby sodium vapor lamp spilled across its darkened windows and struck the porch of the little house next door where Quickson lived.

As he parked behind Moses's cruiser at the curb, the sergeant hopped out and hurried over. He was a short, muscular guy, except for his infamous beer belly, and was bundled up like an Eskimo. "Haven't seen no one, Lew. There hasn't been a car on this road since I got here."

"Any lights in the church or the house?"

"Nope." His glasses had fogged up; he removed them and wiped them clear with a handkerchief. "Maybe he never came back after he left the clinic."

"If he's smart, he's over the state line by now. You got the warrant?"

Moses patted his parka. "Sure enough. Assault and attempted rape, just like you said. I still can't believe it."

"The doc says he's got the same shit on his skin that Ben Nash had."

"You think this stuff makes people freak or what?"

"I don't know." They'd reached the front door of the house. "But just in case, be ready to cover me."

Oliver punched the doorbell. He heard it ring—one of those fancy *ding-dong* songs—and when no one came to the door, he knocked and rang the bell again. They walked around to the back to check the garage; Quickson's Pontiac was gone, but the back door of the house yawned open.

"Reverend?" Oliver called as he stuck his head into the utility room. His voice echoed. He hit the light, and he and Mo stepped inside.

The house looked as if it had been ransacked, but whether

Quickson or someone else had done it was initially unclear. Dishes had been swept out of the cabinets and shattered on the floor. The stereo had been tipped over, the TV screen had been smashed, religious icons had been pummeled to smithereens. In the bedroom, a large crucifix had been snapped in half and tossed on the bed. Clothes had been torn off hangers and some of them were puddled in an open suitcase on the floor.

In the bathroom sink, Oliver found pages from a Bible that had been partially burned. When he smoothed them out, he realized they were from Revelations. Sections had been highlighted in yellow and all of them dealt with Armageddon, God's wrath, punishment, plagues, the end of the world.

"Looks to me like the reverend took off," Mo remarked.

Oliver agreed, but they went next door to the church just to make sure. The side door was unlocked, and just inside the hall Oliver found the light panel. He hit a couple of the switches, and he and Mo continued into the church.

The only sound was that of the wind rattling the stained-glass windows. On the floor in front of the pulpit, scrawled in what looked like crayon, was: THE WEB WANTS ME THE WEB WANTS THE WEB NO GOD NO PAIN HUNGER PAIN HELP ME HELP PLE.

"Let's get the fuck outta here," Mo whispered.

As they hurried back out to the curb, the bell in the tower pealed nine times, marking the hour. Oliver knew it was connected to an electric timer, but just the same it spooked him. It was as if Quickson, wherever he was, was laughing at them.

13

Developments

1.

The inside of the Nameless smelled of coffee and fresh rolls and was absolutely deserted when Nash and Fay entered. "Hey, Andy, you closed?" Nash called out.

Horn's head poked out of the kitchen; he grinned when he saw them. "Not to friends. Grab a seat and I'll be with you in a second."

As if by mutual consent, he and Fay headed for the same table, one that was away from the front window. "Did we plan this or what?" she asked with a laugh, shaking the melted snow from her hair.

He chuckled. "Warmer back here."

"But no safer." The mirth vanished so quickly from her eyes, he wasn't entirely sure he'd really heard her laugh. She glanced quickly toward the window and blew into her hands, warming them. "I have a feeling they aren't going to find him, Scott."

"You and Samson are welcome to your choice of more than thirty rooms at the inn."

Even though she smiled at the invitation, he could tell she was about to say thanks, but no thanks, and who could blame her? He had avoided her ever since Ben's memorial service. It was partly the finality of it all; he could no longer deny that Ben was dead. But their protracted conversation afterward had more to do with it than he wanted to admit. At some level, he was afraid that his attraction to her was misdirected, perhaps even a little perverse, given her role in his brother's life. It was as if a part of him believed that through Fay, he could keep something of Ben alive and maybe even understand what had happened to him in the last months of his life. And yet it was more than that. He'd thought of little else but her since the last time he'd seen her.

"If this keeps coming down like it is," he said before she'd spoken, "you may not get out of your driveway in the morning. At the inn, you're assured of getting out. There's a plow in the garage that I can connect to the front of the Jeep."

"Thanks, but there's no need if Lew picked him up. But if he didn't, then it sounds awfully tempting."

It was better than a flat-out *no*, he thought.

"Here we go," boomed Horn as he hurried up the aisle wearing a chef's apron that was dusted with flour. He was carrying a tray with a pot of coffee, mugs, and a basket of fresh rolls on it. He set it down, pulled out a chair, and looked hard at Nash, at Fay, at Nash again. He sat back, frowning, his arms folded at his chest.

"So you going to tell me what's going on, or am I supposed to play twenty questions?"

"Who says anything's going on?" Fay asked.

"Shee-it, girl. Neither one of you can lie worth a damn. What happened?"

As Fay related the story, her voice was far calmer and detached than it had been earlier. She seemed, in fact, so removed from the situation now, she could have been talking about something that had happened to someone else. It was the physician in her, Nash thought, that capacity to distance herself from what was in front of her so she could diagnose it, treat it. He envied her the ability.

For the most part, Horn seemed rather sanguine about the story. Nothing about preachers, he said, ever surprised him, especially fanatic Bible-thumpers like Quickson. "It's just a good thing Scotty showed up when he did," Horn said when she'd finished. "And that you run fast."

"Why *did* you stop by the clinic?" Fay asked.

"To show you some photos."

"They're in the Jeep?"

He nodded.

"Go get 'em, boy," said Horn.

Outside, the snow wasn't falling quite so furiously now. The streetlights illuminated the entrance to the park across the street and the trellis that covered it. All of the roses that had flourished with such wild abandon on it were dead. Their vines had withered. The great hulking live oaks, branches draped in Spanish moss now flecked with snow, looked like they were in shock. It seemed to Nash that he could hear them weeping for the end of summer, for the fall that had never come.

A peculiar hush cloaked the town. It was almost as though Lagoon had drawn in on itself, huddled against a danger that remained invisible, hidden, but whose presence it sensed as surely as he did. For a moment, as he stood there with the snow whispering around him, he felt as if he was in the center of a vortex that had not yet begun to spin. But he sensed the violent motion building at its center and knew it involved more than what had happened to Ben, to Quickson, more than the strange mutations and the abnormal weather. These things were connected somehow, but the heart of it remained tucked away, a closely guarded secret. Perhaps Suffield was right. Perhaps Nature *was* getting even.

As he retrieved his briefcase from the Jeep, a red Firebird slipped into the parking space behind him. Katie and a young man hopped out. For a beat or two, in the muted light, she so strongly resembled his image of what his daughter would have looked like at sixteen that his heart caught in his throat. Then she and her companion stepped into the wash of light from the café and she was simply herself again, and not nearly as serious as she had been that day in the meadow.

She introduced him to Ray Bosque, whose name Nash recognized from Bosque Garage, which his old man owned. He was a handsome kid of nineteen or twenty who was clearly taken with Katie and overly polite. Everything was *Yes, sir*, and *No, sir*, and *That's right, sir*. Even a while later, when they were all seated inside and Suffield showed up on his way home from work, Bosque addressed him in the same way. Suffield seemed embarrassed by it and finally asked him to knock it off.

"You're making me feel real old," he griped. "So just to set the record straight, Ray, we're Hank, Andy, Fay, and Scott, okay?"

Ray laughed, his face loosening at last. "Okay."

"Good. Now that we've got that straightened out, let's see these photos, Scott."

The photographs were 8 × 10s and were divided into three batches. The first consisted of the physical mutations they'd found that day in the meadow: the hive, the butterflies, the rose-like flowers. The second batch was of blowups of the moon buggies. Nash had caught head-on shots of a pair of men in one of the buggies, and despite the graininess of the enlargements, the men were clearly visible. The driver was perfectly bald, husky, and had a hawkish nose and a generous mouth. He was wearing headphones with a mike that swung back and forth in front of his mouth. His companion was younger, leaner, with a full head of red hair and spare features.

Nash pointed out something that had not been apparent in the negatives or in smaller versions of the photographs: a kind of spectral image that surrounded each of the physical mutations. When he'd first noticed it in the darkroom, it had reminded him of what you saw during a solar eclipse, when the corona of the sun blazed around its circumference. Now it just looked eerie.

He went over the obvious explanations: an abnormality on the paper or the film, an odd refraction of light that the blowups had exacerbated, faulty chemicals, improper temperatures during the development process. "So just to make sure, I tossed out all the chemicals and paper and printed them again. I got the same thing. It could be a light leak in the camera, but in that case the images wouldn't be so uniformly consistent. What's curious is that all the pictures with the ghost images on them were taken with a red filter on the lens, which increases contrast."

"But what do these images *mean*?" Fay asked.

"I don't know."

Ray twisted the gold post in his earlobe. "Maybe that's just how the mutations photograph."

"If so, that doesn't explain this." Nash removed the third batch of pictures from the envelope and separated them into two piles. He lined up photos from the first stack in the center of the table, with identical pictures from the second directly under their counterparts. They were ordinary scenes: the post office, a shot of the inn taken from a canoe on the lagoon, the library, the Nameless, the Kroger's grocery store, the lagoon.

"The photos in the top row were taken when I was here a little over a year ago: no ghost image, no filter. I shot the second group five days ago with a red filter. They all have ghost images. Even the lagoon itself."

"But what good is it if we don't know what it means?" asked Horn.

"I was hoping Hank might have some ideas."

Suffield had worked the elastic band off his ponytail and now he combed his fingers back through his long, glossy hair and shook his head. "Hey, I'm a biologist. This is way outta my line. These are *buildings*."

"But the lagoon and the trees around it aren't, Hank," objected Katie.

Suffield picked up the two photographs of the lagoon, comparing them. Something flickered across his face, but Nash didn't know the man well enough to interpret what it meant. "I don't know," he said. "The only thing it reminds me of is Kirlian photography. You familiar with it?"

Nash nodded. "But I've never tried it."

"What is it?" asked Ray.

"A means of photographing, with a special kind of camera, the energy that a living thing radiates. You could put your hand on the film, for instance, and snap a picture of your particular energy field. We've used it in the lab with plants. Some people claim to be able to read breaks in the energy field that indicate ill health or whatever. But to my knowledge it can't be done with a regular camera."

Fay sighed and sat back. "Look, there's got to be some explanation. These things don't just *happen*. And that goes for the mutations, too."

The physician speaking, Nash thought. *Give me facts and I'll diagnose.*

"Of course they don't just *happen*," Suffield replied. He tapped the photos taken in the meadow. "These mutations indicate design and intent, Fay. They indicate awareness."

She smiled. "I've read your books, Hank. They're brilliant in their originality. But I just don't agree with them any more than I agree with your interpretation of Kirlian photography images."

"Fine. But let me ask you this." He leaned forward, his dark eyes as calm and inscrutable as the surface of the lagoon at night. "What the hell do you think is causing all these eczema cases? These incidents of violence and aggression? What caused the abnormalities in Ben? You're a doctor. I'd like to hear your thoughts on it, Fay."

The change in her demeanor was instantaneous and not at all subtle. Her spine went rigid, her voice clicked into its *controlled, professional* mode again, and her face looked as though it had calcified. "Personally, I think it's some sort of new strain of virus that—"

"A *virus*?" Suffield burst out laughing. "A fucking virus? That's bullshit." He started firing questions at her. How was this virus transmitted? Was it contagious? Did she think it tied in with the abnormal weather?

Color rushed into Fay's cheeks; fissures appeared in her control. "I didn't say I had the answers, Hank. I'm just telling you what I think is involved."

"Hell, you've got blinders on. You're only seeing one facet of it. To understand what this thing is, you've got to look at how it's related to everything else that's going on. Until you do that, you're deluding yourself."

"Excuse me." Horn held up his hands, a referee signaling time out. "I say we all have something to eat and break out a couple of brews." He glanced around the table. "How about it, folks?"

"Not us," said Ray, touching Katie's arm. "We're going to shove off."

Nash, wanting to avoid further unpleasantness, glanced at Fay to see if she was ready to split as well. But she and Suffield had settled back to wait for the beers and looked as eager as pugilists for the second round.

2.

Ray patted the seat beside him. "I don't bite, you know."

"But I do," Katie replied.

He laughed. "Thanks for the warning."

She scooted over beside him and adjusted the car's air vent so the heat blew directly on her feet, which felt like they were frozen solid. His arm rested along the back of the seat and his fingers stroked her hair.

"Your old man always so intense?" Ray asked.

"Only when he's not stoned and he's talking about something he believes in. I hate it when he gets like that in front of other people."

"You think he's right? About what's going on?"

"I don't know. But *he* thinks he's right."

"At least he believes in something. The only thing my old man believes in is the inside of a bottle of bourbon. He used to beat up on my mother when he got loaded, but that stopped when she left and went to live with her sister in Chapel Hill. So now it's just him and me in that house, and I'm moving out at the end of the week."

"To where?" *Don't say out of state.*

"I found a place over near the railroad tracks. You want to see it tomorrow?"

"Sure."

He looked over at her. In the flickering spill of streetlights, his face seemed infinitely mysterious, a face she could look at a thousand times and always find something new, something she hadn't noticed before.

"You're not at all like your friend Dani, Katie-o."

"Is that good or bad?"

He laughed. "Good."

"Why?"

"If I want to know what you're thinking, all I've got to do is look at you."

"That doesn't sound good."

He gave the back of her neck an affectionate squeeze that sent goose bumps down her spine. "It is. Take my word for it."

The Firebird turned onto Hawthorne. In the dark, the trees and brush seemed to huddle closer to the road, like a crowd of people seeking refuge from something. Overhead branches sagged with the weight of the snow. Now and then one of them gave way and a clump of snow hit the roof of the Firebird, startling her.

She hadn't felt the same about this road since the morning on her bike when the dark smell had chased her. It was like the bridge in the children's story about trolls, something she had to cross to get from point A to point B. But it was unsafe, and at any second, it might betray her and the trolls would get her.

That was how she thought of them, of the people to whom the dark smell belonged. They were trolls, creatures of the dark who lived somewhere on the lagoon, hidden in the trees. Ben had become one of them when he'd gotten sick; maybe there were other people in town who were also getting sick and would join the trolls. Maybe her sense of smell meant *she* was becoming one of them and that was what had attracted the trolls to the house. They'd been looking for her. But the odor of garbage had distracted them and they'd pillaged the cans.

Her theory didn't explain how the trolls had gotten here to begin with, but so what? Trolls—like leprechauns and fairies—had always existed. And these were particularly bad. It made more sense to her than Hank's theories.

When they got to the house, she invited Ray in. Hank, she said, wouldn't be back for a while and Jo was probably asleep; she'd been sick. They could make popcorn and watch the tube or something. She knew she was babbling, and why had she suggested watching TV when they'd just gone to a movie? But Ray smiled and asked her to show him the canaries she'd told him about.

Katie hung their jackets in the hall closet, and they went into the kitchen. When she switched on the overhead light, she saw Ike perched on the edge of a Tupperware container on the counter pecking at the brownies inside. Tina was in the sink fluttering in a bowl half filled with water, singing sweetly.

"Far out." Ray laughed. "You just let them fly around the house?"

"Not usually." Katie caught Ike. "And especially not when Jo's around. How'd you get out, boy? Hmm? Did Hank leave the door unlatched?"

Ike trilled a couple of notes. Tina responded with a trill of her own and lifted up from the bowl. Water flew from her feathers as she zipped for a ceiling beam, where Katie couldn't catch her.

"Jo's going to have a fit if she realizes they've gotten out of the cage."

"What's Tina like to eat?" Ray asked. "Maybe I can lure her down that way."

"Strawberries. She loves strawberries. There're some in the fridge. Be right back. Let me put Ike in the cage."

When she returned to the kitchen, Ray was standing on a chair, holding out a strawberry that Tina was eyeing with obvious interest. Katie circled to the other side of the table, climbed onto the chair, and whispered, "When she comes down, I'll nab her."

Ray clicked his tongue at Tina; she cocked her head from left to right and fluttered her wings. But she didn't descend. From the other room, Ike sang two short notes, three long, and Tina replied with a piercing whistle. It was as if they were talking to each other, planning their next move.

Suddenly, Ike swooped into the kitchen and raced toward the beam where Tina was. It wasn't possible; Katie knew she'd latched the door to the cage when she'd put him back inside. But there he was next to Tina, the two of them preening and singing and ignoring Katie and Ray completely.

"They're making fun of us," he said with a laugh.

"I locked the latch on the cage."

"So maybe Hank taught them how to *un*lock it."

"No, he wouldn't. Because of Jo."

Just as they hopped down from the chair, Jo shambled into the kitchen. Her copper hair needed combing, and she had deep circles under her eyes. Her terry-cloth robe fell open in front, revealing her long, soiled nightgown. She blinked against the bright light, knuckled an eye, glanced at Ray, then at Katie. "Where's Hank?"

"At the Nameless."

Her mouth pursed with disapproval. "Swell. Here I am sicker than a dog and he's at the Nameless. How considerate of him." She opened the freezer, took out a package of frozen steak, stuck it in the microwave. Then she stood with her back to them, watching the meat through the glass window. "He always does this to me, you know. He doesn't like being around sick people. Never has. Not that he'd admit it. Ha. No way."

Thoroughly mortified, Katie looked at Ray and mouthed, *Sorry*.

"Don't worry about it," he whispered. "I'd better split."

She suddenly hated Jo, hated her for intruding, for her whining, for being such a jerk. They walked past her and into the hall. Katie got Ray's jacket from the closet. "I'm really sorry. She's just so weird."

He smiled, fixing her with those dark, liquid eyes. Something deep inside her went soft and strange. "Don't worry about it, Katie-o. She doesn't hold a candle to my old man in the weirdness department." He kissed her then, lightly, gently. "See you tomorrow," he said, and slipped out the door.

Katie floated back toward the kitchen, elated, touching her mouth with her fingertips, unable to stop smiling.

"You're not supposed to bring boys home, young lady," Jo snapped without looking at her. She was leaning over the sink, her back to Katie. "You know the rules."

"Hank's never told me that."

"*I'm* telling you." Jo spun around, the slab of raw steak in her hand, the top chewed off. Blood bubbled from the corner of her mouth, her eyes were glassy, her lips stained pink. "Next thing you'll be fucking these guys in the family room. I know how it is. I know." She tore into a corner of the steak, gnawing at it, making strange animal sounds. Her cheeks were bright pink, feverish, rivulets of blood were trickling down the side of her arm. "You think I can't remember what it's like to be sixteen and pretty?" she mumbled in between bites. "I know. I remember. I sure do. Guys always wanting to touch and kiss and suck . . ."

She tore at the slab of meat again, wiped her hand across her mouth as she chewed. Katie struggled against the thick, stale odor of sickness that Jo radiated, a stink like wet moss, like old rotting leaves. She was certain this was the same odor she'd smelled outside the house that morning. She backed up to the wall, trying to distance herself from it, but it crashed around her in waves, swirling into her nostrils, coating the inside of her mouth.

"Jo, I don't think you should, uh, be eating raw meat," she stammered. "How about if I fix you something? A sandwich. Soup." She moved toward Jo, breathing through her mouth. "Here, let me have the steak." She reached for it, but Jo snatched her hand away.

"No," she whined. "Mine. It's mine." The sleeve of her robe slipped down to her elbow, exposing her arm. It was red and puffy. Pus or something like it was seeping out.

"My God, your arm. What happened to your arm?"

The slab of steak slipped from her hand and into the sink as she twisted her arm around to look at it. "Oh. That." She sniffled. "Poison ivy. I've got it on my leg, too, see?" She turned and, with her bloodied hand, pulled up the hem of her robe in front. The top of her thigh was covered with the rash. "There's even a patch on my tummy."

Now she lifted her gown, showing Katie her stomach. "It spreads, you know. Poison ivy spreads like crazy. Where's my steak?" She looked around, frowning, confused, rubbing at her bloodstained mouth with the back of her hand. "Hungry. I'm hungry and the steak's gone."

She started to weep. Her shoulders shook. Katie went over to her. She didn't want to touch her, to connect with the smell, but she couldn't just stand here doing nothing. Katie slipped an arm around her, grimacing as the odor thickened around her. She nearly gagged. "C'mon, Jo, I think you'd better get back to bed. I'll call Fay. She'll give you something to make you feel better."

"No." Jo wrenched away and whipped her head from side to side, her voice getting louder, more hysterical. "Nonono. I'm hungry, that's all. Just hungry. No doctors. It's poison ivy and the flu. The flu. I've got the flu and poison ivy. I want my steak. Did you take my steak?" Her eyes narrowed and she screamed, *"Where's my goddamn steak? You took my steak!"*

She lunged at Katie, slamming her back against the refrigerator, her fingers hooked like claws around Katie's throat. She kicked and tried to fight her off, but Jo was too strong and Katie couldn't catch her breath. The thick, sickly odor sucked away what strength she had. The stink was everywhere. It pounded against her. Her lungs screeched for air. The light in the room winked off and on. Black dots swam before her eyes. Her ears rang. Panic exploded in her chest.

She's going to kill me.

Katie grabbed Jo's hair and yanked on it. Jo shrieked in pain but didn't let go of Katie's throat; she kept squeezing it, harder, harder. Then suddenly she flew back, and Katie, released, stumbled forward, gulping air, coughing, rubbing her throat, her eyes tearing. She saw Hank clutching Jo in a bear hug as she screamed and struggled, shrieked and kicked. They twirled through the kitchen like clumsy dancers, bumping into the table and knocking things to the floor as Hank tried to restrain her. Jo got her hands loose and beat her fists against his chest, his face. She clawed at him. Katie grabbed the frying pan from the stove and, without even thinking about what she was doing, slammed it over Jo's head.

It made a sharp, terrible sound. Jo gasped and went limp in Hank's arms. Neither of them moved. The only sound in the silence was his breathing and hers. Blood oozed from a scratch on Hank's cheek. Then the frying pan slipped from Katie's hand and clattered to the floor, startling them both from their torpor.

"You all right?"

"I think so." She was trembling.

"Call Fay. And 911. We need an ambulance."

She's a troll, Katie thought wildly. *One of them.* "She attacked me, Hank. She was eating raw steak and attacked me, I don't know why she did it, I didn't do anything to her. I didn't provoke her, I mean, I—"

"I know you didn't do anything. Don't worry. Just make those calls. I'm going to keep an eye on her."

Katie spun toward the phone.

14

Hazards

1.

"I'm dying, aren't I," whimpered Jo, staring up at Fay from the couch where she lay. "I want to know the truth. If I'm dying, I want you to tell me."

"You're ill, Jo, you aren't dying. There's a difference. I'd like to take a look at this rash you mentioned, okay?"

Her lower lip thrust out in a pout, as if to say this was all someone else's fault, but she didn't know whose yet. When she spoke, her voice was small, choked. "Nothing helps it. I've tried everything. Calamine, aloe, salt water. I even went to the health-food store and got some stuff, but nothing works." She sat up, throwing off the afghan that covered her, and rolled her nightgown to her upper thigh. "Just look. Two weeks ago, there was just a little speck here. Now look at it."

Sweet Christ.

This wasn't any rash. This was similar to what Quickson had shown her, but much worse. On her upper thighs, it was at least half an inch thick, then it tapered off around her knees and worsened again on the backs of her arms and legs. It was a faded brown, the color of old foam rubber, and, at its thickest points, looked as porous as sponge. Fay didn't want to touch it, to get too close to it, wanted suddenly to be as far away from this woman as possible. But the doctor in her wouldn't let her budge. The doctor in her rapped a ruler against her knuckles and said, *Control.*

She snapped on a pair of latex gloves, ran her hands over the rash, and thought she was going to vomit. She swallowed hard.

Even though the condition had been more widespread on Ben, this was the first time she'd seen such a severe case on a living person. She took advantage of the opportunity by firing questions at Jo. Was she in pain? Did it itch? Was she having diffi-

culty using her arms and legs? No, no, no, Jo replied. It felt
. . . well, strange, that was all.

When did she first notice the rash? Two weeks ago? Was that
what she'd said? No, that was just on her thigh. The first time
was about three months ago, when there was just a little
bitty patch on the inside of her wrist. That was how it stayed
until a couple of weeks ago, when the rash became inflamed.
Then, four or five days ago, it started to spread. To thicken. To
ooze.

"When did you start feeling sick?" *When did you develop
this taste for raw meat?*

"On and off for a couple of weeks. I thought I was getting
the flu, but then I'd feel better again. I started feeling really sick
when it began to spread. That's when I got the fever and . . .
and . . ." Her face squashed up and she started to cry again,
straining Fay's patience.

Was she dying? she asked again. She deserved to know, it
was her right. Fay assured her she wasn't dying and did it with
more conviction than she felt. She coaxed Jo back against the
couch and drew the afghan over her.

"Have you had any other symptoms? A sore throat? Cough?
Anything like that?"

Jo hiccuped and yanked a piece of Kleenex from the box on
the coffee table. "No. But bright lights have started bothering
my eyes in the last couple of days. And I'm, uh, turned on all
the time. Like I'm in heat or something." She gave a strange,
clipped laugh. "But I didn't want Hank to see me like this, so
I've . . . I've been telling him I thought I was contagious and
he's been sleeping in the den."

"Anything else?"

She frowned. "Dreams. I have these weird dreams."

"What kind of dreams?" Fay stripped off the gloves and set
them on top of a magazine on the coffee table.

"I hear people talking, but I can never see them. They tell
me things."

"Such as?"

Jo rubbed her nose with the back of her hand. "That it's going
to be okay if I just let the voices help me."

"Help you how?"

She looked away. "I'm not supposed to say."

Delusions, Fay thought.

"Is Katie still out there?" Jo asked.

"Yes."

"She made me awful mad. She took my steak."

"Why were you eating raw steak, Jo?"

"I was hungry." She looked down at her hands. "Real hungry. Katie shouldn't have taken my steak." Now she raised her eyes. "Who else is out there?"

"Hank and Scott Nash."

"Ben's brother."

"Right."

"Why's he here?"

"He drove me over."

She curled her hands tightly against her chest and whispered, "Am I going to end up like Ben? Am I going to end up crazy? The voices say that happens sometimes, Fay. Sometimes people can't stand the . . . the change and they . . . they do things like Ben did."

The back of Fay's neck prickled with alarm. "What change, Jo?"

She threw off the covers and held up her arms so that the sleeves of her nightgown slipped back. Her voice turned sharp and ugly; color flashed into her faded eyes. "*This* change. What the hell do you think I'm talking about?"

"It's a skin condition that's probably caused by a virus. It's not permanent."

"It's not?" She seemed genuinely perplexed. "But I thought . . . the voices said . . . I mean . . ."

"Look, I'm going to admit you to Franklin General for some tests. The ambulance should be here shortly."

"No. No hospital. Please. I hate hospitals." She grabbed Fay's hand. "Don't send me to a hospital."

Jesus, don't touch me. Don't touch me. Fay repressed the urge to jerk her arm free and managed to pull it back gently. The skin all over her hand seemed to tingle from contact with Jo. She knew it was her imagination, that it had to be, but she didn't care. All she could think of was scrubbing her hands with something strong. "You need tests I can't run and treatment I can't give you, Jo. It's for the best. I'll send Hank in now."

She quickly retreated and, in the kitchen, got rid of the magazine that held the latex gloves, then scrubbed her hands in the sink. "How is she?" Suffield asked.

"Bad. She's got the worst case of the rash I've seen yet. I think it's best if she goes to Franklin General."

"You know damn well they aren't going to be able to do anything for her, Fay, so what the hell's the point? And it's not just a *rash*, for Christ's sakes. I saw it. It's . . .'' The revulsion that swept over his face had no counterpart in spoken language.

"All I'm saying is that I can't help her, Hank. We need other people working on this. She'll be better off in a hospital."

"I don't want her here," Katie said quietly. "She could've killed me. She's *strong*, Hank. Really strong. I'm afraid of her and I don't want her here."

Suffield looked torn, but not for long. When it came down to Katie or Jo, there was no real decision to be made. "Don't worry about it, kiddo." He pushed away from the table and went into the living room, shutting the door behind him.

While Fay, Katie, and Nash waited for the ambulance to arrive, she called the station to find out if Quickson had been picked up. Oliver said he'd left a message on her machine at home; didn't she get it?

"If I'd gotten it, Lew, I wouldn't be calling you." It came out more sharply than she'd intended, but she was beyond caring. She knew Oliver was fishing for information about her whereabouts—specifically, if she was at the Blue Inn with Nash—and it irritated her. "There was an emergency at the Suffields'. So did you arrest Quickson?"

"No. We couldn't find him. His place looked like he'd packed up and split. But we've got an APB out on him."

He said it as if this was supposed to comfort her. "Great."

"Don't worry, Fay, we'll catch him. I'll be in touch."

"Yeah, thanks." *For nothing.*

2.

It seemed to Nash that the night conspired to keep him awake. First it was the wind, whining along the edges of the windows and blowing branches against the glass. Then it was the silence when the wind died, the kind of deep, penetrating silence he imagined existed in the underworld of Greek myths. It saturated the air, and the harder he strained to detect something inside it, the more pervasive it became.

But deep down, he knew the wind and the silence and all the rest of it had nothing to do with his difficulty in sleeping. It was Fay's presence three doors down that was doing it, the idea of her being so close—and yet so distant.

They had stayed up for a while when they'd gotten back here, talking about Jo, Quickson, Suffield's theories, trying to fit everything that had happened into a larger picture. By the time he'd fixed up a room for her just down the hall, it was past midnight and he was bushed. But as soon as he was in bed, his fatigue had abandoned him and he'd lain in the dark, thinking of Fay, of Ben, of Ben's hands against her hips, of Ben's mouth at her breasts, of Ben inside her.

Nash sat up and threw off the covers. The creak of the springs in the mattress was a welcome sound—company in the silence, evidence that he hadn't gone suddenly deaf. He thought he heard Samson sighing or snorting down the hall, as though he were dreaming, and listened for something that would tell him that Fay was also awake. But the only other sound was the whisper of heat through the vents.

At the window, Nash gazed out at the lagoon. It had stopped snowing. The sky was still soupy, but the light on the back deck provided enough illumination to see the whiteness of every-thing, a whiteness that would blind by morning. The lagoon burned like a pale eye in the center of the dark trees that em-braced it. But the heart of the lagoon, where the water hadn't frozen, looked like a dilated pupil.

Scattered along the east shore were glimmers of light and puffs of smoke billowing from invisible chimneys. To the south, he could just make out a pinprick of light like a star that was probably coming from the Menninger place. To the west, he saw only darkness. The few homes back there had been shut up since the weather had turned cold.

And when are you going to shut down the inn, Nash? Or put out a FOR SALE sign and go back to your own life?

When he knew the truth.

He started to turn away from the window but thought he glimpsed something darting through the trees at the western edge of the lagoon. He rubbed his palm over the glass. He still couldn't see clearly enough, so he opened the window and leaned out into the cold silence, wishing for more light, sharper eye-sight. There. He saw it again, something flitting into the trees.

He hurried over to the closet, flicked on the light inside, and worked loose the secret panel in the wall. Here Ben had stashed important documents and papers, memorabilia from his mar-riage, survival gear, and guns, including the Uzi he'd used dur-ing the final moments of his life. His brother had collected guns for the same reason he collected anything else: he enjoyed it. At one time, they were displayed in a case in the bar downstairs. But shortly after his wife had died, Ben had moved them all up here. Nash suspected it was because he was afraid he might use one of them on himself. The irony was that he'd died by his own hand despite the precaution.

Nash found a pair of binoculars, switched off the light, and on his way back to the window, shrugged on his robe; it was chilly in the room now. He focused on the spot where he'd last seen the animal, then moved slowly along the shore. Trees swam into focus, but it was too dark on the west side for him to make out much else. He swung the binoculars east, saw the edge of the Suffields' back deck, and then south again to the dock that jutted off the Menningers' beach. He swept the west shore again and moved slowly south until he thought he saw something.

He adjusted the lenses, trying to bring the animal into focus. But the binoculars were old and the lenses were scratched and the creature was much farther away now, slipping through the trees. Nash leaned farther out the window, trying to track it. He didn't see it again until it reached the curve in the shore and stepped away from the shelter of the trees.

It moved upright like a bear, but it wasn't as large, as bulky, and he couldn't even tell if it had fur. There was a certain grace about it that was almost human and yet it loped like an animal accustomed to four legs, not two. For just an instant, the creature turned, almost as though it sensed him watching, and its head filled the binoculars. It was a malformed thing, hideous in its proportions, like something that had been broken and ineptly slapped back together, a Humpty Dumpty head after the fall.

Gooseflesh raced along Nash's arms as he dropped to his knees and balanced the binoculars against the top of the window-sill to steady his hands. He focused the lenses again. The creature had gone utterly still, like a deer impaled by headlights, and Nash was certain that it saw him.

How? It's too far away.

But his body wasn't listening to his head. The hair at the back of his neck stood up, his skin turned cold and clammy, his heart pounded to a feverish, primal beat.

He ducked down under the sill, pulling the binoculars with him, and nearly leaped out of his skin when a voice whispered, "Scott?"

He jerked around. Fay stood silhouetted in the doorway by a night light in the hall, one arm clutched at her waist, and the other at her throat, holding her robe closed. Her hair was a dark, wild nimbus around her head.

"Jesus, you scared the hell out of me."

"What're you doing on the floor?"

"C'mere, there's something I want you to see. But get down."

Her robe rustled as she came over and crouched beside him. "What is it?"

"I'm not sure." He handed her the binoculars. "It's almost directly south."

She peered through the lenses and focused the sight. Nash scanned the far shore, but the creature wasn't visible without the binoculars. "See anything?"

"Just trees and . . . My God, what *is* it?"

"A bear?"

"Not in these woods. Part of it is . . . stretched out on the ice at the edge of the lagoon and its hand is in the water. It's fishing, Scott. The damn thing is ice-fish—" She suddenly pulled her head down under the sill, her eyes wide, frightened, her voice the barest whisper. "It saw me. But it couldn't have. We're too far away."

"I know. I had the same feeling. C'mon, let's go up into the attic to take a look. It has a better view of the lagoon."

They found Samson at the end of the hall, paws perched on the sill as he wheezed and clawed at the glass. "What is it, boy?" Fay whispered.

Nash rubbed the window with his hand and peered out, but couldn't see anything. Samson whimpered and was halfway down the stairs before he stopped and glanced back, as if asking to be let out.

"We're going up, guy." Nash opened the door that led to the attic and Samson flew up the stairs ahead of them.

The attic was cold, musty, and black, except for the dim light that seeped through the windows at either end. Nash had been up here a few days ago, cleaning and sorting the things Ben had stored. The bed at the window was stacked with old magazines he intended to toss out, and he moved several piles to the desk to make room for himself and Fay. Samson leaped up and wedged himself between them, whimpering until Nash opened the window.

Fay raised the binoculars to her eyes.

"See anything?"

"Nothing. It's gone."

"You sure?"

"Take a look." She unhooked the strap from her neck and passed him the glasses.

He scanned the lagoon from west to east and back again.

There was no sign of the creature. Even Samson seemed to be having trouble picking up a scent; his nose was working furiously at the silent, gelid air.

"Nothing," he said, setting the binoculars aside.

"Those are Ben's, aren't they?"

"I found them in his stash." He paused. "You know about that?"

She nodded and sat back against the wall, arms hooked around her legs. "Lew was real curious about where the Uzi had come from. I never told him about Ben's collection of guns."

"Good. It's none of his business, anyway."

"Actually, it *is* his business, but the idea of Lew poking around in Ben's things turned my stomach."

"Was he quizzing you over the phone earlier about where you'd been?"

"Sure." She smiled and stroked Samson as he gave up at the window and stretched out on the bed, his head in Fay's lap. "He asked me out the first week I was in town and I turned him down. He's been bugging me ever since, except when Ben and I were seeing each other. Lew really resented him for that." She looked up at him. "And now he resents you for the same reason. He thinks there's something going on with us."

A warning or an invitation, Nash couldn't tell which. But it had never seemed so important to say the right thing to a woman, to do the right thing. "*Is* there something going on with us?"

She laughed softly and leaned into the sill, an elbow resting against it, the robe at her throat falling open. "Maybe I should be asking *you*, Nash. You've been avoiding me since the memorial service."

Her directness was a surprise, and somewhat unsettling. Nash was accustomed to south Florida women, who had polished coyness to an art form. "I guess I didn't want Ben to be the basis for the attraction."

"He isn't. Not for me."

For an awkward moment, they just looked at each other, then they both laughed. "Did we do this backward or what?" he said.

"We could have breakfast and start over again," she suggested. "Bacon and eggs and seduction."

Nash laughed again. "Or we could just pretend."

"I think I like that option."

They leaned over Samson at the same moment and she touched his face. Nash's fingers slipped into her hair. Their mouths touched, parted, touched again. His tongue slid along her lower lip; her mouth opened against his.

For long moments, his entire being seemed focused only on the simplicity of the kiss, the coolness of her tongue curling around his, the scent of her hair and skin. Then Samson squirmed between them and they moved apart, laughing again, as the dog stood, shook himself, and jumped off the bed. He settled on the floor with a sigh, a wheeze, and was silent.

"Such discretion on Samson's part," she remarked, her thumb moving along Nash's lower lip as if to define it.

"Good manners." He untied the sash at her waist and slipped the robe off her shoulders. "You raised him well."

"It's easier with only children, you know." They moved back against the bed, neither of them speaking for a long time.

In lovemaking, Nash discovered that Fay became the perfect amalgamation of all the women she was. The cool, controlled physician knew precisely where to touch, how to touch, but she did it with the seductress's hands and mouth. The flirt teased him into a high-pitched fever, and the bookworm prolonged the pleasure, drawing back at the right moment, holding him still, whispering to him.

Sometimes she led and he followed, and sometimes it was the other way around. Beneath his hands, she became cool, damp clay that he molded and sculpted, elongating her limbs, altering the shape of her hips, her breasts, her thighs. Her musky scent mixed with the smell of water and smoke until he was drunk with it and didn't think he could hold back any longer. He slipped out of her and kissed his way down the length of her body, lingering at a breast, a hip, until his tongue moved in a slow, hot glide across the flat plane of her tummy, and lower.

Her taste was so exquisite, he suddenly couldn't remember other tastes. She gripped the sides of his head, holding him there, pressing him against her with a desperate greed, a gluttony that demanded, that begged to be sated. Her soft, broken moans seemed to mock the tight silence beyond them and became a kind of music that transported him, filled him. Nash wanted to climb into her, to turn her and himself inside out, like umbrellas, like a magician's cloak, as though the act itself would whisk them to some other planet, some other time, another universe. As the muscles in her thighs tightened and quivered, he stopped, suspending her there, and she gasped, an aerialist in a free-fall between heaven and earth. Then Nash touched her again and her breath exploded and he moved inside her, into that soft, sweet music, into a tide that was hot and electric, a pleasure so extreme it became pain.

The geometry of their bodies grew into a complexity of limbs, sensations, noises, until he was burning, burning, lost in a white blaze of desert, beyond need, desire, beyond everything except the moment.

He came suddenly, his insides collapsing like the walls of an old building, and as she clutched at him, her skin released a scent unlike anything he'd ever smelled. It weaved around them, cloying, strange, wonderful, a witch scent that drugged and mystified and permeated the room.

They both went utterly still, tangled in each other. Nash heard their labored breathing and the rush of his own fevered blood as the scent clamped down over him completely.

Much later, he bolted awake to a high-pitched keening that rippled through the dark like the bay of a wolf calling its mate. He moved quietly away from Fay and sat up, rubbing his hands over his arms to warm himself. The room was freezing.

He peered out the open window at the lagoon. Streaks of gray light sliced across the sky to the east, tipping the treetops. Everything was sealed in white and absolutely soundless. He found the binoculars on the floor, fixed them against his eyes, and swept the shores once. Nothing. And he didn't hear the keening again, either.

Nash shut the window, left the binoculars on the sill, and fixed the covers over himself and Fay. She was on her side, her back to him. "What?" she asked, her voice drowsy with sleep.

"I thought I heard something, that's all." He fitted himself against her so that they were lying like spoons. She snuggled back and moved his hand to her belly, where the skin was soft and warm. His fingers burrowed lower, and she laughed softly and turned on her other side, facing him, her legs sliding apart, admitting him. He found a rhythm that made her purr; she nibbled at his ear, whispering things that excited him.

Now the witch scent materialized again, shifting around them, a sweet, invisible tide. Her hands sought him, but he was already hard, and she lifted up to straddle him. Instead, he coaxed her back against the bed, wanting to arouse her with his hands, at a distance, so that he could watch her face, as though something in her private expressions of pleasure could explain the provenance of the scent.

The covers slipped to her waist. Her arms stretched languidly over her head; she was a cat unfolding in warm sunlight. Her skin was the color of pearls, slick and cool, like a damp leaf, but inside she was hot, feverish, wet, a rain forest the sun never penetrated. His fingers were lost in that darkness, sliding through it, in and out, exploring blindly as her eyes fluttered closed, as she abandoned her body to him, to the sensations he aroused in her, and floated in a dark tide of sentience, in a strange, solitary passion to which he was only incidental.

Her expression changed. Her hips moved, rotating, grinding, lifting slightly until she was impaled. The scent thickened. It seemed to take root in the very air, and blossomed with all the exuberance of flowers in a spring meadow. This time it wasn't sweet or sour or anything else he could identify. It simply bewitched. He felt as if he'd inhaled a gallon of nitrous oxide and could lift up out of his bones, his blood, and soar.

When she came, the scent scattered, a dandelion in the wind.

Nash dreamed of hazards, both physical and spiritual, of Ben rising from the dead, of animals that walked like men but couldn't be men, and of the witch scent, thickening until it choked him.

15

What Happened at the Junkman's

1.

At 8:30 P.M. on September 16, the Mobile Medical Unit pulled out of a village twenty miles north of Lagoon and headed home. Mona was at the wheel and Fay was slumped in the passenger seat. They were nearly four hours behind schedule and she was tired, hungry, and cranky.

They'd gotten started late this morning because the van wouldn't crank up. It had taken the mechanic forty minutes to find the problem, which temperatures in the twenties last night had exacerbated, and two hours to fix it. Then throughout the afternoon there had been numerous minor delays that had accrued like interest on an unpaid debt. Now here they were, on a two-lane country road as desolate as the moon.

This was backwoods Georgia, where trees hugged the road a little too closely and the snow-covered hills in the distance loomed like fat, luminous apparitions against a nearly starless sky, and where, in between, thrived a world straight out of *Deliverance*. Poverty and moonshine, incest and banjos. Even though the van serviced this area and she'd treated some of these people, the prospect of breaking down on this road made her uneasy.

"I hate this road after dark," said Mona, shifting gears as they started up an incline.

"I was just thinking the same thing."

Mona lit a cigarette and cracked her window. "Are the doors back there locked, Fay?"

"I'm sure they are, but I'll check again."

"Thanks. I've got a bad case of the spooks tonight."

"That makes two of us."

Fay made her way back through the van, checking windows and doors, feeling like a kid alone in the house at night, taking precautions against the arrival of the bogeyman. When she was sure the van was sealed up tight, she ducked into the restroom and turned on the light.

The room was barely larger than a closet, but when you were in the middle of nowhere, it served its purpose. She used the toilet, then dampened some paper towels under the faucet and pressed them against her cheeks. It eased the hot throb behind her eyes but did nothing for her hunger cramps or her disposition.

She wadded the towels, tossed them in the basket, and scrutinized herself in the mirror. *What're we looking for tonight, Fay? Which symptoms? Are we shifting into high-gear paranoia? Sliding into hypochondria again?*

Well, so what if she was? It was inevitable. Even though she'd seen no new cases of the skin condition since Jo Englert, the rash on some of her other patients was gradually spreading and beginning to thicken. And there were other alarming developments as well: three incidents of domestic violence at the northern end of the county in families where at least one person was afflicted; the disappearance of Jo Englert, who'd checked herself out of Franklin General four days after she'd arrived and hadn't been seen since; and the fact that Quickson still hadn't been found. In short, the pathology of this thing was following what Lance Blair at the CDC had described.

No wonder she stood in front of mirrors, examining her own skin for changes.

She turned her head right and left and lifted her hair at either side to look at her neck. She unbuttoned her cardigan and the blouse under it and leaned closer, touching her throat, her chest, seeking spots of dry skin that hadn't turned red yet. She didn't see or feel anything.

Fay watched her hand moving carefully over each breast, looking for abnormalities that didn't show. And as she watched, her hand became Ben's, slow and sure and gentle. Her nipples hardened. A slow, erotic burn started somewhere deep inside her, melting through her. The hand was now Scott's, and it glided over her skin the way his had every night for the last four, rolling a nipple between his fingers, slipping down against her belly, and . . .

I feel so turned on all the time, like I'm in heat or something: Jo's words. Fay jerked her hand from her body. She quickly snapped her bra, fixed her clothes, and hurried back to the front of the van, her breath thick in her throat, cheeks hot, her nipples straining against the fabric of her bra.

"Hey, Fay, the gas gauge is brushing *E*. You think old fart Obie would spare a few gallons?"

Obie. Now there was a dose of reality for her. "If he doesn't, we'll camp in his yard."

Obie considered most people in the medical profession to be greedy butchers. But his opinion of Fay and Mona was a bit more forgiving because a year ago they'd treated one of his ailing cats for free. So from time to time, he presented them with a supposedly valuable antique from his junk shop or invited them in for coffee or brandy. Tonight, with the cold dark rubbing up against the windows of the van, a brandy sounded awful tempting.

And we won't think about disturbing things, will we, Fay? We won't think about rashes or Quickson or the weird odor your skin releases when you're turned on. We'll pretend.

Mona slowed as they approached the wooden sign that pointed the way to the junk shop and hung a right. The van bounced as it hit the unpaved, slushy road. The headlights danced across the trees on either side of them, creating spectral shapes that seemed to float against the dark green, then vanish. Mona hummed a few bars of the theme from *The Twilight Zone*, and she and Fay laughed.

"We're hopeless, Mona."

"Don't I know it. *The Invasion of the Body Snatchers* was on the tube last night. The old one, you know? And I couldn't take more than fifteen minutes of it."

She stopped in front of the shop, and they climbed down from the van, zipping up their jackets. The temperature felt as if it had plunged several more degrees since the sun had set.

"Hey, Obie, it's us. Mona and Fay," called Mona as they trotted up the steps of the junk-filled porch.

"God, don't warn him. If he's in his I-hate-medical-people mood he won't open the door for us."

"Ha. The old coot's got a crush on me."

A calico cat, huddled down on some blankets in a rusting washtub on the porch, meowed plaintively and followed them up to the door. Mona knocked aside a black iron frying pan that hung from the porch ceiling and rapped hard on the door.

"Ahoy, Obie. We're in need of brandy," she said.

Fay glanced at Obie's shack off to the right. It was a two-room hootch built thirty or forty years ago and looked more impoverished than she remembered. There weren't any lights on. No smoke billowed from the chimney. Either Obie had started in on his vodka early today and was sleeping off a drunk or he just wasn't home. Whatever. She suddenly didn't want to be here. There was something deeply unsettling about the air, the texture of the dark, the quality of the silence.

"You sure we don't have enough gas to make it back to town?" Fay whispered.

"Even if there's anything in the reserve, we'd be lucky to make it two miles. C'mon, let's try the house."

Obie's pickup truck was parked between the shop and the shack. The driver's door stood open, as if he'd hopped out in a big hurry; the keys were still in the ignition. The rear was loaded up with crates and pieces of furniture.

"I don't like it," Fay said.

"Hey, there's nothing to be spooked about. Obie was so bombed, he didn't bother unloading his truck. Now he's sleeping it off. Take my word for it. Let's have a look."

Fay followed her up to the shack. When Obie didn't answer their knocks, Mona tried the knob, turned it, and the door creaked open. "Obe?" Mona patted the wall just inside for the light switch.

A lamp blinked on. The front room was jammed with furniture and things, but there was no sign of the old man. "He's probably gone into town with someone else," Fay said. "Let's just pump a gallon of gas into the van and leave him a note and ten bucks."

"He locks the pump."

"Terrific."

Mona headed for the tiny kitchen to the left, which was separated from the front room by a low counter. The fridge door was ajar. "Goddamn, Fay, look at this mess."

The floor on the other side of the counter was strewn with packages of frozen food that had been swept out of the freezer. Everything had thawed, including the packets of meat, which had bled and turned the puddles of water a bright pink. The garbage had been overturned. Drawers had been emptied. The pantry looked like a tornado had torn through it. Cans had been ripped open and scooped clean—not all of the cans, only the ones that contained meat. Vienna sausage, ham, pork and beans.

Jo ate raw steak.

"I'm leaving, Mona. Now." She spoke calmly, but with such urgency that she caught Mona's full attention. "You coming?"

"Okay, okay. But it doesn't solve our problem, you know. We're still going to run out of gas."

"I'll call Scott." Of course. She should have thought of it before. She would call Nash. She would ask him to bring a can of gas and meet them at the juncture a mile or so down the road. Surely they had enough gas to get there.

"And Lew. You'd better call Lew and tell him to come 'out here and take a look around. Obie's obviously not here and someone broke in. I think Lew should take a look."

Fine. But Nash first. She went into the crowded front room, reached for the phone. It was dead. The van. She would use the phone in the van. As she started toward the front door, one of the cats outside shrieked. The steps creaked. *Someone's out there.* She leaped toward the far side of the kitchen counter, ducked down beside Mona, and looked around for something to use as a weapon. Anything would do.

Her fingers closed over a plastic container of bleach. She twirled off the lid, waiting, listening. She heard another sound, then the window exploded, showering the front room with glass, and something thudded heavily against the wooden floor. A weird chattering noise filled the darkness outside, a chant, but not of words, at least not of words she could distinguish.

Fay's fingers tightened on the bottle of Clorox. She forced herself to peek around the corner of the counter into the front room. Obie was sprawled on his belly in the glass, legs and arms twisted at odd angles, broken beyond repair. He was close enough so she could see his face, which was turned toward her, eyes wide, vapid. His neck looked as if it had been ripped open and chewed. *Same as the Fenuzo kid, but worse.* Muscles and tendons protruded from the gaping hole like ragged electrical wires from a faulty socket. Gorge swelled in her throat. She swallowed it back and moved behind the counter again.

"What the fuck's going on?" Mona whispered.

"It's Obie in the front room. He's dead. Is there another way out of here? A cellar? Is there a cellar?"

Blood drained from Mona's face, turning it almost as pale as her hair. "Dead? Obie?"

Fay nodded and repeated her question. Mona rubbed a hand over her eyes. She swallowed so hard, Fay heard it. "Yeah. A cellar. Where Obie made moonshine. It's around the other side of the pantry."

Fay found the top for the bleach, spun it on, tucked the bottle under her arm. "Let's go."

Outside, a window shattered, and the strange sound churned through the darkness again, a chattering in fast forward, the noise of a dozen frenzied rats. Fay realized they—*Who? Who's out there?*—had broken into the van, cutting her and Mona off from their one sure escape route. As they crawled out from behind the counter, a torch sailed through the broken window. There was so much clutter in the front room that the flames caught immediately.

The chattering rose a decibel.

She rounded the corner, rolling the bottle of bleach along in front of her, and looked back once to make sure Mona was behind her. She was clutching a pair of scissors.

Smoke thickened in the front room.

Fay reached the door to the cellar, opened it, tucked the bottle of Clorox under her arm, and motioned Mona to go down first. They descended into the dark, into the belly of the smoldering beast. They didn't dare turn on a light. But Mona had stuffed her pockets with matches from one of the overturned drawers upstairs and lit a couple. She held them up, tiny, flickering torches.

The cellar was an obstacle course of junk. Fay weaved around it, moving toward the rectangular window facing the back of the shack. The matches went out. Mona lit more. They squeezed through the narrow aisles, climbed over chairs. Fay accidentally kicked over a bottle of moonshine, and the smell of hundred-proof grain alcohol mixed with the stink of smoke, of fire. The dark clamped over them again as the matches blinked out. Mona struck several more. The noise outside got louder. Louder. Smoke seeped through the cellar ceiling.

They reached the window and Fay scrambled up onto an old bureau. She removed the screen, tossed it aside, shucked her jacket, and wrapped it around her right fist. She slammed it against the center of the window, knocking out the glass. It fell soundlessly onto the grass outside. She tapped her bound fist around the jagged edges, working them loose.

"Obie's pickup is our only chance," Fay whispered.

"I know." Mona passed Fay the scissors and a box of matches, scrambled up onto the bureau, and stuck her head through the opening. She wiggled out, turned. "Pass me everything. Hurry."

Fay's control slipped a notch as she shoved her way out into the cold; fear scuttled like a bug across the floor of her gut. She shook it off, leaped up, fled to the corner of the shack, right behind Mona.

Tongues of fire curled from the windows, hissing and crackling like living things. It wouldn't be long before the nearby trees went up and someone in the vicinity saw the fire and called it in. But it wouldn't happen soon enough to help them.

They peered around the corner. The glow of the flames spilled over onto the pickup truck, and beyond it, lights blazed in the van's windows. Outside, a person in dark clothes was shouting to whoever was inside. She couldn't hear what was said; the crackle and hiss of flames was too loud.

"We're going to have to go right through them," Mona said, drawing Fay back behind the shack. "There's only one road out."

"I'll drive."

"Forget it. I drive the van all the time. I'm a better driver. Once I'm inside the pickup, you get into the rear. Knock on the glass when you're in. Let's just hope the old clunker doesn't take a dump before we're outta the driveway."

Mona shoved everything into Fay's arms and hit the ground, scampering on all fours toward the truck. Fay gripped the bottle of Clorox and followed.

The far side of the shack crumbled. Part of the roof caved in. Embers lit up the blackness. Plumes of greasy smoke rolled into the alley, burning her eyes. She pressed her arm across her mouth and nose and reached the truck seconds after Mona had vanished inside it. The rear door was down, a flat, protruding tongue, and she hopped onto it, adrenaline pumping through her as she scaled furniture and old cartons. When she reached the window, she rapped against it. Mona's head popped up; the pickup roared to life and shot forward.

For long, breathless seconds, there was only the sound of the cold wind rushing past her head and the fury of the flames devouring Obie's shack. The truck fishtailed in the slush, knocking the cartons around in the back. Firelight washed over the truck, flames leaped from the roof of the shack, funnels of smoke sprang for the trees. Then the truck swerved violently to the left to avoid the medical van and bounced onto the shoulder, back onto the road again.

Two men appeared behind the truck, lumbering after it at astonishing speed. They were wearing nothing but shorts and T-shirts and they were both barefoot. In a moment of absolute clarity, thanks to the firelight, Fay could see the crust on their faces. It raised the planes of skin and bones, distorting features, altering them, creating something only remotely human, and she knew she was staring into the face of Ben's future, had he lived. Her control snapped, terror seized her, and she slammed her feet against one of the cartons.

It shot off the rear of the truck, barely missing the man closest to her. Its contents spilled across the road but didn't stop either of their pursuers.

The man in the forefront gained. He was less than two yards away when he suddenly vaulted, arms outstretched, and lifted into the strange orange light, a human torpedo. Fay shoved another carton off the truck and hurled the open Clorox bottle at him. The box missed him, but the bottle struck him in the forehead. Bleach splattered his face and he fell back, howling in pain, clawing at his cheeks and eyes.

The second man, undaunted, kept on coming. Grinning. Gaining. Shouting at her. Fay pushed an old chair off the rear of the truck; the man swung around it.

He ran faster, dust flying up around his legs. He was less than four feet from the rear of the truck. Three feet. She fell back on her buttocks, pressed her feet against another carton, but nothing happened. It was too heavy.

He was two feet away when he sprang.

For a second, he seemed to be frozen in the firelight, legs paralyzed in a wide gait, body tilted slightly forward, arms curled at his sides, eyes wild, manic. Then he was flying toward her again, and Fay leaped up, threw her arms around an upright mirror, and hurled it away from her at the same instant the truck swerved savagely to the right. The man and the mirror collided. Glass exploded. Shards rained through the dark, sparkling like fireflies as the glow of flames struck them.

The truck swung left, then right again. Fay stumbled back, arms windmilling, and crashed into the carton and furniture behind her. Her hip struck the corner of something and a flash of pain seared through it. She pushed forward and sprawled across the tops of two boxes, clinging to them, the rear door bouncing up and down, things around her shifting as the truck skidded into another turn.

She couldn't see the fire now. It was only a hot, orange radiance against the black sky, a layer of thick, quivering color that shimmered above the trees. They were going to make it. They were going to get out of here alive, they were—

The truck hit something and the impact threw the boxes she

was clinging to out onto the rear door. She scrambled back and was thrown to the floor when the truck lurched again. Her cheek scraped against the metal floor. The scissors she'd dropped earlier poked into her cheek and her fingers closed around them. She rolled onto her knees, dizzy, weak, spitting out blood. Suddenly, she was struck from behind and understood what they'd hit moments ago. *He sailed over the roof.* . . .

She screamed as she fell into the cartons and tried to cast the person off. But he rode her like a demon, clinging to her with terrifying strength, one hand clamped around her forehead, the other pulling her arm back, back. Fay slammed her elbow into him, and for an instant, he loosened his grip on her and she twisted around and stabbed blindly at the air with the scissors. The blades sank into flesh. The man bellowed and let go of her. Fay spun and reared up and thrust the scissors into his throat.

His mouth opened in a silent scream and he fell back, hands fluttering like huge, misshapen moths as they tried to reach the scissors. Then he tumbled off the truck and lay still, a dark smudge in the slush.

The truck raced away.

16

The Web

Hungry, hungry, hungry

The chants filled Bud's head, a hideous, primal chorus that horrified him because he identified with it. He knew that hunger. He knew. Even now as he drove the medical van wildly toward the main road, the hunger grew inside him, multiplied like a cell run amok, demanding to be sated.

Hungryhungry

The silent chants were coming from the lab at the back of the van where the supplies were, chants that reverberated through the web. He knew what Betty and the others were doing. Their faces and bodies expanded across the inside of his eyelids, flickering like heat lightning. He saw them as clearly as he would have if they'd been standing directly in front of him.

Betty was sprawled on the floor with the others, feasting on packages of frozen blood, drunk with the odors, the taste. Blood smeared her mouth, her hands, and oozed down the sides of her misshapen arms. It sickened him. His own hunger throbbed and ached and screeched inside him as he watched, as he thirsted, as he drove like a maniac to get the van someplace safe, someplace where he, too, could gorge himself.

He tried to think about something else, about what had happened to the two wounded members of the group—*the fuck-ups*—after they'd fled into the woods. But he couldn't focus on them, didn't care about them; it simply didn't matter. What mattered was his hunger.

Cold air poured through the busted passenger window; he didn't feel it. His new skin was a thick, impenetrable cloak that insulated him from the cold. Papers fluttered and lifted from the counter just behind him. Some of them flew through the broken windows and floated off into the dark like angels. Every time he hit a bump in the road, something crashed to the floor at the back of the van.

Hungerhunger

In the rearview mirror, he saw the headlights of the VW van, his and Betty's van. One of the twins was driving; he didn't know which one. It didn't matter. They were as interchangeable as a pair of copper pennies. He couldn't even remember where they'd come from. He couldn't recall where any members of the group were from, not specifically, not so that he could look at one of them and think, *He's from Toledo* or *She grew up in Frisco*. Those kinds of details didn't seem to make much difference to anyone anymore. All that mattered was that they were part of the web.

They were an amorphous group banded together only because they were changing and needed each other. The web brought them together, unified them, governed what they did and how they did it and made things known to them.

Hungryhungryhungry

The hunger tore through him again and he clutched his side, gritting his teeth against the pain. The headlights struck a sign that said CAMPGROUND, NO RVS ALLOWED. Bud swung left into a knot of pines, down a narrow road. Mounds of dirty snow lined the shoulders like bags of laundry. The trees all seemed to bend inward, their branches weighted with ice and snow.

Bud slowed as he approached the camping area and stopped in front of the rest rooms. He shut off the headlights as the VW pulled in alongside. His gut cramped so fiercely now, it hurt when he stood, when he moved.

Food oh God give me food I need food fast please.

Sure you do, lamb chops, back this way. Betty's voice echoed in the web: Betty laughing at him, coaxing him back, back through the ruined van, through shattered glass, tubes, slides, back through broken microscopes.

The door creaked as it swung open behind him and one of the twin's voices riffled through the web, soft and melodious, almost feminine. *Din-ner, din-ner.* He repeated the word over and over again, the web amplifying it until it blended with *Hungryhungry* and sounded like *Din-hun, ner-gry*. Bud spun around and hissed, "Shut up, just shut the fuck up."

The twin grinned. It stretched the new skin around his tiny rosebud of a mouth until it cracked. He patted Bud on the shoulder. "Relax, Bud. It's not good to get uptight before you eat."

Bud jerked away from him. He heard Betty and her friends laughing as he made his way to the back of the van. There she was, sitting up against a counter, a pint of blood tipped to her mouth, empty pints scattered around her. Blood stained her shorts, her shirt, her deformed face. She belched when she saw him and giggled.

All kinds of flavors here, lamb chops. Tell him, Willy. She glanced at the man to her left. The reverend. *Tell him about the flavors.*

The reverend held up two pints. "Type A and type O." He laughed. "What's your pleasure?"

Bud couldn't take his eyes off the blood. Its odor was a sweetness that made his bones ache, that made his eyes burn and his mouth water. Twin pushed past him and took one of the proffered pints.

"That leaves type O for you, Bud." The reverend taunted him with the pint.

"Saver of souls to vampire, huh, Reverend Bill." Bud's voice was tight and quiet.

Quickson's mouth twitched; his glasses caught the light, fracturing it. "Blood is sacred, Bud."

"Don't be nasty to the reverend, Bud," admonished Betty. "He's been real good. He knew there was stuff here we could use." Her thick fingers worked at something wrapped in foil. "I saved a little goody for you. Something that belonged to the junkman." She patted the floor beside her. *Just for you and me, lamb chops.*

The hunger chewed at him, the odors pushed him closer to the sweet, sweet blood that promised an end to the pain. The human in him urged him to flee, but the beast jerked him down, down to the floor beside Betty. His eyes fixed on the foil. It made a strange crinkling sound as she unwrapped it.

"It's okay, Bud," cooed the woman to his right. Jo Someone. She wasn't even looking at him. Her eyes were glued to the foil. Saliva drooled from a corner of her bloodstained mouth. "It's okay. Really."

Next to her, another woman nodded agreeably. Catherine. Her name was Catherine. But Bud couldn't remember anything else about her. It didn't matter. Nothing mattered but the treasure Betty held out. Nestled in a pool of blood in the foil was the junkman's heart. The beast in him forced his hand to reach for it as Quickson laughed and Betty chanted, *Eat, lamb chops, you're no better than us.*

And he ate, and it suddenly didn't matter anymore if this was the last act that separated him from them. It didn't matter because nothing had ever tasted so good, so succulent, so *right*.

17

Bogeyman

1.

Never mind, Katie thought, that the old county road was the
most direct route between Lagoon and the city of Franklin. At
night, it was also the darkest, and if Jo's battered Pinto decided
to break down, she was going to be in a world of trouble.

She wished now that she'd taken the feeder extension to Route
16, which would have brought her right into the center of town—
and taken her twenty minutes longer. But when she'd left the
Franklin Mall at nine, all she could think about was getting
home before Hank did. He disliked her being out on a school
night. Even though it was unlikely he'd get on her about it, she
wasn't taking any chances. Since Jo's disappearance, she could
no longer predict Hank's moods.

Some days he seemed fine, just like the old Hank before Jo
had ever come into their lives. But other days a black, angry
scent seeped from his pores and he was unapproachable. He
would shut himself in his den, smoking one joint after another
as he supposedly worked on his book, and in the evening after
supper he would just leave, saying he would be back later. She
was never quite sure which Hank would sit down across from
her at breakfast.

This morning it had been the old Hank, upbeat and excited
because in a few days the egg Tina had laid would hatch. Katie
sensed the new addition to the family—whom she'd already
dubbed Turner—had something to do with Hank's current book.
But whenever she questioned him about it, a strange, secret
smile crept across his face. *I don't want to talk about it yet.
We'll just have to wait and see if I'm right.*

She downshifted as she rounded a curve. The Pinto sputtered
and wheezed, an asthmatic gasping for air, then backfired and
started to lose power. "C'mon, car, don't do this to me, please."

161

She gripped the steering wheel and shook it as her foot pumped the accelerator. The car gained some speed as it started down an incline. Katie shifted into third, hoping that whatever was wrong would correct itself before she reached the next plateau in the road. But the engine started to rattle and she smelled smoke.

She rolled down the window and stuck her head out, expecting to see flames shooting from the exhaust pipe. There weren't any, but anything was possible with this stupid car. It was almost like Jo was getting even with her, as if she were somewhere out there in the dark having a good chuckle over how Katie was about to get stuck in the middle of nowhere.

Alone.

At night.

On the darkest road in the county.

She kept pumping the gas pedal as the Pinto chugged out of the curve, and shifted into fourth. The speedometer needle brushed forty-seven, fifty, fifty-two. "C'mon, you're doing great, just a little farther." She made deals with the Pinto. If it got up to fifty-five and held it as far as town, she would take it to Ray tomorrow and he would fix it up as good as new. If it got her all the way home, she'd toss in a fresh paint job as well. What color did it want to be? Red? No? How about blue? Not good enough? Well, then, how about silver? Yes? Perfect. A shiny, metallic silver with black racing stripes, how would that be?

As if in response, the needle hit fifty-seven and she let out a triumphant whoop. The car gulped down a mile without stopping. Two miles. Three. She was going to make it.

She swung into and out of another curve without tapping the brakes. The road began to level out. The speedometer needle dropped back to fifty-five. *No, please, you promised. You were doing great.* The smell of smoke was much stronger now, but it wasn't coming from the Pinto. She realized it was belching from a fire two or three miles ahead of her, where orange ribbons streaked the black sky like luminous paint.

Swell. The car was about to die and she would be stranded near a forest fire. But a fire meant firemen and cops. At the most, she would have to walk a couple of miles and she did almost twice that when she rode her bike to school. A cinch.

She glanced down at the speedometer. The needle was barely brushing forty-eight. The Pinto sputtered again and black smoke poured from the exhaust pipe. The death rattle deep in the engine's heart quickly escalated to a loud, terrible clunking, and the needle plunged from thirty-six to thirty in nothing flat. She shifted into third, cursing Jo for neglecting the car and herself for driving it. At night. Alone.

When the needle hit twenty, she steered the Pinto closer to the shoulder of the road. It died a few minutes later, shuddering, hissing, and emitting one final clunk that sounded like the engine had fallen through the casing. Then it was still.

Katie shut off the headlights. Removed the key from the ignition. Glanced out the window. The road was as empty as a pillaged tomb, and except for the distant firelight, the darkness was thick. She didn't want to leave the safety of the car, and yet she couldn't just sit here and hope that someone would come by and give her a lift into town. She wasn't so sure she'd accept a ride, anyway; hitchhiking was a sure ticket to trouble.

She plucked her bag out of the backseat and zipped up her parka. Purse, keys . . . what else? A flashlight? She looked in the glove compartment. It was stuffed with junk: gum, Kleenex, a half-smoked pack of Marlboros, torn maps, an old tube of lipstick. Nothing as useful as a flashlight. Of course not. Not for good ole Jo.

She stepped out, pulled on her gloves. The cold bit at her hands as she locked the door and dropped the keys into her purse. She fixed the Macy's bag over her shoulder, then stood with her back against the side of the car and peered up and down the road.

Get moving, coward.

She walked quickly, sniffing at the smoky air, trying to burrow her way through it to other smells. But the smoke hung in the darkness, a cloud that sucked odors into it like a vacuum cleaner. She kept to the shoulder and didn't get too close to the trees. They grew in clusters so dense through here, the distant firelight couldn't penetrate the blackness between them. The memory of the terrible odor that had pursued her that morning was still much too vivid for her to seek whatever protection the trees might offer.

And yet, what could possibly harm her out here? Perverts didn't lurk in the woods when it was this cold, and there were no *huge* animals like bears or tigers or anything.

But the trolls . . .

Kids believed in trolls; she wasn't a kid.

But that ugly smell on Hawthorne that morning . . .

She'd imagined it.

People like Jo . . .
What people?
Her shoes crunched over gravel and old snow. The cold stung her cheeks. The shriek of sirens in the distance comforted her; it meant that people weren't that far away. And since she was in Lagoon County, the sirens had to be those of Lagoon firemen and cops, some of whom she knew. One of them would drive her to a phone so she could call Ray.

He was working late at his father's garage tonight and would borrow a tow truck to come out here and pick up the Pinto. While he was doing that, she would call Hank so he wouldn't worry.

"A" would happen, which meant that "B" would follow, and the result would be "C." That was how the world worked. The world was like those logic problems they'd reviewed in math tutorial to get them ready for the SATs. It was ordered, reasonable, comprehensible.

So if she really believed all that, how come she was almost running? Why had the skin at the back of her neck gone tight and prickly? Why did she feel the *tickle* inside? What was that noise she'd heard? Why was she sniffing frantically at the air?

Nothing. She was about to freak over nothing, she thought, and suddenly stopped. She turned slowly in place, gravel crunching underfoot, until she faced the trees. Her heart thudded against her ribs; the cold wrapped around her, tight and cruel. Her breath plumed in the air.

Come out if you're in there, bogeyman. Come out, come out, wherever you are.

And then, almost as if her silent dare had been heard, a heavy, leaden odor as blunt as a hammer slammed into her and nearly knocked her to her knees. For a long, agonizing second, she couldn't breathe, couldn't blink, couldn't move. Fragmented images hissed into her, filling her like poison, images she didn't understand, couldn't seize. A dreadful, debilitating cold seeped into her limbs, her bones, her very blood, and crawled through the spaces behind her eyes. She felt it stalking the edges of her brain, her heart, then tightening its grip, squeezing. . . .

She screamed, and the scream released her. Her feet tore away from the gravel and she raced across the road, away from the trees, the smell, the rustling. But when she jerked her head around, she saw a figure charging out of the trees after her. A man. It was a man in shorts and a T-shirt who was as fleet as the wind, flying through the dark as though he were born to it.

A floodgate of terror opened inside her; adrenaline surged through her blood, her muscles. She tucked her arms in at her sides and ran straight down the middle of the road, praying that a car would come by, that she could somehow outrun him. Her shoes slapped the pavement. Her purse banged her hip. The Macy's bag got heavier and heavier.

She stole another backward glance. Panic erupted in her chest. He was rapidly closing the gap between them, and in the firelight, which wasn't quite so distant now, she saw a man who was not a man. *A troll, Jesus God, it's a troll.* His body was bulky and misshapen, covered with a hideous something that seemed slick and shiny in the firelight, like moss but not moss. It reminded her of Jo's skin; this was how her skin would have looked in firelight. That was how she'd smelled.

The odor radiated from his weird skin and leaped toward her, trying to seize her, crush her, suffocate her. She ran faster and so did he. The smell fell over her like a net and pictures poured through her, all of them incomplete, chopped up, grotesque. She saw a slice of face that was human but not human, with the same dense, raised skin. She glimpsed a pig or a hog that had been sliced open, its organs dug out, and tongues of fire licking at a wall, a ceiling, a pane of glass.

Then an image of a truck filled the insides of her eyes, a complete picture. The truck careened wildly through firelight, and someone—a woman, yeah, a woman—was shoving things off the back of it. Metal flashed—a blade, maybe part of a scissors, she couldn't tell for sure—and she felt a sudden, white-hot pain in her throat, as though something sharp had pierced it.

She gasped, stumbled, and then laughter seared through her skull. *Hungryhungry pain hurt bad hungryhungry.* The words rang out inside her as clearly as the laughter had. She knew they were coming from the man-thing and she didn't need to look back to see how close he was. She *felt* his nearness, the heat of his body, his skin, the heat of his madness.

Katie darted for the trees and felt him do the same, as though they were connected by a loose, invisible wire. She cut back to the right and he mimicked her, playing with her now, a cat teasing a mouse. She dashed left, right, left again, over and over, to the shoulder, the road, the shoulder, the road, and sensed that he was slowing. A look back confirmed it. For some reason, he moved more quickly in a straight or nearly straight line and, like an alligator, lacked the capacity for rapid turns and switchbacks.

She kept moving in the same way, her hand digging into the Macy's bag. She clawed at the package that held Hank's gift, knowing it would buy her time, maybe enough time to get to the firemen and cops before the man-thing reached her. She loosened the lid.

Her fingers sank into a box filled with marbles of every shape and size and color. They were part of a do-it-yourself science model that, when assembled, was supposed to be an illustrated history of man's evolution. Four and a half million years of evolution reduced to marbles. She didn't understand it. She didn't need to.

She grabbed a handful and flung them over her shoulder. They rained around her, striking the pavement like stones, like hail. Another handful. Then another and another. The man-thing made a sound that was utterly human, a yelp of surprise, and when her head snapped around, she saw his bulky arms pinwheeling for balance, his legs sliding out from under him, saw him falling. She stopped long enough to hurl a last handful of marbles at him, her chest heaving for air, sweat streaming down her face.

The marbles bounced off his head, his cheeks, his arms. He slammed into the ground and rolled on the carpet of marbles. Then she spun around and flew down the road, running as she'd never run in her life, pausing just long enough to get a second wind that carried her to the next curve. And the next.

2.

By the time Oliver arrived at Obie's, the old man's shack and shop were nothing but crackling rubble. The hogs and pigs he'd kept in the pen out back had panicked and escaped. Some of the surrounding trees had been partially destroyed, and firemen were still trying to contain isolated blazes. The stink of smoke and burned wood clung to the cold air.

Oliver poked around the periphery of the ruin with a long stick, overturning half-burned objects blackened beyond recognition. Now and then something Fay or Mona had said drifted through his thoughts: a description of what had happened, of one of the creatures that had chased them. But he didn't want to examine any of it too closely. Not yet. Maybe never.

He and Sergeant Moses had met them at the gas station two miles away, where Fay had placed the call to the fire department. He'd sent Moses on to Obie's and had stuck around to take their statement. Since both women were badly shaken up, he'd made it as brief as possible and asked them to stop by the station tomorrow morning. Now he wished he'd gotten more details; he didn't have any idea how to even write up a report on this.

Just what the hell was he supposed to say? That *creatures* had killed Obie, burned the shack, and stolen the county medical van? Yeah, the mayor and the county commissioners would love it. *Creatures.* Sure.

Where was the *creature* Fay had supposedly stabbed with a pair of scissors? And the one who'd gotten Clorox tossed in his eyes? The only corpse they'd found was Obie's, and it was so badly burned, Oliver wasn't even sure it qualified as a corpse. And what had happened to the medical van? The big boys were really going to ride his ass about that. To them, the death of an eccentric old coot like Obie wasn't going to mean squat. But the loss of a medical van worth at least a hundred grand . . . Ah, well, that would be different. That would be serious. That would demand answers yesterday.

Oliver rubbed at his burning eyes as he turned away from the rubble. He tossed the stick aside, thinking of the words scrawled on the floor of Quickson's church. *The web wants me . . . No God no pain hunger pain . . .* He thought of Ben Nash. He thought of the rumors he'd heard about Jo Englert, walking out of Franklin General, her skin looking like something reptilian, and of the dozen or more people who'd disappeared from the county in the last two weeks. And he felt the dark rubbing up against his back and suddenly wanted to flee, to get as far away from this place as he could.

Just as he started across the driveway, someone burst from the dark at the end and careened toward him, arms waving frantically. In the spill from the fire truck's spotlight, he saw that it was Hank Suffield's kid, Katie. She looked like a refugee from a nightmare.

She stumbled before she reached him and lay in the dirt, gasping for breath, trying to get up as he ran over to her. "Back there . . . oh, God . . . back there it was after me and I had to leave the car . . . it broke down and . . . it came out of the woods and . . . Hank's present . . . the marbles are all over the road and . . . and . . ." She stopped suddenly, sucking air in through her teeth, and looked at him and then beyond him and whispered, "The fire . . . the scissors . . . oh, God . . ."

Oliver helped her into his truck, then ran over to the ambulance and pulled out one of the canteens filled with water. She would have guzzled the entire thing if he hadn't stopped her. "Hold on, Kate, not so fast. Here . . .''

He poured some into a towel, and she pressed it to her face and the back of her neck, then drank from the canteen again. When she finally sat back, her breathing was almost normal, and he said, "Now, why don't you just tell me nice and slow what happened . . .''

And she did.

3.

A dream awakened her and it was gone as soon as she opened her eyes. But her heart was thudding in her chest, the muscles in her legs had tensed up, as if she'd been running, and she sensed she'd been dreaming about the troll. About what had happened earlier on the old county road.

Katie tugged the comforter up to her chin and tried to go back to sleep. She was bone tired, but now that she was awake, she was afraid to close her eyes again. She was certain she would find herself back on the old road, running again, and this time she wouldn't get away. This time the troll would catch her, wrestle her to the ground, and—*What?* What would've happened if it had caught her?

Hungry pain bad hungry

She snuggled down deeper into the cocoon of her covers and pressed her hands over her ears to still the echo of the man-thing's voice. *I could've ended up like the pig.*

She hadn't told Oliver or Hank about the smell, the pictures in her head, or how she'd heard what the creature had been thinking. But she needed, desperately, to tell someone. It wasn't normal, and it scared her. It was one thing to track Hank's scent or Ray's or those of people she knew; then, it was a kind of game that *she* controlled. But this was different. This time a scent had been thrust on her. It had trapped her, imprisoned her, nearly gotten her killed, and she hadn't been able to shut it off, to wrench free of it.

Why had her sense of smell developed in the first place? Was it a form of mutation, like the trout with the extra eyes or the roselike flower? Was it connected somehow to the way Jo's skin had changed? Had Jo mutated? *Am I mutating?*

She threw off the covers, leaped out of bed, and hurried into the bathroom. She switched on the light, shut the door, and leaned close to the full-length mirror on the back of it. She touched her face, turned her head from side to side, examined her throat, her arms.

Katie pulled her flannel nightgown over her head and stared at herself—front, sides, rear. She didn't see any sign of a rash like Jo had in the beginning. But what did that prove? Maybe the change had already started but wouldn't manifest itself for days or weeks. Maybe the smell thing happened first.

Then why hadn't Jo mentioned it? Or Ben? Maybe it was just a phase she was going through, like adolescence. Any number of things could cause it, she thought. Screwy hormones, improper diet, contaminated air, bad water . . . Sure. A doctor would be able to tell her what was wrong. But what kind of doctor did you go to for something like this? Eyes, ears, nose and throat? An internist? A *shrink*?

Thinking about it made her head ache.

She put on her nightgown again, and when she was back in the bedroom, she pulled the comforter off the bed and draped it around her shoulders. She opened the window and settled in the rocker in front of it, legs pulled up against her, the cold washing over her.

The air was still and soundless, except for the distant hoot of an owl, a solitary, almost plaintive sound. The moon gleamed against the icy surface of the lagoon, a surreal, ghostly eye. Its light varnished the trees on the far shore and made them look as if they were trembling.

Katie sniffed tentatively at the chill. She wanted to understand this capacity she'd developed, to test it, even though half the time she was sure she imagined the images it seemed to produce. But the only unusual scent she detected now was Hank's, coming from the open window next door. Otherwise, the night smelled exactly as it should have: of woodsmoke and winter, ice and evergreens.

She poked her head out the window and inhaled deeply. The air seeped into her tissues, her blood, her very bones. She thought she caught a faint tendril of something different, something that was out of place, but it wasn't strong enough to track. She wondered if she'd conjured it.

Another breath, then . . . *there*. It rode the stillness like a bird on a current of wind. It seemed to be waiting for her. She closed her eyes, taking slow, carefully measured breaths that she held to the count of five, then released. She gradually felt a part of herself detach and float out into the scent.

There was something vaguely familiar about it, yet she couldn't place it, couldn't puzzle through it. Since it didn't frighten her, she followed it as far as she could without going outside to physically track it.

The scent twisted and roamed, as though it couldn't make up its mind where it was going. Once, it looped back on itself like a pretzel and another time it suddenly seemed to divide and go off in two separate directions, which was clearly impossible. Scents couldn't divide like that, any more than people or animals could. But it was almost as if this smell had acquired a life of its own and didn't play by the rules as she understood them.

Katie followed the stronger of the two smells until it started to thicken, to darken, to congeal like blood. Then she jerked away from it, and her eyes flew open, fastening on the west shore. She was suddenly certain that the scent belonged to Jo, to a changed Jo, a mutated Jo, a Jo like the man-thing that had chased her, and that she was somewhere in the dense woods on the west side of the lagoon.

18

Pairs

1.

When Nash had first visited Hartwell Research during his last trip here, he'd expected a sterile, forbidding place where scientific types hustled through ivory towers, faces skewed with intensity. But the grounds, which covered about fifty acres, resembled a small ivy-league campus. Trees. Brick buildings. Paths that twisted through snow and cold sunlight. Frozen ponds that gleamed against the red Georgia clay like mirrors in fairy tales.

The computer center where Ben had worked was at the far end. It was a simple three-story building with large floor-to-ceiling windows that looked like a college dorm. He nosed Delilah into a parking spot in front, grabbed his briefcase, and went inside.

The cavernous lobby had polished marble floors, soft lights, quiet music, and an S-shaped desk manned by two uniformed security guards. One kept tabs on a half-dozen computer-controlled video monitors. The other was shuffling through a clipboard jammed with papers and muttering to himself. When Nash said he was here to see Karl Granger, the guard didn't bother to hide his annoyance at the interruption.

"I'll be with you in a second."

Nash waited while the guard sorted through the papers on the clipboard, answered calls, and had a conversation about the clipboard mess with the other guard. Four minutes passed. Five. Six. He wished he'd arranged to meet Granger in town, but he'd wanted the element of surprise in his favor. He finally walked over to the end of the counter, where the guard had parked himself. "Where's Mr. Granger's office?"

The man's face was a complete blank, as though he hadn't understood the question because he didn't speak English. Nash's blood pressure crept upward. He started to say something, but the guard rolled his eyes and sighed and slapped his hand over the clipboard papers.

"Do you have an appointment with Mr. Granger, sir?"

"Yes," he lied. "The name's Scott Nash."

The guard called Granger's office, got the okay, then asked for ID. Nash dropped his Florida driver's license and his American Express card on the counter. The guard scrutinized them and looked at Nash to compare his face with the photo on his license.

"I guess you get a lot of terrorists through here, huh."

Not amused, the guard said, "Regulations." He slid the ID back across the counter and directed Nash down the hall, where the elevators were. He picked up some of the free brochures on the desk and walked away.

Hartwell Public Relations was typical of most corporations, public or private. *We are a private institution dedicated to the advancement of mankind through the improvement of the quality of life. . . . Latest developments in technology, pharmaceuticals . . . Medical-school grants for the brightest minds in the nation . . . Blah, blah, blah.*

According to Ben, Hartwell's main interest was profit through pharmaceuticals. *Drugs, bro. That's the future. Drugs to boost, drugs to bring you down, drugs to cure, drugs to regulate, drugs drugs drugs.*

At the end of the hall, Nash had to walk through a metal detector and send his briefcase through an X-ray machine. The area was manned by another guard who could have been the first turkey's clone. Nash figured they were all Quantico rejects who'd attended the same security school.

He rode the elevator to the second floor, where the administrative offices were, and Granger's attractive secretary made a point of letting him know that her boss usually didn't see people unless they had appointments. But she knew he was anxious to see Nash and, fortunately, he had a light schedule today. He would be along shortly.

All of this was delivered pleasantly but firmly, as though Nash were a young child who'd broken a rule but was still in everyone's good graces. She ushered him into an office that was surprisingly modest for a V.P.: thick gray carpeting, a teakwood desk, numerous potted plants, and a lovely view of the grounds. Would he like something to drink while he waited? Coffee? Tea? He demurred.

Her smile was as pleasant and efficient as her manner. "I'd just like to offer my condolences about Ben, Mr. Nash. He was well liked around here."

He thanked her and was relieved when she left.

He sank into the cushions on the couch, picked up a *Business Week* magazine, paged through it, set it aside, stood, sat, stood again. He ended up at the window, watching several golf carts putt across shoveled sidewalks. The last time he'd been here, it was spring and everywhere he'd looked there had been green and brilliant explosions of color. Now the place looked dead. Considering his reason for being here, it seemed fitting.

One of the golf carts pulled up on the sidewalk in front of the building and Granger stepped down. He was a tall, rather thin man of sixty with hair the color of ash. He was impeccably dressed in a three-piece suit and a dark dress coat. Nash couldn't see his companion until they moved closer to the steps. And then he recognized that bald head, that hawkish nose. This was the guy in his 11 × 14 blowup of the moon buggy. The one with the headphones on. One of the boys from the meadow. He was about Nash's height, six-four, outweighed him by fifty or sixty pounds, and from the looks of him, it was all muscle.

Nash ducked back behind the window, waited a beat or two, looked again. The two men were shaking hands, then Granger trotted up the steps and Baldy crossed the street. He got into the passenger side of a gray BMW with darkly tinted windows, and the car pulled away from the curb.

Nash quickly lowered himself to the couch and picked up the *Business Week*. He was looking through it when Granger breezed into the room a few minutes later.

His greeting was a shade too hearty, and his smile smacked of anxiety. Nash couldn't tell if it was because Granger simply had a lot on his mind or if his unexpected presence had something to do with it. He said the right things about Ben—how sorry he was, what a tragedy it was. But the topic seemed to make him as uncomfortable as it did some of the townspeople. He didn't hang up his coat. He didn't sit down.

"You go away for six weeks around here and get back to a million things that should've been done yesterday." Granger shook his head: a busy man letting Nash know his free time was limited. "How about if we head over to the cafeteria for some coffee?"

"Sounds good." Nash picked up his briefcase.

"Ben didn't really have a work area here," Granger said as

they left the office and started down the stairs. "But my secretary gathered up some books and whatnot from the desk he used. You can pick it up after we get back, if that's okay with you, Scott."

Nash nodded. "What was he working on, anyway?"

"He was working out glitches in some of the computer programs in the bio department."

His vagueness irritated Nash, particularly because he was the man who'd hired Ben. "What kind of programs?"

"I really don't know."

Nash let that pass for the moment and pushed through the double doors, into the chilly air.

"You want to walk or take the cart, Scott?"

"Walk."

"Good." He patted his midriff. "I could use the exercise."

As they strolled toward the park across the street, Granger talked about his trip to the Galápagos: the giant tortoises, the iguanas, the flora, the incomparable beauty of the place. "Was it a professional or a personal trip?" asked Nash.

"Both," Granger replied. "Hartwell and the Ecuadorian government are involved in several joint research projects, one of which is on the Galápagos. I combined the trip with a lifelong dream to duplicate Darwin's original journey through the islands. It was an absolutely thrilling experience, Scott. Have you ever seen the islands?"

Nash nodded. "A couple years ago I did photographs for a travel story that ran in *Travel & Leisure*."

"There's literally no place like it on earth. I mean, think of it, Scott. Hundreds of species of wildlife and plants that just don't exist anywhere else. If I ever had any question about the validity of evolution or the survival of the fittest, that trip dispelled it."

"I'm sure Hank Suffield would disagree with you."

Granger chuckled good-naturedly. "Hank and I have had our share of debates. His theories are really quite brilliant and I admire his courage for publishing them. He's a tremendous asset to Hartwell simply because he doesn't think along conventional lines. But his theories have never been proven, and frankly, I doubt they ever will be. I think he's dead wrong."

Granger waved at a group of people on the other side of the road as he and Nash turned down a walk to the cafeteria. Inside, they went through the line for coffee and rolls, then found a table next to a window that overlooked a pond and a running track for employees.

"So you don't think nature possesses consciousness or memory," Nash said as if there had been no interruption in their conversation.

Granger smiled and shook his head. "Absolutely not. That's metaphysical mumbo jumbo, Scott. Darwin proved that natural selection was responsible for choosing the best designs and adaptations from all of those that nature spontaneously created. But he also said natural selection doesn't imply intelligence or conscious choice. These designs just happen."

"Then Darwin basically substituted blind occurrence for the mechanistic view that God was the intelligence behind the great machine of the universe."

"Yes." Granger's white head bobbed. "Exactly. I can see you've been reading Hank's books."

"I found the material fascinating." Even though it was hardly light bedtime reading, he thought.

"It is. It definitely is. I just don't agree with it."

"Didn't Darwin also believe that things in the universe changed gradually? Over a period of eons?"

"Yes."

"But that doesn't explain why the dinosaurs disappeared so suddenly. Or why other forms of life *appear* just as suddenly." *Like snakes with feet, Karl. And butterflies that emerge from ground hives and trout with an extra pair of eyes. You know anything about those things, Karl? Did Baldy mention them?* "In fact, I think Darwin and the present genetic theories leave a lot of unanswered questions."

Nash was trying to goad him, but Granger seemed to find it all quite amusing, coming from a layman. "It sounds like Hank has another convert."

"You have to admit he raises some intriguing questions."

"I've never disputed that."

"Well, Hank and Darwin do have some notions in common. Like the idea that acquired characteristics can be inherited."

"Which is one area where I totally disagree with Darwin." Granger stirred three heaping teaspoons of sugar into his coffee. "With that particular idea, he was a victim of nineteenth-century thinking, that's all. It was a commonly held belief back then. Take camels, for instance.

"Camels," he said, "have thick calluses on their knees, which, to someone who doesn't know about such things, would appear to be caused by abrasion, from kneeling down. But they're born with the calluses, something Darwin and a nineteenth-century zoologist named Lamarck believed was an acquired characteristic that was eventually inherited. It's just another example of a chance genetic mutation.''

''That just *happened* to produce pads in the right places.'' Nash shook his head. ''I can't buy it.''

Granger flashed his most patient smile. ''Look, Scott. I've been having this same argument with Hank for as long as I've known him. You're not going to change what I believe and I won't change what you believe. It's like politics or religion. What's the point?''

''The point is this.'' Nash unsnapped the briefcase and removed six 11 × 14 meadow photographs. ''I think you know about these. And I can't quite shake the feeling that this is all mixed up with why Ben did what he did. I just don't understand the connection yet.''

Nash fanned the photos in front of Granger, who stared at them for a long, uncomfortable moment. His fingers stepped through the pictures, separating them, then he rubbed a hand over his jaw and looked up at Nash. ''What are they?''

''Okay, let's try this one.'' Nash reached into the briefcase again and brought out the blowup of the moon buggy, Baldy clearly visible inside. ''Who is this guy, Karl? And please, don't tell me you don't know him because I saw you with him outside.''

Granger's long, narrow hands stacked the photos, tapped them against the table to straighten them, set them in front of Nash. His gaze was as earnest and intense as his voice when he spoke. ''I'm not at liberty to discuss any of it, Scott. But I assure you it has absolutely nothing to do with Ben.'' He glanced at his watch. ''And now I've really got to get back to the office.''

Nash gathered up the photos and dropped them in his briefcase. They were silent until they were outside again. ''So who's the bald guy, Karl?''

''A colonel. Steve Fielding.''

''How do you know him? And what's the army's interest in Meadow Creek?''

Granger sighed. ''Please, Scott. I told you I can't discuss it. I'd be glad to give you the colonel's number and you can talk to him directly.''

Nash laughed. ''Thanks, but I'm not in the mood for bureaucratic doubletalk.''

Granger's pale gray eyes sought Nash's. "Take my word for it. None of this has anything to do with Ben."

He sounded and looked sincere. But Nash knew he was lying through his teeth.

2.

By three that afternoon, Fay finally managed to break away from the clinic to run a couple of errands and get a bite to eat. Her head pounded from hunger, her sinuses were dry from the heat in the building, and what she wanted most of all was to go home.

But today was family day at the clinic, which meant there would be a lull now until around six, then another wave of mothers and kids would arrive. She'd be lucky to see her last patient by nine and get home by ten.

She pushed through the double doors to the street. The crisp air was a welcome change from the stuffy clinic and cooled her burning cheeks. A wind had kicked up. Trees bent under its pressure, dry leaves and twigs swirled through the streets, windows rattled, doors swung open in shops as she passed.

Fay slipped on her sunglasses. The painful throb in her head slid off to one side like an orb of mercury suspended in a thermometer and lodged in her right temple. It beat hard and fast as she walked the few blocks to Castleton's Army/Navy and promised to bloom into a migraine before evening.

She hadn't really felt right since that night at Obie's a week ago. Her litany of symptoms could have fit a dozen afflictions and diseases. But she couldn't deny that they fit most closely into the emerging profile that ended, ultimately, with the skin condition. A deep, consuming hunger for foods that were high in iron, light-sensitive eyes, which probably caused the headaches, an overactive libido, and a growing imperviousness to the cold.

At the moment, she could think about it with her usual professional detachment, as if she were one of her own patients. But at times, especially at night, she imagined her skin changing, thickening, darkening. She saw herself becoming one of the creatures—the *things*—that had chased her and Mona at Obie's. And then her detachment crumbled and she lay awake trembling, terrified, scratching at her arms, her legs, her face, until she couldn't stand staying in bed any longer.

Last night had been like that.

But her first thought this morning was that she lacked the most important symptom: eruptions on her skin. Without that, everything else seemed secondary. But there could be changes occurring in her organs, like what had happened to Ben, and the effects might appear in any number of tests she could run on herself. Maybe that was next step. *Do the bloody tests and be rid of the paranoia once and for all.*

It was warm inside Castleton's, and fairly busy, considering it was a weekday during the off-season. Shoppers with pink cheeks pushed carts along the aisles, stocking up on items that were ten to fifteen percent cheaper here than elsewhere. She had intended to buy a ten-pound bag of Samson's dry food and to replenish some of the canned goods she kept in the pantry for emergencies. But the sales were too good to pass up, and by the time she turned down the last aisle, her cart was nearly full.

"Hi, Dr. Fay," called Harness. He wheeled his cart toward her, one foot resting on the low horizontal bar at the bottom, the other propelling the cart forward until it had gathered speed. Then he leaped on and rode it, that lopsided grin cutting cleanly across the bottom half of his face. He screeched to a halt, missing her cart by inches.

"Hi, Harness. You picking up some things for your mom?"

"She's next door." He passed his hand through the air over the cart, indicating the things inside. Lanterns and a couple of sleeping bags, an army blanket, a pea coat. "For vacation."

"Where're you going?"

"Air-zona. Better than here. No one sick, no one disappearing, no one changin'. Poor Joe, poor Obie." He shook his head; a drop of spittle caught on his lower lip. "But more will go. Believe, Dr. Fay, believe. More. Change or die. I know. I know. I saw terrible cold. Listen, listen." He leaned so close to her, she could smell his faintly sour breath. His plump, dimpled fingers closed around her wrist and he tapped her knuckles with his thumb. "Not safe here, Dr. Fay. Not safe. Never again. Go. Go fast."

"*There* you are, son," said Harness's mother, waddling toward them as fast as her short, stumpy legs would carry her. Harness had let go of Fay's hand and was picking at his thumbnail. "I hope he didn't bother you."

"He was just telling me you're going to Arizona on vacation."

She brushed nervously at strands of her gray hair. "To see my sister, actually. But not until late October or so."

Harness's head snapped up; his dove-gray eyes widened with alarm. "*Must* leave. *Must.* Bad cold coming, changes, death. *Must* leave."

His mother winced and looked as if she wished the floor would open up beneath her. "Really, Harness. I asked you not to—"

He jerked away from them, the cart trundling noisily over the floors. His mother dug her hands into her jacket pockets, her eyes flickering anxiously from her son to Fay. "Ever since that business at the Blue Inn, he's been so insistent about leaving. All this nonsense talk. I blame Ben Nash. He was an evil, evil man who—" She stopped suddenly, as if she'd just remembered that Fay had known him, then hastily excused herself and hurried off.

Change or die. . . .

The place Harness had touched on her wrist was cool and seemed to tingle. But between her thumb and forefinger, everything burned and itched—the skin, the muscles and tendons, the bones. She scratched at it until the spot was red and angry, and yes, her fingers slid over the skin, seeking a rash, expecting to find it, and yes, some of last night's fear seeped through her, and yes, Christ yes, Harness spooked her.

"Not safe. . . ."

She hurried to the front of the store and got into one of the lines. Charlie Castleton and his wife, Luanne, were manning the registers. Since they were old-timers here and knew everyone and loved to chat and gossip, Fay knew it was going to take forever to get through the line.

"Never again. . . ."

The longer she stood in line, the warmer she got. She stripped off her jacket, fanned the back of her neck, stepped out of line, and drank water from a nearby fountain. It helped, but not enough. She began to feel weak and strange, as though she had no control over her own body, as though it belonged to someone else and her essence just happened to be inside the casing of flesh and bone. Any second now, the muscles would let loose, the tendons would snap, her stomach would heave, her tongue would loll from her mouth, saliva would drool over her chin. She was ravenous. She itched all over. The heat baked the skin under her clothes.

Fay gripped the side of the cart to steady herself and smiled at Charlie when she reached the front of the line. He reminded her of Elmer Fudd: small, short, and plump, with a mouth that moved like a fish's. She saw it moving but couldn't hear what he was saying. Her ears were ringing, blood rushed from her face to her toes and then back up again.

". . . run on everything from blankets to kerosene," he was saying, shaking his head as he rang up her purchases. "Gets cold like this and people go strange, Fay. Don't rightly know what to think about it all, what with Ben and Joe Fenuzo and the reverend just disappearing like he did. . . ."

Ding, sang the register. *Ding ding.*

". . . hear about the Wilkin boy walking off his job at the north end of the county two days ago and no one's seen him since?" Charlie looked up at her then, his round, wizened face like an elf's, his clear blue eyes frowning. "You okay, Fay honey? You look pale."

"Fine, I'm fine," she managed to say. "Just a little tired."

"Understandable."

Ding ding.

"That's fifty-two sixteen, Fay. You have your car or you want to pick it up later?"

"Later, thanks."

She wrote a check for the amount; her hand trembled. In her rush to get outside, she collided with another customer and the jolt set off tiny explosions of pain that rode the back of her skull like a demon. The heat in the store tightened around her, a vise, a sealed coffin, and for a second or two, before she reached the door, she thought she was going to be sick. But then she was out, the cold soothing her feverish cheeks, a benediction. It swirled into her nostrils, through her lips, burrowed into her eyes, her ears, and suddenly her body was her own again, as though the cold had returned it to her.

Her strange elation seemed to transport her through the windy street in seconds flat. One instant she was outside Castleton's, and the next she was in front of the Nameless, with no clear memory of getting there. She was ravenous.

Inside, the lunch crowd had diminished to three tables of customers. Two were occupied by truckers. At the third sat a pair of men who seemed vaguely familiar to Fay. One was bald, with a hawkish nose, and appeared to be in his early or mid-fifties. His companion was younger, thinner, with thick, curly red hair and freckles. It took her a few moments to place their faces. Nash's photos. The men in the moon buggies.

She found Horn in the kitchen, singing along to a blues tune on the radio as he scraped at one of the grills with a sharp-edged spatula. He winked when he saw her and stabbed a thumb toward the front room; she nodded and shut the door to the pass-through, ensuring their privacy. Only then did he turn down the radio's volume.

"When did *they* show up?" she asked, keeping her voice soft.

"About twenty minutes ago." He wiped his hands on his apron and pulled up a stool for Fay. "Sit yourself right down. What's your pleasure?"

"The specialty. Make it rare." *Very rare.*

"Rare it'll be." He talked as he cooked, explaining that the two men had driven up in the gray BMW parked out front. His waitress said she'd seen them around town yesterday and found out they'd been staying at Prudy's Place for three days. It was a bed-and-breakfast inn at the edge of town, the only place to stay now that the Blue Inn was closed to business. "I gave Prudy a call just to see what she knows. She tells me Baldy's name is Col. Steven Fielding. His buddy Red is Bruce Lattimer. Don't know if the boy's got a rank or not."

"Anything else?"

"Yeah, they make a lot of phone calls, especially to the Center for Disease Control and to an army base outside Atlanta. How about some fries?"

"Just the steak, Andy, thanks." The aroma alone was enough to make her mouth water, but Horn was browning it too much and she asked him to flip it. He clucked his tongue against his teeth and shook his head.

"It's your gut, girl." He flipped the steak. "Prudy says Red was trying to be real casual the other morning, asking questions about what happened up at Obie's. He seemed to know a lot about the fire and the medical van being stolen and even about the Suffield girl showing up."

"Then he's talked to Lew."

"Naw. Prudy said he'd spoken to the mayor. She wanted to know how come he was asking *her* questions since he seemed to know so much about it already, and that shut him up fast."

"Good for her." Fay laughed.

Horn slid her steak onto a plate, garnished it with radishes, lettuce, and slices of tomato, and set it in front of her. She lit into it as though she hadn't eaten in weeks. Her body responded instantly: her stomach seized up like a hand, grabbing greedily at the chunks as she swallowed them; the dull throb at her tem-

ples vanished; and that sense of elation she'd felt outside rushed
into her again.

When she finished, when she'd wiped the last pool of blood
off the plate with a slice of bread, Horn said he wanted to show
her something. They went out the rear door and across the driveway to a garage. It was so old and decrepit, it looked as if it
would fold up like a beach chair in a strong wind. Light filtered
through the dirty window to their left and spilled over the old
furniture Horn refurbished in his spare time. On the counter
where he kept his tools was a large bird cage with a pair of
lizards inside. They weren't very big and were munching away
on lettuce leaves and bits of fruit on the floor of the cage.

"Your new pets or something, Andy?"

"More or less. Abe and Bo. They look normal, huh, just
your regular garden-type-variety lizard."

She wondered what the punch line was going to be. Lizards
that talked? That stood upright on their tails? That spouted fire
like dragons? Lizards with wings?

"I'm going to lower that blind and you just keep watching
those critters," Horn said.

"Gotcha, boss."

A dusky twilight settled through the garage as Horn dropped
the blind and came back over. "Give them ten or fifteen seconds."

"For what?" she asked.

"You'll see."

Ten seconds later, both reptiles started to glow. The light was
steady, soft, almost ethereal, and the most astonishingly beautiful thing she'd ever seen.

"After a minute or so," Horn whispered, "the glow fixes
itself to the light in the room. If you want it bright, you do this."
He reached into the cage and drew his fingertip down the length
of Abe's body. The glow intensified. "And if you want it dim-
mer . . ." His finger touched the lizard's head; the glow dulled.

"Where'd you find them?"

"Outside here, under some leaves."

"Do they glow like that all night?"

"Uh-uh. Only for about two hours after they've eaten. Then
the glow shuts off. It has to be turned on again by more food or
by stroking their backs. Each feeding provides about four hours
of light."

Watching them, Fay felt a curious mix of wonder and dread.

"So what's it mean, Andy? Are these two guys like the snake? The butterflies? The strange rose?"

"Not as mean as the snake, not as pretty as Scotty's pictures of the butterflies, but the same kind of thing, I reckon." He stroked one lizard, then the other, shutting off the glow. "Maybe the devil's loose, Fay, or maybe God's rolling the dice. I like to think that magic's come back to the world."

But as he said it, something cold and unpleasant that had nothing to do with magic trailed across the muscular plains of her heart, and she shivered.

19

At the North End

Too many brews last night.

Oliver dug around in one of his desk drawers for a bottle of Tylenol and downed a couple with a gulp of coffee. He massaged his throbbing temples as he waited for the pills to kick in and silently damned Moses, who'd insisted on hitting just one more bar before closing time last night.

One more bar, one more tequila, one more beer chaser equals one mammoth drunk.

Jesus. Never again.

He pushed away from the desk to close the blinds, wincing as the movement drove a spike through the center of his forehead. A blast of heat struck his face, and on his way back to his chair he adjusted the thermostat to sixty-five. But neither of those things did much for him now; not even the Tylenol seemed to help.

Oliver rested his head against the back of his chair and closed his eyes. The parade of the dead, wounded, and those who had disappeared marched noisily across the inside of his eyes like soldiers, pounding drums and blowing horns, demanding that he count them, that he pay attention to them, that he avenge them. He knuckled his eyes, trying to get rid of them, but they shouted and clamored and made such pests of themselves, that he finally reached for the folder jammed with their photographs, their vital statistics. He didn't have to look in the file, though, to know who they were. Or how many they were.

Sixty-four, if he counted the twenty-nine people Ben Nash had mowed down that night at the Blue Inn. And that figure was probably low because he was sure there were others he didn't know about, deaths and disappearances among backwoods folks that hadn't been reported and never would be. And just how the hell was he supposed to solve all of these cases when he had only four full-timers in the department?

No wonder he needed to be loaded to sleep at night.

"So now I know the truth," said a female voice behind him. "My taxes go toward you sitting around on your fat ass. Can't say I'm surprised, Lew, but I gotta tell you, it pisses me off."

Not now, Jesus, not now.

He turned and glared at Obie's daughter. She stood in the doorway with one hand on her hip and the other leaning against the jamb. Polly had her old man's small, deeply set dark eyes, long nose, lanky frame, and cantankerous disposition. Her auburn hair was frizzy and wild, pulled carelessly away from her face and fastened with an elastic band. She wore a sequined suede jacket the color of a palomino, jeans so tight he could see the line of her panties, and boots.

Like her old man, she handled a rifle as though it were part of her anatomy. Polly's problem, other than the fact that she was Obie's offspring, was that she'd been born in the wrong time. She belonged in the Wild West of a century ago.

"Shit from you I don't need today."

"Ain't that too goddamn bad, sweetie." She strutted into his office and stabbed her cigarette out against the inside of the trash can. "By the way, you look like hell."

"I *feel* like hell."

She smiled knowingly. "Lemme guess. Tequilas, right? With beer chasers."

Oliver didn't say anything.

"Well, anyway. I've got some news you should welcome. In fact, I've been doing your job, Lew, so you oughta be thanking me."

"Yeah? And which job is that?"

"Looking for who killed Daddy, that's what." She rolled one of the chairs close to him, turned it around, straddled it, rested her elbows against it. Tough Polly. "Looking for clues, you know?"

"And I suppose you found who killed him."

"Not yet. But I asked myself, for starters, where the medical van might be. Me and some of the guys over at the saloon launched a two-day search. . . ." She smiled now, reached into her jacket for another smoke, and lit it with a one-handed flick of a match. "And we found it, Lew. Ain't that something?"

"Sure you did." He opened his middle drawer, worked his fingers into his pouch of tobacco, pinched some, and pressed it up against the inside of his cheek. "We searched every square inch of the woods within a five-mile radius of your pa's place and didn't find squat."

"Only 'cause you don't know how to look. You should've expanded it a few miles. We found it at the north end of the county."

He waited for her to go on, to give him directions to the place. When she didn't, when she didn't say anything more, when she just sat there flicking ashes on the floor, he said, "So how do I get to this place?"

"You don't. Not without me."

A dull throb pulsed between his eyes. "Uh-huh."

"I'm free now." A small, coy smile.

It irritated him. "Uh-huh."

"Free for the rest of the day." Her face softened and she touched his knee. "And night."

When she leaned close to him like this, she ceased to annoy him. It was like seeing another Polly just beneath the surface of the woman who'd strolled through the door a few minutes ago. This hidden woman was softer, seductive, a sweet dream of oblivion.

"So let's go," he said.

"Since I'm doing your job for you now, you owe me a dinner, Lew." She rocked toward him as they stood and touched her index finger to his mouth: a bedroom gesture. "Something expensive. Like lobster."

Oliver nibbled at the tip of her finger. "Let's see that van first."

Out in the hall, Harness crossed their path. That was exactly how Oliver thought of it, too, as though the fruitcake were the equivalent of a black cat. An omen, like salt spilled on a full table, like an umbrella opened in a house.

He flashed his lopsided grin and leaned on his mop. "Hey, mate."

Oliver nodded hello. "You know Polly?"

"Sure. Poll's a doll."

Polly laughed and slapped Harness on the back. "Any time you want to leave this shithole and come work at the Brazen Saloon, Harness, you got a job. And you won't be mopping floors, either."

"Good deal."

"Bet your ass it's a good deal. I'd pay you more, too." She whispered something in his ear. Harness's head bobbed up and down, then he straightened and his eyes went soft, sliding back and forth in his face before settling on something just over Oliver's left shoulder. "Hungry," he whispered. "They're hungry."

"Who's hungry?" Polly asked.

"Changers."

"The changers were hungry when they attacked Daddy?"

Aw, shit, Oliver thought. "C'mon, Polly, let's split."

"Harness isn't finished yet, Lew." Her voice could have sliced through lead. "Go on, Harness."

"Harness sees faces. Many, many faces. All the same. All changed."

Polly frowned. "I don't understand. What's that got to do with Daddy?"

"Changers. Changers and dangers." His eyes seemed to focus again, and he grinned. "Got to work. Poll take care." With that, he swished his mop across the floor and his bucket clattered as he pushed it down the hall, away from them.

"Goddamn fruitcake," Oliver muttered.

"Yeah?" Her glance was as barbed as her voice. "You think so, huh?"

"Hey, if you want to make something out of what he says, that's your business."

"That *fruitcake*, Lew, has a better idea of what's going on in this town than any of us."

"So fill me in." He crossed his arms at the chest. "I'm listening."

"Sure you are. Let's take my truck."

She strutted forward and Oliver stared appreciatively at her receding figure: a wisp of a waist, jeans hugging the curve of her hips, an ass as tight as a fist. A fine woman to look at (but not as fine as the doc), and even finer in the sack. If she'd just keep her mouth shut.

Sunlight glinted off the snow, the hood of Polly's truck, the windshield. It lanced through Oliver's shades, into his eyes, and felt like it was frying his brain. But thanks to the trees, there were long miles of respite when he felt almost normal. If it was possible to feel normal in sticks as deep as these, with a hangover that had left miniature elephants stampeding across the floor of his gut.

Even to a Georgia cracker like Oliver, the north end of Lagoon County was backward, depressing as hell. There were a few shacks with tin roofs set back in the pines or an occasional lone gas station that stood at the edge of the road, a struggling bastion of progress. But mostly the terrain was as empty as the moon. It was as if civilization had leapfrogged from the town of Lagoon to the nearest hamlet in the center of Franklin County thirty-three miles away and everything in between was waiting for progress to find it.

"I thought you said it was just a couple miles, Polly."

"I lied."

"Then how far is it?"

"Relax, Lew. You're not being kidnapped. It's not much farther."

She lit another butt, Oliver packed his cheek with tobacco, and they continued on without speaking. She smoked; he chewed and spat. The road, bordered by patches of dirty snow, rose and dipped in a series of gentle swells, which Polly negotiated at seventy. At the crest of one, Oliver saw another four hills rolling through brilliant sunlight and deep shadows, a surreal landscape of asphalt and pines against a sharp blue sky. They raced down into it, and Polly hung a sharp left onto a dirt road that twisted through naked birch trees and descended into a ravine.

Oliver spotted a creek, iced over along its shores. Beyond it was a flat, barren stretch of land with an abandoned barn in the distance. He knew where he was; as a kid he'd played in that barn. It, like the land that surrounded it, had once belonged to a farmer whose name Oliver couldn't remember. Now it was owned by a couple of Atlanta businessmen who were looking to develop it. Condos, town houses, a man-made lake, yuppie paradise.

"It's in the barn." She gunned the accelerator, and they tore through the creek. The rear wheels bounced up, slammed down. His bones came unhinged. The pain in his head shot out his left ear. Now they were clear of the creek, racing toward the barn, and Oliver was laughing because he felt good. The pain really *had* left him. The Tylenol had kicked in.

Polly pulled up in front of the barn and plucked a flashlight from the glove compartment. She unhooked the rifle from the gun rack behind them, spun it once as she got out, a regular Annie Oakley, and peered across the roof of the truck at him. "You feel it?" she whispered.

He wanted very much to laugh, to hold on to the good feeling, but yes, damnit, he felt it, a *wrongness* about this place. It was as if he and Polly were the last people on a devastated earth who hoped this shithole barn might hold food or weapons or provide shelter for the night. Wind whistled across the open field. It nipped at his cheeks and hands as he and Polly pushed the old doors open.

The air inside held vestiges of aromas: manure, hay, grain, and a faint odor of gasoline that seemed to hang over everything. Streaks of light fell through the splintered beams in the roof onto the medical van. It was parked in the center of the empty barn, a hulking white elephant with a shattered face and mud-splattered haunches. It looked as if it had been broken in some long-forgotten war.

"I figure they're going to come back for what they didn't take with them the first time." Polly nudged the van's door open with the end of her rifle and climbed in. Oliver was right behind her.

Shattered glass blanketed the floor; cabinet doors yawned open; storage compartments had been smashed and cleaned out; and jars and containers on the counters had been toppled, spewing cotton balls, packages of gauze, rolls of adhesive tape. One of the computer screens lay on its side on the floor, next to a microscope, but otherwise the equipment seemed to be untouched.

Strewn across the floor in the lab were plastic bags that had once contained emergency blood and plasma. Streaks and patches of dried blood stained the vinyl. Polly snagged one of the plastic bags with the end of the rifle and held it up, a flag, a white hanky of surrender. "Pretty bizarre, huh." She flung it away; it smacked the wall to her left. "There's more shit I want you to see back here, Lew."

They made their way to the rear of the van. This area had once been the equivalent of a lobby in a doctor's office. Now it resembled the lobby of the Blue Inn after Ben Nash's rampage: cushions torn away from the couch and chairs, blinds ripped from the windows and tossed in a corner, the glass in the windows nothing but jagged edges. The coffee table had been overturned and the glass jar that had contained candy had exploded when it struck the floor. Caramels, lollipops, and chocolate mints were everywhere, sprouting from the debris in a rainbow of colors. Ants swarmed over and around them, more goddamn ants than Oliver had ever seen in one place before. They seemed to make a kind of high-pitched buzzing that brought goose flesh to his arms and sucked the moisture from his throat.

"See those critters?" Polly gestured toward the ants with her rifle.

"I'd have to be blind not to. You hear them?"

She grinned. "Have to be deaf not to. And they're not ants. At least not like any ants I've ever seen, Lew. If you look at them real close, you'll see they aren't shaped like ants."

"I'll take your word for it."

"Watch this." She pulled a pack of matches from her jacket pocket, tore off five or six, and tossed them, unlit, next to one of the swarms. The black mass instantly shifted directions and covered the matches. "Now isn't that something? But this is the part that really gets me." She lit a cigarette, edged closer to the swarm, and set it on a piece of glass on the floor. "It'll take a bit. Just watch."

Ten or fifteen seconds passed. The buzzing got louder. That sense of *wrongness* crept over him again and he stepped back quickly from the closest swarm, his eyes sweeping the floor around him to make sure he wasn't standing in a throng of them.

"Here we go," Polly whispered, and pointed toward the torn cushions.

Feathers and flecks of foam rubber stirred as though someone had breathed on them, then parted as five bright red spiders half the size of his hand crawled out. Gooseflesh burst along his arms. These things reminded him of the giant weaver-spiders he'd seen when he was growing up. He didn't know if that was their real name, but it was what he and his buddies had called them. The huge, hideous things had been common in the backwoods swamps and had spun tremendous webs between trees in which to catch their prey. He'd gotten tangled up in one on his way home from fishing one night and to this day, could still see the weaver scampering toward him as he struggled to free himself. But these creatures were somehow worse because they seemed intelligent, lining up on the edge of the cushion like birds often did on phone wires, buzzing loudly, their antennas twitching this way, that, reading the air.

The largest crawled down the cushion and the other four fell into pairs behind it, a maneuver that was almost military in its precision. Now they inched their way toward the burning cigarette. Both Oliver and Polly moved back quickly. Her rifle swung up, ready. Oliver's gut rolled over; he pulled out his .38.

"Ugly fuckers, aren't they," she whispered.

"Where the hell did they *come* from?"

"When I was here earlier, I lit a cigarette and they just came outta nowhere. The smaller guys you called ants . . . I think those are the babies, Lew. It's like the sulfur in the matches attracts the babies and the smoke or the fire attracts the big guys.''

The troop advanced, circling the burning butt. Their buzzing was so loud now, it churned through the room, echoing, thickening the air, transmuting it until Oliver felt as if he were inhaling liquid glue. Sweat popped out on his forehead, his upper lip.

He took another step back.

Pressed his hands to his ears.

The noise became a slow, debilitating torture; he didn't know how much more of it he could stand. The urge to bolt surged from some deep primal well, nearly overpowering him.

But suddenly the buzzing stopped. Silence collapsed around them, a silence so total, so complete, he felt as if he were suspended between breaths, between life and death, swaying at the edge of a black abyss.

''Jesus,'' Polly hissed.

The sound of her voice released him. He blinked. His left arm jerked to his forehead, wiping the sweat. Now the lead spider darted forward, nipped at the glowing embers, and retreated as a second spider scuttled toward it. Back and forth they went, again and again, a bizarre relay race, each of them eating away at the glowing embers until the tip of the butt was gone. When the last spider slipped back into place, the five broke their circle and lined up side by side, facing Polly.

They're watching us. Waiting for us to make a move.

The buzzing started up again—not as loud as before or as high-pitched or as painful, but more menacing. The swarms of babies shifted across the floor, an oozing black stain that moved toward the five adults, answering a summons.

Dirty Harry wouldn't run. But fuck Harry. ''Let's split,'' he said, his voice flat, hard.

''My thoughts exactly, Lew.''

But the closest door was on the other side of the spiders, and there was no way in hell he was going to wade through them to get to it. That meant they had to make their way around the troops, into the hall, and to the front of the van.

They both inched away; the five adults crept forward. The black smudge of babies quivered like wet sand or loose flesh as they neatly divided into three distinct groups. One remained aligned with the adults and the other two split off to either side like bodyguards. They were a regiment about to march into battle.

"You get the feeling they're playing with us, Lew? That they're waiting for us to light out for the door?"

Sweat trickled into Oliver's eyes; he flicked the safety off his gun. "It's not going to be the door directly in front of us."

Her laugh was choked and very, very soft. "Let's try the one just past the lab."

They'd spoken without looking at each other, and now Polly took another step back. So did he. The spiders didn't move. The low buzzing sound continued, a dull, almost hypnotic noise. The air in the van heated up, tightening like sunburned skin. It seemed that the room was shrinking.

They kept moving back until their spines touched the wall. Now they sidestepped toward the corner, Polly in the lead. Just as she started to ease around it, the buzzing turned high-pitched and frenzied. It was the sound of a hundred fingernails raking a chalkboard simultaneously, and doing it over and over again, faster and faster. The groups converged and the dark mass swelled toward them, a rushing river, a living tide.

Polly swung the rifle up and fired. The explosion rocked the van, blew a hole in the floor, and shocked Oliver into a bone-white terror. He shoved Polly forward and they lurched into the hall, the dreadful noise rising and falling and echoing around them. He didn't look back; he didn't dare.

As they burst out of the van, Polly stumbled and fell to her knees. Oliver grabbed her arm and yanked her to her feet and that was when he saw it, a black quivering wave that rippled across the floor of the barn to their right, coming straight toward them. Another wave oozed out of the broken windows.

They tore into the cold sunlight, slammed the doors shut, and Oliver knocked the rusty bolt into place. When he reached Polly's truck, she was already at the rear, hauling out two cans of gasoline and some old rags. She tossed him a can, he grabbed some rags, and they ran back to the barn.

They scattered the rags around the front and sides of the barn, and Oliver stuffed some into the cracked walls. They doused them, splattered gasoline on the doors, the ground, then he shouted for her to get the truck started. He stood about six feet away and squeezed off two shots.

The gasoline ignited. Flames leaped up against the doors and sped through it. Within seconds, the old wood was burning. *Feast on them flames, fuckers.*

He sprinted back to the truck, leaped inside, and Polly gunned the accelerator. They shot away from the shithole, and only when they were on the other side of the creek did she slow down. She swung the truck around and they watched the flames consume the barn.

Beams toppled. A wall crumpled. Part of the roof caved in. And then the van blew. The explosion rocked the air and hurled a fireball through what remained of the roof, spewing debris seventy feet into the sun-struck sky. Tongues of smoke leaped upward.

"What're you going to say happened?" Polly asked without looking at him.

"That we were out driving around and saw the smoke."

She rolled her lower lip against her teeth. "You think the fire killed them, don't you?"

"Nothing could live through that goddamn fire, Polly."

"Yeah, you're right." She jabbed her fingers through her wild hair, pushing it off her forehead. "You're absolutely right."

But he knew she didn't believe it for a minute and neither did he.

20

Underground

In the cold, sweet darkness of the cellar, the web cradled and restored him. Its threads rippled with movements, whispers, dreams, connecting Bud to those who were changing, who were coming.

Some were still a great distance from Lagoon, traveling at night in groups like his, seeking refuge during the day in places where the light couldn't reach them. Others were much closer and traveled in pairs or threes or fours. For all of them, the journey was slow and hard, complicated by the gnawing need for food that their accelerated metabolisms demanded.

But their hunger wasn't his problem. His job was to get them here quickly. So he called to them through the web, urging them forward, ordering them to move faster, faster. Most would obey because they had no choice. They couldn't silence him, couldn't ignore him, couldn't pretend his voice didn't exist. He was already too powerful. He was not sure when he'd become aware of the power he possessed, but he knew that each time the web closed around him, invisible, inexplicable, yet real, the power increased. Soon, he would know how to use the web to crush those who resisted him and to lure those who resisted the change.

Some would be of no use to him or to the group. But others had talents Bud needed, abilities that would enhance his power, like the girl who tracked smells. Bud wanted her very badly. The doctor would also be useful; they needed her skills, her access to blood and plasma. And through her Bud would snare the photographer, a non-changer, who would serve as a protector later, in the final stages.

He did not question his visions. He did not question anything. Since the night at the junkman's, he had moved beyond doubt into a realm unsullied by humanity. He understood his mission. He would fulfill it. And in return the web would make him omnipotent.

* * *

Feed me. Hungry. Feed me.

Betty's voice whispered through the web, weak and wistful, the voice of a child, drawing him up, up, from the black hole of sleep. He swung his legs over the old couch where he'd been stretched out and peered through the dark at the cot on the other side of the cellar.

Feed me.

He walked over to the cot and lit the candle next to it. Even though he didn't need it to see, Betty liked the flickering light. She followed it eagerly with her eyes, as though she'd never seen a flame before. The soft glow spilled over her face, her naked body, illuminating the tiny silken threads that grew from the pores in her skin and fluttered as she breathed. Some of the filaments were long and had started to wrap around her at the waist. The fibers sprouting from the backs of her hands had already enveloped them, bending her thumbs under so they rested against her palms.

As Bud sat beside her, she lifted her arm and stroked his bare thigh and then his face. The fibers were softer than rain against his cheek, and yet so strong she couldn't have broken them even if she'd wanted to. *Hungry hurry hungry.*

He picked up a knife from the floor and passed the tip of the blade through the flame until it glowed red-hot. He let it cool, then pressed it to the underside of his right arm and sliced deeply into the skin. The blood that bubbled to the surface was scarlet, thick, like syrup. He touched his fingertip to it, then let Betty suck the blood off. She smacked her lips. The web reverberated with her soft, pathetic cries for more, more, always more. Bud held his arm to her mouth, wincing as she sucked, as she worked her tongue into the wound, licking, digging, poking, then sucking again.

Her skin released a powerful, erotic scent that curled around him, commanding him just as the web flowed through him. It surged through his nostrils, burned into the primal center of his brain, pulled at him like gravity. His arm dropped away from her mouth. Her legs fell open. *Now now now.* She groaned and writhed as he climbed on top of her and shoved himself inside her. Blood from his arm soaked into the silken threads and mixed with her scent, driving him into a mindless fever-pitch until they rutted like animals.

When it was over, some of the threads had folded across his back and caressed his spine like tiny, slippery hands.

21

On the West Shore

At nine on the morning of October 4, the temperature in Lagoon stood at fifty-two. Water from the melted snow ran through streets and rushed down drainpipes. It seeped into beds of fallen leaves and splashed up against the sides of the Pinto as Katie drove across town, headed for Ray's apartment.

Even for a Saturday the roads seemed too empty. There were hardly any trucks whizzing past on Route 16 when she crossed it. In the Four Corners, there were a few cars at the curb in front of the Nameless, several in the Kroger's parking lot, and the Castletons' Jeep in front of the Army/Navy. A garbage truck trundled past the library to one of the nearby neighborhoods.

A handful of pedestrians were out and about, but not like you'd usually find. It was almost as if the break in the weather wasn't fooling anyone, that people felt it was just temporary and tomorrow or next week winter would roar in again, more folks would fall ill or vanish or commit some unspeakable act the rest of them might or might not hear about.

Katie wasn't sure what to think anymore. She wanted desperately to believe that whatever malignant presence she'd sensed in Lagoon had moved on. But she had only to remember the *thing* that had chased her that night on the old county road or the charred smell of the air at Obie's to know that nothing had changed. This was a lull in the storm, that was all. But she intended to take advantage of it.

She parked at the curb in front of Ray's apartment building. It was a refurbished freight warehouse that stood on a hillock across the street from the old railroad tracks. Just beyond the tracks, the land sloped down to Cow Creek, where she, Hank, and her mother used to picnic. She could see it from here, twist-

196

ing through the sunlight, its gleaming white surface breaking up as the ice melted.

Water streamed over the sidewalk that led up to the building. It was exuberant, sweet-smelling, tricking her for a moment into believing that it was spring, that time had rushed ahead without her knowledge. But then she passed the pair of weeping willows in the yard whose bare, gnarled branches were the color of soot, and knew better. It was October and the world should have been burning with color.

Three flights up: Ray's door was open. "Hey, Katie-o," he called. "Come take a look at this."

His voice echoed under the loft's cavernous ceiling and rang out in the virtually empty room. Light poured through the eight tall windows that filled two of the walls, streaked across the faded wooden floors, and stopped just short of the old wooden table where Ray was stripping down an engine. "This baby's going into the bike in the spring," he said, motioning her over to the table.

She pulled up a stool and propped her chin in her hand as he explained what the different parts were and what they did. She listened as much with her nose as her ears, tracking his enthusiasm through memories of motorbikes and cars that were every bit as vivid as other people's memories of families, lovers, friends.

"You think there's going to be a spring?" she asked when he'd finished.

"Doom and gloom. You're beginning to sound like Hank." He crooked a greasy finger under her chin and kissed her. "For *us* there'll be a spring."

This reference to the future, to the two of them having a future, usually would have thrilled her. But his scent darkened and a blurred image flitted through her head, as elusive as a lightning bug. Even though she didn't see it clearly, it frightened her. She reached for it, but his smell shut down completely. It happened so quickly, so abruptly, she felt momentarily disoriented, dizzy, as if she'd just stepped off a tilt-a-whirl at a carnival.

"I wish you wouldn't do that," she said irritably, pulling back.

He frowned. "Do what? Kiss you?"

"Cut me off like that."

"Like what?" He had a funny look on his face. "What the hell're you talking about?"

She realized that she'd spoken without thinking and that of course he didn't have any idea what she was talking about. How could he? She'd never mentioned the scents—his or anyone else's. But she'd come here to ask him to hike into the woods on the west shore of the lagoon with her so that she could track what she believed was Jo's scent. Just how had she planned on explaining it to him, anyway? Had she hoped he would come along without asking questions? Had she really believed he wouldn't think anything of it when she pressed her chin to the ground and sniffed through the leaves and brush like a bloodhound? How could she be so stupid?

Katie gazed across the table. The distance was only a couple of feet, but it felt like miles, like a yawning chasm she somehow had to bridge, to cross. "I smell things," she blurted out.

"You smell things." His voice was as flat as old Coke. "Hey, that's swell, Katie."

"No, you don't understand."

"You're right." He sat back, arms folded at his chest. "I don't."

"I smell moods, feelings, like that. And sometimes there're images connected to them, usually of the past, but not always. Not that night at the Blue Inn when Ben went berserk. That night was different." She had his full attention now and rushed on, explaining what had happened. Ben in the doorway. The dark scent. The pictures in her head. "There were different images, some real hazy, and I think those were . . ." She paused, seeking the right word. "Probabilities. Things he *might* have done. But the clearest picture was of him with the Uzi. And that's when I shouted at him . . ."

Ray didn't laugh, didn't smile, didn't do anything except sit there, staring at her with an expression she couldn't read.

"You don't believe me, do you," she said.

"No, I do," he said quickly. "Really. I'm just having a hard time understanding it, that's all." He sat forward, arms parallel to the table now. "When you said I cut you off . . ."

"Your scent shuts down."

He smiled at that. "But what's that mean?"

"It's like you jerk the smell back into yourself and I can't track it."

"You mean you just go around *tracking* these smells?" There was an unpleasant edge to his voice. "Digging up people's memories?"

"What're you so pissed about?"

"I'm not pissed." He started picking up his tools and dropping them into the toolbox on the floor. "I just don't think it's right." He slammed the lid shut and made a lot of noise as he swept parts of the engine into a box and cleaned off the table. "It's an invasion of privacy or something."

"Hey, Hank and I wouldn't even be alive if it hadn't been for Ben's smell that night." Her voice rose. "And I sure as hell wouldn't be alive if I hadn't smelled something on the old county road when the Pinto broke down. So don't talk to me about invasion of privacy, Ray. In fact, just forget I said anything at all."

With that, she slung her purse over her shoulder and left, slamming the door behind her. Before she made it to the second floor, tears gathered in the corners of her eyes.

"You jerk, you stupid jerk," she muttered, swiping at her eyes with the back of her hand, uncertain whether she was referring to herself or to him or to both of them.

She should have just kept her mouth shut. You didn't go around telling people you smelled moods and feelings, not even people you were close to, she thought. But if *he* had told *her* the story, she wouldn't have gotten mad, she wouldn't have . . .

He felt threatened. He's hiding something.

"Katie, hold on," Ray shouted.

The front door of the building opened and slammed shut, but she didn't stop, didn't turn around. He caught up with her just as she reached the Pinto and grabbed her hand.

"Wait."

She pulled her arm back. "Leave me alone."

"Look, I'm sorry." He leaned against the hood and raked his fingers through his dark hair. His eyes had turned liquid with regret. "I didn't mean to get pissed. This just takes some getting used to, that's all."

She didn't reply.

A cool breeze skipped between them, rustling dry leaves in the streets. "Say something, will you?"

"I already said too much."

"C'mon." He sighed. "I said I'm sorry. Let me take you to breakfast. I want to hear the rest of it."

What're you hiding, Ray? What're you afraid of?

"Should I beg? Say I'm sorry fifty times?"

Be honest with me.

"Jesus. Okay. I'll beg." He dropped to his knees, kissed the top of her boot, and said, "I'm sorry, I'm sorry, I'm. . . ."

She stared down at his head, at the curve of his back, and burst out laughing. Ray scrambled to his feet and spun her halfway down the street, humming a funny, disconnected tune as they whirled through sunlight and shadow. They finally fell back, side by side, in a mound of damp leaves piled up against the curb, and lay there laughing, her hand in his. She peered up through the branches, sunlight burning her eyes. The dampness soaked through her blouse. But she didn't want to move, to say anything that would disrupt the moment. It was simple right here. She didn't have to think. She didn't have to do anything at all.

He turned his head finally and looked at her. "Friends, Katie-o?"

"That depends."

He rolled onto his side, picking leaves from her hair. "On what? Continued good behavior?"

She laughed. "I'd like you to go someplace with me."

"Sure. Where?"

"I'll tell you over breakfast."

He kissed her, a long, slow kiss she felt all the way to her toes, then helped her to her feet. "Deal."

The west side of the lagoon belonged to the Barlows, a wealthy family in Atlanta who had once owned all of the land around it. Fifteen years ago, they'd started selling off parcels of property to the north, south, and east, but had refused all offers for the sale of the west shore.

As far as Katie knew, their land extended from just beyond the Blue Inn to the north, back through nearly fifty acres of woods to the edge of a state park that lay in South Carolina, and south to the property line of the last cabin at the opposite end of the lagoon. The Barlow summer place was somewhere in the middle of it all. Katie had never been inside it, had never even been near it. But she'd heard that it was pretty rustic; supposedly, old man Barlow liked things simple when he came up here.

Simple was apparently synonymous with *difficult* to the old man; he'd made it nearly impossible to reach the west side of the lagoon. Unless you went in on foot, there were only two accesses. One came in through the state park. The other approached from a dirt road to the northwest, which was where Katie and Ray were.

They'd gotten a late start because when they'd gone by the garage to borrow a Jeep, Ray's father had asked him to tackle an emergency transmission repair. Now it was nearly four, but it was worth it just to have the Jeep. Nothing else could have negotiated this road.

It was little more than an overgrown footpath the melting snow had turned to mud. Towering pines bordered it at either side, their branches long and lush, reaching out like the arms of Christmas trees as if to embrace lights, decorations, tinsel. Rays of sunlight shot through the branches and seemed to float in the shadowy air in front of them, ethereal, magical, a little eerie.

"You got any idea just where in here you, uh, picked up Jo's scent?" Ray asked.

She could tell he wasn't quite comfortable talking about it despite his assurances over breakfast to the contrary. "I just know it was coming from this side of the lagoon."

"Lots of woods back here, Katie-o."

"Yeah."

"We've got to narrow it down somehow."

"I haven't smelled anything yet."

"You sure?"

She turned her head toward the window and sniffed at the air. Pine, water, earth: that was all. "Positive."

"You're sure she smelled like this thing that chased you on the old county road?"

"Yes."

"So in other words she's become one of them."

"I think so."

"But what *are* they?"

Trolls. "I don't know."

"Mutants? Like the trout? The rose?"

"I think so."

That word, *mutant*, suddenly possessed a terrible power that it had lacked when referring to plants and animals. It was as if the mere act of saying it aloud, of sharing it here, in this place, had imbued it with a reality beyond Hank's theories.

She rubbed her hands over her arms, warming them, and watched the ghost reflections in the windshield dance across the glass: trees that sprang from a slice of blue sky, the deep green of a low-hanging branch melting into a curve just ahead. She imagined Jo's face floating in the blue, the green, a pale moon with faded celery eyes and copper hair. She blinked and the face became that of the thing that had chased her: discolored skin, features misshapen and squashed together.

"What're we going to do if we find her?" he asked.

If we find them: that was what he was really asking. She looked over at him, at the sunglasses riding on top of his head, at the deep furrow between his eyes, at his large, gentle hands resting against the steering wheel. She thought she caught the faintest trace of the darkness she'd smelled so briefly in him earlier, but then it was gone.

"Kate?"

"I don't know. I don't know what we'll do if we find her." *Or them.* She glanced away.

During their first hour in the woods, they traveled only ten miles because the Jeep got stuck in the mud and it took them a long time to push it out. Then they reached a spot where the road had washed out, leaving huge, gaping holes in the red clay that would swallow the Jeep's wheels whole. So they backtracked, seeking another route—a path, a foot trail, anything would do.

By five-thirty, they found what looked like a narrow tunnel through pines and brush. "The Jeep will get scratched to shit if I take it in there," Ray said. "And since it's not my Jeep, I think we should hoof it. I need to get some stuff out of the back."

The idea of leaving the safety of the Jeep, such as it was, didn't appeal to her in the least. But when she stepped out into the now cooling air, the dark odor rushed at her from the wet pine needles, the red clay, the bark of the trees. It was like a child's concept of God, everywhere at once, a silent voice in the wilderness that swept around her in waves. She couldn't have ignored it even if she wanted to.

She found the spot where it seemed strongest, dropped to her knees, inhaled deeply, and seized a tendril. No pictures, but it didn't matter. This was something she could track. This was the darkness that was in Jo, in Ben, in the man-thing. This was the malignancy in Lagoon.

"You found something?" Ray's voice as he came up behind her was soft, incredulous, maybe a little afraid, but most of all it was riddled with curiosity.

"This way." She moved swiftly through the trees to her left.

Now and then the brush was too thick and Katie had to detour or Ray had to hack through it with a machete he'd pulled out of the back of the Jeep. Sometimes the scent tricked her and divided, just as Jo's had that night, or worse, it split off into several different directions. Then she was forced to choose which fork to follow, never knowing for sure if it was the *right* one because there were no images. She needed the images. She understood their importance now. They were a means of comparison, of distinguishing nuances among similar scents.

She lost all sense of time. She barely noticed the growing chill in the air or the darkening sky or the rising wind. For a while, she even forgot that Ray was with her. The smells and the woods were all that existed. They were a rhythm, a pulse, a heartbeat, and she was inside them, wedded to them like muscle to bone.

The wind strummed branches. Leaves blew. She stopped, suddenly cold, and looked around. What had happened to the light? When had the temperature plunged? Where had all the clouds come from?

"Ray?"

"Ssshhh." He was standing three feet from her, head cocked to one side, gazing off to his right, listening to something. "You hear that?" he whispered.

"The wind, that's all I hear." She unfastened the sweater tied at her waist and pulled it over her head. She was ravenous. "What time is it?"

"Nearly seven."

No wonder she was so hungry.

She sniffed once at the air, just to make sure the scent hadn't vanished, then moved to Ray's side. He was still peering off to his right, into the dusky light that swam between the trees. The machete was tucked under his arm as he held out the canteen, even though she hadn't asked for it. She took it, twirled the top off, drank.

"What is it? What do you hear?"

"Nothing now. But before . . ." He turned his head, looking at her, his eyes wide with alarm. "It was a high-pitched sound, like a dog whistle you can suddenly hear or something. It was weird." He slipped an arm around her shoulders, a gesture that anywhere else would have been romantic. But here, now, there was something almost desperate about it, as if she were his conduit to life on the other side of the lagoon. "I think we'd better get out of here. It's going to snow or rain or something."

"But the scent is—"

"Fuck the scent. You've been tracking it for an hour, going around and around in circles, Katie. *Something's* out here, but I sure as hell don't want to find it. Not at night. Let's split."

She glanced toward the general direction of the scent. It angled off into trees that were denser, spaces that were darker, gloomier. Although she was reluctant to leave, she was unwilling to be out here in the dark. "Where's the Jeep?"

He stabbed a thumb over his shoulder. "Back that way."

It didn't seem right. "You sure?"

"Yeah, I made marks on the trees." He ran his fingers over a slash on the trunk of a pine. "Like this."

Just then a high-pitched keening rippled through the woods. The noise was neither animal nor human, but something else, something primal and fierce that raised the hair at the back of her neck and gooseflesh on her arms. Suddenly she and Ray were running, the wind at their backs, the sound echoing around them.

Branches slapped and clawed at them. Shrubbery seemed to spring out of nowhere, grabbing at their ankles, their legs. Trees closed in on them with the ruthlessness of a marauding army. Rocks appeared where she was sure none had existed before. It was as if the woods now conspired against them, trying to trap them, hold them, prevent them from reaching the Jeep.

The woods exploded with movement. Startled birds lifted from trees, their wings beating frantically at the air. A panicked deer leaped across their path. Rodents fled through damp leaves. Then the keening stopped just as abruptly as it had started, and they pulled up short, breathing hard, listening as the wind blew through the silence.

Trees creaked, branches scraped against each other, clumps of leaves tumbled across the ground. And now the black smell swelled in the wind, rode it like an invisible horseman who chanted *Hungry, hungry*. The words surged in the quickening darkness, surrounding them, flying at them from every direction, momentarily paralyzing them both. Then Ray grabbed her hand and they lurched to the left, crashing through thorny thickets, bushes, mud.

The odor had clamped down over Katie like a drug. She couldn't snap free of it, couldn't outrun it, couldn't defend herself against it. The wind fanned it. The impending darkness fed it. The chant churned through her again, *Hungry, catch, eat.* Ray ran faster, faster, still gripping her hand and the machete, and she knew he heard it, too, that it wasn't just in her head.

Then Katie stumbled, her ankle turned, and she went down, dragging Ray with her. She landed hard on her left side. Pain flashed through her ankle, her hip, her shoulder. The odor slammed into her, crushing the air from her lungs. She coughed, rolled, sat up, and saw Ray a yard away, scrambling to his feet. She shouted at him and he spun.

He looked like a caveman, charging toward her through the twilight, brandishing the machete, yelling something the wind gobbled up. The odor swirled like a dervish around her, and the chant got louder as she tried to get up. *". . . out of the way!"* Ray yelled.

She jerked her head to the right. Something was loping toward her from the trees, and oh, Jesus God, she knew what it was, she knew. Its face was a mass of ridges and protrusions that had once been a nose, a forehead, a chin, cheekbones. Its skin gleamed as it shot toward her, a bullet, a torpedo, a projectile launched from a nightmare.

Katie screamed and leaped up just as Ray sped past her shrieking like a madman. His feet left the ground and, a second later, struck the thing's chest, knocking it back. Ray swung the machete into the air. The blade glistened above his head in the waning light, then dropped like a guillotine into the thing's shoulder.

Its screech tore apart the twilight, and in its agony, in its struggle to wrench the blade from its shoulder, the thing released a thick, terrible smell that filled Katie completely, choking her. She stumbled back, unable to breathe, her eyes tearing, the twilight blinking off and on like a strobe. She whirled blindly, desperate to get away from the odor, her need for oxygen greater than the white-hot pain that radiated through her ankle, greater than her fear, greater than anything she'd ever known. She fell, scrambled up, fell again, her face squashed into a pile of wet leaves, pine needles, mud, soil. For some reason, these odors broke the hold of the other smell and she burrowed her face into them, deeper and deeper, sucking in huge lungfuls of the loamy scent of woods, water, pine.

When she finally lifted her head, it was as if she'd broken through the surface of a lake after being trapped underwater. Her breath exploded from her mouth, she coughed, she sputtered, and then Ray was jerking her to her feet, shoving her forward, shouting, *"C'mon! Jesus, c'mon, it's not dead!"*

She ran. It started to drizzle. The dark closed around her, a tight, cold fist, and her thoughts flew out of her head, scattering like pigeons until she was nothing more than nerves and bones and raw fear. She had no clear memory of reaching the Jeep or of getting out of the woods. One moment she was running and the next she was in Ray's apartment, bundled in a blanket in front of a space heater. Nothing seemed to connect the two events.

The steady drum of the shower, the warmth from the heater, and the bourbon Ray had splashed in her tea made her drowsy and lethargic, like an overfed cat. But she pushed herself up and padded over to the window.

The rain had turned to ice. It stuck to the willow trees at the side of the building, to the Pinto's windshield and roof. It varnished the sidewalk, the street, the hill beyond the railroad tracks, and by tomorrow, the world would be utterly white, transformed, flipped inside out, just as it was now, inside her.

The memories invaded her, swam around inside her like germs or viruses, like protozoa. *That skin, the smell, the horrid shrieking . . .*

They should go to the cops. They would search the area, call out the dogs, the choppers. . . .

The way it moved . . . those chants. It lives back there with others of its kind. . . .

The cops would laugh. The cops would think she was just a kid and that Ray was just a dumb mechanic and that they'd been drinking or doing drugs and had imagined it all.

A lot of others.

Hank would believe her. He'd know what to do.

It wanted us.

She covered her face with her hands, no longer sure if she should tell anyone at all.

It wanted me.

Part IV

THE TOWN

"In Nature, there are neither rewards nor punishments; there are only consequences."
                              —ROBERT B. INGERSTOLL

1.

Every Saturday night for fifteen years, Sam Loman had closed up the Kroger's grocery store in town promptly at nine-thirty and driven out to the Joker's Dozen for a couple of brews. Tonight was no different.

Joker's on Saturdays was a ritual, like eating chicken wings on Wednesdays when the deli had their special or having bagels with coffee on Friday mornings as soon as they popped out of the bakery oven. It was one of those points that connected the events in his life, and you didn't go breaking rituals just because of a little freak weather, he thought.

Route 16 was probably the safer road out of town, because it had been sanded. But five days ago Loman had bought snow tires for his Camaro and felt pretty secure about taking the old county road, which was faster. The tires had cost him a bundle, and his wife, Jackie, was still griping about it. She figured it was a waste of bucks since the bad weather was going to break, the snow was going to melt, and they'd get the Indian summer they'd been cheated out of. She had made this pronouncement like she had the inside scoop from the weather god himself. But Loman knew better. He knew about the dark corruptions in Lagoon. Ever since that morning when Quickson had confronted him in the meat aisle, he'd been hearing things from his customers. They trusted him, confided in him, knew they could tell him things that would die with him.

From Sergeant Moses's wife, he'd heard what had *really* happened to Joe Fenuzo, the story the *Lagoon Bugle* didn't print. The kid was found in the cooler, his dick hanging out, his jugular sucked dry. From the girlfriend of an orderly who worked at Franklin General, he'd heard about Joe Englert's admission with some sort of grotesque growth on her skin and how she'd walked out four days later. Over a couple of beers a week or so ago, Polly Oberman had told him what had really gone down that night at her old man's place and the day she and Captain Oliver found the medical van.

There was something mighty wrong in Lagoon, all right, and to Loman's way of thinking the weird weather was the least of it.

Five miles north on the county road, he hung a right at the blinking light and bounced down a dirt road for three hundred yards. Joker's stood in a small clearing, surrounded by naked river birches that bent under the weight of ice glistening from their branches. It looked like it had been teleported out of the Old West—horse troughs at either end that had once been filled with feed, a wooden porch that sagged like an old filly's back, wooden hitching posts on the railings. It had been decades since anyone up here had ridden a horse to a bar, but what the hell, Loman thought. A part of Joker was still living out a childhood in the fifties.

The glow of light from the front windows spilled into the parking lot and made the falling ice sparkle and glisten like something out of a fairy tale. The cars parked in front looked as if a child had chipped them into being from blocks of ice.

Loman slipped his Camaro into his usual spot closest to the driveway, then dashed inside.

Half a dozen of the Saturday-night regulars were at the bar, a young couple he recognized as teachers at the school were playing pool, and another couple had claimed a booth. Joker, standing behind the bar, was huddled over a chess game with Haskell, who owned a feed shop at the north end of the county. He looked up as Loman came in.

"Sammy, get over here quick. Haskell's just taken my rook. I need advice."

"His rook, four pawns, and his bishop." Haskell laughed, combing his fingers through his graying beard. "And in another couple moves, his queen's going to bite the dust."

"I think he's cheating." Joker set a draft on the counter for Loman as he shrugged off his jacket and gloves.

"You always think the other guy's cheating when you're losing," Loman said, laughing.

He'd known Joker since high school, when they'd paired up during a poker game at a party one night. If you could ignore the gray in his sandy hair and mustache, the deepening wrinkles at the corners of his eyes, and the bulge of his beer belly, he didn't look much different now than he had twenty years ago.

Joker's old man had owned this place then and the family had lived upstairs. Now his father was a county commissioner and Joker lived in town with whomever his current woman was. He used the upstairs apartment only when he was too drunk to drive home, which was most Saturday nights.

"Just look at this mess." Joker gestured toward the board. "What the hell should I do next?"

"Learn the game," Loman quipped.

Haskell laughed. "You got that right."

"C'mon, Sammy. What's my next move?"

As Loman studied the board, the front door blew open and two men swept in with a gust of wind. One was white, the other black, and both wore boots and heavy navy pea coats that reached to their shins. Thick scarves wrapped around their necks and part of their faces; their hands were lost in leather gloves. They looked, Loman thought, like extras from *Dr. Zhivago*.

They claimed stools at the end of the bar. Both men undraped their scarves, but only the black man removed his gloves. "What'll it be, boys?" Joker asked.

"Just two coffees." The black man enunciated the words crisply, clearly, like an actor, thought Loman.

"Two coffees coming up," Joker said. "How're the roads out there?"

"Not too bad unless you get off the main drag," the black man replied. He slid a quarter across the bar to his companion, who got up and shuffled toward the jukebox. Water had beaded on his coat and dripped on the floor as he crossed the room.

"Hurry up," Haskell said. "Make his move for him, Sammy. I've got to finish up here and get my ass home before the wife comes out looking for me with a shotgun."

Loman nodded, reluctant to take his eyes off either of the men. They made him uneasy, although he couldn't have said exactly why. He moved Joker's bishop and Haskell murmured, "Shit, I was afraid you were gonna do that. Hey, Joker, you just gained an edge."

" 'Bout time," Joker said, returning to the game.

Loman sipped his beer and glanced in the mirror. His own lean face gazed back at him, but it looked haunted by some secret tragedy. Shadows grew from the sockets of his eyes and spilled onto his cheeks, oozing across them until it seemed that the shadows originated inside him and weren't a trick of the light. He quickly turned his attention from himself to the man at the jukebox.

He still hadn't taken off his gloves.

Loman's focus now shifted to the black man's reflection; their eyes met. A chill feathered Loman's spine and he averted his gaze.

He excused himself and walked to the back of the bar to use the rest room. ''Hey Jude'' came on. The guy at the jukebox glanced at Loman as he passed. His eyes were as vacant as a sky at high noon in August.

No one home in there, he thought. *The dude's worse off than Harness.*

A window in the rest room was open, and through it Loman heard a car idling in the lot behind the bar. He peered outside but couldn't see much. The yellow bulb that usually lit the back porch wasn't on. He switched off the bathroom light and, as his eyes adjusted to the dark, saw a VW bus parked parallel to the Dumpster. Its headlights were off. But a light glowed inside, silhouetting several figures against the blinds that covered the side windows.

The bus back here, the two strangers up front. . . . He didn't like it. He wasn't usually paranoid, but these weren't normal times in Lagoon and even the mundane, the ordinary, was suspect.

Loman left the light off, used the urinal, then stepped out into the hall again. He walked to the rear door and peeked around the edge of the curtain that covered the pane of glass. The van's windows were now absolutely black.

So what's that prove, Sammy?

Maybe nothing. He was starting to feel somewhat foolish, but he couldn't shake his apprehension, so he engaged the dead bolt on the door. He realized he didn't want to return to the bar, that he was *afraid* to, that his fear was a massive, debilitating tumor pressing against some strategic nerve center deep inside his body.

You fucking coward.

Yes, Christ, yes, he was, but he couldn't help it. Every time he tried to move down the hall, he couldn't get more than a few steps. But he needed to warn Joker, to tell him to close the bar, to get those two guys out, to barricade the doors, the windows, to . . .

Stop it.

Loman pressed his hands over his face, torn by indecision.

Like most people, he'd been raised to believe that reality was what you could see and touch, taste and hear and smell. If you experienced something that didn't fit into those parameters, then you weren't normal. So while Loman's head told him he was creating something out of nothing, he couldn't deny the insistent urgings of his body. He couldn't deny what he sensed.

He broke loose from the torpor that had paralyzed him and lurched for the door to the apartment. He would call Joker from the phone upstairs. And if he had to, he would come back down here with that thirty-ought-six shotgun Joker kept over the fireplace and order the two men to leave.

Loman shut the staircase door quietly behind him, locked the dead bolt, fastened the chain, and stole silently up the stairs.

2.

In the dream, Bobby Peters was with his mom at the Franklin Mall. His *real* mom. She was holding his hand and chatting gaily about the pretty displays in the windows they passed. She didn't seem to notice that they were the only people in the whole place. When Bobby mentioned it to her, she got cross with him and told him it didn't matter, what difference did it make, it was nicer like this, having the mall to themselves. Didn't he like being with his mommy? Didn't he love her? Huh? Didn't he?

Yes, he said, yes, he loved her, really he did. But she didn't hear him. Her voice turned mean, and she jerked on his arm and squeezed his fingers until they hurt so much he was crying. She pulled him along behind her, pulled so fast he stumbled over his own feet. She said she was going to show him what happened to bad boys who didn't love their mommies. Uh-huh, he was going to learn the hard way.

Her hand went dark and soft, like a sponge, and his sank into it, sank deeper and deeper until his fingers seemed to be growing into her skin. He screamed and wrenched away. She laughed and laughed as the skin on her face puffed up and thickened. It squashed her mouth into a tight little O, shoved her eyes closer together, covered her cheeks and nose until there were only two tiny holes for nostrils.

Hungry hungry, she whispered, and lunged for him.

Bobby whirled away from her. The mall vanished. He ran through the dark, the snow flying around him, the chants following him. He saw a light ahead, and as he raced toward it, it got larger. A door appeared in the center of it and he burst through it, into the sound of a pounding heart that beat rapidly, loudly.

His mom was inside, his fake mom, the mean lady in her ugly skin. She was with other people who looked like she did, and everywhere there was blood, so much blood, blood on the floors and the walls, blood smeared on the mean lady's face and hands and arms. Bobby screamed and came to in his own bed, his dad holding him.

"It's okay, son, it's just a nightmare. You're okay."

"Mommy," he cried. "Mommy . . ."

"Ssshhh," his dad whispered.

3.

Andy Horn shut off the lights in the Nameless and flipped the sign on the door from OPEN to CLOSED. He parted the blinds with his hand and gazed out into the empty, windswept road.

Ice glistened from the electrical wires, winked like stars from the bare branches of trees in the park, and shone in bright, glossy patches on the road. *Ice, m'man. Not rain, not snow, but ice.* Not once in his sixty-four years had he seen an ice storm in Lagoon County.

He let the blind fall back into place and sat down at the table with his mug of coffee. Light from the street lamps seeped through the slats and fell in perfect stripes across the surface of the table, chopping it into eighths. Precise, evenly spaced, geometrically perfect eighths, as if they'd been measured and drawn with a ruler.

An *exact* design, he thought. Like Nature.

If he reached out and shook the blinds, the precision would slide into chaos as the stripes trembled and quivered and melted together. But the underlying perfection, the *order*, would remain even if he couldn't see it and would restore itself when the blinds stopped moving. Again, like Nature.

Just say it, ole man.

He pushed up the sleeve of his shirt and let the stripes fall across his upper arm, where the skin was raised and swollen and filling with pus. An *exact* design, he reminded himself. An underlying *order*.

Comforting words. But they didn't make the rash any easier to look at, to touch, to understand. They didn't help him sleep. In the end, words were simply words, with no more significance than what a man attached to them, and the nature of the design, whatever it was, remained hidden, lost to him, as irrefutable as the slowly spreading aberrance on his skin.

4.

"Joker's Dozen."

Loman was on the phone upstairs; he could hear "Imagine" playing on the jukebox now. A regular Beatle marathon was in progress down there. "It's me. Sam. I'm upstairs in the apartment. I—"

"What the hell you doing up there, Sammy? Haskell just took my other rook, man. C'mon, I need your help."

"Listen to me, Joker. There's a VW bus parked out back with some people inside. I think the black dude and his buddy are with them and . . ." *And what?* He had the feeling they were going to rob the place? Plunder it? Worse? No matter what he said, it was going to sound crazy. ". . . and I don't like it. I think they're planning something."

Joker's laughter said he was well on his way to being blasted. "What the hell're you talking about, Sammy? What bus?"

"Out back. I locked the rear door just in case. I think you should just close up shop for the night. Get those two guys outta there. They're trouble. They're—"

"Hey, what the fuck do you think you're—"

Haskell's voice in the background was cut short by a woman's scream, a scream Loman knew he would remember for the rest of his life. Then Joker—it had to be Joker, it couldn't have been anyone else—shouted something unintelligible. Bottles shattered. The line went dead.

He slammed down the phone, stumbled through the dark to the fireplace, grabbed the thirty-ought-six from its rack. A box of shells was on the mantel and Loman was shaking so badly, he nearly spilled it. He loaded the rifle and shoved a handful of shells into his shirt pocket as he rushed over to the window.

He parted the curtain with his hand.

The door of the van stood open.

Shrieks from downstairs vibrated against the floor under his feet. He pressed back against the wall, sweat springing across his back, blood thundering in his ears. *Sweet Christ, do something, they're killing them down there.*

He ran to the door, but his hand refused to turn the knob. Instead, it threw the dead bolt and fastened the chain, acting as if with a volition of its own. He watched as it did these things despite repeated demands from his brain to do the opposite, to do what was right and noble and courageous.

He cursed himself even as he was stepping back from the door, blinking hard, afraid that in the next moment or the next the wood would explode inward. When nothing happened, when the hideous shrieks downstairs just went on and on, searing through him, scorching him raw inside, he looked frantically around the room, at the outline of objects, trying to remember what was up here, what might be heavy enough to use as a barricade.

There was an empty mahogany display case against the wall, about six feet from the door. Once, years ago, it had taken three of them to move it from one end of the room to the other. But Loman, despite his slight build and fueled by surges of adrenaline, managed to shove it in front of the door. Only then did he return to the phone and punch out 911. But when he held the receiver to his ear, there was nothing. No dial tone, no hollow sound, just a black hole deeper than space.

Huge, startled gasps burst from his mouth and collapsed, almost instantly, into groans. "Aw, Christ, sweet Christ, what—"

He clamped a hand over his mouth as the shrieks diminished, as the jukebox needle scratched across "A Day in the Life," as silence clamped down over the building, deep and vast, as impenetrable as his terror. He took an involuntary step back and grimaced when the floorboard creaked.

Did they hear it?

He slipped off his boots and picked his way slowly across the room, a man moving through a mine field. At the window, his heart pounding furiously against his ribs, he slipped two fingers behind the blinds and lifted them an inch away from the glass. No more. Just an inch.

The doors of the VW bus were still open, and two figures stood outside. The only thing he could tell about them was that they were wearing shorts and T-shirts and seemed impervious to the ice, the cold. Two more stepped into his line of vision; one of them was dragging something behind him. When Loman caught a flash of blond hair and realized the something was a woman, he yanked his hand away from the blinds and pressed his back against the wall, his eyes squeezed shut, his right hand frozen on the rifle, a shudder ripping through him.

They're taking the bodies away.

A door slammed. A blast of wind rattled the glass. Downstairs, he heard pounding, things breaking, a thumping sound, then a crash in the stairwell. Loman knew they'd just broken through the downstairs door that led to the apartment.

Their footfalls echoed on the stairs.

He cocked the rifle, fixed the end of it against his shoulder, sighted down the barrel as he moved back. How many were there? Did he have enough shells? Could he mow them all down before they got to him?

The rifle dropped to his side. He grabbed his boots, spun, and flew into the guest bedroom. *Porch over parking lot. Camaro directly below me. Long fucking drop.* But it was either drop or fight.

He couldn't get the porch door open, it was stuck, so he threw open the window. The cold rushed in, harsh and brutal. Something slammed against the front door of the apartment, then silence tightened around the building again. He shut the bedroom door, turned the flimsy lock in the knob, jerked on his boots. He was wearing only a shirt and jeans and was already shivering from the cold, so he yanked the quilt off the foot of the bed and wrapped it around his shoulders.

Out, fast. C'mon, c'mon.

As he scrambled through the window, soft explosions of cracking wood filled the front room, followed instantly by a strange, haunting chant. It was as if he'd stumbled into a sixteenth-century monastery at vespers, except there was nothing holy about this sound. It surrounded him, invaded him, and would have claimed him if he hadn't slammed the window shut, muting it somewhat.

Ice had turned the porch into a treacherous terrain riddled with hidden perils that his boots couldn't detect. He moved hand over hand along the railing, the rifle tucked under his armpit, his palms sticking to the ice, his fingers nearly frozen by the time he reached the end.

He peered down at his car.

I can't.

But he would.

It's too far.

No other way out.

A fist shattered the glass behind him. Loman turned, raised the thirty-ought-six, fired. A screech of pain sliced through the dark. He cocked the rifle and fired again. And again.

Then he swung his left leg over the icy railing, fit his heel between two slats. Now his right leg. One hand still gripped the banister. The Camaro blurred beneath him, and he dropped.

Wind whistled in his ears. The quilt flapped at his back like a cape. He held his breath. His heart stopped. He struck the hood feet first. His right foot slid out from under him and he slipped back, tumbling to the ground. Air rushed from his lungs. The rifle flew out of his hands. His teeth bit through the tip of his tongue. He rolled, seized the rifle, lurched for the car, jerked the door open, hurled himself inside.

Doors locked. Keys. Ignition. But his fingers were so stiff, he couldn't hold on to the keys and they dropped. He grappled for them, his breath coming in bursts like hiccups, like gasps. *Oh, God, please, let the car start, please. . . .*

It cranked up on the first try. The wipers whipped back and forth across the icy windshield as Loman revved the engine, slammed the gearshift into reverse. The Camaro fishtailed and crashed into the back of one of the parked cars. Loman shifted into first, mashed the accelerator to the floor. But the bumper was caught and now the engine strained, shrieking as the people in the bar had. Reverse again, first again, reverse, first. The car sprang free and shot forward.

The headlights impaled two figures racing toward him from the ice, the snow. One was a naked woman, her hair riding the wind. He saw her breasts. Her thighs. He saw that she was not human.

The Camaro struck her a second later, and she vanished over the roof. Loman swung the wheel violently to the right, toward the exit. The left fender barely missed the man who'd been with her and swerved out onto the main road, spinning like a top, the tires kicking up clouds of snow.

When the car stopped spinning, its nose was pointing north. Loman took off.

He didn't stop until he was a hundred and eighty miles from Lagoon, the only car in a well-lit K Mart shopping lot, and he didn't get out until the sun was rising.

Part V

ECHOES

"The more often a pattern of activity has been repeated, the stronger its influence will be."
—RUPERT SHELDRAKE

22

The Morning After

1.

The brilliance blinded, dazzled, mesmerized.

Nash stood on the open deck, in a world so white, it had been stripped of dimension, depth, definition. The lagoon was a flat white island of ice surrounded by the tall shapes of white trees. The sun had washed the blue from the sky.

Gradually, his eyes adjusted to the glare and he could detect details in the surreal landscape: icicles hanging from branches like diamond pendants, gnarled bushes the ice had sculpted into things of incomparable beauty, docks that jutted out into the lagoon like anemic tongues.

The thermometer registered eighteen degrees.

His toes curled up against the cold that seeped through the rubber soles of his running shoes. Only masochists and madmen ran on days like this, he thought.

"Hey, Nash, if you don't stretch, you get nasty things like shin splints and pulled muscles," Fay called from indoors.

Through the open door, he watched her on the rug in the lobby as she rolled onto her stomach, bent her right leg up, and dipped her head back until her toes brushed her hair. His muscles ached just watching her.

"I'd end up as a cripple doing what you're doing."

Now she rolled into a lotus position, slowly raised her left leg, and hooked the foot behind her neck. She did the same with the right and held the position for two or three seconds. She reminded him then of the street beggars on the streets of Calcutta or Rio, the kind who pushed themselves along on tiny carts with wheels because they had no legs. Nash was relieved when she untangled and stepped out onto the deck, Samson at her heels.

"You feel like racing this morning?"

"I'm not even sure I feel like running unless the road's been plowed."

"It has. I heard the plow come through about five this morning."

"Loser fixes breakfast."

"Fair enough. Best time starting from the bottom of the hill?"

"Sounds good."

She locked a hand on the railing on either side of him, rolled onto the balls of her feet, and kissed him. "I'd like an omelet and bacon and a couple of cinnamon rolls."

"Optimist." Nash laughed. "If it's a tie, we toss for who cooks."

"You're on. Let's go."

The word *go* propelled Samson to the front door. The second Nash opened it, he dashed outside and shot for the trees.

They walked down the slope, ice and snow crunching underfoot. The snow was packed and marked with tire tracks, a sure sign the mayor's brigade had definitely made the rounds, plowing and sanding roads with equipment borrowed from a utility department in North Carolina. The plowing was probably unnecessary, since it had only exposed the layer of ice under the two or three inches of snow that had fallen. But the mayor was like a kid with a new toy; he couldn't resist a chance to try out his equipment.

At the bottom of the hill, they synchronized watches, then Nash set his on the second timer. At the count of three, they took off. For the first couple of minutes, they were neck to neck, equally matched despite Nash's advantage of longer legs and Fay's lighter weight.

But as soon as they passed the live oak that marked the half-mile point, Fay shouted, "I'm changing my order to pancakes, Nash," and tore out in front of him, shoes pounding the road, arms tucked tightly at her sides.

He opened up wide, but in seconds he knew it wasn't fast enough. She was nothing but a streak of blue through a white tunnel. Adrenaline poured through him. He drew on a reserve he didn't know he had and picked up speed. Five seconds passed. Eight. Ten. Thirty seconds later, despite his increased speed, the distance between them was even greater than before. It was like a Hyundai racing a Porsche, a 747 trying to catch a phantom-jet fighter. She rounded a curve and Nash lost sight of her.

He unzipped his jacket.

Sweat streamed down his face.

His shoes pounded against the road.

The muscles in his legs started to cramp.

At the mile point, he clocked himself: six minutes and ten seconds, about twenty seconds faster than usual. Fay had already looped back; he could see her at the mile-and-a-half point hurtling toward him.

He stopped, panting for breath, and flicked his fingers at his watch, certain it was wrong. It had to be wrong. He looked at the watch, at her, at his watch again, and then she soared past him, a vision, a hallucination. He ran after her, anxious to know the exact moment when she reached the two-mile mark. If he remembered correctly, the women's world record for a mile-run was about 4:18, and according to his watch, Fay had just done *two* miles back to back in 8:38.

When Nash reached her, she was on all fours on the ground, her breathing loud, ragged. She lifted her head to look up at him. Her cheeks were bright red. Strands of hair were plastered to her forehead and temples. She tried to speak but was too winded, and promptly turned her head to the side and vomited. She started to shudder, to rock back and forth, her arms clutched to her waist. Nash helped her to her feet.

"You didn't have to kill yourself for pancakes," he said.

She tried to smile but stumbled instead. He picked her up and carried her back to the house. She didn't protest, didn't tell him that she was fine and could make it on her own. She simply went limp in his arms.

He got her situated on the couch, worked off her shoes, drew the afghan over her. She said she would be okay, she just needed to lie here for a minute. Could he get her a glass of water? He did, and she downed half of it, then fell back against the pillows, too exhausted to move.

In minutes, she was asleep.

Nash took her pulse. It was a nice, steady fifty-eight, ten points lower than his was when he got out of bed in the morning. The readout on her digital watch indicated that she'd run the last mile, her *third mile*, in 4:18, tying the record.

2.

Oliver awakened to Polly's hands fluttering over his skin like the wings of a butterfly, to her tight, pale thighs opening to him, to her wild hair falling around his face like a curtain. When the phone pealed and his arm shot out to answer it, her hand descended over his, hot and dry as a wind.

"No, don't answer it." Her voice was still husky with sleep, but it possessed the quiet pleading of a woman at the edge. "They'll call back."

"Relax," he said, and she rolled off him and plopped back against the mattress with an irritated sigh. The phone rang again and he picked up the receiver.

It was Sergeant Moses. "Sorry about the time, Lew. But we just got a real strange call from Sammy Loman. He was calling from someplace in North Carolina and said he'd been driving since he left Joker's last night. He wasn't too coherent, but near as I can figure, something happened out at Joker's. Something bad. I called out there, but the line's dead. I called his apartment here in town and no one answered."

Oliver sat up and swung his legs over the edge of the bed. "You get Loman's number?"

"Yeah, it's a pay phone in a K Mart lot." Moses reeled it off and Loman jotted it on the back of an envelope. "I told him to stick around for five or ten minutes, but he said he didn't know if he could. He thinks someone is after him."

"Who?"

"I don't know. He sounded real paranoid. He wanted me to call his wife at her mother's and tell her to stay there. He said he's not coming back to Lagoon."

"Terrific. You at the station?"

"Yeah."

"I'll call you right back." He hung up, punched out the number Moses had given him. After twenty rings, he gave up and called Moses back. "I'll meet you at Joker's in fifteen minutes. Don't go in alone."

"Right."

"I'm coming with you," Polly said, throwing off the covers.

"This is police business."

"Don't give me that macho horseshit, Lew. Joker's a friend of mine."

With that, she reached for her clothes, and Oliver knew there was no point in arguing with her. She would end up at Joker's with or without him.

Moses was already waiting when Oliver's truck swung into the lot. He was standing next to a maroon truck with HASKELL FEED written on the side in faded black letters and was scribbling on a notepad. He hurried over as Oliver and Polly got out. Although Moses rarely drank, he always looked like he was coming off a three-day drunk: hooded eyes, a square, shadowed jaw, a bulbous nose as bright as a Christmas bulb. "We've got Haskell's truck here, a Chevy that belongs to a social-studies teacher at the high school, Joker's pickup, and three other vehicles I'm about to run a make on."

"Is anyone in there?" Polly asked.

"I don't think so. I shouted for Joker, but there wasn't any answer. Other than that, I haven't done anything. I got here just before you two pulled in."

"Let's go take a look," Oliver said.

That familiar sense of *wrongness* permeated the air; it reminded Oliver of the barn where the medical van had been stashed. He pulled out his .38 and approached the building warily, as though it were a wounded thing that might strike out at any second to defend itself.

The sagging porch moaned as he and the others crossed it. Oliver took up a position to the right of the door, Polly directly behind him, Moses to the left. He nodded at the sergeant, who touched the knob, turning it slowly. The door swung open.

"Jesus God," Moses whispered.

There was so much blood that at first that was all Oliver saw. Blood on the walls and the floor, on the bar, booths, and tables. Then other details crept into his awareness: toppled stools, smashed bottles of booze, glass glistening against the floor, the face of the jukebox caved in like a piece of rotten fruit. There were no bodies.

As he stepped into the room, the stink of blood and alcohol pressed up against him, nauseating him. He threw open the front windows, then stood there as the cold air swept over him and into the room. Neither Polly nor Moses moved or spoke; they seemed to be waiting for him to tell them what to do.

"Where're the bodies?" Polly whispered.

No one answered her. Oliver forced himself to walk forward. His boots crushed shards of glass; blood pulsed behind his eyes, sweat dampened his hands, his face. "Joker?"

His voice sounded small and disembodied in the silence, a mockery. He already knew Joker wasn't here. No one was here. No one.

He and Moses moved slowly toward the back hall, following trails of blood that led past the jukebox. The door to the apartment stood ajar. The wood in the center had been punched in and the chain was snapped in two. Oliver poked his head through the entry, turned on the light, peered up the stairs. The door at the top was in the same condition. "Joker?" The silence tossed his own voice back to him.

"I'll check up here," Moses said, and brushed past him, looking grateful that he had something definite to do.

Oliver walked to the end of the hall, where Polly had already opened the rear door, and stepped outside onto the porch where she stood. "They broke in here." She pointed at the busted glass in the door. "And also pulled the bodies out this door."

"Who?"

They looked at each other; her face was as white as the ice around them. "The same goddamn *things* that killed my old man and chased the medical van that night and the Suffield girl, Lew, who the hell do you think? You figure some crazed killer is going around doing this stuff, Lew?" She let out a harsh, ugly laugh, flicked her wild hair off the collar of her jacket, and pulled out a smoke. She lit it and puffed with a vengeance. "Jesus, all I do is tend bar and I know more about what's going on here than you do."

"Yeah? And just what's going on, Polly? All I've heard so far are tales about bogeymen. The doc and her nurse and the kid supposedly get chased by some dudes in Bermuda shorts who have weird shit on their skin. So what's that mean, huh? Just what the hell does that mean? The Fenuzo kid ends up in a freezer with a chewed neck, your old man is already dead when he's hurled through a window in his shack, people are just walking out of their lives for no apparent reason, spiders that seem to be intelligent chase us out of the van, feds are talking to the mayor, the weather's gone berserk . . . Fine, I know all that. But tell me what the fuck it *means*, that's all I'm asking."

His outburst released the deep, abject fear that he'd been trying to repress for weeks. It had grown with his dread of the dark, with his certainty that whatever was going on in Lagoon was something he couldn't control or prevent or stop. Now, as he stood on the cold stoop with Polly, the fear tore down whatever meager defenses he'd erected against it and stripped him bare. To his utter horror, he felt tears build at the backs of his eyes, the tears of a child in desperate need of comfort and assurance that bogeymen existed only in the mind.

"I don't know what it means." She spoke with an atypical gentleness that indicated she'd seen more than he wished she had. "But I don't think the meaning matters very much, Lew.

The point is that something terrible is loose in Lagoon and it's getting worse, and something's got to be done.''

Moses came back downstairs and reported a broken window, a smashed bedroom door, a dead phone, some blood on the bedroom floor. But no bodies. Oliver asked him to radio a dispatcher and get some forensics people out here pronto. Polly gave him a look that said *What good are they going to do?* and walked back inside to use the rest room.

Relieved of her presence and alone again when Moses left to radio in, Oliver recovered himself in bits and pieces. It was like patching together memories the morning after tying one on. The fear receded, but not very far. He sensed it crouching in a corner of his mind, a jack-in-the-box that would spring when he least expected it, a clown with a hideous grin that would leap on him some night while he slept.

He walked out toward the white field, eyes glued to the ground as if the snow would yield its secrets. But whatever clues it held—tire marks, blood, footprints—had long since vanished. Right now, Sammy Loman was his best lead, and Christ only knew where the hell he was. Oliver figured he could track him down through his wife, but the mayor and Joker's father were going to be on his ass for answers long before then.

He reached the Dumpster and threw open the lid. For a second, the neurons between his eyes and his brain seemed to misfire and what he was seeing made no impression on him at all. Then something clicked into place—he could actually hear it, a soft, quick sound like a lock when it opened—and he stumbled away from the Dumpster. His mouth opened to shout for Moses, but nothing came out. The fear cackled someplace deep inside him, then vaulted out of the shadows and leaped onto his back. He whirled and ran straight through the bar, the fear pounding his spine like hammers, his mouth opening and closing, sucking at air, trying to form words.

When he reached the front lot, he fell against Moses's car, doubled over, and puked. The only word his mouth could form was *Dumpster*.

3.

Ten bodies.

They lay on gurneys lined up against the wall in the morgue, sealed in bags that Fay didn't want to touch—not now, not tomorrow, not ever.

"Where do you want to start?" Mona asked.

"I don't. This isn't my idea of a fun way to spend a Sunday evening."

"Moses suggested we start with the weird one."

"Since when is *he* an expert on anything?"

"I knew that'd get a rise out of you." She pulled a gurney away from the wall and wheeled it over to the aluminum autopsy table. The body bag had a red tag on it. "He said all of the bodies they found in the Dumpster except this one had been gutted."

"Then that should make it the only ordinary one in the bunch, not the *weird* one. Leave it to Moses to get his adjectives screwed up."

They snapped on latex gloves, tied masks around their faces, and hoisted the body bag onto the aluminum table. Fay adjusted the mike over the table, which was connected to a tape recorder on a cart to her left. Then she unzipped the bag and they rolled the body out. A female. *The weird one.*

A part of Fay instantly detached and retreated into that other place, that safe white space that had served her so well as a physician. But another part of her remained rooted just where she was, focused on a picture unrolling in the upper corner of her right eye, a picture of Ben as he had been the day he'd lain on this very table. This creature, this alien being, this terrible abomination in front of her was the end result of what had afflicted Ben; this was what he would have become if he'd lived.

She had stared into the face of that future the night at Obie's but, in the weeks since, had denied what she'd seen. Her salvation lay as much in that denial as it did in her need to believe that these changes were caused by a virus. A virus could be treated. A virus spelled hope. To believe in Suffield's theory of an indifferent intelligence called Nature was the road to madness.

Mona's eyes met hers across the table, eyes that were bright with alarm, with fear, with many of the same thoughts Fay had. There was no need to speak. Fay pulled the overhead light closer to the body and examined the thin, fibrous hairs that grew out of some of the pores. She held out her hand and Mona passed her an instrument that looked like a pair of long tweezers. Fay plucked out one of the hairs and held it up to the light. It was absolutely white and looked more like a thread than a hair.

"Can you get me a slide? I'd like to look at this under the microscope."

A few moments later, Fay peered through the eyepiece of the microscope. The fiber wasn't animal or human hair. But it couldn't be what she thought it was, either. "Take a look," Fay said. "Tell me what you think."

A couple of minutes passed. Mona finally raised her head, shook it. "This is going to sound strange, Fay, but it looks like a silk thread to me."

"Yeah, that was my feeling."

They exchanged a glance, but neither of them said anything more. They returned to the autopsy table. The threads were longest at the woman's sides, growing out of enlarged pores just under her breasts, at her upper thighs, and just behind her earlobes. Fay plucked out a dozen more, then excised several by removing the pore itself.

Blood ran freely. It was such a deep red, it was nearly brown. She withdrew four syringes of blood from the woman's arm, a tricky maneuver that took three attempts because no veins showed in her skin.

When she took a sample of the skin by making a lateral slice on the woman's hip, it was like cutting through sponge cake. And yet the flesh was hard and tough to the touch, rather like the belly of a pregnant woman.

She started to turn on the recorder, then thought better of it and asked Mona to get the Nikon. She wanted photographs before she started cutting. She wanted *proof*. For herself. For Nash. For Suffield. In fifteen or twenty years, she wanted to be able to pull out these photographs and say, *This is what that virus did*, and marvel at the ingenuity of medical research and technology that had found a cure.

The camera was already loaded with color film. She used up the fourteen pictures that were left, then removed the roll and slipped it in the pocket of her lab coat. Nash could develop them later in the darkroom; she wasn't about to trust these to the local drugstore.

As Mona put the camera away, there was a knock at the outer door. "Fay? It's Captain Oliver."

Captain: an official visit. "Want me to send him packing?" Mona asked.

"No, it's okay. I'll handle him." Fay pulled off the gloves and shut the door to the autopsy room on her way out.

Oliver wasn't alone, and she immediately recognized the two men who were with him: Baldy and Red, the same two she'd seen that day at the Nameless, the ones from Nash's photographs, the boys from the meadow.

Bad news, Mona. Get rid of the slides.

"What can I do for you, Lew?"

Dressed in wrinkled navy slacks with a sloppy pullover, Oliver looked about as uncomfortable and unsure of himself as she'd ever seen him. "Mind if we come in?"

"Yeah, I mind. I've got ten bodies to autopsy in there, Lew. You said you needed the results by tomorrow afternoon."

"That's what we'd like to talk to you about, Dr. Donovan," said Baldy.

He smiled politely as he spoke, but it was the sort of smile you might see on a mugger's face before he knocked you out. He was dressed in jeans and a brown leather jacket straight out of World War I. A flying ace jacket, the kind Snoopy wore. All he needed, she thought, was a stupid red scarf trailing from his neck.

"This is Colonel Fielding," said Oliver. "Steven Fielding. And his assistant, Bruce Lattimer."

Lattimer nodded. "Evening, ma'am. Sorry to intrude like this." He looked younger than his photograph, with thick, curly red hair and freckles. He bore a strong resemblance to Dennis the Menace and wore a jacket identical to Fielding's, jeans, boots, and a belt made out of alligator skin. Nouveau tacky, she thought, and stepped aside so they could enter.

"What did you gentlemen want to discuss?"

"The CDC would like to autopsy the body that wasn't mutilated and we're here to pick it up," Fielding said.

"None of the bodies leaves here without written authorization." She kept her voice just as pleasant as his.

"Got it right here." Lattimer pulled an envelope out of his jacket and handed it to her. "It was faxed a little while ago."

It looked legitimate, particularly with the loose, florid signature at the bottom that Fay recognized: Lance Blair, courtesy of the CDC. "We were just about to start the autopsy. I'll have my assistant get it back into the body bag for you."

"Don't trouble yourself, ma'am," said Lattimer. "We'll do it."

The door of the autopsy room opened just then, and Mona, bless her sweet eavesdropping soul, wheeled the gurney out. The body was already in the bag, which was zipped up, sealed. With luck, the boys wouldn't notice the missing slice of skin from the woman's hip until the body had reached its destination.

Mona's eyes met Fay's briefly; they glinted with triumph. "Here you go, guys." She sounded as if she were addressing a couple of Cub Scouts. "You've made our Sunday."

Fay barely suppressed a smile as she introduced Mona to the two men. "I didn't realize the CDC had colonels in its ranks," Mona remarked, gazing at Fielding in that open, implacable way she had.

"It doesn't. The military is just helping out." Then the colonel nodded at Lattimer, who unzipped the bag just enough to make sure this was the body they'd come for. If he felt anything about what he was looking at, he gave no indication.

"This is it," he said.

Fay shook her head. "Not quite." She pulled open a desk drawer and brought out a release form. "You need to sign this, Colonel."

He gave it a quick once-over and scribbled something illegible at the bottom. "I understand you and Ms. Stawson were at Oberman's the night he was killed and his place burned," Fielding said as he passed the form back to her.

She glanced at Oliver, who was staring at the floor, then looked back at Fielding. "We'd stopped to get gas. Why?"

"According to the police report, you claim you were chased by several men who had . . ." His eyes flickered to Lattimer. "What was her description, Bruce?"

Lattimer cleared his throat, obviously delighted that he'd been asked to contribute. "If I remember correctly, you referred to them as men with severe skin deformities, who were wearing shorts and T-shirts, even though the temperature that night was in the low thirties."

"That's right."

"Did they look anything like the woman in the body bag, Doctor?"

"Why?"

Fielding blinked. "Excuse me?"

"Why? What's your interest, Colonel?" *What're you and the CDC hiding?*

"Like I said, we're just helping the CDC." He smiled pleasantly. "And we would all appreciate it if you kept what you've seen to yourself."

"Seen here? Or at Joker's?"

"Both."

"Why?"

The colonel's expression wasn't quite so pleasant now. "To avoid feeding the rumor mill, Doctor."

He thanked her for her time, then he and Lattimer hoisted the body off the gurney and left without another word to anyone. Oliver didn't seem to know whether to follow them or to stay where he was. He leaned against the jamb, ran a finger over his sandy mustache, looked down at the floor, up again.

"So what's the deal, Lew?" said Mona. "How'd those two bozos get involved?"

"This came from the mayor and Joker's old man," he replied. "I didn't have nothing to do with it. They all showed up at the bar."

"Are they army?"

"A.I."

Mona laughed. "Arrogant idiots. I couldn't agree more."

"Army Intelligence," he said.

"That's it?" Fay's irritation was as evident as Oliver's unease. "That's all you know?"

"What the hell do you want me to say? I was just doing what I get paid to do."

Despite her dislike for the man, Fay felt sorry for Oliver just then. "Oh, forget it. I'll try to have something for you on these bodies by tomorrow."

She started to turn away, but Oliver asked if he could talk to her. In private. He looked pointedly at Mona, who held up her hands. "I was just leaving. I'll be upstairs, Fay. Buzz me when you need me."

Something peculiar happened to the air when it was just the two of them alone in the cold room. It seemed that the very molecules that swirled invisibly around them had suddenly thickened, as though they were about to materialize.

"I'd, uh, like to know what you think about that." He tilted his head toward the door where Baldy and Red had vanished. "Off the record."

"About the body or your buddies?"

His mouth twitched. "The body."

"If I'd been able to do the autopsy, Lew, I might've had some answers for you."

"I didn't have any choice about that."

She didn't say anything.

"I was just following orders."

Squirm, Lew, c'mon, lemme see you squirm some more.

"Commissioner Jokerzy and the mayor thought it was best if we cooperated with the CDC."

"They're not telling everything they know, Lew. Not to you, not to any of us."

But Oliver didn't want to talk about sins of omission. He rubbed his jaw. "The stuff that covered the body—isn't it what Ben had?"

"It looked similar, yes."

"And Reverend Quickson?"

"His wasn't that bad."

"Is it contagious?"

"I don't know. If I'd been able to complete the autopsy, I—"

"Yeah, yeah," he said. "I know."

Then he turned and shuffled out into the hall, his shoulders stooped as if under a crushing weight.

23

Little Truths

1.

For nearly two weeks, the only person Katie told about what had happened on the west shore was Dani Menninger.

Dani, however, didn't have much to say about it one way or another. She was more interested in the fact that Katie had been with Ray. When she admitted they'd been seeing each other, Dani didn't get mad or huffy about it like Katie expected her to do. She quickly confided that she'd started dating that *gorgeous* new senior with the snappy little Mercedes. Even her old man approved of him, she added, as if to say who needed Ray, anyway. Not surprisingly, she began to avoid Katie after that.

It hurt, but not like it would have several months ago. After all, she still had Ray, and the events on the west shore had tightened their relationship. It had divided their lives into a before and an after, as if the Katie and Ray who had escaped from the woods were not the same people who had entered it.

But then two things happened that forced her to confide in someone else about what had happened that day.

On Thursday afternoon when she got home from school, a gray BMW was parked behind Hank's Mustang in the driveway. It belonged to the two men who were in the living room with him, a pair she recognized: Baldy and Red from the meadow. Hank introduced them as Colonel Fielding and Mr. Lattimer, who were with Army Intelligence, whatever that was. They had some questions about what had happened to her that night on the old county road, he said. His expression clearly signaled that she didn't have to tell them a damn thing; he'd recognized them as well.

"What night?" she asked, settling next to Hank on the couch.

"When Mr. Oberman was killed," Lattimer replied. He sat

234

forward in his chair, twirling his shades between his thumb and his forefinger. "You were included in the police report."

He had eyes the same color as Jo's, and she didn't like the way he smelled. Two strikes against him. "I was?"

"According to Captain Oliver, you showed up around nine, racing down the drive like you 'had a ghost on your tail.' Those were his words." When Lattimer smiled, he smelled like seaweed and dead fish baking in a hot summer sun: strike three. "Then you proceeded to tell him about something that had chased you after your Pinto had broken down."

"I did?"

Lattimer's smile was sucked into his thin cheeks; he didn't have much patience. "You saying none of it happened? That you lied?"

"No."

"Then what *are* you saying, young lady?" Fielding asked.

"That I don't feel like talking to you guys."

She got up and went out into the kitchen, where her schoolbooks were. She spread them out on the table, then helped herself to a snack from the fridge. She heard Hank apologizing to the two men—*"You know how teenagers are"*—and wished they'd just leave. But now the colonel was questioning Hank about Jo. Hadn't she been admitted to Franklin General with severe skin lesions? Did Mr. Suffield know why she'd checked herself out? Had he heard from her since she'd left?

"I think you'd better check with Dr. Donovan. She admitted Jo to the hospital, Colonel. And no, I don't have any idea why she checked herself out of the hospital, and no, I haven't heard from her, and what I'd like to know is what business any of this is of yours."

"The Center for Disease Control is behind this investigation, Mr. Suffield. We're just helping them out. . . ."

Katie didn't hear the rest of it; Lattimer's scent distracted her, reaching her before she heard him coming up behind her. *Sneaky little shit.*

"Mind taking a look at this?" Lattimer reached over her shoulder and dropped a folder in front of her. He went around to the other side of the table and sat down, waiting for her to see what was inside.

"I've got homework to do, you know."

"C'mon, just take a look." His smile was the kind she always saw on the faces of adults who thought kids were stupid. "Then I'll leave you alone."

She flipped open the folder. Inside was a glossy 8 × 10 color photograph of one of the man-things that had chased her on the old county road. It seemed to be running out of the picture, coming after her, the eyes searing through her. She slapped the folder shut and shoved it across the table.

"Leave me alone." She looked down at her social-studies book. The page blurred. "I have work to do."

Lattimer tapped the photo and went on as if he hadn't heard her. "This freak used to be human, Katie. He was a school-teacher, a pretty regular guy until he started having these weird compulsions for raw meat. Then his eyes became real sensitive to the light, and when it got real bad, he couldn't go out during the day anymore."

But at night, the man went hunting, except that he didn't use a gun. "No siree. This fellow didn't need a gun." Lattimer's voice was low and soft, almost lewd, like the voice of a tele- phone perv. "He was able to kill rabbits and deer by running them into the ground and strangling them with his bare hands. One time, he brought his wife a dead squirrel, just like cats did with a kill. Have you ever seen a cat do that?"

Katie didn't say anything.

"Well, that's what this guy did, young lady. Another time, he flew into a violent rage and knocked his wife and kids around. Someone called the cops and he ended up in the VA hospi- tal. The docs ran all kinds of tests on him, just like they did on your dad's girlfriend. Only he didn't check himself out of the hospital like she did. He was in an isolation ward because he looked like this"—Lattimer tapped the photo—"and he killed two nurses and an orderly when he broke out. It's a disease, see, and we don't know how it's spread or how contagious it is, but we're trying to find out and we need your help. Yours and Dr. Donovan's and your dad's and anyone else who's had any ex- perience with this. We're on your side."

All the time he'd been talking, his scent had wrapped slowly and steadily around her like a tendril of smoke, of seaweed, a tongue of wind. Now that he'd announced they were on the same side and awaited her reaction, the scent drew her into a memory of Lattimer in a rage, hurling a neighbor's marmalade cat by the tail and flinging it against a wall. It had nothing and everything to do with his sitting there and telling her he was on their side.

"You broke the cat's back."

His astonishment felt almost as good as the moment when she pushed away from the table and walked out of the room.

She took refuge under the headphones in her bedroom, listening to a Minor Threat tape Ray had given her. The music was loud and weighted and crushed the echo of Lattimer's grim little story.

Hank walked into her bedroom a while later, wearing jeans and a bulky sweater. Knock-around clothes. His hair was still damp from the shower and hung loose to his shoulders, making him look younger, more relaxed. He switched off her tape player and sank into the rocker near the window. "We need to talk."

She hadn't seen much of him lately—he wasn't home very often in the evenings anymore—and she was sorry his 'We need to talk' was prompted by the feds' visit. "You're not mad, are you? About what happened with those two guys?"

"Them?" Hank laughed. "No way. You handled it just great. I don't think they'll be bugging us again." He rubbed his jaw, growing serious again. "I heard part of that rap he gave you about the diseased schoolteacher. He's wrong, you know. It's not a disease. It's not caused by a virus. It's a mutation, same as the snake Fay found, same as the tricks Ike and Tina do."

She didn't know what to say. She never did when Hank was stoned and slipped into a fevered defense of his theories.

"Jo mutated. Reverend Quickson mutated. So did Ben and Bobby Peters's mom. So have dozens of other people in this town. The creatures that attacked the Joker's Dozen last weekend were also mutants. Maybe people we knew, maybe people who've come here from somewhere else. I've talked to Sammy Loman since he came back, and what he described seeing out there fit the description you gave of what chased you on the county road that night. It fit Fay's description of what was after her and Mona at Obie's. There's a pattern, Kate." He paused; the only sound in the room was the soft creak of the chair as he rocked. "What happened to you and Ray a couple weeks back? The night of the ice storm?"

The question caught her by surprise and her *What?* came a beat too late. Hank's smile was a little crooked; it threw his face out of balance. "I've never seen people act as weird as you two did when he brought you back here that night. I've been thinking that maybe you had started, uh, you know, sleeping together, and that was why you were acting like that. If that's the case, fine, that's your business. You're old enough to know what's what and you don't need lectures from me. But if it's something having to do with all this"—his hands made a lazy circle in the air—"then that's something we should talk about. It concerns all of us."

She didn't say anything. She was staring at her hands.

"Is that a yes? No? A maybe?"

"It's hard to explain."

"It's important, Katie."

Something in his voice—a certain softness, a quietude that was usually lacking, or perhaps a trace of fear—caused her to raise her eyes. Hank had pushed up his left sleeve; now he turned the neck of the floor lamp so that it shone directly on his arm. On the long and thin erratic red ribbon that extended from his elbow to a spot just short of his wrist. It looked like a worm. Or a burn. Or a scab. It was like one of those designs on an IQ test that were supposed to measure imagination or perception, she forgot which, and she could create whatever she wanted out of it.

Instead, she froze up inside, and her mind locked on an image of Ray sinking the machete into the man-thing's shoulder. Then a black fright seized her, shook her, emptied her of everything except the ugly truth of what she was looking at.

Her eyes brimmed with tears. She sank to the floor at his knees, her arms closed around his waist, her cheek pressed against his sweater. She burrowed into the familiar scent of wool, skin, father, as he stroked her hair, rocking and listening and then sharing his secrets as well.

2.

"Hank didn't say what this is about?" Fay asked.

Nash shook his head. "Just that it's important."

"A pontificating powwow, in other words."

She made it sound obscene, he thought, and wondered why Fay always took such personal umbrage over Suffield's theories. "I guess so."

"Shit. I'm really not in the mood." She pushed away from the kitchen table and started clearing the dishes, her dark mood as palpable as her perfume.

They were at her place and had just finished a dinner he'd cooked and which she'd barely touched: chicken in a creamy wine sauce that had taken him an hour to prepare. For the last few weeks, it seemed she'd hardly eaten anything. She was like a fussy child when it came to food, picking at what was on her plate, pushing it around, finally giving most of it to Samson.

Nash scooped Fay's leftovers into the dog's bowl. Samson didn't eat it; he sucked it down and sat back, panting for more. "You're going to be a tub, big boy. Look at that. You're already getting a belly."

From the sink, where she was rinsing off dishes, Fay said, "I really wish you wouldn't give him the leftovers all the time, Scott."

"What's bugging you, anyway?" He spoke to her back, his tone sharper than he intended.

Her voice when she replied was just as barbed. "Something has to be bugging me because I don't feel like doing what you want to do?"

He sensed that another remark from him—from either of them—would hurl the evening into the dark, treacherous waters that had become much too familiar to him during the death throes of his marriage after his daughter had died.

In the past weeks, these moments had become much more frequent. It was as if they were rushing toward the edge of an abyss from which one or the other had so far pulled away from just in time, before saying something that couldn't be taken back. So he didn't bother dignifying her question with an answer. He wiped off the table, helped her stack the dishes in the dishwasher; the silence between them stretched on, an unrelieved desert.

"I think I'll go over to Hank's for a while," he said finally.

She shrugged. "Suit yourself."

Count on it, he thought, and went into the hall for his jacket. Samson followed him and nuzzled his leash, which hung on a hook on the inside of the door. "Not tonight, guy. You keep the lady company."

As he left, Fay was in the living room watching TV—something she rarely did, that she derided as a waste of time, utterly boring, the pursuit of empty minds, and so on. For some reason, the TV business disturbed him as much as the argument they'd barely avoided.

3.

She heard him leave.

She heard the garage door trundle open. Now the Jeep cranked up.

Her fingers tightened over the armrest of the chair, tightened until her knuckles were white and the tendons ached. She felt

as if she were bracing herself against a sudden shift in gravity,
a doubling of G forces. She squeezed her eyes shut as she heard
the Jeep pull out of the driveway.

Now.

Nonono. Not yet. She would give him a minute or so just to
make sure he didn't come back. *I can't wait a minute.* But she
forced herself to sit there. Drew in deep lungfuls of air. Counted
backward slowly from a hundred. Sweat popped out on her
upper lip. She began to hurt all over, in her bones, her blood,
the depths of her soul.

When she was sure she couldn't stand it an instant longer,
when she knew she would plunge into madness if she didn't
move, if she didn't respond to the terrible blackness inside her,
she leaped up and stumbled into the kitchen. She shut the door
so that Samson couldn't follow her and threw open the freezer.
She yanked out a package of liver, tore off the cellophane,
popped it in the microwave to defrost.

One minute.

One long, horrible, endless minute.

She paced, arms clutched at her waist, grateful that Nash had
left, that he didn't see her like this. Tears backed up in her eyes
as the pain, the need, the blackness, deepened.

Her knees felt weak, spongy, insubstantial. She grabbed a
chair, pulled it over to the microwave, sank into it, bit back a
groan. *Hurry, please. Jesus, hurry.*

The fridge hummed in the silence.

The clock ticked.

Branches scratched at the windows.

Then the bell rang and she snatched the liver out of the microwave. It was cool and slippery to the touch, tricky to hold,
a little blob that seemed to pulse in her hands. Blood ran down
the insides of her arms. She licked it off. The taste was so sweet,
she let her tongue slide over the slab of meat, around it, sampling.

She started to bite into it, but a sudden image of what she
looked like just then made her hesitate. *Control,* whispered the
voice of her father.

Eat. Quickly, whispered the other voice, the voice that swept
through her dreams at night like a hot wind.

Control.

She dropped the liver onto a plate. Cut it into small, chewable
pieces, delicate pieces, as if she were preparing a plate of hors
d'oeuvres. Her hands trembled. Her breathing quickened. Sa-

liva bubbled in a corner of her mouth. Tears coursed down her cheeks as she hurried over to the table. She jerked out a chair. Sat down. Stabbed a chunk of the raw meat. Lifted the fork. She shook so badly, she had to steady one hand with the other as she guided the fork toward her mouth.

The smell alone was enough to drive her into a near frenzy. But when her teeth sank into the meat and blood oozed down the back of her throat, her control snapped completely. The fork slipped out of her hand, clattered against the floor, and she grabbed at the bits of meat, stuffing them into her mouth, chewing and swallowing as fast as she could. When the place was empty, she licked at the swirls and pools of blood, licked until the plate was clean, and then her sobs crashed against the silence, sobs of relief, of horror at what she was becoming.

24

The Telling

When Nash arrived at the Suffields', Horn and Ray were already settled in with mugs of hot cocoa near the crackling fire. They asked where Fay was, asked as if she and Nash were now permanently paired in their minds, an inseparable duo, mates on the Ark. He said she wasn't feeling well, but ten minutes later the doorbell rang and it was Fay.

She looked cool and complacent in jeans and a black wool sweater, dark hair gathered at the back of her neck with a colorful scarf. "I decided it'd probably be a good idea if I didn't miss this."

"My favorite opponent," Suffield said with a laugh. "Glad you could make it."

She claimed the seat next to Nash on the couch, her eyes seeking his, telegraphing her apology for what had happened earlier. But he wasn't in a forgiving mood and averted his gaze.

Suffield rubbed his hands together, as eager as a professor who wanted to get on with his lecture before the bell rang. He started to pace as he told them about the visitors he and Katie had had that afternoon. No one was surprised. They all knew about Fielding and Lattimer and the body the two feds had claimed from the morgue after the slaughter at Joker's. Nash suspected that most of the people in town had heard Sammy Loman's version of what had happened at the bar that night. He'd recounted his tale to anyone who would listen.

But none of them had heard the story Katie and Ray told about their experience in the woods on the west side of the lagoon. As they took turns talking, each one picking up where the other had left off, Nash began to feel like a kid at camp, listening to ghost stories under the watchful eye of a full moon. He thought of that high-pitched keening he heard from time to time at night, echo-

ing across the dark silence of the lagoon. He thought of were-
wolves, vampires, things that went bump in the night. That was
easy to laugh off; this was not.

Horn wanted to know what had prompted their excursion.
Ray replied that Katie should really explain that part. But she
was evidently uncomfortable about it and looked at Suffield for
support.

He shook his head. "It's your ball game, kiddo. You know
more about it than I do."

She stared at her hands, fingers curling against her thighs.
She seemed uncertain about where to start until Suffield prodded
her, then she blurted out a convoluted story that wandered,
looped back on itself, dead-ended. Scents she tracked as though
they were footprints, scents that were often accompanied by
mental images: Ben on the deck of the inn during the final moments of his life and what she had seen.

As incredible as it would have sounded to Nash two months
ago, it was now no more bizarre than snakes with feet, butterflies in ground hives, people covered in crusted skin, or his
brother mowing down twenty-nine people and then turning the
gun on himself. For the first time since he'd gotten to Lagoon,
he was forced to *name* what had happened to Ben. That he had
mutated.

For weeks, he'd referred to it as a *change*, a vague term that
meant virtually anything. To tag it beyond that would have given
it too much power. But now Ben was one of many, a piece in a
larger puzzle, no longer isolated in Nash's mind as a freak, an
abomination.

The obvious questions—what had caused it, if it could be
prevented from happening in others, why it was happening in
Lagoon—were what Suffield attempted to answer.

"We've talked about some of this before, about whether these
human mutations are caused by a virus or are part of the same
design we've seen in the plant and animal mutations. From what
the feds say, they believe it's a virus. A disease. I think they
were looking for answers near Meadow Creek, probably trying
to find some correlation between the plant and animal mutations
and the human ones. When we saw them, they were working in
a sterile environment within the moon buggies; they apparently
thought the virus was extremely contagious. Obviously they
don't think that anymore, or they wouldn't be here in town.
Personally, I think the virus theory is way off the mark—"

"Hank, we know what your theories are," Fay said.

He refused to be rankled. "Now I'm going to prove them. Kate, could you get Turner and the other stuff I'll need?"

She returned a few minutes later with a paper bag and a cage, which she set on the coffee table. Inside the cage was a small yellow and orange canary, Ike and Tina's offspring. From the bag, Suffield removed a glass jar partially filled with sugar cubes. He spun off the lid, covered the top with clear plastic, and secured it with tape around the edges.

Several months back, he explained, he'd isolated Tina from Ike to teach her a particular trick. Within a few weeks, he discovered that Ike had learned the trick as well even though he had never seen Tina do it. On a hunch, he'd checked with breeders in different parts of the state and found that some of their birds were also able to perform the maneuver.

"Turner's now about three weeks old. He's never seen either of the canaries do the trick, and yet he's able to duplicate it."

Fay's patronizing smile was like that of a parent whose child had said something amusing—and patently ridiculous. "C'mon, Hank. Learned abilities can't be passed on genetically."

"It's never been proven using old paradigms. But I think what we've all been experiencing here in Lagoon is the emergence of something that's going to make our old ideas about science obsolete."

Suffield removed Turner from the cage and put him down near the jar of sugar cubes. He sang sweetly, his little throat throbbing, and hopped toward the jar. He pecked at the side, then fluttered his wings and flew toward Katie. He landed on her head; she gently disengaged him and set him on the table again.

"He doesn't get it," she said.

"Give him a few minutes."

Now Turner hopped back to the jar, pecking furiously at the sides. He suddenly lifted up from the table and flapped around above the jar. He touched down on the plastic, testing it, flew up again, then hovered, pecking at the plastic. Nash realized the holes he made weren't random; they created a specific pattern. When he finally landed on the plastic, his claws fit perfectly into the openings.

Turner jerked up his left foot, right, left and right, over and over again until the plastic ripped. He tore pieces away from the jar, shredding one strip after another until the hole was big enough to peer into. But since it was upright, he still couldn't reach the cubes, so he tipped the jar over. He tried to get at the cubes and failed. Now he landed on the side of the jar and rolled it, a lumberjack riding a fallen log. The cubes slid closer and closer to the opening. He finally stopped, stuck his head through one of the holes, and pecked at the nearest cube.

"He was born knowing how to do that?" Horn exclaimed.

"Yeah."

Suffield pulled a legal pad and pen from the paper bag and drew a couple of squiggles. He enclosed them in a dome, then sketched half a dozen curved lines on either side that looked like parentheses within parentheses. He turned the pad around so they could all see.

"I'm not much of an artist, but let's say this thing in the dome here is Tina. She has a field of energy around her; I call it an echo. Everything has one: stones, trees, cells, nervous systems, animals, man." He tapped the parenthesis outside the dome. "Tina's 'echo' can be heard by other canaries. In a sense, they tune into it like we'd tune into a radio or a TV station."

Just as an electrical impulse carried voices and music from the station, so did these echoes carry information. "When I taught Tina to get at the cubes in the sealed jar, that information became part of her energy field and, in a larger sense, part of the echo of all canaries. By tuning into the field, other canaries learned the trick. As more canaries master it, the trick will become easier and easier to learn until this particular ability is simply something all canaries will be born knowing how to do.

"It becomes part of the canary echo, part of what they inherit. Even before Turner had hatched, his particular echo had tuned into that of his parents' and drew on the knowledge, coding it into his genes."

Fay didn't look quite as skeptical now. "Wouldn't this sort of thing take generations to occur?"

"It depends. I think there's an energy vortex or something in Lagoon that accelerates the mutations. I don't have any proof of it, but maybe the cold line in the meadow marks the place where the energy starts or ends. Maybe that's why Scott's photos of the buildings have that ghost image around them."

Suffield set the pen down and crossed his legs Indian style. For a moment here in the firelight, he could have been a shaman imparting wisdom for members of his tribe, the diviner, the interpreter of the events, the man who placed their lives into perspective within the cosmos.

"Is there any precedence for this?" Nash asked. "For what Turner learned?"

"A lot of incidents like this have been observed, but hardly any have been systematically documented. The one that comes to mind involved blue tit birds in Europe."

In 1921, a blue tit bird in Southampton, England, was observed pecking open a milk bottle that had been delivered to someone's house and drinking about two inches of milk inside. Between 1930 and 1947, the habit was recorded among eleven species of tits, and had spread all over the United Kingdom, as well as to Sweden, Denmark, and Holland.

At first, scientists believed the habit had been spread through imitation. But that was ruled out because the blue tit didn't travel more than a few miles from its breeding places. It also didn't explain what happened in Holland. During the war, milk bottles practically vanished from that country. And yet attacks on them resumed in the late forties, when bottles became common again, even though it was unlikely that any blue tits that'd learned the habit before the war had survived.

"In other words, it was some sort of rapid evolutionary change in response to man's human activity. It seems that habits acquired by some animals can make it easier for other similar animals to attain the same habits, despite there being no known communication between them."

"Because of the echoes?" Ray asked.

"And because habits strengthen an echo. The more animals or people or whatever that acquire the habit, the stronger its echo grows."

A simple example existed in competitive running. Since 1954, when Roger Bannister first broke through the four-minute-mile "barrier," it had gotten easier for people to do, and runners had been cutting the time by seconds ever since. The same could be said for the number of women over forty now having kids for the first time. Once a few famous women had done it, other women realized it wasn't the big deal the medical establishment had said it was, and that removed the barriers.

"In the same way, the mutations among human beings that we've seen are part of an echo effect. As soon as there was *one* mutation, it was inevitable there would be more as echo fields tuned in on the new information and used it. Again, as the numbers of mutants grow, the echo fields strengthen and the faster the mutations occur. In other words, what we're dealing with is rapid evolutionary change."

"But it's not happening all over," Horn said.

"Not yet. It's focused in Lagoon and in a few other small

towns, like the ones the CDC guy mentioned to Fay. We know those places are experiencing unusual weather, that there've been mutations, an acceleration in violent crimes and so on. And I'm betting they've also got cold lines that mark the beginning or end of an energy vortex. *This* is Nature's experiment. If it doesn't work, it self-destructs somehow and vanishes just as fast as the dinosaurs did. And if it works . . ." His voice trailed off. "I don't know. I don't know what happens if it works because I don't know what the hell the point of the experiment is."

"Maybe Nature is just getting even," said Ray.

"Yeah, maybe." Suffield started pacing again. "This could be her reaction to what man has done to her—the pollution, the depletion of the ozone, the razing of rain forests, the extinction of her animals . . ." He smiled sadly. "She's got a long memory and she's been pretty damn patient for a lot of years. It's possible her final goal is just to eliminate man entirely."

"By making her look like those . . . those things in the woods?" Katie exclaimed.

"Those mutants aren't necessarily in their final form. The threads Fay found on the body Fielding and Lattimer took from the morgue indicate there's another stage to this."

Fay blanched. "Then you're saying there's no way to stop any of it. That we're all going to mutate."

"There may be some people who don't mutate at all or some who mutate in different ways. But the point, Fay, is that we don't control it. Nature does."

Her eyes turned the color of marble, and when she spoke, the fierceness in her voice resounded with utter clarity in the room. It was as though Suffield's conclusions offended Fay at the most basic level.

"No. You're wrong. It's a disease caused by a virus, Hank. It *behaves* like a virus. It *infects* like a virus. There are specific symptoms and parameters to this thing. It's a new disease, something that seemed to appear suddenly, just like AIDS, but which has probably lain dormant for a long time in certain segments of the population. The plant and animal mutations don't have anything to do with what's happening to human beings. That's—"

"Separate?" Suffield's sardonic smile altered the shape of his mouth. "C'mon. Man doesn't exist in a vacuum. We're *part* of Nature, not separate from it. As for the symptoms, they aren't uniformly consistent in everyone. Some people don't develop a sensitivity to bright sunlight or a need for iron until the rash has already appeared. Others get those symptoms first, and still others might never develop them or could experience things your parameters didn't include, Fay, like Katie's sense of smell. Maybe that's a symptom also.''

"And why doesn't everyone become violent or aggressive? Why doesn't everyone hear the voices Jo talked about? There's an element of individualism to all this that has to do with the different ways people react to things like extreme hunger, an overwhelming need for sex, or weird shit growing on their skin. Ben reacted with violence. Quickson reacted by trying to act out repressed sexual urges. Jo reacted by turning against the person she was jealous of—Katie. Others just go crazy or kill themselves or whatever. Again, we're part of an experiment.''

For every person who reacted in a perverse way, you had others who were fighting it quietly, Suffield continued. They hadn't gone to doctors, hadn't walked out on their families, hadn't killed anyone.

"Since when have you had such extensive contact with people who're infected, Hank?'' asked Fay.

Her sarcasm failed to get a rise out of him. "It's a matter of listening. This is a funny town, Fay. You'd be surprised how many people are reluctant to talk to the county physician because they don't want anything on their records that might be used against them. We're not the only ones who've known about the feds or who've pieced together a picture of what's happening. And if we're going to come through this thing with our humanity intact, we need to ban together just like the deviants that slaughtered everyone at Joker's.''

"That's a real nice sixties rap, Hank. Free love, communes, drugs for everyone. It didn't work then and it won't work now, especially against a disease.''

"Personally, I'd like to hear what Hank's got in mind,'' said Horn.

When Nash and the others agreed, Fay looked as though she didn't know whether to leave, scream, or just sit back and listen. In the end, she stayed, a reluctant observer who listened to what Suffield had in mind but contributed nothing unless she was asked.

According to Suffield, there were about three dozen "quiet fighters'' in Lagoon who were in various stages of the mutation. They had created a loose network among themselves that served as a support group. They purchased red meats wholesale from a local farmer, supplied cortisone cream for those in the group

who developed skin lesions, had a hot line that was manned
twenty-four hours a day by one or more members, and donated
their own funds to families where the primary breadwinner was
too deformed to work.

But the group was getting to the point where it needed outside
help. There were some people for whom red meat no longer
satisfied the increased need for iron or the deep, debilitating
hunger Jo had experienced. Suffield believed they might benefit
from blood transfusions.

Three of the women, including one in her sixties who'd gone
through menopause more than fifteen years ago, were pregnant.
For obvious reasons, they wanted to terminate the pregnancies.
But because of the skin lesions, they couldn't go to a clinic.

"And those are just the immediate problems." Suffield's eyes
fixed on Fay, the message implicit.

"Hank, I may run the clinic, but I don't control it. I have
people to answer to. There are government and county regulations that—"

"Fuck regulations. I'm asking for your help, Fay."

She raked her fingers back through her hair, her face no longer
seized up with anger and indignation. "I don't know. I've got
to think about it."

Suffield quietly ticked off a list of names that included the
Castletons, Sammy Loman's wife, the Peters boy and his father,
the local pharmacist, the woman who owned Prudy's Place, one
of the librarians, several employees at Hartwell—in short, people Fay had known since she'd moved here. And then, as though
that weren't enough, he said, "And you can add me to the list."

The silence deafened for the moment it lasted. "And me,"
Ray said quietly.

"Me, too," said Horn.

Emotions flitted across Fay's face with the rapidity of light,
then seemed to dive into the shadows around her mouth. "I've
got to think about it." With that, she shrugged on her jacket,
picked up her purse, and left.

Nash lay alone in the darkness of his room at the inn, Fay's
face as bright and clear in his mind as a blind man's memory of
the sun.

A face that's going to change.

He wasn't sure when the suspicion had first rooted in him.
Maybe it was the morning of her extraordinary run. Perhaps it
was earlier, the first time they'd made love and the witch scent

had swept over him, as powerful as some ancient curse. But tonight, when Suffield, Ray, and Horn had included themselves in the list of victims, he had known for sure that Fay was also changing.

Mutating, Nash. Say the word. Mu-ta-ting.

It explained her violent reaction to Suffield's theories. In her mind, it meant she had no control over what was happening to her. It nullified her abilities as a physician. *You knew and chose not to see it, just like with Ben.*

He pressed the heels of his hands against his eyes, trying not to see the prints he'd developed of the corpse Fielding and Lattimer had claimed from the morgue. But the images marched through him with impunity, and, God help him, he didn't know if he loved Fay enough to love her still when she was no longer human.

To touch that skin . . .

Make love to her . . .

I can't. . . .

He rolled out of bed and threw open the window. The cold wind swept around him, a blessing, an anodyne that soothed his burning cheeks, his eyes. It blew across the lagoon, making a hollow, plaintive sound. As he listened, it filled him with nostalgia for something he couldn't name, for the life he had lost when his daughter had died, for the years of knowing Ben that death had stolen from him, perhaps even a yearning for something he might never experience: a life with Fay.

He watched the moon, perched low in the western sky, a sliver of gold that crowned the tops of trees like a Christmas ornament. He wanted to see it move, needed to see its solitary slide across the black sky toward dawn so that he would know time hadn't stalled, that his own life possessed a forward thrust that would catapult him into a safer future.

You've got the answers you came for. It's time to split.

He listened for the eerie keening, the music of the mutants. But there was only the mournful bay of the wind, and beyond it, a silence deeper than death.

25

Turning Point

1.

At seven-thirty on the morning of October 20, the sky was overcast, the temperature in Lagoon stood at fifteen degrees, and there were six inches of snow on the ground. Forty minutes later, the sun was summer bright, it was a balmy seventy degrees, and the snow was melting faster than it had come down the night before. For the rest of that day and for the next three, the temperature climbed steadily upward until, on the twenty-fifth, the mercury hit ninety-four.

The inside of the Pinto that afternoon was like a furnace. Katie had to wrap a scarf around the steering wheel before she left the school parking lot so she could touch it long enough to drive. The air-conditioning in the car didn't work and even with the windows down the heat was oppressive. As she drove toward Bosque Garage, through the sweltering streets and the rivers of red mud the melting snow had left behind, a part of her longed for the cold again.

She saw a film crew from CNN talking to passing pedestrians in front of the city park: another night that Lagoon's weather would make national news. At the garage, a van from an Atlanta TV station was parked in front of one of the work stalls, steam billowing from its open hood. The driver, who looked hassled and hot, stood off to the side with Ray's father. As Katie approached, she heard him say, "I don't care what it costs. I just need the damn thing fixed by this evening."

"We'll do what we can, sir," Mr. Bosque replied.

The man thanked him profusely and hurried off.

"Is Ray around, Mr. Bosque?" Katie asked.

He looked up from his clipboard, his dark eyes like Ray's. But that was where the resemblance between them stopped.

"Haven't seen him, kid. Not for a few days. You'll probably find him at his place."

"Okay, thanks."

She started to turn away, but he said, "Hey, kid."

"The name's Katie."

Bosque's smile seemed to cut the lower part of his face off from the rest of it. "Katie. Right. Suffield's girl. Seeing how your old man's such a bright guy, that probably means you're pretty bright yourself. So what the hell're you doing with a loser like Ray?"

He stepped closer to her as he spoke. His scent was thick and ugly, easy to track, and it didn't take her long to understand why Ray hadn't been around: his father had fired him. "*You're* the loser," she snapped, and walked quickly back to the Pinto.

She hadn't seen Ray or heard from him in a week, since that night at the house when Fay had left in a huff. Even Hank, who'd been working with him in the group, hadn't been in touch with him. She was afraid that when she got to his place his Firebird would be gone and his apartment would be as vacant as the day he moved in.

But the Firebird was in its usual spot in front of the building. It was parked at a weird angle, one of the wheels up over the curb. He'd been in a big hurry. The thought alarmed her and she raced up the walk and into the building. She took the stairs two at a time and was nearly out of breath when she reached the third floor.

Heat beat against the only window on the landing, baking the stale, humid air. She rang the bell and pounded on the door, but he didn't answer. "Ray? It's me. Katie." She jiggled the knob, which was locked, then remembered he had given her a key to the back door. She dug it out of her purse as she rounded the corner into the tiny nook, slipped it into the dead-bolt lock, turned it.

The door yawned open into a cool, eerie twilight. He'd drawn all the blinds and had the air conditioner on low enough to frost the windows. She slipped quietly past the old washing machine and the stained sink and stopped in the kitchen doorway.

The only light was that which seeped through the slats of the blinds. But it was enough to see the jars, plates, and cellophane wrappers that littered the counter. A kitchen drawer had been overturned and utensils were scattered across the wooden floor. Several clay pots of geraniums that had once sat in the kitchen window, lapping up sunlight, had been squashed into clumps of black earth and torn petals near the refrigerator door. The steady *drip drip drip* from the faucet and Ray's ragged breaths seemed to echo.

He was hunched over a stool at the tiny table, his back to her. "Ray?"

"Go away, Katie. Please." His voice was soft and hoarse, and he smelled of pain, a raw, uncontained pain that flashed around her like neon. "Just go away."

"What's wrong?" She stepped closer to him, wanting desperately to touch him, but the pain brushed up against her. It was like a mild electrical shock, startling her more than it hurt her. "What's going on?"

He shifted on the stool now, turning slowly, like an old man. Despite the dim light, she could see the deep hollows in his cheeks, the dark circles under his eyes, and the crud that was slowly claiming the side of his neck. Tiny white hairs stuck out of it. His shirt was stained with blood. He clutched the gnawed remains of a steak bone in his hand; blood pooled in the plate it had been sitting on.

"Get. Out. I don't want to hurt you." The words slapped the air. Then Ray's face seemed to cave in and he began to weep. The steak bone slipped from his hand and clattered against the plate. He pressed his hands to his face, his shoulders shuddering with silent sobs, the smell of pain oozing from the pores of his skin like a thick oil.

She rushed over to him, holding him, whispering to him, wincing as his pain melted through her bones, her blood, becoming her pain. It delivered her into the black, solitary clutches of the world where his hunger had driven him, a place of utter bleakness and despair. She helped him off the stool and to the couch in the front room.

He didn't protest, didn't tell her to leave, didn't fight her. He sank into the cushions, trembling with the violence of his need, his haunted eyes following her as she rushed back into the kitchen and rifled through the freezer and the fridge, looking for more meat.

"It's all gone. I ate all of it. Raw. I ate it raw." His voice broke beneath the weight of his shame, his humiliation, his fear. "And I'm still hungry."

Katie grabbed a soiled towel from the counter, ran it under the faucet, hurried back to him. She cleaned his face and hands, as though he were a small child who'd soiled himself. "Leave, Katie. I don't want to hurt you. Please leave."

"You're not going to hurt me. That'd make you like them, and you aren't like them. Got that?" She took hold of his chin, forcing him to look at her. "You aren't like them."

The fierceness in her voice almost made him smile. "You don't understand. . . ."

"I'm going to Kroger's for meat. I'll be right back."

"No." He shook his head. "The . . . the meat doesn't do anything now. It's beyond that, it's—"

He clutched himself at the waist as a pain tore through him, then stumbled to his feet and into the kitchen, the pain blinding him, deafening him to everything but his need. He clawed through the freezer, tossing out ice trays, plastic containers, ripping open packages of food wrapped in foil. His groans were thick and rabid, and the smell of his pain saturated the air, suffocating her. Katie grabbed a knife from the sink, pressed the blade to her forearm, and slashed open the skin.

She shouted at him, and he spun, eyes wild, breath slapping the air like he'd been running. He looked at her, at the blood bubbling from the wound, at her again, and something of the old Ray swept across his ravaged face. "Jesus. No. Get away from me."

He backed into the open fridge door and it banged against the wall, knocking out a bottle of mayonnaise that burst when it struck the floor. Katie moved toward him, her bleeding arm extended, an offering to calm an enraged animal. His face glistened with sweat. His eyes widened. He made soft, pathetic sounds that were part whimpers, part gasps, then his hands jerked up, grasping her arm at the wrist, the elbow. He crushed his mouth against the wound and sucked.

2.

The air conditioner in Oliver's office didn't work, and the ceiling fan did little more than stir the hot, humid air that wafted through the open windows. It hurt to breathe. To move. To reach for the can of Coke on his desk that was practically floating in a pool of its own sweat. He sipped; it was warm and disgustingly sweet. He dropped it in the trash can and wished he was a million miles from Lagoon. Anywhere would do. Alaska. A beach in the Caribbean. Hell, he'd settle for a trip to Atlanta.

His phone rang, but he ignored it.

"Hey, mate."

Oliver swiveled his chair around. The fruitcake looked like

he'd dressed himself—his checkered shirt clashed with his baggy striped pants, and he wore two different socks. "Hey yourself, Harness."

He shuffled into the office and pulled his paycheck out of his shirt pocket. "Last one, mate. Mother and I go the week to come."

"To Arizona, right?"

"Air-zona, uh-huh. You best to go, too, mate. Before the hard cold, the end."

Oliver jerked a thumb toward the window. "No hard cold out there today, Harness."

He jammed his hands in his pockets and rocked onto the balls of his feet, back onto the heels, forward and back, a human pendulum. A patina seemed to glaze his soft gray eyes as they narrowed to slits, their focus turning inward to some secret place where he read the universe like a deck of cards.

Despite Oliver's best efforts to dismiss the fruitcake's riddles, his insides tightened like a spring, a coil, a clock that ticked too fast. His fingers dug into the armrests of his chair. The air around him suddenly seemed hotter, thicker, a grumous clot of something that stuck to his cheeks, his eyelids, his mouth.

Harness's voice possessed an erratic cadence, like the sound of the sea during a storm. "After the saints march in, the cold goes hard, the fires burn, and that begins the end, friend, the end." Tears spilled out of his eyes and tracked down his cheeks as he fixed his gaze on Oliver. "Believe, Lew. Flee. Quick. Quick. You're my friend." Then he touched an ice-cold hand to Oliver's, squeezing tightly. "A friend who hurts. A friend in pain. Remember Ben. Remember Joe. Remember, Lew, remember."

He left so fast, he nearly collided with Moses, who side-stepped to avoid him and stared after him with a wry smile on his face. "What the hell was bozo babbling about *this* time?"

The inside of Oliver's mouth was so dry, it was difficult to form words. "Damned if I know."

After the saints march in . . .

Moses picked up the spittoon on Oliver's desk and spat a wad of tobacco into it. "You on strike or what?"

"Strike?"

"What's with you, man?" Moses rapped his knuckles against the phone. "Your good buddy the colonel just called, and when he couldn't get through to you, he called me. He wants you over at Prudy's Place pronto."

Fielding and his sidekick were nothing but trouble. "He wants to talk to me, he can come over here."

"It sounded important, Lew." Moses rubbed his square, stubbled jaw. "Real important. C'mon, man, I'll go with you."

The fires burn . . .

"Lew?"

That begins the end . . .

The end of what?

"Earth to Lew."

"Yeah, yeah, I heard you. Let's go. You drive."

When Oliver was a kid, Prudy's Place was a local brothel called Hannah's. His old man, who'd never been big on explanations of any kind, had brought him here on his sixteenth birthday, told him to have fun, and left. He spent the night in the arms of a woman ten years older than he who introduced him to every sexual position known to man and then some, and with whom he was madly in love for about two days.

The place had changed a lot in the years since. The red brocade curtains had been replaced with sensible Levolors; the expensive Persian throw rugs had given way to the natural hardwood floors; the formal drawing room was now a dining room. The Steinway piano that had sat near the far window, and which Hannah had played with such haunting beauty, had been auctioned off with the antiques when she'd died. A homey comfort had displaced the grandeur.

Lattimer was waiting in the lobby for them. Gone were his brown leather jacket and jeans. He wore navy-blue pants and a short-sleeve shirt with a tie and looked like a traveling salesman. "The colonel's upstairs with the mayor and the county commissioners, gentlemen. I'll take you up there."

The two men exchanged a glance, and Oliver knew Moses was thinking the same thing he was. The fact that Fielding had phoned him—and not the mayor or one of the commissioners—meant the feds were calling the shots. And that could only mean trouble.

Big trouble.

3.

Fay had drawn the blinds on her office window, turned the air conditioner as low as it would go, and locked the door. *A junkie in hiding.* She tried to laugh at the thought, but couldn't. It was too close to the truth.

The colder air in here assuaged the painful throb in her temple and took the edge off her hunger. Her hands didn't even tremble as she laid out the syringe and the needle, still in their packaging, the alcohol swab, and a vial from the pint-sized fridge against the wall. She felt a certain satisfaction at the precise way she lined up the items on the counter, just as she'd done six hours ago at home. *And six hours before that and before that and . . .* It provided her with a sense of continuity, the illusion of control.

She broke open the wrapping, filled the syringe, swabbed her upper arm, and injected the iron. Four shots a day for seven days: she hadn't felt even a glimmer of that deep, gnawing hunger since the night she and Nash argued. She hadn't touched a piece of meat since then, either. She was afraid that if she did, it would stir the great slumbering beast of the hunger, and this time it would crush her.

But the iron supplements had done nothing to prevent the appearance of the rash. The first spot had shown up the same day she started the iron shots, a tiny patch on her shoulder. It had spread at an alarming rate, almost as if the deplorable heat had accelerated it, and now covered most of her back. The cortisone cream had proven ineffective against it. So had everything else she'd tried.

Out of desperation she'd made an appointment with a dermatologist she knew in Atlanta and, three days ago, had left Lagoon before sunrise to make the three-hour drive. But halfway there she'd started feeling too ill and weak to continue. It got progressively worse as she drove back, and by the time she reached the house, her bones felt like foam rubber, her vision was blurred, and she had a fever of a hundred and three.

But within an hour of her return, the symptoms were gone.

She refused to dwell on what it meant, but she hadn't left Lagoon since.

"Fay?" Mona's voice at her door sent a spurt of panic through her.

"Just a second. I'm on the phone." She quickly wrapped up the spent syringe, needle, and vial, stuck them in her purse to dispose of later, and straightened her clothes. "Right, I'll call you back later, Mom," she said loudly, as though she were on the phone.

Had she forgotten anything? Did she look guilty? Ill? Did Mona suspect?

Stop it. Unlock the door. Smile. You're fine now. The hunger's gone. Nothing to worry about.

When she opened the door, Mona apologized for the interruption and gestured at Katie Suffield, who stood next to her. "She insisted on talking to you, Fay. I'll ask Sumo to take your next patient."

"Okay, thanks. C'mon in, Katie."

She stepped into the office but didn't sit down. Her blond hair was bundled up in back, damp strands curling at the sides of her face, her cheeks flushed from the heat. Fay noticed the bandage on her left forearm.

"So what's the problem?"

"Ray needs a transfusion."

She wasn't Suffield's daughter by blood, Fay thought, but she certainly was in temperament. "I told your dad I can't help in that way, Katie. I'll be glad to take a look at Ray, but—"

"No, you don't understand." The blue of her eyes blazed with sudden intensity. "He *needs* blood. If he doesn't get it, he's going to become like . . . like them. Like the others."

"Look, I'm sure it's not as bad as you think. Tell him to come over to the clinic later this afternoon and—"

"He can't stand the heat. Or the light. The light hurts . . ." She stopped. Her eyes flickered to the drawn blinds, to the air-conditioning unit in the window, pumping furiously to keep the room cool, and back to Fay's face. She leaned into the edge of the desk, her nostrils flaring like a horse's on a cold morning as she sniffed at the air, *sniffed*, for God's sakes. Fay pushed away from her, but Katie's words leaped at her.

"You're changing. You know what the hunger's like, you *know*, you're taking shots for it . . ." She grabbed Fay's arm. "You've *got* to help Ray. And Hank. And the others." Her voice had risen to a fever pitch. "Why can't you help them if you're helping yourself? Why not?"

Fay yanked her arm free of Katie's grasp. "I think you'd better just calm down and—"

"*No!*" she screamed, backing toward the door. "It's not fair! You're a coward, you're nothing but a coward. . . ." She threw open the door and ran into the hall.

Fay just stood there, numb with anger, shame, humiliation, blinking rapidly against the light that flooded into the room. Tears sprang into her eyes. She sought refuge behind her hands, in the familiarity of her own skin, the smell of her palms, the texture of her fingers. She tried to find the safe, white space inside herself, that harbor, that continent, but she no longer knew the way there.

She thought of Nash, whom she hadn't seen since she'd stormed out of the Suffields' that night, and of Horn, who'd been avoiding her, and of Ray and the others who needed something only she could give them. The reality of her hypocrisy, of her isolation from herself and the people she cared about, was suddenly more than she could bear. Something broke inside her. She felt it like a physical pain, a swift, clean break in the center of her soul. Her hand fluttered to her mouth, stifling a sob, and she pushed away quickly from her desk to shut the door when her phone rang.

It was one of the nurses at the front desk, informing her she had a visitor. "Schedule whoever it is for later. I've got patients to see."

"I think that's going to be a little difficult, Dr. Donovan," the nurse said quietly. "The gentleman says he's Lance Blair, from the CDC."

"Here?"

"Yes."

Not now, please, not now. Not Blair.

But she heard herself say, "All right. Send him back."

4.

The mayor, Fielding, and the county commissioners were seated around a conference table. They looked, Oliver thought, like members of a tribunal, a jury of priests and high lords who were about to pass sentence. The mayor, a short butterball of a man, was usually as jovial as Humpty Dumpty before he fell off the wall. But he was oddly subdued today and spoke in a slow, measured voice.

"Colonel Fielding, as you know, has been working closely with the Center for Disease Control, monitoring the, uh, situation here in Lagoon. Certain facts have come to their attention, which they've shared with the commissioners and me. We feel it's necessary to implement something that's going to put a strain on your department, Lew. But we've allocated emergency funds you're free to use to hire additional personnel. Also, the colonel has offered us two dozen of his men, who would be under your authority, to be utilized in whatever way you think would be most effective.'' The mayor smiled at Fielding, acknowledging the debt, and was about to continue when Oliver interrupted him.

''Just what is it that's going to be implemented?''

''A quarantine,'' said Jokerzy, Joker's old man. ''Starting at six A.M. tomorrow.''

''A quarantine?'' Moses's tongue curled around the word as though it were a piece of food he'd never tasted before. ''I don't understand.''

''For everyone's safety,'' said Fielding. ''We need to find out what we're dealing with here.''

The remark irked Oliver because it told him exactly nothing. ''I thought that was the reason you people removed the body from the morgue.''

''That autopsy only raised more questions, Captain,'' said Fielding. ''We still don't know how this disease is transmitted or how contagious it is. And we don't know why it seems to be confined to only a handful of communities like Lagoon.''

Prickles of fear chilled the back of Oliver's neck. ''So you've determined it *is* a disease?''

''No one's determined anything for sure,'' said Lattimer. ''All we have are theories, suppositions. Right now, we suspect it's caused by a virus, and Hartwell Research is trying to isolate it so that a drug can be developed to arrest it.''

To the tune of a tidy sum, no doubt. ''You going to quarantine the whole county or just the town?''

''For now, the quarantine area will cover the town and everything around it within ten miles. Hartwell employees who aren't infected will be issued special badges, so they can still go back and forth to work. Wholesalers who supply stores in town will be permitted to make deliveries at several specified areas. But the unloading and disbursement of goods will be handled by you and your men, Captain. The town will be off limits to everyone else, including the press.''

If the disease was contagious enough to impose a quarantine, Oliver thought, then why let anyone in or out at all? When he asked, Fielding was the one who replied, confirming Oliver's suspicion that the colonel was the head honcho. The mayor and his boys were nothing but figureheads.

''The quarantine is being imposed for a variety of reasons, Captain. Right now, we don't think this thing is spread by casual contact or that the virus is airborne. So there's no reason not to allow the free transport of things like food and supplies.''

"Then why impose a quarantine at all?"

No one seemed particularly eager to answer the question, but Fielding finally said, "It's what the CDC believes is the best course of action right now."

Translation: There're some things we can't tell you, Lew. Dem's da breaks, Lew.

"How're you going to determine which Hartwell employees are infected?"

Fielding started to reply again, but Oliver snapped, "If you don't mind, I'd like to hear it from the mayor."

"We're going to, uh, test them." The mayor had paled. He was beginning to look like Humpty Dumpty after the fall. "And all county employees as well. It'll take a few days."

"Test them how?"

"Examine them. With the CDC's help. We, uh, need an accurate count of just how many people have contracted this thing."

Then what, guys? And just what the hell are you not telling?

The questions hung in a corner of his mind, as bright as a remembered face with no name.

26

Preparations

1.

The real-estate woman wandered through the inn's downstairs rooms, nodding to herself, touching things, jotting notes. She couldn't have been more than forty, yet there was something distinctly matronly about her, as though she'd been born to tailored suits, lace blouses, and sensible shoes. Now and then she murmured, "Uh-huh, uh-huh," which Nash supposed meant that something had met with her expectations. But he didn't know if it was good or bad. Didn't much care, either. All he wanted to do was get the property listed.

Finally, when they were on the third floor, she said, "I have to be honest with you, Mr. Nash. I don't think we'll get any local takers on the inn, what with the scandal and all. But I have clients in the Carolinas who're always looking for investments, and this *is* lakefront property, after all."

That word, *scandal*, almost made him laugh. It was so Victorian. It made it sound like the inn was known for orgies and debauchery rather than as a site where ten murders had occurred.

She wanted to know his asking price and balked when he told her. "That's *much* too low. My feeling is that you should always ask high and in your mind set a rock-bottom price you'll accept." She named a figure that smacked of highway robbery and he shook his head. They tossed the issue around and settled on a compromise. She handed him a listing form, which he glanced over and signed.

"If you can sell the place in ninety days, it'll mean an additional two percent on your commission," he said as they went back downstairs.

Her eyes lit up, and she assured him ninety days should be more than enough time. Did he, by the way, want to sell it

262

furnished? Partially furnished? Empty? As it was, he replied, except for some of his brother's personal things. Fine, so much the better.

Nash walked her outside into the humid dusk. The sky to the east had darkened to streaks of plum, of crimson, and a few early stars were visible. To the west, the sun's last light burned level with the trees, as though they were on fire. The deep, fructuous scent of the earth suffused the air, mingling with the fragrance of pine, a throwback to summer.

"I heard we're going to be on national news tonight or tomorrow night," the real-estate woman remarked.

"Again?" It would be the fourth night running. "Which network this time?"

"CNN. One of their people was in my office today asking about the housing market. He said they've got crews in a couple other areas across the country that're experiencing real unusual weather for this time of year."

We're an experiment . . . Suffield's voice haunted him.

". . . guess it'll be a roundup of weather weirdness," she finished with a small laugh. He thought it held a trace of unease. "I'll be in touch, Mr. Nash." She scooted into her Cadillac, waved, and was gone.

He stood in the fading light, listening to the summerlike stillness. It crackled with an undercurrent of noises: the cries of crickets, the melancholy warbles of unidentified birds, the restless chatter of squirrels, the buzz of an occasional mosquito. But no keening. He hadn't heard that shrill, eerie sound since the weather had turned hot.

But more than once these last few nights, he'd bolted awake to what sounded like the final, lingering note of that hideous sound and had lain motionless in the black pitch of his fear, waiting for it to repeat itself. It never did. But the longer he waited for it, the more aware he became of a deep moiling within the heart of Lagoon, as if the town were twisting and screaming to escape its own nightmare. And invariably, Suffield's words floated through him, prophetic or mad, he didn't know which.

And it didn't matter. The sooner he got the hell out, the better. He didn't belong here. He had stepped into the life his brother had vacated, zipped himself up inside it, and deluded himself into believing it was his. But it wasn't. It never would be. Nothing would change that.

As he started back toward the inn, he heard a car tearing up

Hawthorne. It whisked around the curve of trees and screeched to a halt in the driveway, tires spewing mud and pebbles. Fay's Jetta. She hopped out and sprinted toward him, her hair loose, frizzy with humidity, the hem of her flowered skirt flapping at her knees.

He hadn't seen her since the night at the Suffields', only a week ago. But it might as well have been a month. Or a year. He had nothing to say to her that hadn't already been said during one lengthy phone conversation three days ago. A call he had made and which she had ended.

She stopped less than a foot from him and didn't speak for a beat or two, as though shyness had seized her, emptied her. In the dusky light, her face was a pale, luminous lantern. "I need your help, Nash."

"That's a switch." A faint tendril of the witch scent reached out for him, curled around him, through him, softening him. He stepped back. "Don't."

She looked as if he'd slapped her; the tendril vanished. She clutched her arms to her waist, as if she were holding the scent inside herself, and didn't move any closer. "As of six tomorrow morning, Lagoon is going to be under quarantine," she began.

For the next five or six minutes, she talked hard and fast, and he listened. The last of the light languished against her cheeks, the shape of her mouth, then disappeared. The mosquitos moved in but feasted only on him.

As she spoke, his thoughts flew out in a dozen directions and coincided somewhere in deep space, in a black hole where time as he knew it collapsed. He saw himself leaving Lagoon and sensed the route his life would take once he did; somewhere that Nash and that life already existed. And then he saw himself doing what she asked and understood he could never return to this particular moment and alter his decision. This was it. One path or the other. The known or the unknown. Here. Now.

He hesitated, then reached for her hand and she grasped it, and they ran up to the inn to get what they needed. Ten minutes later, they were inside Delilah, headed for town.

He had chosen. There was no going back.

The clinic was dark, sealed up as tightly as a government secret. He parked in the alley that paralleled the far side of the building, where the Jeep wouldn't be seen from the road.

Fay hurried off to unlock the back door while he got the cooler, a backpack, his flashlight, and a pouch of tools from the backseat. When he was inside the cool, dark hall, he used a screwdriver to splinter the doorjamb and scrape at the edge of the dead bolt, making it look as if the lock had been jimmied when someone broke in.

He caught up with Fay in the clinic stockroom. She was already crouched in front of the refrigerator, removing pints of blood and plasma, vials of drugs and iron, and anything else that might be of use to them. She started stacking the items on the bed of ice as he went through the cabinets and drawers for syringes, collapsible IV poles, alcohol swabs, tubes of cortisone. Except for the poles, everything went into his backpack.

They worked without speaking, each aware of what the other was doing, as though they were two parts of the same brain. Once they had what they needed, they overturned drawers and swept things out of cabinets until the stockroom looked as if it had been attacked by a madman.

Fay went to the front of the clinic to tackle the main computer while Nash damaged the lock and jamb on the stockroom door so that they'd also look as if someone had broken in. Then he carried everything outside and loaded the Jeep.

The air was cool enough now for a jacket. It didn't surprise him; the heat a week ago had started this suddenly. But to Nash it portended a shift in the power that manipulated Lagoon like a puppet. It was almost as if Nature were retaliating against the feds by gearing up for a new twist, an unexpected surprise, and it scared him.

He hastened back inside to the front of the clinic, where Fay was still seated at the computer. The ghostly blue glow from the screen made him feel like the room was surrounded by water, as though they were trapped in a diving bell leagues beneath the sea.

"What all are you deleting?" he whispered, leaning over her shoulder.

"Every file on eczema. Those are the ones the CDC wants."

"I think you'd better delete more than that so it's not so obvious."

She glanced at him, her face so close to his that he could see the light reflected in the pupils of her eyes, a blue flame. "Like what? This data bank goes back at least four years. Files on every patient, treatments, recommendations, prescriptions . . ."

"Everything. Delete everything."

Fay sat there a moment longer, gazing at the screen, worrying her lower lip between her teeth. Then she gave a small nod, a reluctant nod. When she finished killing files and directories, she switched off the computer, picked up her chair, and smashed it into the screen once, twice, three times. Glass exploded, sparks flew, plastic snapped. The violence of the assault echoed in the silence, clawing at his nerves, and as she lifted the chair to hit the computer again, he grabbed her arm.

"That's enough. It's dead."

She dropped the chair quickly, as though it had burned her.

"Were there backups?"

"In my bag."

She plucked her purse off the floor, slung it over her shoulder, and they fled back down the hall, clumsy and frantic, with none of the grace of thieves.

2.

"The most erratic weather in the nation today was in Lagoon, Georgia, with a high of ninety-four and a predicted low tonight of thirty-one. . . ."

Katie glanced at the TV, where the jovial announcer on the Atlanta weather station was pointing at Lagoon on a map dotted with the day's highs and lows across the U.S. "The sixty-three degree drop in temperature is due to a rapidly moving Arctic air mass that's expected to leave up to ten inches of snow in northern Georgia and the Carolina mountains. . . ."

She kept waiting for him to mention that the temperature had plunged forty degrees in just the last half hour. More than a degree a minute. She had watched it happen, watched the mercury tumble in the thermometer outside the kitchen window as she washed dishes. It was still dropping, down, down, down, a free-fall, a bad joke that had brought a chill to the air in the house that even the fire Hank had built hadn't conquered yet.

She could hear him on the phone in the living room, talking with Sammy Loman. It was the fourth call since dinner from someone in the group whose spouse or lover or kids had taken a turn for the worse, just as Ray had. They called Hank, she supposed, because they didn't know who else to call. Because they thought he had answers. Because he listened.

"Want me to dry those?" Ray asked as he came into the kitchen.

"Thanks, but I'm almost done."

He picked up the dish towel anyway, and started wiping dishes. His face still looked pinched and thin, and the fine silver threads at his neck seemed longer. But he wasn't as pale now and that haunted expression in his eyes was gone. Maybe what she'd fixed him and Hank for dinner had helped: a pound of raw calf's liver chopped into fine bits and dumped into a blender with milk, yogurt, and a nutrition drink that had about fifty different kinds of vitamins in it.

"How's the arm?" he asked.

She held it out. A Band-Aid had replaced the bandage. "Okay. The cut wasn't that deep."

Ray brought his hand up under hers, as if to support it, then folded her fingers and turned her hand over and kissed the knuckles one at a time. A tingle ran up her arm; something caught in her throat.

"I appreciate what you did, Katie."

"It scares me," she whispered.

He slipped his arms around her, hugging her, his mouth warm against her hair. "Whatever happens, I love you, Katie-o."

She squeezed her eyes shut and held him hard, wanting desperately to believe that tomorrow or the next day she would wake up and find everything back to normal. But in her heart she knew it wasn't going to happen. This wasn't a movie with a happy ending; it was her life and it seemed to be getting progressively darker.

The doorbell pealed. She and Ray moved apart quickly, as if they'd been caught doing something they shouldn't. He gave her hand a quick squeeze, and she peeked through the window to see who it was. Fay and Nash. *Surprise, surprise.* A chilly gust of wind that smelled of impending snow followed them in. Fay carried a paper bag and Nash a cooler.

Fay's eyes pinned Katie's for a split second, telegraphing an apology for what had happened in the clinic that afternoon. A powerful scent radiated from her skin. It was part sorrow, part fear, part something else that made Katie want to weep. "Is Hank around?" she asked.

"He's on the phone."

"Can you get him? It's really important."

"So is the phone call."

An awkward stillness seeped into the air, and Katie immediately regretted her sharp tone. Fay just stared at her. Nash cleared his throat. Ray studied his shoes. "I was wrong and I'm sorry," Fay said quietly. "That's why we're here." She set the paper bag on the table and Nash put the cooler next to it. He flipped back the lid and took out a dozen vials. Fay pulled syringes and needles from the bag. "These are iron supplements for you and Hank," she said to Ray. "I'll show you how to give yourselves the injections. I also need to type your blood and show you both how to give yourselves transfusions. I don't think either of these things will stop the skin condition, but it'll alleviate the hunger and some of the other symptoms."

"A change of heart, Fay?" Hank asked from the doorway.

She glanced up. "The CDC is—"

"Yeah, I heard. That was Sammy Loman on the phone. He said you left his place a little while ago."

She gestured toward the items on the table. "Scott and I hit about a dozen homes, delivering supplies and alerting people to the quarantine. We've got enough here for everyone, I think, but need help dispersing everything. I want to get it done before six tomorrow morning."

Hank surveyed the array on the table, his smile sliding across his face like a ray of light, then looked up at Fay. "Welcome to the group, doc."

3.

A light snow was falling when they left the Suffields' and with it came that soft, muted stillness unique to winter, the silence of a world sealed up in its own solitude.

In years past, it was a quiet that Fay enjoyed, that she anticipated with a kind of sweet longing. It meant a good book in front of the fire, a long walk, snuggling under the quilts at night, and a host of other small pleasures. But tonight it felt claustrophobic, as if the town were being sealed up with them inside it. Like a coffin. Like some final countdown toward a future she couldn't imagine.

"You don't have to do this, Scott." They had reached the Jeep and she spoke to him over Delilah's roof.

"Do what?"

"Stay here. Go around delivering supplies to these people." She held up their list of names. "It's not your battle."

"It's not yours, either."

"Yeah, it is. I'm changing. You're not. I live here. You don't. And once the quarantine is in effect, there's no telling when you'll be able to leave."

He leaned forward, elbows resting against the edge of the roof, snow flecking his black hair like a harbinger of advancing age. "The only way I'm leaving here is if you come with me. Tonight. After we finish making our rounds."

"I don't know if I can."

"If we drove all night," he rushed on, "we could be at least four hundred miles from Lagoon by the time the quarantine goes into effect."

As though she hadn't spoken. She opened the door and climbed into the Jeep. Nash swung behind the wheel and touched her shoulder. "You will have done your part, Fay. You can't accomplish anything more by staying here. Maybe if you got away from Lagoon, the rash would—"

"No, Scott." She touched his arm. "That's not what I mean. I don't know if I *can* leave. I don't know if there's a choice anymore."

"I don't understand."

She told him about her attempted trip to Atlanta. "It could've been some side effect of the mutation we don't know about. Or it could be that there *is* an energy vortex here, as Hank says. Maybe when you change, your body becomes dependent on it. That's how it felt at the time. I mean, within an hour of my getting back here, all the symptoms were gone."

It was too dark in the car to see his expression. But she felt his need to deny what she was saying, felt it in the tightening of the muscles and tendons in his hand, in the light, quick strokes of his thumb across her knuckles. "But you're not sure."

"No."

"Then we could try. Later. After we've finished delivering supplies."

Even the thought of it stirred the memory of how ill she'd felt, how weak, how the fever had swept over her, a black, burning tide. But yes, she would try, yes, of course. A trial run. After all, no one else she'd spoken to had mentioned such a thing. And every day Suffield, who was changing, drove to Hartwell, eight miles outside of Lagoon, and *he* hadn't said anything about feeling ill. If anyone were going to report something like this, he would. Suffield never held anything back.

The weight of the gloom she'd felt for the past week lifted. "Yes, okay," she said with a laugh, and Nash hugged her.

"Then let's get this show on the road."

4.

It took Katie more than an hour to call people in the group whom Nash and Fay hadn't seen earlier. She told them about the quarantine and that supplies would be delivered. Some, she knew, were going to pack up their cars tonight and head out of town. Others, like Horn, would stick around because Lagoon had always been home. And still others, like Hank, would remain because they saw no point in leaving. And if he and Ray stayed, so would she.

But she wished they would hurry back. The idea of being alone in the house until two or three in the morning made her uneasy. Especially with the snow fluttering down outside and the vast silence hugging the windows and pressing up against the house, an invisible beast.

She poked at the fire, put on another log, made herself a cup of hot tea, checked the thermometer again. Twenty-eight and holding: the weatherman had been wrong about the temperature and right about the snow and wrong about the reasons.

She fixed herself a snack. Turned on the tube. Checked on the canaries. Glanced at the clock, the TV, the phone. She decided to warn Dani about the quarantine and picked up the receiver to dial. Katie hadn't seen her for more than a week, which meant her parents had probably left for Europe to open Mrs. Menninger's line of fall clothes. She always cut school when they were out of town. She got away with it, too, because the housekeeper didn't care what she did as long as she didn't make trouble.

She reached the answering machine, a sure sign that Dani was stoned on something and lost in her headphones. She would drive over there, then. It didn't matter that they barely spoke to each other now; Dani needed to know about the quarantine.

Katie pulled on her boots and shrugged on her parka, patting the pockets to make sure she had the keys to the Pinto. Then she switched on the answering machine and left.

Only the upstairs lights were on at the Menningers' house, a pair of rectangular eyes peering out into the dark and snow. It was so quiet, Katie could hear the beat of her own heart. She left the keys in the ignition and hurried through the snow to the front door.

It must have been the housekeeper's night off or something. She rang the bell but wasn't surprised when no one answered it.

If Dani was in the basement with the headphones on, it would take a nuclear blast to grab her attention. The door wasn't locked, so she walked in.

It was freezing inside and the air smelled strange. She focused on the scent, trying to decipher it, to find something she could follow, but it kept getting away from her. Katie flicked on the hallway light and walked into the living room.

The quiet spooked her.

It shouldn't have been this quiet even if Dani was in the basement.

The living-room curtains were closed and the smell, whatever it was, seemed stronger in here. Again she tried to seize something in the scent that would lead her into it, but it continued to elude her, a playful kitten that wasn't ready to be caught.

She peered up the staircase, into the dim light at the top, and called Dani's name. When she took her hand away from the banister, cobwebs stuck to her fingers. She brushed her hands together to get the stuff off and wondered if Dani had fired the housekeeper and been staying here alone with her *gorgeous* senior or maybe with some college guy. That would be Dani's style, all right.

She went into the kitchen. The sink was filled with dirty dishes; the trash can was jammed with garbage, empty bottles of booze, and beer cans; and the floor was tracked with dirt. No wonder the house smelled weird. On the counter was an ashtray stuffed with butts. Next to it were a pack of matches and a Bic lighter. She tested the lighter and stuck it and the matches in her pocket just in case Dani had unscrewed all of the light bulbs in the basement.

The windows over the sink were wide open and the door to the cellar, where Dani's room was, stood ajar. Katie stepped onto the landing and leaned over the railing.

"Hey, Dani," she shouted. "It's me."

No answer.

Katie trotted down the stairs. A blue bulb burned at the entrance to the cellar. It cast a watery light across the colorful bolts of fabric that hung from the ceiling, dividing the room into numerous cubbyholes. There was a nook where Dani partied, one where she slept, another where her desk was set up, a compartment for every imaginable activity. And everywhere around the cellar she had posted signs that said NO TRESPASSING and KEEP OUT and ADULTS NOT WELCOME HERE.

"Dani?"

But Katie already knew she wasn't here. Just the same, she pushed aside one curtain after another, making her way through the maze and the wash of blue light. She veered around dirty dishes, stacks of albums, books, spilled makeup, cellophane wrappers, empty Coke bottles. The smell grew stronger. She tracked it to the far corner of the room, where the air-conditioning unit for the house was located. Above it were exposed wooden beams and a web of pipes that reflected the eerie blue light.

The air here smelled like earth after a hard rain, when the soil released an overwhelming fragrance of richness. But there was something else at the core of the scent, folded inside it, concealed. She stepped a little closer to the air-conditioning unit. Why was her heart thudding so hard against the cage of her ribs? Why had sweat broken out along her upper lip? Why was the *tickle* so strong?

She touched the corner of the unit to peer behind it into the pooled shadows, then drew her hand quickly away from the gummy cobwebs that caught on her fingers. Katie tried to brush it off, but it stuck like adhesive. She rubbed her hands together, hard and fast, until the cobwebs rolled off in long, damp strings the color of mucus. She flung them away from her and climbed onto the air conditioner, careful not to touch it.

The cobwebs fluttered over the tops of her boots.

Her nose worked frantically at the air, and now the scent drew her eyes up the paneling, into the geometry of pipes and beams. There, suspended from the ceiling, were three oblong-shaped objects larger than she was, the same color as the paneling. She didn't know what they were; she'd never seen anything like them.

Katie moved a little closer and reached out to touch the end of the one nearest to her. Her fingers sank into cobwebs and she jerked her hand back. She dug into the pocket of her parka for the lighter, flicked it, held it up.

Her lungs shut down. Her brain closed up as tight as a fist. The scream that shoved up from someplace deep in her chest died before it struck the air. She just stood there, paralyzed, staring at the things in front of her, at the opaque shapes inside them: feet and legs pressed firmly together, arms tucked slightly in front of the body, shoulders hunched in close together, heads bowed as if in prayer. . . .

Cocoons, three huge cocoons, Jesus God, it can't be.

The lighter burned her fingers and went out as she leaped

back, toppling off the air conditioner, her arms flapping wildly to maintain her balance. She fell into one of the lengths of fabric, tearing it off the ceiling, and when she struck the floor, it folded in around her like giant wings, trapping her. She screamed, clawing at it, twisting and rolling around inside it to escape. She found an opening and crawled out, sucking air in through her teeth, her chest heaving.

Suddenly, somewhere upstairs, a door slammed. The floor creaked. She went utterly still, fingers digging into her thighs, eyes wide, and then the dark smell slammed into her, nearly knocking her back.

They're here. In the house. Upstairs.

She jumped up, looking around wildly for someplace to hide. *Think, c'mon, think. You know this room.* But her fear was a black blood that filled her. She tore blindly toward the walk-in closet and pressed back into Dani's clothes—so many clothes, skirts and slacks and blouses, jumpsuits, dresses, sweaters, and coats. Something was wrong with the door; it wouldn't close all the way. So she hunkered down and pressed back as far into the closet as she could, covering her knees and legs with a coat that nearly brushed the floor.

And then she waited, the floorboards above her head creaking, the smell moving closer.

Closer.

Part VI

THE TOWN

"At the bottom of the abyss comes the voice of salvation. The black moment is the moment when the real message of transformation is going to come. At the dark moment comes the light."
—JOSEPH CAMPBELL

1.

Luanne Castleton stood in front of the full-length mirror on the back of the bathroom door. The glass had steamed up when she'd showered and her reflection was as blurred as an unfocused photograph. She looked like a connect-the-dots picture with some of the lines missing, and she hated the way the incompleteness taunted her, mocking her cowardice.

For weeks, she had avoided mirrors.

But she moved toward it suddenly, before she could change her mind, and rubbed her towel over the glass in tight, jerky motions. Her face appeared, a pale, damp moon with dark splotches across it that might have been shadows. But weren't. Her eyes were an excessive blue, pools that threatened to spill over onto her gaunt cheeks. She touched her mouth, her jaw, and brushed strands of her gray-streaked hair away from her temples, where patches of the dark skin bloomed like birthmarks.

Now her neck and shoulders appeared. They were unchanged. Now her breasts.

They were engorged, pendulous, and striated with pale blue veins that weaved through the dark, thicker skin like miniature creeks. The nipples, which were still her own skin, were hard as walnuts and black. Not brown as they usually got during pregnancy, not merely dusky, but *black*. She pinched the right one and a pink liquid oozed out that was viscous to the touch, with the consistency of glue or tar. She rubbed her fingertip against the liquid and sniffed at it.

Blood. My God, it's blood.

She swiped at it with the towel, not allowing herself to speculate about what it meant, and quickly finished rubbing the glass clear. Then she stepped back and stared at herself. The new skin had claimed more than half of her body. It was porous, the color of old lead, and when she poked at it, her finger sank into it as if into foam rubber or sponge or a wad of cotton. It stretched thinly over the bulge of her belly and seemed smoother there, shinier, as though it had been varnished.

Luanne turned sideways and ran her palm slowly over the protrusion. She looked like she was six or seven months pregnant, but she knew she couldn't be further along than three. And the shape was all wrong. Instead of a rounded swell that curved gently at the sides, the contours were elongated, starting high—just under her breastbone—and ending low, almost touching her pubic bone.

She squeezed back tears and spun around, spine pressed to the glass, and pressed her face into the towel to stifle the bursts of air that erupted from her chest like gasps. She raked her nails across her stomach, clawing at the thing inside her, hating it. It wasn't part of her and Charlie. It was an abomination, a corruption of nature, something alien that had invaded her and was now feeding off her, sucking the life from her, claiming her, and she wanted it out.

Tomorrow. Fay said she would take it out tomorrow. She gave me her word. She promised. Fay was one of them now. When she and Nash had delivered supplies earlier, she'd examined Luanne and said she would return tomorrow with the machine. She would vacuum the thing out of her womb, her memory, her life. And then . . . She didn't know. She didn't know what would happen. She hadn't thought that far ahead.

The thing inside her suddenly slammed up against her. The skin bulged at the navel, then seemed to ripple from top to bottom in fast, painful contractions.

"No," she whispered, bearing down on her womb with her hands to stem the pain, to stop the contractions. "Please, no. Please . . ." *I can't be in labor. It's too soon.*

She pushed herself to her feet, grabbed her robe off the toilet, and jammed her arms into the sleeves. As she threw open the door, a white-hot agony flashed through her womb and into her chest, robbing her of breath. She doubled over, wheezing, and when it passed, she stumbled into the bedroom and screamed for Charlie.

2.

In the dream, his mom's voice was soft, sweet, the way it was before she got sick and went away. She was calling to him, telling him to follow her voice; she missed him, she loved him, didn't he want to be with his mommy?

Bobby Peters started to cry and reached out to the voice. It lifted him from the bed and he floated like an angel toward the window, into the music of his mom's voice. He knew he was dreaming, but everything seemed so real—the way the blinds rolled up and the windows opened and how, suddenly, he was outside in the snow, wearing just his pajamas, but he couldn't feel the cold. "Mommy?" he whispered.

This way, Bobby. Follow the sound of Mommy's voice. That's right, sweetheart, come to Mommy.

"But what about Daddy?"

Daddy can't come where we're going.

He hesitated. Weren't he and Daddy supposed to go someplace in a little while? Before the sun came up? He remembered his dad talking about it with Mr. Nash when he was here with Dr. Fay, but he couldn't recall exactly what had been said. Was it a vacation? Were they going up to the mountains?

C'mon, sweetheart, whispered his mom's voice.

"Daddy and I are going away," he said. "You come, too."

We'll all go away together, Bobby. But I want to show you something first. I'm in the woods. C'mon.

The woods weren't far; he could see them from where he was. He would go see Mommy, and then they would come back to the house and get Daddy and the three of them would go on vacation.

He moved through the falling snow and into the trees and there was Mommy, wearing a cloak and hood like some sort of princess. He ran to her and she swooped him up in her arms, laughing, hugging him, telling him what a good boy he was. But then the hood slipped off her head and the cloak fell away from her body, and Bobby screamed.

It wasn't his mom at all, but a monster with her voice and skin like dried mud with long white hairs growing out of it. The hairs fluttered around him, sticking to his face, scratching his skin, hurting him. As he screamed again and struggled to get away, the hairs drifted into his mouth and down his throat, reaching deep inside him until he couldn't scream anymore.

Now the threads tightened around his face and shoulders,

sapping his strength, pressing him back into the monster's arms as it whispered, *We'll be fine, sweetheart, we'll be just fine now.* It ran farther into the woods, and the hairs spun around them, squashing Bobby against the monster's chest until he seemed to be sinking into the terrible skin, melting into it.

The threads had covered his mouth, sealing it shut, but he could still see the dark, the snow, and he could hear the voice saying, *It won't be long now and it won't hurt, I promise, it won't hurt. Mommy and Bobby will be together for a long, long time. Isn't that what Mommy's boy always wanted?*

They stopped next to a huge tree, a pine that seemed to shoot upward forever. Its long branches hung close to the ground, hiding them as the monster pressed up against the trunk. It tightened its arms around Bobby as more threads snaked out of the pores of its skin, wrapping around them both like rope.

In his mind, Bobby screamed, *Wake up, it's only a dream, wake up, wake up.* But he knew it wasn't a dream because now the threads broke through the skin on the monster's hips and made a soft, crackling sound. The lower fibers wound around the trunk, binding them to it. He struggled to break free, but the hairs held fast; they were as strong as wire, cut into him like wire, they hurt, and when he tried to scream, they poked through the skin at the back of his throat and bent upward into the roof of his mouth and glided up into his nostrils.

Don't fight it, honey, whispered his mom. *Don't fight it.*

He heard the soft, crackling sound again and twisted his head to see what it was, where it was coming from. Hairs broke through the skin on the monster's shoulders and swept around the trunk, binding them to it. More hairs punched through the top of the monster's skull, growing fast and furiously until they leaped for the nearest branches, seized them, tightened around them like hands, lifting him and the monster several inches from the ground. Then the hair slithered across his eyes, blinding him, and filled his nostrils and ears so he couldn't breathe or hear.

He grew stiff and cold and sleepy. Distantly, he heard his mom's voice whispering to him. *You're with your mommy now, where you belong.*

3.

Katie huddled in the closet, surrounded by silk and cotton and satin clothing that had slipped off their hangers. She breathed into the coat that covered her knees, filling her lungs with the scents that lingered in the coat's lining: traces of Dani's perfume, her sweat, spilled booze, smells that helped to disguise the odor of the intruder on the stairs.

It wasn't as foul as the man-thing that had chased her the night the Pinto had broken down or as crazed as the smell of whatever it was that Ray had attacked with the machete. But it was blacker, denser, as impenetrable as the deepest reaches of the sea, and she knew it would suffocate her if she smelled it too long or too hard.

Something brushed up against her in the dark. It took her a moment to realize it wasn't physical, that it wasn't a bug or the hem of one of Dani's dresses. It was a scent—different from that of the intruder, yet a part of it as well. She reached, and it quivered when she found it, seeming to expand like a net, receiving her, welcoming her.

Katie opened herself to it, and it was as if she'd been plugged directly into a computer that was dumping everything from its disks into her. Information rushed through her—in symbols, images, sentences, in fragments that flashed in her skull like lightning. It came at her so quickly, she didn't know how she could possibly contain it long enough to remember it all.

But she understood it came from the power that ruled Lagoon, that it was a link, a web, a bridge to the vortex of energy Hank had mentioned and which Nash's photographs had captured. It emanated from the very heart of Nature, from a sentient being that had been dying slowly for decades, suffocating in man's indifference. Now She was fighting back the only way She knew how, by putting man out of commission.

Who's there?

The words purled through the web, soft and persuasive, a melodic sound like water tumbling over rocks or eddying across hot sand. But she sensed the darkness behind the words and knew it came from the intruder, that he was inside the web with her. She scampered out of the web, head throbbing, mouth dry with fear.

He was in the basement now, his scent preceding him like a procession of attendants. Through the partially open door, Katie saw him—or her, she couldn't tell which—pushing aside the sheets of fabric. The blue light washed his naked back, exposing the uneven moonscape of dark, porous skin that covered him completely. His thighs were thicker than her torso, his shoulders were massive, his hair was gone, and his head was misshapen from the crusted skin. Despite his bulk, he moved with surprising grace.

He ripped down some of the sheets, kicked aside bottles and cans and plates, and although he was obviously agitated, he didn't seem to be in any hurry. Now and then he stopped to examine something on the floor, and once he stopped and turned slowly, head cocked to the side as if he'd heard or sensed something.

He knows I'm here.

Katie's hand tightened over the hanger on the floor beside her. Sweat rushed across her back and her leg muscles tensed up, prepared for flight. Now he faced the closet: definitely male.

The blue light pooled between the ridges that his features formed: a forehead like a cliff between his eyes, cheeks that swelled on one side and looked concave on the other, a chin as bulbous and pitted as a rotting potato. The bundle under his arm was a cocoon like the ones suspended from the ceiling, but it was smaller and white and not fully formed yet. He set it on the floor as he walked slowly toward the closet.

Please God please make him go away. . . .

The hanger was in her lap now. She twisted the hooked end this way and that, straightening it, making a dagger of it. The scent pushed up against her. She thought she was going to cough or gag or choke or maybe all three at once and pressed her hand over her nose, not daring to take her eyes from the door.

The man, the being, the entity, whatever he was, stopped and looked away from the closet door, distracted. Then he moved back toward the cocoon, as though it had called him.

He walked out of her line of vision, but she could still see the cocoon on the floor where he'd put it a few moments ago. She tightened her grip on the hanger. The smell reached her again. She felt around on the floor for the fallen clothes, grabbed two silk blouses. She wrapped one tightly around the end of the hanger and stuffed the other inside her parka. Then she pulled out the Bic lighter and the matches.

One chance. That's all you'll get.

She snapped the Bic in two; the lighter fluid seeped into the silk. Carefully, slowly, she raised up, praying her knees wouldn't crack, that her head wouldn't hit against the hangers, that she had this figured right. She struck a match and held the flame to the blouse wrapped around the end of the hanger. It caught instantly. A tongue of fire sprang to a dress hanging nearby, and within seconds, smoke filled the closet.

Katie threw open the door, wielding her torch. The man shouted something. Blue light glowed in all the smoke. The white threads of the cocoon caught it, reflected it as brightly as moonlight on snow or ice.

The man lurched toward her, blocking her path to the stairs. Katie stabbed at the air above the cocoon and yelled, "Stay away from me or I'll burn it, I swear I will!"

For a split second, neither of them moved.

Behind her, flames jumped out of the closet, hungrily seeking something to consume. She felt the heat against her back, her eyes teared from the smoke, her torch was dying. The man suddenly emitted a shrill, desperate keening, the noise of a thing in pain, and lunged for her. Katie thrust the torch at him. The flames sizzled and hissed like bacon on a griddle as they grazed his skin. He bellowed, stumbled back, and she dropped the torch to the cocoon.

It burst into flame, burning white, a star going nova. The light flooded through the blue and the smoke and she saw him clearly, his hands gripping the sides of his head as he shrieked in agony. Then he hurled himself toward her and the cocoon.

Katie jumped to the side still clutching the hanger, the spent torch, and charged toward the stairs, but he was faster. He grabbed the hood of her parka and jerked her back with such force, her feet literally left the floor. She collapsed on top of him. Her teeth sank through her lower lip. Blood poured into her mouth and down her chin. His black stink closed around her and she heard his voice in the web shouting, *The girl with the smell get the girl with the smell kill kill* . . .

She kicked and struggled, but the stink choked her, sucked at her. His arms were crushing her waist, her ribs. She felt something snap inside her. Pain flashed through her. Adrenaline poured into her blood, galvanizing her, and she somehow found the strength to wrench her hand loose. The hand still clutching the hanger. She slammed it back and it sank into him, sank deep, and his arms slackened enough for her to break free.

The echo of his anguish resounded in the web, she heard it, she would hear it for the rest of her life. It pursued her with a mugger's diligence through the stink of smoke, of the cooked flesh that had been in the cocoon, and pushed her harder and faster toward the stairs. Toward freedom.

When she exploded into the kitchen, she flung the basement

door shut, knowing it wouldn't stop him, that nothing would stop him or any of it. But it would slow him up.

She shot for the front door.

4.

"There, see?" said Nash.

He glanced at Fay. She was sitting close to him, close enough so their shoulders touched, her legs drawn up against her, arms hooked around them. Light from the dashboard collected in points on her face—her forehead, the tip of her nose, her chin, one cheek—and left the rest of her in shadow, as though she were an organic part of the dark landscape beyond them.

"We're not that far out of town," she said. "When it happened before, I was on the road an hour and a half before I started feeling sick." She smiled at him and touched her hand to his thigh. "You prepared to drive halfway to Atlanta to make a point, Nash?"

"*This* point, yeah."

"And then back to pick up Samson and my things and your things?"

"Yes."

She laughed. It was a soft, pleasing sound that seemed totally at odds with everything else that had been going on, and loosened the tightness between them. Her hand warmed his leg and, for a beat or two, the witch scent brushed up against him. But it retreated hastily, a thief who'd decided against a break-in.

"I can't always control it," she said.

This was the first time she'd ever referred to the scent or even hinted that she was aware of it. "You mean just in general?"

"Yes. Tonight at Luanne and Charlie's, when I was examining her, she asked me about it. She wanted to know if I'd been experiencing anything like it. She said it's been happening to her for at least four months."

The lights of a car passing them in the other direction flashed in the windshield and streaked the glass like luminous paint. "What about you?" he asked.

"Once, with Ben, I think it might've happened. As early as February or March, around then. Luanne thinks it's comparable to the scent some female animals release when they're in heat," Fay went on. "Nature's way of ensuring the continuation of the species."

"In this case, the *new* species," Nash remarked.

She let out a sharp, bitter laugh and ran a hand over her face. "He's right, you know. Hank's right. It's not a virus."

His head swelled with the disquieting tone of her voice, the whisper of the tires against the pavement, the whistle of the cold wind against the windows. These noises were a code he broke down and absorbed like nutrients, as though they could tell him what to expect tomorrow or next week or next month. But the future was as closed to him as what Ben had been thinking during the final moments of his life.

"How do you explain a sixty-one-year-old woman conceiving?" he asked.

She rested her head against the back of the seat. "She's not the oldest woman to ever conceive—I think the record is sixty-seven. But in this case it looks like Nature's making sure its female mutants are fertile regardless of age." Fay turned down the heat in the car and cracked her window to admit some fresh air. "When the skin condition starts getting worse, Scott, I don't want you around, okay?" She spoke softly, her head averted. "It'd be easier for me."

"It's not going to get worse. We're getting out of here, remember?"

She looked at him, her eyes liquid with emotion, but didn't reply. It was just as well. He wanted to marry her, not lose her, but now obviously wasn't the time to talk about it.

As they crossed Meadow Creek and the cold line, Fay moved closer to her window and rolled it down all the way. The difference in temperature was barely noticeable now, a few degrees at the most. But it stopped snowing a couple of miles past the creek, and now and then the headlights struck clusters of trees that still had autumn foliage.

Nash's eyes burned with fatigue; he felt as if they'd been driving for hours. It seemed that the road was running through him now, as if he weren't quite solid, and his molecules were moving even farther apart. Maybe in another hour he wouldn't be here in the Jeep at all. His being would be scattered like so many seeds through the billion miles of space above them, Nature's gift to the non-changers, transformation without mutation, an end of the physical self but not to consciousness.

"Scott?"

"Yeah?"

"I think you'd better turn around."

"You feel sick?"

She was holding a wad of Kleenex against her mouth and nose. "Yes."

"Like before?"

"Worse."

She took the Kleenex away from her mouth; it was soaked with blood that was oozing from her mouth and nose. She tipped her head back to stop the flow, and Nash grabbed a rag from under the seat, thrust it in her hands, and swung off onto the shoulder. He scrambled in the backseat for an old towel and the bottle of distilled water he kept in here for the radiator, then hurried around to Fay's side and opened her door.

· She got out and leaned against the Jeep, head still tilted back as he cleaned off her face and hands. Her gums were bleeding and blood was streaming out of her nostrils as fast as he wiped the stuff away. She was hemorrhaging.

Jesus, I'm going to lose her. "Tell me what to do." He sought to control the panic in his voice but knew it was useless. "Just tell me what to do. It's bleeding a lot."

"Snow." She sat at the edge of her seat and stretched out, wedging her body between the gear shift and the seats. "Cold will help. And then get me back to Lagoon."

5.

Luanne lay propped at a forty-five-degree angle, back propped up by pillows, legs drawn up, hands clutching her knees. Charlie was to her right and Mona Stawson was at the foot of the bed, and both of them were telling her to push, to push, but she was already pushing and straining so hard she was drenched in sweat. Her heart felt like it was going to erupt through her chest.

Another contraction seized her and she screamed. It hurt, oh, God, it hurt so much, like she was being eaten from the inside out by a raging fire that burned hotter and brighter every time she pushed. She fell back against the pillows, sobbing, "Just get it out, get it out of me!"

Mona ordered her to push again and again, harder, harder. Luanne hated her and Charlie and the travesty inside her, and her hatred fueled her strength, boiled through her like the pain, competing with the pain, shoving it aside until only the hatred existed, blazing like a sun in her head.

She pushed and screamed again as something warm and wet rushed out between her thighs. She wanted to see what it was, but Mona had draped a sheet over her thighs and snapped orders at Charlie to get this, get that. Then her face went bone white and she gasped and jerked back, and Charlie said, "What? What is it?"

"I . . . I . . ." Mona stammered.

Luanne bolted forward and tore the sheet away from her. There, lying between her thighs, was a cocoon, and the shape of a tiny mouth inside it was sucking at the blood smeared across the pale threads.

6.

Katie made it to the driveway before the man-thing burst out the front door and tore through the snow after her. She flung open the car door and dived inside, slamming her fist against the lock. As she reached to turn the ignition, she prayed that the Pinto would start, knowing she was dead if it wouldn't.

He reached the car just as the engine turned over. He leaped, landed on the hood, a ball player sliding into home. She threw the car into reverse and swung into a violent turn, hoping to hurl him off. But he clung like a spider and inched his way toward the windshield, grinning.

Katie gunned the accelerator and the car blasted forward onto Hawthorne, a projectile, a missile, a bullet. But the man kept coming, grinning, those misshapen hands somehow finding purchase on the slippery hood. She flicked on the wipers and snow flew into his face; it didn't bother him. She swung the wheel violently to the right, to the left, trying to throw him off, but it did no good.

He grabbed one of the wipers and bent it back with his hand until it snapped off. His grin widened. He slammed his fist against the windshield. The blow echoed inside the car and bounced around inside her, a noise as huge as her terror. He struck it again. And again. A web of lines sped through the glass. Katie smashed her foot on the brakes, and for an instant, his hold seemed to loosen. He slipped to the side, then the dashboard lit up as the Pinto stalled.

The stench of gas rushed through the car.

She whimpered, she swore, she pumped the accelerator and flooded the engine. The man's grin was a black hole in his face as he raised his fist and brought it down against the windshield again. The web of cracks in the glass multiplied. She flicked the key once, twice. The car burped and stuttered to life, then lurched forward again.

The speedometer needle leaped to twenty, forty, forty-five, fifty. She couldn't see the road. The man blocked her view. But she knew every twist and curve on Hawthorne, and as it veered to the right, she steered the Pinto up over the curb and headed straight for the front yard of one of the cabins that had been closed for the winter.

The tires tore over dead shrubs, kicked up damp pine needles, spat out gravel and snow. The man was no longer grinning. The wind ripped at his eyes and his fingers scrambled for new holds as he started to slip and slide again.

A second later, the car struck a wooden gazebo.

The fence around it crumbled like dry sod, a beam snapped like a toothpick, the car bounced up onto the concrete floor, and Katie slammed on the brakes. The man soared back off the hood, a one-dimensional cartoon character that seemed to slide through the glare of the headlights as if across a slippery, invisible floor. Then he hit the ground.

She jerked the gear shift into reverse, the tires spun, caught, and she roared down Hawthorne.

Part VII

COLD STORAGE

"Nature has no principles. She furnishes us with no reason to believe that human life is to be respected. Nature, in her indifference, makes no distinction between good and evil."

—ANATOLE FRANCE

27

Quarantine

Silence echoed through the streets like the memory of some ancient curse. It was as oppressive as jungle heat, maddening in its consistency, a triumph of disguise that masked the very heartbeat of Lagoon.

Oliver listened to it with the tenacity of a man who knew he had no ear for music, but who hoped to understand, perhaps through osmosis if nothing else, the difference between Bach and the Beatles. He knew the silence could tell him something if he only had the key. It wasn't just the quarantine or the absence of trucks and semis on Route 16 or the fewer number of people on the streets, trying to attend to business as though things were normal. It wasn't just the gray, drooping skies that had dumped fifteen inches of snow on Lagoon in three days. Those things were part of it, yes, but didn't tell him the full story.

The source of the silence was something else, something subterranean, hidden. It was like venturing into an ocean as a kid after repeated warnings about the undertow, but not really understanding the concept until you were in it. Until the roiling tide was dragging you under and down and you were sputtering for breath and sucking in seawater. That kind of something. He listened and heard only the noisy silence. He peered into the faces of people he had known for years, seeking whatever they knew, but he could no longer read their expressions. He was as helpless as a seer who had lost his powers.

Whenever he stopped at the Nameless for coffee, hoping he might hear something that would banish his ignorance, conversation inside abruptly ceased. Eyes looked the other way. Customers sometimes got up and left. Even Horn, who had always been friendly, was now merely cordial. Everything was *"Yes, sir," "No, sir."* The division between them that had once been a matter of color was now something deeper, stronger, almost fierce.

At the Brazen Saloon where Polly worked, the story was much the same. He was no longer asked to join the poker games in the back room with guys he'd gone to high school with. When he struck up conversations with some of the regulars, he might as well have been talking to himself. Although Polly remained what she had always been—irreverent and saucy and thoroughly irritating—she no longer came on to him.

One night Oliver suggested they go back to his place and she looked at him as if he'd lost his mind. How the hell did he think they could manage even lousy sex, she asked, when the feds probably had every place in town wired for sound? He laughed and said they were under quarantine, for Christ's sakes, not in a prison camp.

Same goddamn thing, she muttered, and turned on her heel and walked away from him.

He waited around until the bar closed at two so he could talk to her alone. But she just sat on the stool beside him, in the dim wash of light, downing shots of bourbon and babbling about how she was leaving this shithole of a town once the quarantine was lifted. He drove her home, and there in the cold stillness of his truck, she told him that he'd made himself an outsider by working with the feds, that people saw him as a traitor, worse than a scab at a picket line.

He already knew that, he said. But what about the other thing? The conspiracy of silence? Did she know anything about that? She shook her head, her wild hair crackling with static electricity, and wouldn't look at him. "You're imagining things, Lew. People are just pulling into themselves, trying to carry on with their lives, trying like hell to function somewhat normally under abnormal conditions."

"Bullshit. It's more than that. I *feel* it, don't you?"

Polly turned her head slowly, as if the movement hurt the muscles in her neck. She looked like she was about to cry as she leaned close to him, reaching for his hand, holding it in both of hers. She gazed at it as she turned his palm up and traced the lines with her nail. "I'm going to tell you something I heard, but if you ever say it came from me, I'll deny it, Lew."

He nodded eagerly and swore he would keep it to himself.

The quarantine, she said, had nothing to do with the sickness. The feds had found something in the cellar at Prudy's Place.

"What kind of something?"

"That depends on who you talk to. The stories range from a dead alien to giant insects. But my best source, a maid at the inn, is telling me it's a large cocoon hanging from the ceiling." It supposedly contained one of those *things* that fit the description Fay Donovan had given of what had chased the medical van that night at her old man's. The feds had taken it somewhere and were now looking for more of them.

"Looking where?" he asked, almost afraid to hear her answer.

"All over town. They've got this idea that there's a connection between the cocoons and the people with the sickness." They believed that if they could identify everyone who'd been infected, she went on, they would be able to locate all of the cocoons. But since the clinic's records had been destroyed during the break-in, the only way they were going to be able to identify who'd been treated for the sickness was through their testing program. So the program actually served a dual purpose—as a convincing excuse for imposing the quarantine to begin with and to track the cocoons.

Why, Oliver asked, did the feds think the sickness had anything to do with these cocoons?

Polly sighed and raked her fingers back through her hair, impatient with him now. "Your buddy the doc probably has the answer to that." Her snide tone let him know that *she* knew he had the hots for Fay. "Or maybe you should ask that space cadet Hank Suffield, Lew. I'd lay bets that either of them or both of them also know what really happened at the Menningers' house the night it burned. And if they won't tell you, why don't you try Suffield's daughter? Or Sammy Loman over at Kroger's? In fact, why the hell are you bugging me when *your* contacts are smack in the thick of it? They can probably even tell you what had happened to the Peters kid, Lew. And if all else fails, well, hell, you can always demand answers from the feds. Now would you mind letting me get some sleep, please? Huh? Do you think you can do that?" And with that, she toppled sideways, a wind-up doll who'd just run out of juice, and passed out.

Oliver carried her inside and put her to bed. The heat was on so high, the room steamed like Africa. It was the warmest he'd been in days, and instead of driving home, he kicked off his shoes and sank into the rocker near the window. He had to share the space with Polly's fat orange cat, who kneaded his thighs with clawless paws and purred as he sat there in the humid dark, watching the snow fall, waiting for sunrise and answers.

In the darkest corridors in his head, Harness's voice echoed: *The cold goes hard . . . The end . . .*

At eight the next morning, his courage boosted by a couple of hours of fitful sleep and daylight, Oliver strolled into the dining room at Prudy's Place and made a beeline for Fielding's booth. The colonel was alone, stabbing at bits of sausage on a plate streaked with egg yolk. His bald head, slippery with gray light, was bowed over a newspaper.

Oliver sat down across from him. "Tell me about the cocoons."

The colonel's eyes as he raised them were a flat brown, two-dimensional, reflecting and revealing nothing. They seemed to slip over Oliver's features, taking in his unshaven jaw, the pinched corners of his mouth, the leaden tone of his fatigue. Oliver expected him to laugh or to say, "The what?" Instead, Fielding nodded, set down his fork, wiped at his mouth, and dropped a five-spot on the table as he stood.

"Let's go."

"Where?"

Fielding leaned into the table and grinned. A fleck of egg yolk clung to a front tooth. "Think of me as the genie in the bottle, Lew. I'm granting your wish."

They crossed town on back roads in one of the army jeeps that had a plow on the front. Its jaws chewed up snow and spit if off to either side, where it piled up at the curbs. The heater blew directly on Oliver's feet, baking them into his boots. A light snow dusted the windshield and the wipers flicked it off almost as fast as it fell.

They passed through the quarantine blockade to the north and turned into Joker's. There were three jeeps and a van in the parking lot and several men in uniform mulling around on the porch, smoking, talking, waiting for something. The light here seemed pale, strange, not quite solid. Everything Oliver looked at possessed a patina, as though he'd been swimming in heavily chlorinated water with his eyes open.

"We ready here?" Fielding asked one of the men on the porch.

"Yes, sir. Just waiting for you. We're set up out back. Poke and Slim are inside."

Poke and Slim were loading things into a canvas bag on the bar. They were zipped into white jumpsuits that reminded Oliver of what the astronauts wore in space. But these didn't have helmets and weren't as bulky. The man named Poke, a short, muscular guy in his late thirties, snapped on a pair of thick white gloves and slung the canvas bag over his shoulder. "We're ready, sir."

"Okay, let's get on with it."

Oliver followed Fielding and the other two men into the cold, dank cellar. Joker used to store booze and supplies down here, but the shelves were now stripped bare. No one flicked on the naked bulbs that dangled from the ceiling. They relied on flashlights and whatever dusky light filtered through the tiny dirty windows. One of the panes, Oliver noticed, was broken. Cold and snow drifted through it.

Crates and boxes were stacked high in the far corner of the room, the darkest corner, and this was where the men stopped.

Slim, who was much taller than his partner, rolled onto the balls of his feet and lifted a couple of wooden crates from the top of a stack. He set them in front of Poke, who pushed with his foot until they were up against the wall, just beneath the exposed ceiling beams. Then he stepped aside as Slim climbed on top.

"Hold it," Fielding said. "I'd like the captain to take a look first."

"Sure thing." Slim motioned Oliver over and made room for him on top of the crate. He held out his hand to give Oliver a boost. "C'mon up, man, that's the only way you'll see it."

Oliver grabbed his gloved hand and scrambled onto the top of the crates. The cocoon was at least six feet long and maybe half as wide and was almost the same color as the stone walls. It hung from the ceiling and was well hidden behind another stack of crates and boxes. The upper part of it was obscured by the low, exposed beams. As Slim shone his flashlight on it, Oliver detected a shape within the translucent threads, and the thing inside quivered with movement, as if turning away from the light.

Gooseflesh zipped along Oliver's arms; the inside of his mouth went bone dry. "What the hell *is* it?"

"It used to be human," said Fielding.

"Commissioner Jokerzy found it when he was out here yesterday." Slim's voice was light, breezy, like it was no big deal, like he'd seen worse in his life. "We think there's probably another around somewhere. They usually come in pairs or clusters. Hey, Poke, pass me the camera."

Poke pulled a fancy 35-millimeter out of the canvas bag, screwed on a lens, and attached a flash. ''She's all set to go.''

The flash lit up the cocoon in a stroboscopic brilliance that seared to the backs of Oliver's eyes and imprinted his brain forever with an image of the thing inside, recoiling from the light. Slim snapped half a dozen photographs, and it was several moments before the spots in Oliver's eyes swam away like little black fish.

''Got to move the crates closer,'' Slim said, handing the camera to Poke, then hopping down.

Oliver followed; his knees felt as if they'd been filled with Jell-O.

Slim and Poke worked quickly now, silently, in what was obviously a familiar routine. Using an extension cord, Poke plugged an electric saw into a wall socket as Slim moved the crates to within a foot of the cocoon and climbed on top again. Poke passed him the saw; it hummed when Slim turned it on.

''Those threads look fragile, but they're tough as nails. Only thing you can cut through them with is a saw or a blowtorch,'' Fielding explained.

Poke fixed his hands at the bottom of the thing, holding it steady as Slim sliced through the threads that held it to the ceiling. He gripped it at the top while Poke opened a white bag under it.

The cocoon slipped inside, making a soft, rustling sound as it brushed against the plastic.

Upstairs again, the men shucked their white suits and everyone went outside, Poke and Slim carrying the bag between them. The men who'd been on the front porch when Oliver and Fielding had driven up were now standing in a half circle around a huge pile of firewood. Their cheeks were flushed pink from the cold, but they seemed oblivious to the snow fluttering down around them. Oliver thought they looked like eager children in green fatigues playing war, toy rifles over their shoulders.

They cheered when Poke and Slim set the bag on the firewood and carefully eased it away from the cocoon. ''Big fucker,'' someone muttered.

''Not as big as yesterday's,'' another man remarked.

''Atten-*shun*,'' ordered Fielding.

The men fell into a formation that jerked the curves of the half circle into straight lines. Two men stepped forward, one with a can of kerosene and the other holding a box of matches.

The man with the kerosene moved ceremoniously around the firewood, dousing it.

The cocoon was quickly changing colors, flickering from the stone hue it had been in the cellar to a white that blended with the snow to shades of green that matched the men's fatigues. Then it was brown, the color of the wood, then white again, green again, faster and faster. It was a chameleon out of whack, a light show in fast-forward.

The thing inside writhed, creating bumps and protrusions on the surface of the cocoon, as though fists and feet and knees were working in counterpoint, seeking a weakness in the threads, a place to bust out of.

The soldier with the kerosene stepped back into line and the match bearer marched to the northern point, struck a match against the box, touched it to the wood. It flared with a sound like wind through a tunnel, bright yellow tongues of fire licking greedily at the kerosene, curling around the wood, throwing off heat that made the thing inside the cocoon twist and kick, as though it were trying to roll the cocoon away from the flames, the heat.

The soldier walked quickly around the firewood, tossing lit matches at the other cardinal points, then stepped back into line. The men now formed a tight circle around the firewood, leaving room for Fielding and Oliver at the south end. The flames danced and hissed, closing in on the cocoon. The whiteness of everything acted as a mirror, reflecting the yellow glow of the flames against the men's lean, hungry faces. Their eyes were riveted on the cocoon, the fire, and now, softly, they began to chant.

"Burn, burn, burn."

The cocoon eddied with colors that shifted so fast, there didn't appear to be any pause between the end of one and the beginning of another. White as a pearl, green as a string bean, brown as bark, yellow and orange like the flames. This soundless carnival of pulsing color went on for fifteen or twenty seconds, maybe longer. But suddenly the cocoon turned pitch black, and an instant later, the flames reached it.

"Burn," the men chanted softly. *"Burn, burn."*

The threads hissed and crackled and popped. The ends curled in on themselves. A dreadful keening pierced the air, a sound that struck Oliver to the core. It lifted the chants to a new height that pounded against the inside of Oliver's head, a drumbeat that was frenzied and hot, a rhythm that evoked flashes of ritual sacrifices, of tribal rites carried out beneath black skies, gold moons, around fires like this one. A wildness spurted like blood through the air and the men suddenly converged on the pyre, a pack of wolves moving in for the kill.

Some of them kicked at the firewood, laughing as sparks leaped onto the center of the cocoon. Others grabbed pieces of wood from the periphery and wielded them like clubs, darting forward to hit and poke at the cocoon. But it had evidently hardened, perhaps when it had turned black, and clattered like metal when it was struck.

This seemed to enrage the men, to fuel their madness. They chanted louder, as though the chant were magical, powerful, capable of splitting the thing in two. The flames surrounded the cocoon now, hurdling it, zipping across its black surface, licking at its sides.

Fielding thrust a length of wood into Oliver's hands, his dark eyes wild with firelight, beads of sweat glistening on his upper lip, his forehead. ''This is how it's done,'' he hissed, and pushed into the circle.

Oliver stood there, the wood heavy and cold in his hands, watching as the colonel darted toward the flames and beat the cocoon once, twice, three times before leaping back from the fire. Someone shoved Oliver from behind and he stumbled into the crowd. The chant swept through him. The fire heated his cheeks. The smell of smoke swirled into him. And then the madness seized him, a force of such raw power, it squeezed everything out of his head except the need to strike, to destroy, to kill the thing that was different, the thing that symbolized the silence in Lagoon, the darkness.

28

Discoveries

1.

For three days, Nash had wandered through town with his camera, snapping pictures of everything through the attached red filter: people, buildings, cars, trees, even the old railroad tracks that bordered Lagoon to the west. He wanted photos of people he knew well and people he didn't know at all, residents and government interlopers alike. The first were fairly easy; the latter took some planning.

When Horn happened to mention that some of the army security boys ate at the Nameless every morning, Nash parked himself in the kitchen and got twenty pictures of them as they scarfed down steak and eggs and pancakes. That very afternoon, from behind Delilah's tinted window, his lens captured four of the CDC people as they were leaving the clinic. Another day, he photographed Karl Granger and a couple of other Hartwell honchos as they entered Prudy's Place, presumably for a pow-wow with Fielding.

On the fourth day of the quarantine, Nash set up the camera on the deck, under a sky that seemed to slouch beneath the weight of an unbearable secret, close enough to touch. He shot half a roll of black and white film of the lagoon, the surrounding trees, the inn. He even got a couple of pictures of Samson, who hammed for the camera, then begged to accompany Nash when he started to leave.

"I'm driving, guy, not walking, so let's go."

When he'd first arrived here, he would have walked or run the distance to the south end of the lagoon. But this was no longer the same road, and hadn't been for some time now, since long before Katie's nightmare at the Menningers'. Even during the day there was a certain vileness about the air here. Nash couldn't shake the feeling that the surrounding woods harbored

299

a perilous something that watched from the shadows, awaiting nightfall.

He felt it as Delilah chugged through the hard-packed snow. He heard it in the susurrus voice of the wind that whispered through the trees. It was as tangible as the steering wheel under his hands, and yet remained nameless, unknowable, an essence as ephemeral as time and as black as a fold in space.

Of the fourteen homes along the lagoon, only two were inhabited now—Fay's and the Suffields'. They were less than a mile from each other, but at night a mile was as distant as the nearest planet. As a result, Fay and Samson had virtually moved into the inn. Ray had vacated his apartment and now lived with the Suffields'. Nash had given them several weapons and ammunition from Ben's stash and made sure they knew how to handle them. At the inn, a .357 and a 9-millimeter Walther were always within easy reach. But even so, he knew that sooner or later, something would have to change.

Perhaps Katie, Suffield, and Ray would move into the inn. Maybe the five of them would pack up and move in with Horn, to the large apartment above the Nameless where he lived. There was, after all, safety in numbers. But Nash wasn't convinced they'd be any more secure in town than they were out here. Maybe the solution was for Suffield's group—what was left of them—to relocate at the inn. There was certainly enough room.

This option, however, wasn't without problems. Some people in the group wanted to stay where they were. They were mostly the ones who'd bought the government propaganda—that the mutations were caused by a virus and that Hartwell was developing a miracle drug that would restore their lives to normal.

Other people in the group preferred to cope within the familiar structure of their own homes and families. They were mixed in their beliefs about the virus versus Suffield's theories.

Then there were a few, like the Castletons, who were receptive to alternatives, particularly as their own situations worsened. But they feared that banning together openly would only make it easier for the CDC to identify them, to tag them. Although testing was not yet mandatory for anyone other than county employees and Hartwell personnel, Nash suspected it was only a matter of time. And probably not very much time: five other towns in the United States were under quarantine.

The American Civil Liberties Union and a half-dozen other organizations had filed civil suits and were managing to keep the issue at the forefront of the news. The CDC was trying to combat the negative press by issuing statements almost daily about the "disease" they now called SES—Systemic Epidermal Syndrome. Symptoms were enumerated. The cortisone treatment was recommended for the skin condition. But otherwise, statements were vague and details scanty. Nothing had been said about how the SES virus was transmitted or its degree of contagion, and of course the cocoons hadn't been mentioned at all.

Nash didn't doubt the rumors that had been circulating about the cocoon found at Prudy's Place or that their discovery was what had prompted the quarantine. He'd heard Katie's account of what she'd seen in the cellar at the Menningers'. He'd listened to Mona Stawson's story about what Luanne Castleton had given birth to—and subsequently flushed down the toilet. It was consistent with the photographs Fay had taken of the mutant before Fielding and Lattimer had removed it from the morgue. The cocoons, he thought, were the end result of the silken threads that had been growing from the mutant's pores.

And we know what that means for Fay, don't we, Nash ole boy.

For Fay and all of the others. But why cocoons? What would happen once they broke open? Would they open up at all? What purpose did they serve? And why were he and Katie evidently immune? He didn't think these photographs would answer all of the questions. But he hoped they would provide vital clues about the energy vortex or whatever it was that prevented the changers from leaving the town.

He pulled up in front of the remains of the Menningers' house. There wasn't much left. Blackened concrete posts shot upward from the foundation as if to boost the sky; metal beams formed a latticework through empty space; steps climbed to nowhere; glassless windows framed the frozen lagoon and trees; chrome sinks and faucets were suspended in space. It was as surreal as a Dali painting.

As Nash and Samson walked around, the wind whistled through the ruin, as if celebrating a victory. His boots crunched over shards of glass, slivers of charred wood, bits of ceramic. He took a couple of pictures of the crumbling structure, then stretched out on his stomach and peered into the gaping hole of what had once been the cellar. Samson mimicked him, front paws dangling over the edge as he whimpered and sniffed at the faint vestiges of smoke. Nash used the flash to shoot another half-dozen pictures of the cellar, concentrating on the corner where Katie said the cocoons had been.

He'd expected to feel spooked here, but there was only a curious absence in the air, as though the fire had purged the place. The official story on the fire was that it had been caused by faulty wiring. Four corpses supposedly had been discovered, burned beyond recognition, but were identified through dental charts as the Menningers, their daughter, and a friend of Dani's, who evidently had perished in the blaze while they were sleeping. Katie, however, swore the Menningers were in the cocoons she'd seen and that the fourth was one the man-thing had. Nash believed her.

On the way back to the inn, he used up the rest of the film on photos of each home along Hawthorne. Then he shut himself up in the makeshift darkroom in the bathroom on the third floor.

He'd bought the equipment last year when he'd visited Ben and had found it stashed in the attic. The one thing he lacked was a metal drum for drying prints, but to compensate he'd strung a fishing line lengthwise in the shower. He fastened the prints and negatives there with clothespins and used Fay's hair dryer to speed up the drying.

He developed the negatives in small metal tanks that were similar to those he'd first used twenty years ago. The process was slow and tedious, and under ordinary circumstances, he simply would have had the negatives developed professionally. But the only place in town that offered a one-hour service had closed a month ago, when the owner walked out of his life. The place was up for sale.

Once the negatives were dry, he selected the ones he wanted to print first, got out the high-contrast paper, and went to work. He promptly lost track of time. The only reality became the soft luster of the safe light, the pungent smell of chemicals, and finally the prints.

By late afternoon, the new photos were pinned to a clothesline he'd strung the length of the bedroom, and the old ones were lined up across the floor, the bed, the desk, wherever there was space. He compared the pictures of buildings first.

The ghost images were far more pronounced in the new pictures than in the ones he'd taken in August. Some structures, in fact, were almost completely spectral. They seemed to float, to hover, to quiver in the light like alien craft that might vanish at any second. The same was true for every photo of the lagoon and the land around it.

The inn and the homes along the lagoon, including Fay's and the Suffields', all had the spectral shapes around them. But the

Menningers' place was the worst of the lot. Beams and posts were practically transparent. Through its cellar walls, he could detect the shape of the lagoon, of trees.

He was afraid to scrutinize the photos of people he knew, and particularly reluctant to look at Fay's pictures or those he'd taken of himself. He decided to save them for last and started with the photographs of the feds—Fielding's men and the CDC. The results were mixed: about half were surrounded by faint auras of light and the others were free of it. Fielding himself was clear, but his buddy Lattimer wasn't. Captain Oliver was okay, but his sidekick Moses wasn't.

He studied the picture of Karl Granger and his two companions from Hartwell. All three were encircled by the ghost light, but Granger's was the most evident. Nash wondered if there was some way of telling from the aura how advanced the change was. If he assumed that faint, narrow bands of light meant the change was only in its preliminary stages, then Granger was much further along. But how far? Had he developed a rash yet? Had any of the other symptoms manifested?

He compared Granger's picture with Suffield's. The intensity of their auras were a little different, but the bands of light around each of them measured an inch and a half. If he used Suffield's change as a gauge, then it meant that about fifty percent of Granger's body was probably covered with the new skin and he was experiencing at least some of the other symptoms. The rash probably hadn't started to show on his face and hands yet. But unlike Suffield, who'd already been tested at Hartwell and suspended from work, Granger would escape detection. After all, he was heading up the drug research. How convenient.

Nash moved on to the other pictures, jotting notes in an attempt to correlate the bands of light with the various stages of the change. He assumed it manifested first in the aura and then physically, but had no way of measuring the lapse of time between one stage of the mutation and another. However, by using people he knew as a base, he might glean some idea of how far the change had progressed.

Nash placed Horn at the low end of the scale and Ray at the top end. He was the worst of the people Nash knew: dark skin on his face and hands and tiny, silken threads poking out of the pores in his chest, neck, and legs. Then he made careful and detailed comparisons.

The results were frightening.

Forty-five out of the hundred people he'd photographed in

Lagoon were mutating. Of these, more than half were about to make the transition into Ray's stage. If this small cross-section was indicative of Lagoon's population as a whole, then forty-five percent were already in some stage of the change.

Nash walked up and down the rows of photographs, collecting his, Fay's, and Katie's, forcing himself not to look at them closely. He carried them over to the desk and turned on the lamp.

All of Katie's photos were clear. In one of them, she was playing around with Turner, the baby canary. A bright halo of light encased him. Turner *was* a kind of mutant and since the plant mutations had had the ghost light around them, it made sense that the animal mutations would, too.

The eight photos of Fay had been taken over a period of several weeks. In each one, the band of light grew wider, brighter, more intense. The last picture, snapped a couple of days ago, placed her somewhere between Suffield and Ray on the scale.

His own photos were as ordinary as Katie's. Even Samson, who appeared in a couple of them, was free of the change. He didn't know whether he felt relief or disappointment. In some ways, it would have been easier if he were also changing. At least then he and Fay would be confronting a common fate and wouldn't be constantly at odds over what he should do.

Her argument was always the same. *Just load up the Jeep and get the hell out, Nash.* His response was that he wasn't going anywhere without her. Since they'd proven it was clearly impossible for her or any of the changers to get out, that left him with only one option. To stay, to ride it out to the end, to . . .

Watch her become a cocoon.

Nash rubbed his hands over his face, cutting off his view of the lagoon, of the dwindling gray light, of the snow that had begun to fall again. He thought of the life he'd left behind, where every event was like a potential photograph, something that begged to be reduced to its simplest form and then rebuilt, layer by layer, balanced and composed into images that told stories. He had married, his daughter had died, his marriage had fallen apart, his brother had killed himself. Simple stories.

Then he had come here and the stories became more complex, involuted, and he was reborn into ignorance, darkness, stupidity. Now he had no easy answers and no more simple stories.

When the phone rang and he lifted his head from the cushion

of his arms, he couldn't immediately remember where he was. The window was dark. Some of the photos had slipped to the floor. The heat had dried the back of his throat to the consistency of tissue paper. He knuckled his eyes, wondering how long he'd slept, why Fay hadn't gotten home yet, where Samson was. When the phone pealed again, he answered it.

"Scott, it's me," Fay said before he'd spoken. Her voice was breathless, the barest of whispers. "Can you get over here right away?"

"Over where? Where are you?"

"At my place. I stopped by here to pick up some more clothes and things and I . . . I found something. Just get over here quick."

"I'm on my way."

2.

Dusk.

Fay waited for Nash at the end of the driveway, in the Jetta. She no longer trusted the house. It was now part of everything that was wrong here.

From this distance, tucked in the folds of trees, the snow falling silently around it, it looked small and white and clean, a doll's house, a house inside a paperweight. It seemed to have no connection to her life at all. Now and then she could still hear the buzz of a voice in her head, a raspy whisper that somehow seemed lewd, unclean, like a leper in biblical times. But it wasn't as loud or intrusive as it had been when she was in the house.

In the cellar.

Where she kept the supply of blood in the old fridge. Her supply. She wouldn't need it now; her hunger had vanished like a bad dream.

Fay rummaged through the glove compartment until she found a pack of Marlboros. They were stale, but she lit one, anyway, pulling the smoke deeply into her lungs. *C'mon, Nash. Please hurry.*

She turned the key in the ignition and flicked on the wipers. Snow flew from the glass and the house appeared in the half-moon arc on the windshield. Lights still shone in the front windows, and there, at the side of the house, she could see a dim glow spilling out of a cellar window. Nothing had changed. But what had she expected, anyway? That the cocoon would suddenly drop from the ceiling and walk up the stairs and through the door? That it would stroll down the driveway and speak to her?

She wanted to laugh at the absurdity of it all, at a cocoon in her cellar, for God's sakes, at the spineless terror that had propelled her up the stairs at the speed of light, at the way she sat out here in the car, smoking and waiting and watching, like a teenager rebelling against her parents. But the laughter wouldn't come. She knew what she had seen. And a part of her believed that it might be capable of doing exactly what she imagined.

Headlights struck the windshield as Delilah swung into the driveway; Fay winced against the sudden brightness. The voice buzzed at her, but it was so faint now, so distant, it was almost like a memory of sound. She hopped out and hurried over to the Jeep.

"What're you doing parked here?"

"Waiting for you."

He didn't ask why. He didn't comment on her clothes: jeans, a cotton shirt, bare feet. He didn't offer her his parka. When he took her hand, he didn't remark on how much warmer it was than his own despite the way she was dressed. There were certain things now that were simply understood; to mention them would be to waste whatever time together they had left.

She told him what she'd found and that she wanted it removed. Once they were inside the house, they collected the things they would need. Hedge clippers. Gardening gloves. A couple of garbage bags. The aluminum trash can. The 9-millimeter that she removed from her purse.

She slipped on shoes—*Don't want to step on the cobwebs, not again*—and they descended into the cellar. The buzz of the voice in her head was louder again, as though proximity to the cocoon powered it somehow. Katie had mentioned something like this happening to her the night at the Menningers'. She'd called it the web and thought it emanated from the energy vortex Suffield had talked about. A hot line to Mother Nature herself. Sure. A bubble of laughter, of hysteria, of disbelief, boiled in Fay's throat, but it popped like a pimple before it reached the air.

The cocoon dangled from a beam in a corner of the cellar where the light didn't reach. It was well hidden behind the air conditioner and a stack of cartons that had never gotten unpacked when she'd moved from Atlanta. She probably wouldn't have seen it at all if she hadn't heard the buzz. If she'd understood it was in her head. If she hadn't turned away from the fridge to see what it was.

It was a perfect clone of a caterpillar's cocoon, but larger—as long as she was tall and half as wide—and the same color as the paneling on the walls, a light pine. It was too thick, too opaque, to see the shape inside clearly even when a light shone on it. But the thing within tried to turn away from the light and its movements made the surface of the cocoon bubble up like asphalt on a hot summer day.

That's what I'm becoming.

The thought wasn't new. But she had never stood in front of the thing she was becoming; her fear and revulsion were so raw, so pure, they seemed to rise from the depths of the earth beneath her feet and shrieked within the loneliness of the stone and wood around her. And yet she didn't utter a sound. She went numb. She couldn't swallow, blink, move, couldn't do anything except stand there staring like an autistic child at her future. Nash asked for a ladder; the crackle in his voice resounded inside her skull, where the buzz was.

"Me. That's me," she said. The words were a dry rattle, a rasp of wind in a desert that had known nothing but wind and sun for centuries.

He grabbed her by the shoulders, spun her toward him. His black eyes glistened. Emotions flitted across his face: anger, denial, pain, love, all of it electrifying the air, shocking her from her stupor. "Stop it," he hissed. "Tell me where the goddamn ladder is."

She jerked free of his hands and moved woodenly across the cellar. She threw aside more boxes, junk, picked up the ladder, carried it over to him. He murmured an apology; she told him to forget it. They didn't look at each other.

They pulled on the gardening gloves, and Nash picked up the hedge clippers. While he moved the ladder closer to the cocoon, she pushed a wooden workbench under it to catch it when it was free of the ceiling. It wouldn't have far to fall, a foot at the most. But she didn't want it to split open, so she dropped a couple of dusty cushions on top of the workbench and stepped back, shining the flashlight up toward the beams.

Nash snapped the clippers a couple of times to make sure they didn't stick, then touched the edges of the blades to the cluster of threads at the top of the cocoon. But when he tried to cut through the threads, nothing happened.

"They're like steel. Do you have a saw?"

"A saw." She rubbed her forehead with the heel of her hand. "A saw. I don't know. Let me see."

She threw open the doors of the cabinet against the wall and went through the toolbox. She found a saw, but it was so rusted that the teeth looked ready to snap off. She didn't see anything else that could possibly be useful, but thought there might be something in her medical kit they could use.

She returned with an instrument used in cauterizing veins. It took six minutes of intense heat against the threads before they started to loosen and another four before they came away from the ceiling. The scorched fibers smelled like smoldering electrical wires and were still glowing when the cocoon dropped onto the cushions. The pine hue went instantly white, then began to blacken around the edges. Fay felt an overpowering urge to touch it and reached out, her gloved fingers pressing lightly against the center of it.

It didn't give at all. She exerted more pressure and the threads sank in a little, like hard plastic. But as soon as she took her hands away, it popped back into place.

"Let's get it in those garbage bags and haul it out to the center of the lagoon," Nash said as he scrambled down from the ladder. "We can weight it with rocks or something and sink it."

"No."

He looked at her, his eyes as deep as craters in his cheeks. "Then what the hell do you want to do with it?"

She longed to wrench her gaze away from the cocoon, but couldn't. She needed to know. Had to know. "I want to cut it open."

29

Glimpses of the Future

1.

The cocoon rested on a tarp on the dining-room table beneath the glare of the overhead lights and a gooseneck lamp with a 150-watt bulb in it. The white was now streaked with black, like hair that was going suddenly and irrevocably gray, Nash thought.

Despite the illumination, the darker coloring made it more difficult to see the thing inside, which suited him just fine. He had no desire to know what it looked like and thought there was something perverse about Fay's obsession to open it up. An obsession that was evidently shared by Suffield, who had arrived a few minutes ago with Katie and Ray in tow.

Neither of them seemed particularly eager to know what secrets the cocoon held. Katie kept wandering away from the table to poke at the logs in the fireplace and Ray just stood quietly, twisting the gold post in his ear and absently touching the fine threads on his neck.

Sometimes, Nash thought, it was best not to know what you were going to wake up to.

"I think you should slice it open along the sides," Suffield said. "Like a walnut."

"Maybe I should X-ray it first."

"But you'd have to take it to the clinic for that, right?" Suffield asked.

Fay nodded. "Yeah, bad idea."

They talked back and forth like this for several moments, as though it were only the two of them in the room. Ray finally interrupted. "I say we just forget the whole thing and dump it in the lagoon."

Suffield's glance was sharp, annoyed. "Don't be ridiculous. We're *obligated* to know what's inside. The more we know about this, the better off we'll be."

Ray's laughter was bitter enough to curdle milk. "Hey, don't you get it yet, Hank? We're not going to be *around* long enough for knowing or not knowing to make a difference. And besides, man, I don't *want* to know what the fuck I'm going to end up as, okay?"

"No one's making you stay," Suffield shot back.

"You got that right." Ray grabbed his jacket off the chair and marched out of the room. A moment later, the kitchen door slammed.

"That was great, Hank, just great." Bright pink splotches blazed in Katie's cheeks as she stuck out her hand. "Give me the car keys."

"You need to know about this, Katie, you need to know what—"

"I don't *want* to know. Now can I have the keys?"

He tossed them to her. When the door slammed again, a gallery of faces flashed across the inside of Nash's eyes, all of them changing, transmuting. He winced. Suffield caught it and said, "You in or out, Nash?"

"You could've handled that better. They're just kids."

"When it comes to this, we're all kids." His lean face had gone rigid. "You in or out?"

Like it had to be decided here and now, instantly. "I'm still here. Just get on with it."

And they did.

2.

Ray banged around the kitchen, attacking the dirty supper dishes they'd left in the sink when Fay had called earlier. He grabbed a frying pan, scrubbed it with a vengeance, rinsed it, slammed it into the dish rack.

Katie dried it, waiting.

"Your old man's fucked up," he said finally.

"Sometimes."

"He's crazy."

"Sometimes."

"He's an asshole."

"Sometimes."

"You think I should've stuck around."

"I think Fay should've said what it was about when she called."

"She's as fucked up as he is."

"It's different for them. They *need* to know. You don't."

He looked over at her, anger bleeding from his scent like color from his face. "I'm afraid," he whispered. "I want to know, but I'm afraid to know. It's just like how it was when my old man was beating up on my mom. I mean, I knew it was happening, but it scared me so much that I didn't want to *see* it going on because then I wouldn't be able to pretend that it wasn't. But that night when he was beating up on her and I walked in, I lost it. I nearly killed him. . . ."

A black despair swept through her, a glimpse of a future without the people she loved most in the world, and she started to cry. She couldn't help it. The tears just welled up and spilled over, leaving hot, wet tracks on her cheeks that she swiped at with the back of her hand. There was so much she wanted to say to him, but language failed her. She couldn't find the words. Maybe she didn't know the words. Maybe the words didn't even exist.

Then suddenly the words didn't matter because Ray was holding her. His mouth was against hers, his breath filled her lungs, his hands were at her spine, her hips, threading through her hair. Without speaking, they went into her bedroom and she shut the door.

Never in her life had she known anything sweeter than this. Her bones came undone. Her body turned weightless. She lifted, she soared, she floated in the soundless white of the snow. She tracked his scent into a thousand places, burrowed into his secrets, and emerged on the other side, a space traveler changed by the voyage.

She didn't care that most of his skin was thick to the touch and discolored. She wanted to sink into it, become part of it, pull it over herself like a blanket. She stroked the fine, white threads that poked from his pores, soft as a kitten's fur, and wound strands around her fingers, wishing they grew from her hips, her ribs, her eyes. She wanted to go where he would go.

And later, when she dozed, her dreams thrashed around inside her, an asylum of undrugged mental patients that cackled and laughed and whispered in Ray's voice, *Too bad, Katie-o, too bad.*

3.

Fay didn't want to use the cauterizing instrument for fear the intense heat might harm the thing inside the cocoon. Suffield agreed and suggested they try an electric carving knife, if she had one. It took her a while to find it. She hadn't used it since last Thanksgiving when she and Ben had eaten here at the house and had stashed it away with her gold jewelery she rarely wore.

She sharpened it, then Nash and Suffield turned the cocoon on one side as she applied the blade to the other and switched on the knife. She moved it up and down the imaginary seam half a dozen times before the knife overheated and shut off. It had barely made a dent in the cocoon and the blade was already dull again. It was like trying to slice through a walnut with a nail file.

Nash sharpened the blade once more. For just a moment or two, while she was waiting for him to finish, the room seemed to hold too much light; it hurt her eyes in the same way the sun did. But then she started working again and the sensation eased off and the light was only a heat, beating against the backs of her hands, her arms.

She felt as she had during her first autopsy in medical school, irritated that the corpse seemed to fight her efforts to enter it, tossing up obstacles that slowed her down; eager to see what secrets the flesh enclosed; nervous about doing the job right, the way it was supposed to be done.

The same stab of awareness that had afflicted her then plagued her now, that there was something fundamentally twisted in the study of the dead. It was as if this need to ferret out whatever the dead could tell her originated from some deep lack within herself, from a dark hole that begged to be filled with something, anything, she didn't know. And this dead cocoon—for it was surely dead now, it had turned almost completely black, had perhaps started to die the moment Nash had removed it from the ceiling—was no different from a corpse. It would yield its secrets, and for a while, that hole inside her would bubble with fullness, completion.

The side began to crack.

The knife's teeth chattered against the impossibly tough fibers, a sound like metal against metal that vibrated through her skin, her bones. Fay smelled the knife heating up once more and paused, then bore down harder. Perspiration stood out against her forehead. Her vision had narrowed to nothing but the black of the threads and the bright silver metal blade.

I need to know.

The side cracked from one end to the other.

She switched off the knife.

While Nash held it at one end, Suffield worked a screwdriver into the crack, moving it quickly up and down, up and down, widening it. But he was unable to pry it open far enough. It fought his efforts like the jaws of a dead fish that refused to surrender the hook that had caught it.

Nash took the knife and started cutting at the end closest to him, the top of the cocoon, and it gave within minutes. As Suffield was doing the same at his end, a fissure suddenly split the cocoon down the center, neat as an apple, as if a hidden button had been pressed that released the tough outer casing. It fell away in three parts, exposing what lay inside.

No one spoke.

Nash sucked air in through his teeth.

Suffield's hand clutched the edge of the table.

Fay's mind flew instantly toward the safety of professional detachment—what little of it she could muster—and crowded into the clean, white space it provided. From there, she quickly made an assessment.

Human in shape and structure.

Semifetal position, on its side. Knees drawn up, head tucked under, arms tight at the sides.

Cranium: larger than normal.

Hair: sparse, like new fur, like the growth that often covered a newborn's crown.

From the center of the skull, roughly where the fontanels on a newborn would be, grew the fibers that had been attached to the ceiling. Fay guessed that aside from the obvious function of holding the cocoon to a surface, they also acted as a kind of umbilical cord, drawing sustenance of some sort—perhaps from the air or from whatever the cocoon was connected to—that sustained it.

Brows: thin lines of down.

Eyes: closed, lids almost transparent, a latticework of veins.

Nose: not fully formed, the bone in the bridge not quite firm.

Mouth: pursed.

Hands and fingers: ordinary, except that the nails were thin, almost transparent, again like a newborn's.

Skin: bright red, as if badly sunburned, no markings whatsoever, arms and hands covered with the same blond down that appeared on the head.

They turned the entity onto its back.

"Aw, Christ," Suffield whispered. "She's pregnant."

Fay quickly checked for a pulse at the woman's neck and thought she felt a faint flutter against her fingers. She snatched the stethoscope from her bag, fitted it against her ears, listened.

There was a pulse, all right. It was weak but steady at thirty-two beats a minute. Fay stuck her finger in the woman's mouth and swept it back and forth, clearing her throat of the webbed stuff. Her lids snapped open. Her eyeballs rolled wildly around in her head, loose as marbles. Her chest heaved, she gulped at the air, and in one tremendous surge of strength that threw off Fay's hands, the woman flew forward, gasping. Her arms jerked up like a puppet's and she clawed at her throat, wheezing now, just the whites of her eyes showing, her swollen belly rippling with movement.

In isolated patches, her bright red skin bubbled up, as if with blisters, and turned thick and porous. The bones in her face and shoulders shifted and slid, bulging against the skin, popping, crunching as they became something else, something vaguely simian. Fur sped across the woman's body. Her mouth opened and shut in silent screams, and someone shouted, "Do something!" But none of them moved.

Now the bones shifted again, faster this time, faster, faster, and the fur vanished and the forehead protruded into a thick bridge of bone that was Neanderthal man. Another shift, and she became Cro-Magnon. Now the shifts came so rapidly, they were like glimmers of light, flickering through the entire evolutionary history of man until they leaped beyond the known, into the future. A large, bulbous, hairless head, a long neck like a swan's that pivoted, slender arms and legs, liquid eyes frantically telegraphing data Fay couldn't decipher, eyes that filmed over with an extra lid like a lizard's.

The image held for an instant, seesawing in the harsh gleam of light, threatening to collapse, the details shrieking to be remembered. The woman's bright blue eyes swam with agony as they pinned Fay like a frog on a dissecting table. The buzz in her head exploded with something like static and she clearly heard the woman's tortured rasp, *Help me.*

Then the woman's bones just seemed to cave in all at once, like the skin of a fruit that had rotted from the inside out, and she fell back against the table, motionless. Her pupils dilated instantly. A soft lavender, the color of the sea at sunset, swept from her feet to her head at a blinding speed, then swiftly darkened to deep purple, as though her entire body had been bruised. Before it reached her neck, her feet and legs were going black, as black as the outer casing of the cocoon.

It happened fast—ten, maybe fifteen seconds. When it was over, the blackened corpse on the table in front of them looked like a slab of charred beef that some lunatic had sculpted into a vaguely human shape. Noises punctuated the silence—logs crackling in the fireplace, Nash clearing his throat, the loud ticking of the clock in the kitchen—marking time this woman no longer had.

After a while, Fay didn't know how long, one of them moved. The sound startled her. Suffield was the first to speak. "I heard her. I heard her plea for help." He rubbed his hands over his arms as he drew his gaze away from the corpse. The glare of the lights sucked the details from his features; he might have been anyone. "I heard her."

"Bullshit." Nash moved stiffly around the table, like a robot whose batteries were running down, and jerked the edges of the tarp up over the corpse. "She could barely breathe, much less talk."

"I heard her, too," Fay said.

Nash didn't comment. He just kept folding the tarp around the woman. When she was covered, he rolled her onto her side, opened one of the trash bags, and worked it over her feet.

"What're you doing?" Suffield asked.

"What we should've done in the first place—sink it. To the bottom of the lagoon."

"But . . . but we can't," Suffield protested. "Not yet. We need to find out everything we can about her. Fay can do an autopsy, we can—"

"No." Fay's voice cut through the air like a knife through butter. "I can't do an autopsy here. And I can't remove anything from the morgue because the CDC's got the clinic under such tight supervision."

"We could break in. Get what we need." An ugly fanaticism suffused Suffield's voice.

"They've got a round-the-clock guard posted there now that—"

"Then you've got to do it here. Now. You can cut her open here and examine the organs, Fay. You don't need special equipment for that. Hell, *I'll* cut her open. We need to find out what we can about—"

"Shut up," Nash snapped. "We're not going to touch her."

Blood rushed into Suffield's cheeks. "This isn't any of your goddamn business, Nash. *You're* not changing. *We* are. *We* have a right to know. And, my God, you saw what happened. That woman . . ." He stabbed an index finger at the bagged corpse, his voice rabid with conviction. ". . . is a *new* species. Not only does she contain the entire evolutionary history of man, but she *proves* every theory I've ever put forth. *She's* the future. You saw it. Nature's putting us in cold storage until we become that future. You saw what she became there at the end, and I want to know everything I can about her. I'm *going* to know. . . ."

He lunged at the garbage bag like a mugger zonked on crack and clawed at the bottom of it, tearing it open as Fay shouted at him and tried to shove him away. Nash grabbed him by the back of the shirt, jerked him from the table, and slammed his fist into Suffield's jaw. He stumbled back and fell into a nearby chair, blood oozing from a cut on his lip. He started to push himself up from the chair, but Nash promptly shoved him back down.

"Now either get the hell out or help me carry her down to the lagoon." His voice was quiet and deadly.

Suffield glared at Nash as he wiped the back of his hand across his mouth, then pulled a handkerchief out of his pocket and held it to his split lip. The fever in his eyes was gone. He looked as meek as a mongrel dog and didn't say anything at all as he came over to the table. He helped them slide a second garbage bag over the first, then the three of them carried the body out onto the deck and down the stairs into the woods.

They weighted it with several large rocks, put it in a wheelbarrow, and made their way carefully along the slippery path toward the lagoon. The silence that had broken out across the darkness was like the inside of a dream, larger than itself, as vast as the galaxy, something that could not be charted. It was the future.

Just as the woman was.

That final version of shifting bones and musculature, of erupting tissue, haunted Fay. Details floated around inside her, hazy, indistinct, but with the force of a subliminal message.

"Nature's putting us in cold storage. . . ."

The ice along the perimeter of the lagoon was thick enough to support their weight despite last week's heat wave. But as they moved out toward the center, where the water hadn't frozen over, the ice started to crack.

"I'll take her the rest of the way," Nash said. He lifted the bag from the wheelbarrow and hoisted it over his shoulder.

Fay and Suffield remained where they were. She didn't know which was worse—a flash of her own future through the woman in the cocoon or this glimpse of Nash's future once she was gone, a solitary figure making his way across ice and snow.

30

Burn, Burn

1.

On November 4, the Lagoon County School Board issued a notice that classes would be suspended until further notice. Katie wasn't surprised.

Since the quarantine had been imposed, the high school had been struggling along with a skeleton staff. The majority of the students and teachers lived outside of town and hadn't attended since the quarantine had started. That left just fifty or sixty students at the high school, and their numbers had been falling daily. With so many teachers absent, Katie usually ended up with more study halls than she did classes.

But just the same, on the morning of the fifth, she drove over to the school to pick up her homework assignments for the week. Homework, after all, was part of her life before, it was ordinary, and she desperately needed a little of that now.

She couldn't even get near the student parking lot at the back of the building. It was blocked off by barricades, and inside were police cars, jeeps, and a fire truck. Several soldiers kept the crowd behind the barricades. She drove around the block, swung into the lot in front of the abandoned 7/Eleven, and hurried over to see what was going on. The bitter cold—it was just a couple degrees above zero—seemed to diminish her sense of smell. The only scent she picked up from the crowd was a vague uneasiness, an anxiety that zipped through the air like static electricity as people moved around to keep warm.

Katie spotted the senior with the sleek Mercedes whom Dani had been dating. She didn't know his name, but he'd been in a couple of her study halls for the past weeks. "What's going on?" she asked.

He glanced at her, his eyes like moist chocolate-mound candies beneath bushy brows. "Hey." He snapped his fingers and grinned. "I know you. Dani's friend."

"Right."

"Really bizarre about what happened to her and her folks."

She could think of a dozen more appropriate adjectives than bizarre, but she just nodded. "So was there a fire inside the school or what?" she asked.

"The janitor found six cocoons in the basement."

"Cocoons?" Her throat went tight.

"Yeah. Like the ones they found at Joker's and in the library basement and at Prudy's Place. Usually they've been in pairs, but, man, *six* at once." He frowned when she didn't say anything. "You haven't heard about them?"

"Just rumors."

He blew into his hands. "Hell, they aren't rumors. I was talking to a couple of soldiers about them. They've even found some in the woods. They think there could be, like, well, maybe a couple hundred around Lagoon. *Human cocoons*, I mean, is that disgusting or what? Everyone says it's the sickness. That the sickness causes it. I don't know if it's true or not, but I can tell you one thing. If I had weird crap growing all over my body, I'd shoot myself. No two ways about it. I'd swallow a bunch of 'ludes and just blow my brains out. Fast and painless."

"What else have the soldiers said?"

"I hear they're organizing some people from town here to search the woods. Kind of like vigilantes, you know?" He jammed his hands into the pockets of his jacket; his eyes gleamed. "I sure wouldn't mind being a part of that. Those cocoons are what fucked things up to begin with. I think that's really why they quarantined the town."

Kind of like vigilantes. She thought of Ray, now practically bedridden because the threads were constricting his movements, and of Hank and Fay, who weren't far behind. They'd all spent last night at the Blue Inn and would probably spend tonight there as well. It was easier and safer.

Someone moved alongside her and nudged her in the ribs. She looked up and Horn winked at her and took her arm, leading her away from What's-his-name to the periphery of the crowd. A thick wool scarf was wound around his neck, hiding the most visible part of his "sickness."

"Your buddy tell you what's going on in there?" Horn asked.

"Yeah."

"I got mighty bad feelings about this."

His eyes were narrowed to slits; the light hurt them. But Katie knew Horn wasn't about to slip on sunglasses. No one in the crowd wore them. They marked you. They meant you were changing. They meant you were one of *them*, even if you weren't.

She wasn't sure when this paranoia had become rooted so deeply within the heart of the town, but it had affected everyone. The meat bins at Kroger's were never empty anymore because there seemed to be an unspoken awareness that someone would notice if you bought more than what was "reasonable" and report you. It was never entirely clear what constituted "reasonable" or who you would be reported to—the feds? the brain police? the local cops?—but details like that had ceased to matter. Anything that might be connected to the "sickness" was avoided.

Even though people tried to maintain a normalcy to their lives—going to work, running errands, clinging to comforting habits, whatever they were—the quarantine had changed everything. It had narrowed not only the physical boundaries of their existence, but the mental ones as well. Fear had tightened around Lagoon, a noose that grew smaller every day, that infected the air with a suffocating claustrophobia.

The two movie houses in town had shut down due to lack of business. Most of the tourist shops had closed. The local newspaper had run its last edition a week ago, after the quarantine was imposed. The county offices and facilities were still struggling along, but with skeleton staffs because employees were using up long-accumulated sick leave and vacation time. Nothing was open once shadows lengthened toward evening, not even the local watering holes, and by dark, the streets were deserted, except for patrols.

"Here they come," Horn said, tilting his head toward the building.

The men were silhouettes that moved through the infusion of light in the parking lot with the certainty of gods. So much light, light that pulsed from the cold sun, from the snow, from the red brick of the school. Now she could make out Captain Oliver, with two soldiers who were carrying a cocoon. They were quickly followed by another pair of soldiers with a second one. From where Katie stood, the cocoons looked like huge, gray eggs, mythical in size, a dinosaur's eggs.

Murmurs rippled through the air. The crowd shifted like a protoplasmic mass as people strained to get better views; the mass surged against the barricades. Horn grabbed Katie's hand

and held on fast, edging closer to the outer perimeter of the crowd. "Move back, c'mon, step back," shouted one of the soldiers.

The mass obeyed. Then, from somewhere behind her, a voice that sounded like What's-his-name's screamed, "Burn 'em, burn 'em!"

A startled hush fell over the crowd. Heads snapped around. Eyes widened with alarm. Despite the cold, Katie caught a swift, disturbing change in the scent around her. Another shout went up. "Burn them, burn them!"

As others took up the chant, the words assumed a mesmerizing power. Fists beat at the air. Blood and fever rushed into white faces, mouths fell open as if with wills of their own, chants echoed through the parking lot and lifted toward the torn blue sky like hungry scavengers.

Colonel Fielding got out of one of the jeeps, conferred briefly with Oliver, then gestured toward the football field. The soldiers did an about-face and marched their treasures away from the jeeps. Oliver sprinted back to the building as the other soldiers appeared with the rest of the cocoons and directed them toward the field. The chant went on and on, growing louder, more frenzied. The fire truck roared to life and headed to the field.

The barricades were removed. The crowd broke loose, a pack of wolves tracking a fresh scent, and thinned out as people raced to get good seats in the bleachers. Horn and Katie hung back with a handful of others. "If we don't go," he said, "someone will notice."

"Everyone's too busy to notice."

"Not so. Look around."

She did, and saw Fielding's red-haired sidekick coming toward them in a jeep. It slowed as it pulled alongside them. Lattimer rolled down his window. He wasn't wearing sunglasses and squinted against the light.

"Want a lift?"

"No, thanks."

"Still pissed, huh, kid?" He laughed.

She didn't say anything.

"How's your old man feeling these days?"

"Okay."

"That's not what I hear." He grinned and ran his finger across his upper lip. "I hear he got laid off from work. That he tested positive for SES."

"You should know."

"You're right about that, kid. Seen any more bogeymen lately?"

She resisted the urge to spit in his face.

"Hey, I'm asking you a question."

"Fuck off."

"Jesus, girl," Horn whispered, tightening his grasp on her arm. "Let it be."

But it was too late. The jeep stopped. She stopped. Horn stopped. Lattimer got out and strode over to them. "I don't think I heard you right, kid."

She peered up at him, at the slits of his faded green eyes, at the freckles that dusted his cheeks. They were bleached nearly white by the light. "Then you're either deaf or stupid or both."

Rage seized his face, his hands clenched into fists, he took a step toward her and would have grabbed her if Horn hadn't moved between them. "Just back off, man. We don't want trouble with you or anyone."

"Outta my way, nigger."

Horn didn't budge. Some other stragglers had gathered around now, and Lattimer didn't seem too eager to make a scene. "I got news for you, kid." He stabbed a finger toward the field. "Those cocoons are the bogeymen."

With that, he hitched up his pants and walked briskly to his jeep. He sped off, siren blaring as he sliced his way through the crowd.

"Let's get outta here," Horn said.

2.

The cocoons were in the center of the football field, stacked up against each other, dark stains against the hard-packed snow. One of the firemen walked around them, dousing them with kerosene, while several other firemen stood nearby, hoses ready in case the fire got out of hand.

The chants from the stands were loud and rhythmic and beat against the inside of Oliver's head like fists, like drums. The inside of his mouth went dry with anticipation as he got the signal from Fielding. It was time.

He dug into his pocket for a box of wooden matches and walked out onto the field, past the firemen waiting with their hoses. He stopped in front of the cocoons, where the kerosene had melted the surrounding snow. Its odor hung thickly in the cold air, a scent he had grown to love, sweet and intoxicating.

It teased his nostrils and stirred memories of other burnings: the sharp crackle of flames, the brilliant orange slowly breaking down the tough, resilient casings of the cocoons, the gradual blackening, the miserable keening of the things inside as they died.

Abominations, he thought, removing several matches from the box. They were incubi spawned by something evil that had started with Ben Nash. He knew. He had seen what was inside the cocoons. He had been present when an army biologist had cut one open and autopsied what was inside.

"Burn them, burn them!" shouted the crowd.

The words filled him, lifted him. He struck the matches on the side of the box, flicked them at the cocoons, but they went out. He lit several matches at once, and this time he crouched and touched the flames to the edge of the kerosene spill.

The crowd cheered as tongues of fire leaped from the ground and sped toward the cocoons, raced across them, around them, licking, crackling, heating them up until the dark outer casings glowed. The intense heat pressed against Oliver's face and he stepped back, but not far. Never too far. He wanted to inhale the stench of the rugged threads as they succumbed, to see the cocoons burst like ripened pods or blacken like pitch or yawn open like the shell of a dead clam. It didn't matter to him which way it happened. Each was uniquely lovely and right and ended in death.

"Burn," he whispered. "Burn."

The crowd stamped their feet against the bleachers. Their fevered cries exploded like gunfire across the football field. They were parts of a single brain, a single entity, a supreme being cheering the end of the evil, and their delirium seized him, whisking him up, up, into a cyclonic whirlwind. His fist shot into the air. His shouts rang out as greasy tendrils of smoke sprang from the pyre, swollen with the sweet scent of victory, of triumph.

3.

Nash opened the cellar door quietly and didn't turn on the light. He grasped the railing and made his way carefully down the stairs, wincing when one of the steps creaked. His nose wrinkled at the stale, musty odor, and despite his heavy woolen sweater, he felt the chill.

The inn's cellar was huge and cavernous and jammed with

old furniture. But Fay had managed to make it fairly comfortable. She, Suffield, and Ray each had a couch to sleep on. Suffield had his books and computer set up on an old desk so that he could work if he felt like it; Ray had his music, which he usually listened to through headphones.

Fay had spent her daylight hours down here for the last three days, since she'd filed for annual leave from the clinic. When she wasn't attending to iron injections and transfusions for herself or the others, she spent most of her time sleeping, lost in a smooth ambrosial darkness of voices and dreams.

She had tried to describe this place to him, to share it with him. But he couldn't even begin to conceptualize it, and in the end, it became just one more detail of her life that the mutation denied him.

As he reached the bottom of the steps, he saw the green glow of Suffield's computer screen in the far corner of the cellar. Nash wondered what he did all day at the computer. Conducted experiments? Worked on his book, his magnum opus? Took notes on his condition?

The faint light was sufficient for him to see Fay, stretched out on her couch, an arm thrown over her eyes. Her mouth was slightly open; her breathing was a dry rasp. He heard the faint tinkling of music from Ray's headphones.

When Suffield spoke, his voice sounded garbled, a faulty radio reception from a distant planet. "I guess you've heard, huh." He didn't turn around; the back of his nearly bald head gleamed like an eye. The computer keys tapped.

"Heard?" The word seemed to stick against Nash's tongue; a dozen questions sprang into his head. "Heard what?"

Suffield laughed, hit another key on the computer that momentarily blanked the screen, and spun around. In the green light, the threads that protruded from the pores in his face glistened like long, thin blades of bleached grass covered with dew. It seemed to Nash that he could hear them as they brushed together, a soft, weird noise like baby crickets whose legs weren't fully developed yet might make. The fibers that grew from his fingers were slowly pulling them together; it wouldn't be long before he had no use of his hands whatsoever. The crust around his mouth caused him occasionally to swallow consonants or vowels.

"T'public burning."

A chill nipped at Nash's neck. He had just heard about it from Horn; how the hell could Suffield already know? He started to ask, but Suffield had already guessed the question. He clicked his tongue against the back of his teeth and shook his head as if to say Nash was hopeless.

"*T'web*, Scott. T'web. How else could we know squat, stuck down 'ere?" He motioned vaguely toward Fay and Ray. "They were in t'sleep, and suddenly Ray wakes up in a total panic and Fay's groaning like she's in real pain and I . . . I kept feeling somethin' in my head . . . agony, oh, Jesus, you wouldn't believe wha' agony." His eyes were dark craters in his raised cheeks, a place light had touched centuries ago and gotten lost in.

"I heard 'em dying," he whispered, his hand tightening on Nash's arm, the crusted palm hard and crunchy and cool against Nash's skin. "Just like I heard that woman in the cocoon we opened." He leaned close, his deformed mouth moving soundlessly for a moment until he was able to form the words. "And when we cocoon, they'll burn us, too."

"Which is what we've got to talk about."

His hand dropped away from Nash's arm and he spun around, facing his computer again. "Nothin' to talk about. We can't leave Lagoon." He paused. "*You* can. Katie can. But the rest of us can't. Y'know that. So don't even bring it up."

Nash pulled over a rickety rocker that had once been in the lobby; it creaked under his weight. "In another day or two, Ray's going to . . . to cocoon." He nearly choked on the word. "We need to find a safe place to put him." Then, more softly, his heart breaking up inside him: "To put all of you."

Suffield threw out his threaded arms. "What's wrong w'right here? It's dark, it's cold, it's perfect."

"It's also obvious. They already know you're changing, Hank. They probably suspect that Fay is since she's on leave. And who knows what they think about Ray. The point is that this is a place where they would look."

"He's right, Hank." Fay's voice was drugged with sleep as she got up from the couch, smoothing a hand over her jeans and shirt. "We need a plan."

She stopped next to Nash's chair and touched the back of his neck. A cool, light touch, this, the same touch that came to him night after night, seconds before the witch scent drew him in, drugging him beyond caring what she looked like, beyond pain. In the green computer glow, half of her face was cast in shadow. The half that was changing. "We need to know what we're going to do when the time comes."

"We'll *know* what t'do when t'time comes." Suffield's voice held that now familiar biting edge that said, *Back off, leave me alone, I don't want to talk about it now.* "The others knew. So will we."

"The others have had guardians who were changing and *they* knew what to do. We don't have that advantage," she said.

"What others?" Nash asked. "What guardians?"

Suffield and Fay exchanged a look that Nash intercepted but which he didn't know how to read. He had the distinct impression that the conversation was continuing, even though he couldn't hear it.

"Some of the mutants who were living on the west side of the lagoon were guardians," she said. "Their primary function was to disperse the cocoons all over the area, in places where they would be safe. They seemed to have the deepest contact with the web, drawing knowledge from it about what needed to be done during the cocooning process."

A kind of giddiness stole over him; Nash felt the sudden urge to laugh. Here he was, sitting in the cellar of his dead brother's inn, talking to the woman he loved about what he should or should not do once she began to metamorphose into a cocoon. This was not the ordered universe he'd been born into. In this universe, he didn't even know the basic rules. He was as naive as a first-time traveler who'd landed in the middle of the Amazon unprepared for the journey.

"Can't you, uh, tap into the web for the same information?"

"If we could, we would've," Suffield snapped.

"Knock it off, Hank. He's just trying to help. We wouldn't have gotten this far without Scott and Katie."

Suffield slammed his fist against the computer keys and pushed himself to his feet. The green light oozed over his misshapen face, sticking to the fine threads like flecks of old food that had spoiled. "It's *our* decision, n'his. N'Katie's. *We're* changing, we're—"

"Oh, Christ, find something else to say, will you? You're beginning to sound like a goddamn broken record. The facts are simple. We'll die if we leave Lagoon and we'll be burned if we choose the wrong place to stay. I figure we've got nothing to lose."

Music boomed from Ray's corner of the room as he unplugged his headphones. It pounded the stone walls, swallowing every other noise in the cellar, then it went off. Ray struggled to his feet, leaning heavily on a cane Katie had bought for him.

His shoulders stooped as he shuffled toward them. White threads floated around his body like ectoplasm. He seemed almost ethereal, a biblical figure who'd suddenly materialized in a burning bush and would vanish at any second. He was the single most pathetic figure Nash had ever laid eyes on, and it hurt to watch him too long.

Ray flicked on the floor lamp to the left of Suffield's desk. It was dim, sixty watts at the most. It cast enough light to make everyone except Nash squint and stripped away whatever illusions the green twilight had provided.

Ray stood there in his shorts and unbuttoned shirt, the fibers already tightening at his arms, legs, and hands, limiting his movements. He had lost most of his hair; he had no eyebrows. His face was almost entirely white with threads; a few strands grew from the corners of his mouth, like a cat's whiskers.

He pulled a gun out of the waistband of his shorts. It was one of the weapons Nash had given to him and the Suffields. He set it carefully on the desk. "A third choice no one's mentioned." His voice was dry and hoarse, and he spoke slowly, like an immigrant who was just learning English. "But not an option for me anymore. I can't stay in Lagoon, Scott. That's my decision." His dark eyes slid to Fay, to Suffield. "You two have to make your own decisions." Now those haunted eyes moved slowly back to Nash. "I'd like to leave with you and Katie."

Suffield sighed and rubbed the back of his neck. "In case y'forgot, Ray, there's a quarantine. Scott and Katie aren't going anywhere."

"*We're* keeping them here. Not the quarantine." The soft, even cadence of his voice seemed to mollify Suffield somewhat. "There're ways out of this town the colonel's men don't know anything about."

"You'll die if you leave," Fay said.

He tried to smile. "I'll die if I stay. And if I'm going to die, Fay, I'd rather be with people I care about when it happens." He switched the cane to his other hand and leaned on it again, his eyes still on Fay. "I'm probably going to cocoon real soon, maybe within the next twenty-four hours. And if Scott's photographs are accurate at all in terms of how fast this thing progresses, then you and Hank aren't far behind me."

"Scott's system of charting the mutation doesn't tell us the time frame. It's different for each person," Suffield said, irritated again. He gestured wildly toward the computer screen. "I've been working on it, trying to chart it, but there just isn't enough information. You can't possibly know when you're going to cocoon."

"Wrong, Hank." His patience snapped like a stalk of fresh celery, and he flicked the lamp shade upward and dipped his head toward it. "Take a look."

On the crown of Ray's head, slightly to the front, a cluster of stubs poked out of the scalp. They resembled stubble that grew in after a close shave. But these were white, hard, tough to the touch. The bone around them seemed to have bubbled up, and long dark lines streaked away from them, like the tracks of a worm burrowing just beneath the surface of dirt. What Nash felt most of all right then was an urge to puke.

"We know what these are, don't we." Ray raised his head again, his eyes oddly serene. "The umbilical cords that attach to some surface and keep us alive. They appear last."

The words hung there, as black and irrevocable as a sentence of death.

31

The Sweep

1.

Oliver and Lattimer arrived like a foul wind two mornings later, sweeping into the house while Katie was packing up some things Hank wanted at the inn. They'd probably expected to find Hank here because she'd parked his Mustang out front. Oliver wore a dark leather jacket similar to Lattimer's, as though the jacket marked him as a member of an exclusive club. He asked if Hank was home; she said he'd gone into town. Lattimer shrugged and whipped an envelope out of his jacket.

He grinned as he handed it to her. "I guess you're old enough to read, aren't you, kid."

The envelope contained a search warrant signed by a local judge. As she read through it, all she could think about was calling the inn to warn Nash to get everyone out of the cellar. "Search for what? We haven't broken any laws."

Lattimer gave an exaggerated sigh and combed his fingers back through his copper hair. "Don't they teach you civics in school, kid? You don't have to break a law to be served with a search warrant. This won't take long. We'll be in and out in no time. Which way to the basement?"

Once they were in the cellar, she called Nash from Hank's den: he told her to stall them as long as she could. She knew it wouldn't take them long to determine there were no cocoons in the cellar and she doubted they would search anywhere else in the house. They would probably hit Fay's place next, and since she wasn't home, they would go on to the inn. At the most, Nash had ten or fifteen minutes to get everyone moved out of the cellar.

And if he doesn't . . .

She didn't complete the thought.

She checked on Oliver and Lattimer, then slipped into the

hall and plucked her parka from the hook and stole into the garage. She found what she needed in Hank's toolbox, raised the garage door just enough to duck under, and ran out to Oliver's cruiser. A quick pull on the handle under the steering wheel released the hood. She stared at the engine, but only for a moment.

Thanks to Ray, she knew a little something about cars now. The least obvious way of putting this sucker out of commission was by loosening a couple of the distributor wires. She did that easily enough, but just to be safe she also snipped the fan belt.

Have fun, jerks.

She lowered the garage door after she'd scooted back under it, shucked her parka, tossed it on the workbench. She made it back to the kitchen before she heard the men coming upstairs and busied herself at the sink, watering the badly neglected flowers on the sill.

"This place have an attic?" Oliver asked, brushing his hands together.

"Nope."

Lattimer leaned against the fridge and pulled a pipe and a pouch of tobacco from his jacket pocket. "Go check out the other rooms, Lew."

"Waste of time," Oliver replied, clearly irritated that Lattimer was going to have a leisurely smoke while he did all the work.

"Just do it."

Oliver tossed him a dirty look but didn't argue. He shambled into the living room while Lattimer stood there puffing on his pipe and watching Katie. She ignored him. She dumped one of the begonias onto a paper towel and picked dried leaves off of it.

"Where's your old man, kid?"

"I told you, he's in town."

"And when's he due back?"

"I don't know." She rearranged the pebbles at the bottom of the pot so they covered the drain hole. "He didn't say."

"You know what I think, kid?" He rocked toward her. "I think your old man's already cocooned and that you've hidden him somewhere. That's what I think."

He blew a cloud of sweet-smelling smoke toward her. Within it swelled the scent that was specifically his, just his. Katie grabbed on to it, riding it as it thrashed through images that were personal and profane, as it tossed up falsehoods, fragments, old memories and new. She clung to it until it delivered the essential picture, the only one that mattered. She smiled and untangled herself from the odor, understanding now just how accurate Nash's photographs were.

"You think the cocoons are funny, kid?"

She broke apart the black dirt around the begonia's roots with her fingers and packed it into the pot. "What I think, Mr. Lattimer, is that you're pretty funny, chasing around town looking for cocoons to burn, hoping you can find them all before you've changed so much you can't hide the new skin anymore."

She looked up at him. His face had blanched; even his freckles seemed to have faded. "Am I warm, Mr. Lattimer? Am I right on target? You don't know? I figure you're hoping that the cocoons are found fast so the quarantine is lifted and you can get out of here before the colonel knows the truth about you. Otherwise, who knows, maybe he'll want to use you as a guinea pig for Hartwell's wonder drug. The one that's not going to work because what you've got isn't a sickness. You're mutating, that's all. Just like other people. And no drug's going to stop that. And guess what else, Mr. Lattimer? People who're mutating can't leave Lagoon. Isn't that something? The town won't let you guys leave. You get sick and have to turn back. Isn't that nice to know?"

Lattimer's pale green eyes had sunk into his cheeks and blinked rapidly, nervously, a prelude to a seizure. "What the—" he stammered.

"The rooms are clean," Oliver said from the doorway.

The stilted tone of his voice indicated he'd heard everything, and Lattimer knew it. He opened the kitchen door, his dead pipe in his hand, and left. Oliver glanced at Katie on his way out, then looked quickly away, as though he were afraid she might see something in him as well.

She locked the door behind them and watched through the window. They walked silently to the cruiser, Lattimer trailing behind Oliver by several feet, as meek as a child who knew he was going to be called to task for an infraction.

It didn't take them long to discover the car wouldn't start. Oliver threw up his hands. Lattimer stabbed an accusatory finger toward the house. Heated words were exchanged. Oliver's door flew open and he stormed out and stuck his head under the hood. A few minutes later, he marched back to the cruiser and got on the radio.

Lattimer sat in the passenger seat and fumed, arms crossed

on his chest, eyes burning through the window, their heat seeking her like a missile.

They were still sitting out there twenty minutes later when she backed out of the garage, Hank's things in the Mustang's trunk. Both men glared at her as she wiggled her fingers at them. *Toodle-loo, turkeys.*

2.

Sammy Loman sat in the cold dampness of his cellar, a gooseneck lamp aimed at the book in his lap. It was a first edition of *Brave New World* and had been in his wife's family for years. The cover had beautifully embossed gold letters on the front, and the edges of the pages were leafed in gold.

It felt, he thought, the way books were meant to feel when you held them, as though it contained something substantial that was to be savored, absorbed slowly, like a fine meal or a bottle of expensive wine. He opened it to the marker and began to read aloud. He didn't know for sure whether his wife could hear him or if she was even aware of his presence. But a part of him believed that if anything could reach her, it would be the timelessness of words like these.

Now and then he paused and gazed at the cocoon hanging from the ceiling less than six feet away from him. In the last few days, it had turned from a bright, pure white to a soft pine, the color of the walls. There wasn't enough light for him to see the shape of his wife inside. But at night, when he couldn't sleep, he came down here and put his arms around the cocoon, pressing his cheek against the impossibly hard surface until it seemed to warm to his touch. And then he thought he could feel her moving against him, yearning for him.

He was grateful the kids had stayed with his mother-in-law since the night out at Joker's. They'd at least been spared this. He talked to them frequently on the phone and made excuses about why Mom couldn't come to the phone. She had the flu. A bad fever. She wasn't home. One day he would run out of excuses, but he couldn't worry about that now.

Loman looked down at the page again and started to read, but the doorbell pealed, interrupting him. He considered not answering it. He was due at Kroger's by ten and wouldn't get back here before six, and he resented it when something intruded on this special time. But when the bell rang again and again, he pushed the tall old wooden cabinet back in front of the cocoon and told his wife he'd be right back.

Sergeant Moses stood on the stoop with a pair of soldiers, his darkly tinted glasses slightly crooked on his nose. He looked ill at ease and kept shifting his weight from one foot to the other as he nodded and said, "Morning, Sammy. Hope I didn't catch you at a bad time."

"Just getting ready for work. What can I do for you, Mo?"

He brought an envelope out of his jacket. "I've got a, uh, warrant here to search your place."

Loman's blood went thin and cold. He somehow managed to laugh, a laugh that sounded almost natural. "A warrant? For what?"

Moses rubbed his stubbly jaw, glanced down at his shoes, then up again. His voice dropped. "It won't take long, Sammy. You got my word on that. I don't like this any more than you do. Here, take a look."

Loman's mind had already flown into some other place, a probe moving at luminal speeds, seeking an escape, a plan, a miracle. But he took the envelope from Moses and opened it. He didn't need to read it to know it was legit, it had to be, that was the way these people did things. He glanced at the name of the judge who'd signed the warrant, and yes, Loman knew him, had known him for ten years. He knew his wife and kids, and he knew that for the last two months the judge's wife had been buying three times the amount of red meat she used to buy.

Someone in the family was in the change, and the judge was signing search warrants without question, probably signing whatever the feds dropped on his desk because it deflected suspicion and because if he didn't, they would find some other judge who would, and the next warrant might have *his* name on it. Politics. In the end, even this came down to politics. *Scratch my back and I'll scratch yours.*

"I'd like to call Judge Tessel first, Mo. If you don't mind."

One of the soldiers shook his head. "Sorry, sir, but—"

"Sure, go on and call him." Moses's voice was razor-sharp, and the look he shot the soldier could have felled trees. "He's got a right to check things out."

Loman stepped back inside with the warrant, closed the door, pressed the heels of his hands against his eyes. *I can't do it.*

But he would. He had to. Otherwise they would burn her, just as they'd burned the six cocoons at the football field.

Forgive me, please, Oh, God, forgive me.

Before his nerve snapped, he ran into the bedroom, jerked open the nightstand drawer, and pulled out the .38 he'd owned for six years and had never used. It would never stand up to the automatic weapons the soldiers had. But it would do the job he had in mind. It would. It had to.

Loman threw the dead bolt on the cellar door and tore down the stairs. He ducked behind the old wooden cabinet and encircled the cocoon in his arms, his cries muffled against the cool surface. "I'm sorry," he whispered over and over again as he climbed onto a chair and then cocked the gun. He pushed the barrel down into the cluster of threads that clung to the ceiling, down against the toughness, and pulled the trigger.

He thought he heard the faintest whisper of surprise, of anguish, thought he felt the essence of his wife slipping into the air, an invisible balloon, as the cocoon went black. Then there was nothing but the whimper of his own terror, the squeak of the chair as he climbed down, the click of the gun as he stuck the barrel in his mouth.

Forgive me, he thought, and squeezed the trigger.

3.

Oliver, Lattimer, and their reinforcements, two soldiers with automatic weapons: Katie watched them from the dry, tall grass in the field across from the inn. She watched like an outcast, an exile, an expatriate who wanted to return home and couldn't.

The inn door opened. They spoke to Nash. Oliver delivered the search warrant. One of the soldiers remained on the porch as the others went inside. Katie dropped low against the ground and scurried back through the weeds. The snow and the rocks cut her hands, her knees.

When she was deep in the cold shadows of the pines, she got up and ran to where she had parked the Pinto. The backseat was folded down, with Ray lying diagonally across the ample space inside. His limbs were completely immobilized by the fibers now, trapping him like a mummy. Only his eyes, mouth, and nose weren't covered. The threads at the top of his skull seemed to be growing even as she folded away the blanket that protected his eyes.

"They're inside now," she said. "It won't be much longer."

His mouth moved. "Li," he rasped.

Li: light. She pulled the blanket back over his face. "Better?"

"Yes."

"You need anything?"

"Find me," he whispered.

Katie stretched out next to him on her side, one arm thrown across the center of his cocoon, roughly where his waist would be, the other arm under his head, supporting it. She waited for him to release the scent that would pull her in, and then she burrowed, deeper and deeper until she found him, an amalgam of the old and new Ray, the Ray who could somehow speak to her through the scent.

The cold light poured through the open hatchback, pooling around the woman and the nearly completed cocoon.

4.

They searched the cellar with the chilling diligence of secret police, Nash thought. They pulled cabinets away from walls, moved crates and boxes and old furniture, shone bright spotlights in every corner, every nook and cranny.

Oliver barked questions like a skilled interrogator. Was the computer one of Ben's? What about the desk it was sitting on? Why was there so much furniture down here? Was there an attic here at the inn? How many rooms were there? Were there storage areas?

Then the questions got more personal and Nash's patience grew thinner. What was Nash going to do with the inn once the quarantine was lifted? Try to sell the place and leave, he said. Where was the doc, anyway? In town, he replied. Wasn't she living here now?

"That's really none of your business, Captain."

The light streaming through the kitchen window struck Oliver's face as he smiled. "I got news for you, Nash. It's all my business. I need to talk to her because we've also got a search warrant for her place."

"I don't know when she'll be back, but I'll be glad to let you into her house. Or I can give you the key and you can let yourself in."

"Fine," said Lattimer, his pale green eyes darting around the room like restless garden insects. "That's fine."

But it was apparent from Oliver's expression that the arrangement wasn't fine with him. "She's got to be present."

Lattimer rolled his eyes. "Bullshit."

"It's the law."

"Whose law? Yours?" Lattimer exploded with laughter. "This town's under martial law."

Blood filled Oliver's cheeks and turned his nose bright red. He looked like he was about to stamp his feet and have a temper tantrum. Nash figured that he wanted to play God in front of Fay, that he wanted her to be standing there when he dipped his hands into the contents of her drawers, when he touched the clothes in her closet. He wanted to get even for the times she had spurned him, rejected him. Under other circumstances, it would have amused him; now it only infuriated him.

"That's how we've been doing things," Oliver argued.

"We'll take the key, Mr. Nash." Lattimer didn't even look at Oliver. "Why don't you go check the garage, Lew."

"Tell your lackey to do it," he said, referring to the soldier who was now upstairs somewhere. "What's in here, Nash?" He strolled over to the door between the refrigerator and the cabinet; Nash's heart skipped a couple of beats.

"The walk-in freezer."

Oliver rattled the padlock on it. "How come you've got it locked up?"

"Because the first night I was here someone broke in through the back door and stole a bunch of the food inside."

"I don't remember seeing anything on that."

"I never reported it."

"Open it."

A hard, tight knot formed behind Nash's eyes. He moved toward the door on legs carved of wood, and in his head, he seized and discarded excuses as quickly as his heart was beating.

"Upstairs is clear," announced the soldier as he came into the kitchen.

"Good," said Lattimer. "Let's split. We've got a lot of ground to cover before dark."

"The padlock," Oliver insisted.

Lattimer's jaw went rigid. "It's a goddamn waste of time. Now, c'mon, man. Let's hit it."

But Oliver, who'd already lost where Fay's house was concerned, wasn't about to lose on this point as well. "The padlock, Nash. Hurry up."

He spun the knob; his fingers felt thick and damp. He dialed in the combination, the lock snapped loose, the door yawned open. Cold air rushed out in a white cloud, and Oliver stuck his head inside.

"You got enough in here to feed the army," he remarked.

Nash's throat had constricted: it was an effort to speak. "Most of it was here when I arrived."

Oliver eyed the ten large cardboard boxes lined along the floor. "What's in those?"

"Freeze-dried and packaged goods like Fritos and potato chips and what not."

"Uh-huh." As Oliver flipped back the flaps on a couple of them, Nash's fingers tightened on the jamb. The air around his head seemed to thin; he felt suddenly dizzy and nauseous. It was as if he'd zipped from sea level to fifteen thousand feet in the blink of an eye.

That's enough, asshole. You've looked around enough.

Lattimer poked his head through the doorway. "You coming or not, Lew? We're finished here."

"Yeah, yeah." He checked one more carton, his eyes swept across the upper shelves, then he walked out, his foul mood trailing him with the reluctance of an abused pet.

Nash shut the freezer door and moved quickly away from it, relief swollen in his chest. In the lobby, he gave Lattimer the key to Fay's, an exchange Oliver ignored, then the three men left. Nash stood at the window, watching the BMW speed down the driveway, tires spitting out dirty snow. Samson ran after it until the car had vanished behind the trees.

When he was sure they wouldn't double back, he returned to the freezer, shoved three of the boxes away from the far wall, and popped open the four-foot-high door that led into an ice bin.

He crawled halfway inside, his breath a haze of white against endless white. Fay was propped up against bags of ice, a snow queen in her element, her hazel eyes and thinning walnut hair the only color in an otherwise colorless world.

Her eyes possessed that languid, drugged look they always had during the day now, and for a moment or two, she didn't seem to recognize him. Then she said, "Safe?"

"For now."

"Maybe they'll be back."

"Not just yet. They're on their way to your house."

When she blinked, some of the threads that had sprouted at the corners of her eyes got tangled in her lashes, thin white ribbons like mucus. "They're sweeping the town for cocoons, Scott."

He didn't ask how she knew. "Let's get Hank."

They had wrapped Suffield in a sheet and were able to pull him out easily. He had no mobility in his legs now, but he could still move his arms from the shoulders down and raised himself up once he was out of the ice bin and in the freezer. When he spoke, the fibers that had sealed the right corner of his mouth created a parody of his speech. "Ga' 'ucky t'is 'ime."

Got lucky this time: Yeah, Nash thought. And as far as luck was concerned, they were now running on empty.

5.

By late afternoon when Horn arrived, the sky was weeping with slush. It fell in great, wet clumps that stuck to branches like wads of white chewing gum and oozed down the inn's windows, as messy as spit. The wind had risen and whistled into the lobby with him, making the flames in the fireplace spit and hiss.

"Gonna turn to ice before nightfall," he said to Katie as he shrugged off his jacket.

She draped it over the back of a chair near the fire so it would dry. "You must be listening to the same weather forecast we are." She tilted her head toward the cellar stairs. "We've got everything set up downstairs, where it's not so warm."

"You make it sound normal."

She looked up at him. "What other choice is there?"

"None." He ruffled her hair. In the saffron swirl of firelight that haunted the gloomy room, his smile was a small, dimming sun on a cold planet. The smudges of dark skin that were slowly claiming his face were hidden in shadow. He was still a man divided, a Janus; the others were more something else than they were human.

"How's Ray doing?"

"Worse just since this morning."

"And Hank and Fay?"

"Worse."

"It's still accelerating then."

"It looks that way."

"For me, too."

There wasn't anything to say to that.

Downstairs, the weatherman on the tube was predicting ten inches of snowfall before sunrise for Lagoon and the surrounding areas. This would be followed by a precipitous drop in temperature, somewhere between ten and thirty degrees below zero. His words sounded hollow and empty in the dimly lit cellar; he seemed about as real to Katie as the ghost light of stars.

A lamp burned in the corner of the room, bright enough for Nash to see what he was doing, but not so bright that it bothered Ray, Hank, and Fay. They occupied three of the four couches, which were lined up side by side, with an IV pole next to each one. Four poles, four bags of blood, the last of it, Katie thought.

Nash hooked Horn up to an IV, then he and Katie pulled up chairs to listen to his report of what was happening in town. The total tally on the sweep stood between thirty and fifty cocoons, depending on which story you wanted to believe, Horn said. He figured the real number fell somewhere in between.

"Who'd they get?" Fay asked.

Horn closed his eyes and recited the list of casualties, which included most of the people who had been in Hank's support group. There had also been one suicide—Sammy Loman, who had shot into his wife's cocoon first, then turned the gun on himself.

"The public burning has been scheduled for tomorrow night around nine. I think that's your best time to make a break."

"But they'll probably double the security," Katie said.

Horn agreed. The obvious exits were going to be well covered. And they had to assume that Fielding knew about the path old man Barlow had plowed from his cabin through the woods to the state park in South Carolina. He'd probably had lookouts there since the quarantine had started. "But no way in hell can he know the route I mapped out for you. It doesn't exist on any map."

"But we still have to pass the Barlow place to reach it," Nash said.

"That's right, boy. And, thanks to Ben, you've got the guns to do it."

Nash glanced at Katie; she read the doubt in his face. "I know how to shoot," she said.

Fay held up her hands; threads trailed away from them, gossamer strands of silk. "I think I can still hold a gun."

"Won't need to," Horn said. "I'm coming with you. So's Charlie Castleton. He's got nothing to lose since they took Luanne. So that makes four of us."

"We need a vehicle large enough to carry all of us and something that's going to be able to make it through those woods," Nash said.

Horn's smile was mysterious. "Charlie and me got just the right thing in mind. All we have to decide is how to get it. After that, I think we'll do just fine."

"*If* the town doesn't kill us when we try to leave," Fay said quietly.

No one replied.

32

The Heist

1.

Oliver stood at his office window, watching as the sun waged a valiant battle against impending dusk.

Light struck the barren trees in the city park, setting them on fire. They burned with almost unendurable brightness, bizarre wooden sculptures some crazed artist had plucked from a nightmare of holocausts and endings. Then shadows rushed into Four Corners with the exuberance of a swollen, muddy river, gobbling up the light bit by painful bit, and Oliver's old fear of the dark shuddered through him. It was sly and insidious, a foe as real as the cocoons and as formidable as the mutants who had killed Obie.

He rubbed his hands over his arms and turned away from the frosted window, silently cursing the faulty heating system that barely took the chill off the air. When he looked up, Polly was leaning against the doorjamb, hands lost in the pockets of her rabbit fur jacket.

"Goddamn, woman. Don't sneak up on me like that," he griped.

"My, my, aren't we jumpy." She shut the door, lit a cigarette, and flicked the match into the trash can. "I guess tonight's executions have got you a bit on edge, huh."

He laughed. "I'd hardly call them executions." He sank into his chair and straightened the papers on his desk, hoping she'd leave. But apparently she wasn't finished. She came over to the desk, her boots clicking against the floor, and flicked ashes into the trash can.

"Maybe assassinations would be a better word, Lew."

"Look, if you don't mind, I've got work to finish up here."

She grabbed the back of his chair, whipped it around, and leaned into his face, a hand on either armrest, trapping him.

"Let's give those cocoons names, okay, Lew? Let's make them *real*. Let's give them *faces*. There's Luanne Castleton and Prudy and . . ."

She began ticking off the names of people he'd known most of his life. Oliver grabbed her wrists, tore her hands from the armrests, pushed her back as he stood. But it didn't shut her up.

"Let's talk about Moses being out sick, Lew. And about why Judge Tessel signed all those search warrants." He stepped toward her, and she stepped back, her cheeks bright pink, her eyes smoldering with contempt. "Did you know his daughter and wife have cocooned? Did you know he and Fielding struck a little deal? That Fielding promised to leave *his* cocoons alone if Tessel would sign the warrants? No? Fielding didn't tell you? Gee, that's too bad, Lew. Did he happen to tell you what he really believes about all this? That the disease stuff is just government propaganda because they don't know what the hell is behind any of it? He didn't tell you that, either, Lew?

"Maybe you oughta have a little talk with your carrot-top pal, Lattimer. He seems to know all sorts of things you don't, and he sure was shooting off his mouth last night when he'd had one brew too many. He was so drunk he couldn't even get it up, Lew, and he was real self-conscious about the shit all over his body. . . ."

"Get out of here." Oliver seized her by the arm and shoved her toward the door. But she jerked free, spun, and slammed her knee into his groin. Stars exploded in his eyes. He doubled over, moaning, clutching himself. She grabbed him by the hair and flung his head back.

"Don't *ever* do that again or I'll blow your fucking head off." Her face swam in front of his eyes. "You're going to listen to me because I'm going to tell you the truth, Lew. I'm the only person who will. Burning those cocoons will be mass murder. Genocide. You *know* who those people were. You *know*, you son of a bitch. And if you don't do something to stop it, you're going to regret it the rest of your life and, I hope it'll be a *short* life, Lew."

Then she let go of his hair and he dropped to one knee. When the door slammed, the noise seemed to rupture the inside of his head.

2.

Nash poked Delilah into a parking space behind Castleton's Army/Navy. From the glove compartment, he brought out a 9-millimeter semi-automatic and tucked it into the waistband of his jeans. He double-checked the tool pouch hooked to his belt, zipped up his jacket, glanced over at Katie. She was tucking vagrant strands of her blond hair up under her dark knit cap and had exchanged her light parka for a darker one. Her jeans, like her boots, were black.

"Any questions?" he asked.

"Nope. I know what to do."

They synchronized watches, then Nash gave her shoulder an affectionate squeeze, and they both climbed out of the Jeep. The cold was a deep freeze almost as bad as Antarctica, a tough, stinging thing that penetrated his thermal underwear, his layers of clothes. Minus twenty-three degrees and still falling, and that didn't take into account the chill factor of the wind that snapped at them with the blind fury of a rabid dog.

Charlie Castleton poked his head out the rear door before they reached it. Dressed entirely in black, he looked like a short, squat gnome. He opened the door wide and gestured toward the things against the wall. Sleeping bags, food, camping supplies, several rifles with boxes of shells, blankets, assorted odds and ends he thought they could use. Although he'd spent a lifetime in this town, the only personal items he was taking with him fit into a knapsack hanging from his shoulder and a leather bag the size of a small dog.

They loaded everything into the back of the Jeep, then Nash and Charlie took off down the alley, their shadows preceding them. One very tall shadow, one very short, a Mutt-and-Jeff duo headed for the warehouse behind the Kroger's supermarket, where the refrigerated trucks were kept.

3.

The street lamps were winking on as Katie circled the block. They steamed like orange Popsicles, spilling light that varnished the icy sidewalks until they shone, and twinkled in darkened store windows, fireflies from another dimension.

The roads were empty. No police cruisers, no jeeps, no soldiers on foot. There was an unsettling tightness in the air, an expectant something that raised the hairs on her arms. She wanted desperately to track the scent it guarded so jealously, but the bitter cold had numbed her peculiar sense of smell. She felt as vulnerable as a saint in a country peopled by atheists.

She drove over to the Nameless, where the CLOSED sign hung in the window. She parked around back, and two quick raps brought Horn to the door. "How're we doing on time?" he asked.

"Perfect."

"Good. It'll just take me a couple minutes to load the Jeep. Go on inside."

She sat in the dark at the front of the café, watching Kroger's and the time. Her eyes made repeated sweeps through Four Corners. She had never seen it so deserted this early in the evening. It was as if Lagoon were under siege by an invisible, soundless enemy and people had gone into hiding.

Now and then a lone car appeared, chugging through the relentless cold, past the library and the park until it turned off. Each time it happened, her heart beat a little faster and she pressed the heel of her hand against her temple or dug her nails into her palms, telling herself to calm down, to stop imagining things.

She tried to remember what Four Corners had looked like during the summer: cars whizzing past, pedestrians on the streets, shops bustling with business. She tried to recall the park in hot spring daylight but couldn't. It seemed it had always been as it was now, filled with gnarled shapes, pooled shadows, the presence of an unnamed sorrow that had curdled into something evil.

A pickup truck drove through the intersection and hung a right, moving toward Kroger's. *Keep going,* she thought at it. *Please keep going.*

But it pulled up at the curb and someone got out of the pickup. The person moved like a woman, but from this distance Katie couldn't tell who she was. She was bundled up in clothes so dark, the pumpkin glow of the street lights was sucked into the fabric. The woman knocked at the door of the army/navy store, peered through the window, rocked back and looked up at the second floor, then sprinted out to the truck again.

When she paused briefly under a streetlight and glanced up and down the road, Katie got a better look at her. Polly Oberman. She didn't know what business Polly had with Charlie, but she got the distinct impression that she intended to warn him about something. A moment later, her pickup jerked from the curb and sped away from Four Corners.

"How's it look out there?" Horn whispered as he came back inside.

"Empty."

"Good. I'm all set."

As they left, he hesitated in the doorway, an aging man with bent shoulders, clutching a bag in his left hand, gazing into the darkened spaces he'd inhabited longer than Katie had been alive. She knew the feeling, all right, and squeezed his arm as he shut the door quietly and locked it for the last time.

Horn directed her down the dirt road behind the café. It ran past slumbering stores and the ghost shapes of birches and clutches of pine. They emerged directly across from the warehouse and the field next to it. Katie gunned the accelerator and the Jeep shot across the street. It plunged into tall, dry weeds that scraped against the doors like husks of corn the sun had scorched, slapped at the tires, the hood, and closed up behind them. When she was just beyond the door of the warehouse, she swung into a U-turn. Now they could see the front of the warehouse as well as the street. Katie killed the headlights, and they waited, watching.

4.

It had taken Nash nearly fifteen minutes to break into the warehouse, longer than he'd anticipated. But the intense cold had frozen the locks on the wooden doors, making them impossible to pick. He had to resort to a hammer and chisel that left the surrounding wood looking as if it had been attacked by a horde of giant termites.

Since there were no windows inside, Nash flicked on the overhead light. It illuminated a pair of six-wheel-drive trucks that had been used to haul goods from Kroger's Atlanta warehouse to the store here in Lagoon. They weren't merely large. They were monsters capable of eating up a flat highway in seconds flat and leveling anything that got in their way. Nash felt as small as a salt shaker beside them. He was used to vehicles whose steering wheels fit comfortably under his hands, to pedals and brakes and clutches that obeyed when his feet touched them, to cars whose length he could see in the rearview mirror. But *this*. Jesus. He didn't even know if he'd be able to drive one of these.

"Here," said Charlie, thrusting a ring of keys into his hand. "Try them."

There were at least two dozen keys on the ring—part of a key-making side service the army/navy store had offered. It didn't take Nash long to find one that opened the door. But they had to go through thirty of the forty-eight keys before locating one that slid into the ignition—and then refused to turn.

"Shit," Charlie muttered. He held his ring up to the light inside the truck, his practiced fingers slipping over the keys as though they were rosary beads. He found one whose shape and size were similar to the key that had fit into the ignition.

It was perfect.

Nash turned it and the engine thundered to life. It echoed in the closed confines of the warehouse, the wail of a beast preparing to wage battle, and slammed around inside the cage of Nash's skull. Smoke poured from the tailpipe. The glass in the windows rattled. He started flipping switches, punching buttons, turning dials, pulling knobs on the glowing blue dashboard. The lights blazed. The side mirrors moved. A panel slid open behind the seats, exposing the massive interior of the storage compartment.

"You ever driven one of these, Charlie?"

"Nope. You?"

"About twenty years ago, during a summer job. And it was a hell of a lot smaller."

"Then I think you'd better do the honors." Charlie pointed at Nash's legs and then at his own. "Besides, I'd have trouble reaching the pedals."

"Then get the door and let's move on out, Charlie."

5.

Oliver felt like Robert E. Lee, charging with his troops toward a final victory.

He was in the first jeep with Fielding, leading a caravan of cars into Four Corners. Beneath the orange light of the street lamps, it looked like a jaundiced serpent, twisting into an S that coiled through the intense cold. He guessed there were fifty cars, all with their horns blaring, their lights flashing. Fists pounded against doors and roofs. Chants filled the air, the same words, over and over again, *Burn, burn*, a hymn to an unknown god.

This music, this madness, belched through the cold indifference of the air, heating it to an almost unbearable pitch that turned Oliver's bones to a warm mush. He felt giddy with redemption, with a righteousness that expunged the specific memory of what Polly had said to him earlier.

And should he begin to remember too much, to doubt, he had only to glance at Fielding, at the bright fever in his eyes, or to peer into the faces of the people around him, and her voice shrank to a faint, irritating noise at the edge of his mind. He was right and she was wrong. Nothing could be simpler.

Now the jeep turned toward the school, the football field, the S following. The chants grew more frenzied. The horns got louder. "You see?" said Fielding, the rictus of a smile slicing his face in two. "You see what I mean? People needed this, they needed an outlet. And we need them on our side."

Lights erupted in the surrounding dark as more cars converged into Four Corners.

Burn, burn.

6.

Nash heard the racket the second the truck trundled out of the warehouse. It sounded like New Year's in Times Square, like the heart of the stock exchange on the best trading day of the century. It permeated the dark, drowned out the noise of the truck's engine, and infused him with an almost paralyzing dread.

"Sweet Christ," Charlie whispered, the dashboard glow seeping into the lines at his eyes and mouth. "They've made a carnival out of it."

Nash heard pain in his voice. Regret. Hatred. "There's nothing we can do about it, Charlie."

He spotted the Jeep nosing through the weeds and hit the lever that lowered the back door of the truck. A moment later, the Jeep was inside. He punched a button; the panel that separated them from the storage compartment slid open; Katie and Horn poked their heads through.

"Anyone got any ideas?" Nash asked.

"Yeah," said Horn. "I say we join the procession. They're headed toward the high school and we can turn off before they get there, as long as we're near the end of the line."

"Suppose someone sees us and we're followed?" Charlie asked.

Nash pulled the weapon out from under his jacket and set it on the seat between them. "Then we shoot to kill."

7.

The truck lurched and stalled all the way down the alley, a
monster with hiccups, until Nash got the hang of driving it. At
the end of the row of buildings, he turned slowly onto the road
and paused at the stop sign.

The string of cars winding through Four Corners seemed endless, a circus of lights and noises. Some of the cars bore banners
that flapped in the wind: BURN THE BLIGHTS OF LAGOON, THE
TOWN BELONGS TO THE PEOPLE, DEATH TO COCOONS. They
didn't say anything he hadn't already known. But this physical
manifestation of mass hysteria, of a hatred that had been swell-
ing since the quarantine was imposed, lanced through him with
shocking clarity. If there was any doubt in his mind about the
risk of leaving, it vanished; to stay was certain death.

He put the truck in gear and moved forward, flashing the
headlights and honking the horn like everyone else. A space in
line opened up. He slid into it, neat as a piece in a puzzle, and
the madness closed around them.

"Two jeeps coming up on the left," Charlie said, his eyes
glued to the side mirror.

Nash saw them. He slid the gun toward him and tucked it
under his right leg. But the jeeps sped past, messengers on an
urgent mission that had nothing to do with them.

They were almost at the army/navy store, where they'd
started out an hour and a half ago. If he swung left and headed
across Four Corners, he'd be moving against the cars that were
pouring toward them from other directions now. It would make
them too conspicuous. So he crept south with the line, and when
they were parallel to the dirt road that eventually came out behind the Nameless, he turned left.

The truck's tires spewed dirt and gravel and kicked up snow.
As they rounded the corner of the first building, they bounced
over a pothole. Nash downshifted and tapped the brakes. But
the engine strained like a horse at the bit that was eager to fly
ahead, and he had to squash the brakes harder.

Now they were behind the row of buildings, hidden from the
procession. The headlights flickered over trees to their right that
the wind didn't touch, birches, pines, hickory, white bark and
black, woods whose spirit and mystery seemed as impenetrable
to Nash as the derangement of what they had just left.

"Trouble," Charlie said softly.

Headlights flashed off and on in the side mirror, signaling

Nash to stop. He told Katie and Horn to lay low and punched the button that operated the panel to the storage compartment, closing it. He stuck the gun in his belt as he halted the truck.

Nash opened his door, stuck his head out. A lone soldier came toward them, rifle in hand, boots gnawing at the gravel and snow, the beam of his flashlight sliding along the length of the truck. "Evening." He aimed the beam right at Nash's face as he stepped down. "You authorized to be driving this vehicle?"

He wasn't a kid; Nash pegged him to be in his early thirties. He had three stripes on his shoulder and a dimple in his chin the size of a crater. "That's right. We're going to be hauling away the remains of the cocoons. But the engine was acting up and I didn't want to break down in line and slow things up. I think it's the radiator. You have any water in your jeep?"

"Nope." The light darted to the side of the truck, then back to Nash again. "I didn't hear nothing about them using a Kroger's truck to haul off the remains."

"I'm just doing what Captain Oliver requested."

"Uh-huh." He strolled past Nash and pointed the flashlight into the truck, impaling Charlie, who looked on the verge of apoplexy. "Could you please step out, sir?"

"Sure thing."

A pulse throbbed in Nash's temple. *Now, do it now.* His hand felt stiff as he pulled the 9-millimeter from his belt and jammed it in the soldier's back. "Drop the rifle and put your hands on top of your head. One sound and I'll blow your spine in half."

The rifle hit the ground. Nash kicked it under the truck as the soldier slowly raised his arms. But suddenly he emitted a high-pitched shriek, spun, and lashed out at Nash with a karate chop that slammed into the side of his head. The impact nearly knocked him senseless, but he somehow managed to stay on his feet, and when the soldier charged him, Nash squeezed the trigger.

The man was still twitching when he hit the ground.

8.

Katie watched Nash and Horn strip the soldier of everything that could possibly be useful. She watched them drag the body into the trees. Although she knew it was real, that it had happened, none of it touched her. It was like watching a movie. It was something she could turn off and on in her head, something she could get up and walk away from.

She helped Charlie kick snow and dirt over the blood and cover the tracks they'd made. Then she climbed back into the truck and moved Delilah farther forward, making room for the other jeep. Since it was army issue, Nash felt it might come in handy later on. Maybe it would. Maybe it wouldn't. It depended.

But the four grenades she found in the glove compartment would definitely be useful. Grenades were like guns. They were power. They were leverage. They depended on nothing except a hand to jerk the pins from them.

Her hand.

For later.

For the unexpected.

For Ray. For Hank. For Fay. For all of them.

She wrapped them in Kleenex and arranged them carefully in the bottom of her bag.

33

Revenge

1.

Nash had thought he would feel safer once they reached Hawthorne. But he didn't. The only difference between here and town was that the enemy was no longer visible.

It lurked in the woods that loomed on either side of them. It watched from between the trees that leaned in close to the road, their branches scratching at the roof of the truck as it passed. It took shape in his peripheral vision, an amorphous thing of transmuting tissue and bone, and vanished as soon as he sought to see it more clearly. He felt its presence, he knew it was hidden nearby, waiting, but he couldn't define it. Perhaps it was Nature Herself, gearing up for the last stage in Her little experiment, Her final surprise, the death squeeze that would annihilate them all.

He pressed down harder on the accelerator, picking up speed. He thought he could smell the soldier's blood on his hands. He imagined the man rising from his coffin of pine needles and red Georgia clay and stumbling to the football field, where he would salute the colonel and give his report on what had gone wrong, blood spurting from a half-dozen wounds as he spoke.

You're losing it, Nash. It was self-defense. You or him.

But the odor wouldn't go away.

It clung to his skin, an invisible powder, a mark, a curse like Cain's.

Moonlight as cold as the air filtered through the branches and struck the glassy surface of the lagoon. Everything was beginning to look as it did in his photographs, as though the spectral shapes were becoming visible to the naked eye. He blinked and thought he could see through the trunk of the giant live oak to his left. He blinked again, and now he could see its molecules shifting, widening, as electrons and photons swirled faster and faster around the nuclei of atoms like planets spinning around a hundred suns. Another blink, and the world solidified again and the truck was swerving off to the right. He jerked the wheel back and felt Charlie's inquisitive glance.

Hey, Charlie. Guess what? Lagoon's dissolving like aspirin in water. He felt an almost uncontrollable urge to laugh, but he knew if he did, it would collapse into fear or sorrow or pain or maybe all three at once.

He took the final turn to the inn and the truck roared up the gentle incline to the garage door. It was immediately apparent that the truck wouldn't fit. It was too high. Or the garage ceiling was too low. *Is the bottle half full or half empty? Is it partly cloudy or partly sunny? Am I half sane or half crazy?* Koans. Imponderable riddles.

He backed up to the front of the inn and pulled the lever that released the rear door so the jeeps could be driven into the garage.

When he turned off the engine, the truck died with a shudder.

2.

Fay heard Nash talking to someone, but his voice was as distant as the star she'd been watching through the window ever since it had risen. Or maybe it was a planet. Yes, of course. A planet. They were brighter than stars, weren't they? And since this planet had appeared first in the sky, then it was . . . *What?* Alpha Centauri.

No no no. That was a star, not a planet. The planets were . . . *I can't remember.*

Of course you can, whispered the voice of her father. *Try harder.*

Panic clawed at her throat.

Earth.

She remembered Earth and . . . Pluto, yes, okay, Pluto was the most distant planet and then a little closer in was . . . *Why can't I remember any of this? What's wrong with me?*

Footsteps somewhere close by. Nash's.

Don't come in here now. Leave me alone. I've got to remember the names of the planets, it's important to know these things, it's . . .

Control, whispered her father. *Control.*

A face rolled into the upper corner of her right eye. Ben's face. She remembered what Ben looked like, but she couldn't recall the names of the planets in the galaxy. This galaxy. This universe. This time zone.

My name is Fay Donovan and I'm a doctor and my social security number is . . . She couldn't remember. *My birth date is . . .* She didn't know. *My address is . . .* It eluded her.

And yet she could name plants and animals she knew she'd never seen; understood certain intricacies about geology, a field she had never studied; and could sketch—if she were physically able to—a place or a state of mind, she didn't know which it was, that had grown progressively more vivid as her change had deepened. It was almost as if the mutation were swallowing some of her old memories and knowledge to make room for what it fed her during the deep sleep.

"Fay?"

The mattress sank as he sat down beside her, blocking her view of the window. His face seemed slightly out of focus, as if she'd been staring into the sun. She lifted her arm and stroked his beard with the back of her hand; the threads at her knuckles eddied across his cheek.

"We're going to start loading the truck pretty soon."

The truck, right, of course. They had stolen a truck from Kroger's. They were leaving Lagoon. She pushed herself up on her elbows. Samson poked his nose between them, whimpering and licking her hand. She patted his nose and told him to sit, grateful that her physical changes didn't seem to frighten him.

Fay swung her legs over the side of the bed. Although she still had mobility in them, the threads had already knitted together at her waist, hips, and neck. "You were gone a long time."

"We had some trouble." He told her about the procession, the soldier, his face betraying nothing of what he felt about killing the man. Emotionally, he was as removed from her as the star, and it frightened her. "The sooner we get out of here, the better." He started to rise, but she caught his hand.

"Wait." She released the witch scent and felt the moment when it reached him, when it curled around him, an ambrosia too sweet to deny. Her mouth was already seeking his, her hands were already working at the zipper on his jeans, sliding up under his sweater. "Please," she whispered. "Now. Please." *One last time.*

His spine stiffened even as he breathed into her, filling her lungs with his breath. He murmured no as his urgent hands said yes, as his hands tore at her shirt, her shorts, popping buttons, a zipper, stripping away her clothes and his own in sweeping, violent motions.

Desire shuddered through him as they fell back against the mattress, the scent like a third person whose limbs tangled around them. His mouth found a breast and suckled at it like an infant. His hands slipped over the soft threads that twisted around her waist, her hips. He pressed his cheek against them and poked his tongue through them and nibbled at them as if he were trying to bite through them to her skin. He wept, he whispered, he rasped, his desire getting all mixed up with his grief.

When she tried to pull the scent back into herself, it was too late. Their fever fed it, powered it. It became something unto itself, a thing with a life and will of its own. It controlled them. Consumed them. Devoured them whole. She moaned and writhed, trying to escape it, not wanting to escape it, hating it, loving it. The assault was so total that she passed out briefly. Then it started all over again, his hands, his mouth, and she came in a flash of heat so intense, it burned her from the inside out, and she screamed. But the power killed it before it reached the air.

She came again the moment he thrust himself inside her and then again minutes later when the scent sucked him dry and he collapsed against her, weeping.

3.

Four of the field lights were on, bright enough to bleach out the cold glint of the stars overhead. They illuminated the center of the football field, where firewood was stacked in a haphazard circle that Oliver estimated was fifty feet across, maybe more.

In the heart of the circle was a length of wire mesh, its spaces stuffed with newspaper that would absorb the kerosene. Two dump trucks had backed up to it, and now cocoons tumbled out of them in a rainbow of colors, like dozens of huge, unbreakable Easter eggs. They bumped and knocked together as they fell, sounding like poker chips raining out of a container onto a table or like rows of collapsing dominoes. The noise rang out with astonishing clarity in the hushed air.

Fielding, seated in the front row with Oliver on one side and Lattimer on the other, stood and turned to address the crowd. He raised his arms, a Messiah blessing the multitudes, his voice as smooth as Scotch when he spoke. Oliver barely heard what he said. He was mesmerized by the cocoons, by their very strangeness, by his fear of them. He yearned for the fever that would consume his fear, for those long, glorious moments when the flames leaped over the cocoons, crackling, hissing, dominating them, killing them.

The crowd cheered when Fielding was finished, and now the chant rose up again, beating the cold air, and Oliver's head began to swell with the music, the madness. But suddenly the lights in the grandstands went out, plunging the field into a darkness so total, it was as if he'd been instantly blinded.

A chill crawled up Oliver's arms. His ears rang in the abrupt silence. That deep, atavistic fear of the dark poured through him. His fingers sank into his thighs and his eyes darted this way and that, seeking to penetrate the dark, to define shapes within it. Beside him, Fielding muttered, "What the fuck, I didn't tell them to turn out those lights." His voice had lost its smoothness. It sounded merely ordinary now, the voice of an enlisted man, a common foot soldier. He instructed Oliver to find out what the problem was and thrust a flashlight into his hand.

Oliver wanted to tell him no, he wasn't about to leave the safety of the grandstand. But he could feel Lattimer smirking, waiting for him to do exactly that so that he could make some cutting, payback remark that would humiliate him in front of Fielding. "I'm supposed to light the bonfire," he said.

"You will," Fielding replied. "The boys still have to douse the cocoons. We won't do anything until you get back. Go on now, I want those lights back on."

Oliver got reluctantly to his feet, the cold somehow worse now, a presence every bit as terrible as the darkness.

His boots clicked against the concrete walk. He passed through the uncertain murmurs from the bleachers, passed one of the dead field lights, passed out of the safety of the crowd and into the taut solitude of the parking lot, and stopped.

The skin across the back of his neck went hot and tight. His gut turned to a puddle of acid. He thought he was going to puke. There wasn't a light anywhere. The entire town was dark.

And now a noise sprang up around him like the chatter of insects on a humid summer night, a sound which filled him with such sudden and acute terror that his bladder let loose and his head emptied of everything.

He stood there shivering, warm piss running down the insides of his legs, eyes rolling loosely in their sockets. His hands were trembling so badly he couldn't grip his gun and the beam of his flashlight bounced up and down, up and down, a horse on a merry-go-round.

The noise got louder. Louder.

Oliver turned slowly, clutching the gun now, his eyes blinking fast and hard against the dark, trying to penetrate it, to find the source of the noise. But it was everywhere, leaking from the asphalt under his feet, seeping from the bleachers three hundred yards behind him, bleeding from the black sky, the glass stars.

And then he saw shapes emerging from the blackness as though the night had spawned them. They moved out from behind the school building on the other side of the parking lot, advanced toward him from the street to his left, from the relentless dark to his right, dozens of them, a troop, a fucking army. They skulked between cars, trees, and lampposts, so many of them that at times they seemed to be a single mass as shapeless as a protozoa. They were in no apparent hurry, but they didn't stop, didn't pause, they just kept coming and coming, making that hideous chattering sound that swelled in volume and intensity.

He knew his weapon would be ineffective against them. He knew he couldn't make it to his car. He had no illusions about anything. He spun and raced back toward the field, his mouth opening in a scream that refused to emerge. His balls shriveled to the size of prunes, his wet pants froze to the insides of his thighs, Polly's voice boomed in his head: *You're going to regret it the rest of your life.*

The noise erupted around him as the shapes, the things, the mutants, broke loose from the dark and stampeded across the parking lot, headed for the football field.

And the cocoons.

4.

Katie and Horn were in the back of the truck, lifting Ray's cocoon toward the roof. Charlie switched the flashlight to a higher setting. It was blindingly bright; Ray recoiled from it and Horn averted his face. Charlie quickly dimmed it.

The cocoon's threads felt soft and pliable under her hands. But when she exerted a little pressure, the cocoon itself seemed hard, cold, mean to the touch. It was perfectly white now, shorter than Ray was tall. In the final hours, his legs had drawn up toward his body and his chin had dipped onto his chest so that he was in a semifetal position. Lost to her now. Deaf to her.

Speechless. Blind to everything except whatever visions the cocoon fed him. She couldn't even find his scent.

"Easy does it," Charlie said. "Okay, that's about the right height. Now just hold it a bit. The fibers will start to attach themselves to the roof."

Katie's gaze dropped to the floor. She couldn't bear to watch. Her heart felt like it was breaking up into a million pieces inside her. What she wanted most was to throw her arms around the cocoon and vent her grief, to wail and scream like Middle Eastern women did when their sons and husbands were killed in war. But she was ashamed to do it in front of Charlie, who had helped his wife cocoon and then lost her to the fanatics, and in front of Horn, who would soon be facing this very thing.

"Here we go," Charlie whispered, and she forced herself to look.

The cluster of threads at the crown of Ray's head were elongating, rising like thin, charmed snakes to a flutist's song. In the beam of light, they glistened damply, eddying across the surface of the roof, swirling the way seaweed did on a beach when a wave rolled in. There was something eerily beautiful about the sleek gracefulness of the tendrils, their singular purpose, their secret knowledge.

Now their ends vanished into the metal. It was as if some subtle change had occurred on a molecular level that allowed the tendrils and the metal to merge, melt together, to become one. She felt a burst of warmth under her hands, then a cooling, then warmth again: the cocoon was adjusting its temperature. The threads started to change color, becoming the same soft silver as the walls of the truck.

"It's okay to let go now," Charlie said quietly.

But she didn't. She couldn't. She clung to the foot of the cocoon, oblivious to the cold streaming through the open rear door, only dimly aware of Horn telling her they were going back inside for Hank. She heard Charlie say he was leaving the flashlight for her. She heard them leave and pressed her forehead to the threads, her eyes squeezed shut against tears. She waited for the soft whisper of Ray's voice that would say, *Find me, Katie-o*, and desperately sought his scent. But even if the intense cold hadn't interfered, the cocoon would have.

She didn't know how long she stood there, how much time had passed before she heard a male voice to her left say, "Leave it be." She nearly jerked out of her skin as she stumbled away from the cocoon.

The man was standing on the sloping platform the door made when it was lowered, close enough for her to see his deformed face and hands and the rifle at his side. "Jus' move away from it."

He came up the platform toward her. She grabbed the flashlight and stepped back, praying the panel to the front of the truck was open. But she didn't dare take her eyes from him long enough to look.

"Some of 'em die if y'remove them once they're up. Y'can't tell which are which till they're down." His speech was impeded by the crust at his mouth; he sounded like a six-year-old who still had his adenoids. "Bu' I guess peo'le 'ave figured that out, huh." He emitted a curt, bitter laugh and reached out to touch the cocoon.

"Don't," she hissed.

"*Don't?*" He laughed again as his hands touched the threads. Touched Ray. "Y'people 'ave been burnin' these as fast as I can find places to hide 'em and you're tellin' me don't touch it?"

"I haven't burned anything." She kept inching back, hands clutching the flashlight. "None of us here have. We're saving this cocoon. We're taking it away from here."

"No no no," he said softly, shaking his head. "That's m'job. I protect. It's not safe 'ere now. Even with t'soldiers gone it won't be safe. You're goin' to 'elp me find a safer place, Ka'ie. That's y'name, right? Ka'ie. Uh-huh. T'girl with t'miracle smell. You and t'at smell are goin' t'help me find a safer place for the cocoons that're left."

His hands dropped away from the cocoon. He moved closer; she stepped back. "I knew 'bout t'smell t'first time I saw you, when y'were on your bike. 'Member? I jus' didn't under'tand then. And it was me t'at night at the t'place t'at burned. And t'day when you and t'boy were in the woods, it was me he got with t'machete. . . ."

He looked at his shoulder, rubbing it lightly, and her eyes flickered toward the panel. *Open. It's open. I've got a chance.*

"T'new skin heals up fast and fine."

Bile oozed up her throat; she swallowed it back. *Keep him talking. Distract him. Buy time.* "Once you've started to change, you can't leave. The town won't let you."

He laughed; it was not a nice sound. "Sure, Ka'ie."

The man-thing moved closer; she took two more steps back. The cold had nearly numbed her feet, her hands, her face, even the inside of her mouth. She could barely swallow. "I can't help you.'' The words sounded thick and clumsy. ''The smell doesn't work like that.''

''Y'don't 'ave any idea how it works. I do. And you're goin' to 'elp me, otherwise everyone in the inn dies.''

''Then you'd be killing the two cocoons in there.''

''One. T'other's not complete.''

How does he know that?

The web, sure, he knew because the web linked him and Fay.

He swung the rifle up, aiming it at her belly. ''Now come back t'is way nice and slow, Ka'ie. Don't want t'shoot you, but I will if y'make me. And roll t'flashlight over here.'' If she hurled the flashlight at him, she would probably miss. He was still too far away. So she did the next best thing. She flicked the switch to the flashlight's highest setting and her arm snapped up. The beam struck his small dark eyes. He bellowed with pain, threw his arms over his eyes, and Katie whirled around and dived through the open panel into the front of the truck. She scrambled across the long seat, the flashlight slipping out of her grasp, her breath coming in great convulsive spasms, and hurled herself out the door.

She forgot the truck was so high off the ground and plunged to the snow, landing hard on her knees. A white pain seared through them as she jumped up and tore toward the inn, shouting. The windows were dark. Shapes pressed in on her peripheral vision from both sides. She had lost the flashlight. The sidewalk was too long, she wasn't going to make it, her lungs ached, the man was charging after her.

The dark exploded; snow flew up at her right side. *He's shooting at me, Jesus, he's actually shooting at me.* She cut left, right, left again. Glass coughed from an inn window. Shots chattered above her head, on the second floor of the inn. Then the door flew open and she burst into the lobby.

Horn slammed the door, bolted it, pushed a gun and an extra magazine into her hand. ''It's automatic. Just squeeze the trigger and keep shooting. They've cut the power, the phone, everything. Cover the kitchen. Charlie and I have got this room.''

She ran through the lobby. Nash had put aluminum shutters on the sliding glass door that led to the deck, defending their most vulnerable spot. But the shutters blocked the starlight and the glow from the fire cast ghastly shadows on the walls. The throw rugs seemed to float against the light, rectangular eyes that absorbed the firelight and threw it off again.

Katie skidded into the kitchen and found Samson at the door, growling deeply in his throat, crouched as if ready to spring. "It's okay, boy," she whispered, checking the dead bolt, the chain. Satisfied they would hold, she quickly shut the door to the cellar and bolted it. Even though there were no windows down there, no possible way the mutants could break in, she wasn't taking any chances.

She sidestepped along the far wall as gunfire burst somewhere outside the inn again. Her heart pounded, her hands were slick with sweat. She fixed her eyes on the window over the sink. It hadn't been shuttered. Starlight filtered through the glass and washed thinly across the counter. If she could find a plank of wood and a hammer and some nails, maybe she could . . .

Footsteps cut the thought short. Her grip on the gun tightened.

"Katie?"

Nash. It was only Nash.

She stepped out of the shadows. "Right here."

He glanced around, his body filling the doorway. For an instant, as he stood there with a rifle in his hand, he looked like Ben, like Ben that night on the deck, like Ben in the uncertain moments before he'd fired into the crowd. She reached for his scent, caught the blackened edge of it, and felt herself sliding into the yawning abyss that had opened inside him. She jerked free, stepped back. "What?" she whispered.

"Get your things and head for the garage. Our only chance is those jeeps. There're too many of them for us to hold off indefinitely."

"I'm not leaving Ray out there in the—"

"We're driving the jeep *into* the truck," he snapped, his black eyes growing blacker, shinier. "Fay's going to help me get Hank into one of them now."

"But suppose they're already inside the jeep?"

"They aren't. Not yet. They're too preoccupied with us. Five minutes," he repeated.

"Wait," she said. "Take these." She dug into her purse for the grenades.

5.

Oliver was pushed back as far as he could get under the bleachers, but it wasn't far enough. It would never be far enough. They would find him. He knew they would. They would find him and he would die here in the mad shrieking of spectators

clambering for safety, here in the explosion of gunfire, here
where the mutants swept out of the night like a tsunami that
crushed everything in its path.

They were armed with automatic weapons and used them like
terrorists, cutting down anything that moved. They fell on soldiers and spectators and tore them apart just as they had done
to Obie and Joker. The stink of blood suffused the air. Bodies
dropped down through the spaces between the bleachers, some
of them dead, others alive and screaming. Oliver scrambled
away from them on his hands and knees, wiggled under the side
of the bleachers, and darted toward the nearby clutch of Jiffy
Johns that had never been removed when the weather turned too
cold for outdoor sports.

He hurled himself inside one of them, locked the door, and
pressed back into the dark, bargaining with a God he suddenly
believed in. The screams and explosions of gunfire echoed
around him, pounding the metal walls. His terror was so acute
that his bladder let loose again and warm piss soaked his jeans.
In seconds, the cold had plastered the denim against his skin.

At one point, a group of people or mutants, he didn't know
which, stampeded toward him and the Jiffy John toppled like a
toy. Oliver was flung back, his head slammed into the ceiling,
the lid on the toilet flew open, and the chemical solution with
its malodorous contents flooded out.

Trapped inside the tight, dark stench, the solution burning
fiercely wherever it touched him, Oliver panicked. He scrambled around inside the metal coffin, trying to find the door latch,
fists beating the walls, boots slamming against them. The blackness crushed him like an insect, he couldn't find the door, the
stink choked him, the chemicals ate holes in his skin, he was
going to die in here, he knew he was. Then something poked
him in the back. *The latch. The door's* under *me*.

He braced his hands and feet against the walls on either side
and rocked, back and forth, again and again, trying to get the
Jiffy John to roll. Sweat popped out on his face, his forehead.
His muscles burned. The liquid sloshed around him. His left
hand slipped and mashed against something. It oozed through
the fingers of his gloves and it didn't take a genius to figure out
what it was. He turned his head and vomited.

The Jiffy John started to roll and he rocked faster, faster, until
it tumbled onto its side. He turned around, patting frantically at
the wall for the latch, found it, slammed his fist against it. The

door swung open and Oliver fell into the cold dark, gasping for breath, coughing, eyes watering, the chemicals pouring out around him. He crawled clear of the stuff and collapsed, cheek against the snow, blood pounding in his ears.

The burning against his skin finally forced him up. He tore off his gloves and thrust his hands into a mound of snow. It numbed the terrible burning, so he grabbed handfuls and rubbed it against his legs, his cheeks, then ripped off his boots and socks and held snow against his feet. He started to shiver. His teeth chattered. He put his socks, boots, and gloves back on and looked around.

The bleachers stood silent and empty in the dim starlight. It was so quiet, he could hear the flexing of muscles in his eyelids as he blinked. His bones creaked as he stood and turned his head slowly, eyes flickering here, there. The landscape was bleak, strewn with bodies.

He moved cautiously forward, one hand on his .38, his eyes darting through the parking lot ahead of him. Fewer cars: some people had escaped. He quickened his pace, senses wound as tightly as a clock, alert for the slightest sound. But there was nothing except the noise of his boots and an occasional whistle of wind.

Bodies sprawled in the snow; he veered around them. He didn't stop to see who they were or if they were still alive. He moved faster, faster, until his boots were pounding the parking-lot pavement, until he was running, a man fleeing his own perdition.

6.

The garage.

Nash and Fay worked silently, rapidly, dividing Charlie's and Horn's belongings between Delilah and the army jeep. As he flopped down the backseat to make room for Suffield's cocoon, Fay's head snapped toward him. Her eyes looked glazed, almost feverish. "The football field," she whispered. "Mutants. They've come for the cocoons. My God, so many."

"*More* of them?"

"From all over. They've converged in Lagoon. We've got to hurry."

They lifted Suffield's cocoon from the floor. His fingers sank into the cold fibers. They made a moist, sucking sound, almost as if the cocoon were trying to pull his hands into itself. His revulsion was instantaneous. He dropped his end and it struck the floor. He pressed his palms against his jeans, rubbing them on the denim, his shoes scraping against the floor as his legs shuffled backward. He couldn't touch it. He wouldn't. He hugged himself, hands tucked under his armpits as his eyes blinked, as they squeezed shut, as they opened again to Fay's accusatory stare.

"I can't. I can't do this." He choked on the words. He didn't know specifically what it was that he couldn't do; he just knew he couldn't do it.

The beam of the flashlight, aimed at the ceiling, cast dim circles of pale light against Fay's sunken cheeks. Tears glistened in her eyes. Her mouth moved around a single word that she didn't speak: *Please.*

She was still clutching her end of the cocoon, and the space that separated them seemed suddenly enormous, an ocean, a continent, a universe. He thought of the threads that circled her waist, her hips. He remembered their taste, as sweet and intoxicating as the witch scent, and how he'd wanted to tear them out of the pores with his teeth. He remembered invading and being invaded, consuming and being consumed, wanting to kill and be killed, to love and be loved, to be separated from her and to become what she was becoming. He understood none of it, but knew that it had changed him, that it changed him even now as he stood here whispering, "I can't, Jesus, I just can't."

She pushed the cocoon into the back of the Jeep, then turned to him. Moved toward him. Touched him. "I need you, Scott."

He understood she wasn't just referring to now, to this uncertain stretch of time between here and escaping, but that she meant later as well, after she'd changed, after she'd become what Ray was, what Suffield was. He thought of his dead daughter, his dead brother. He thought of the life he had lived before Lagoon, the life that had expired like a library card.

I can't.
Please.
No. Don't ask it of me.
It won't be forever.

He didn't know who was saying what or if they were even speaking out loud. His head ached, his heart ached, his bones ached as she slipped her arms around him. A beat or two passed before he returned her embrace, before the chatter of gunfire pushed them apart.

She gazed at him for a long moment, and he couldn't read

her expression, didn't want to read it, was afraid to. Then she crawled into the Jeep and fixed sleeping bags and blankets around Suffield's cocoon to protect it. Her movements were slow, languid, constricted; the process had speeded up in her just since they'd come downstairs. It hurt him to look at her.

It was time.

He cranked up Delilah's engine and Katie started the army jeep. He hit the remote-control switch for the garage door and it trundled noisily upward, a gate opening into another world.

34

Breakout

1.

For Nash, the race to the truck happened in quick flashes that froze instants in time like snapshots.

He saw Delilah tearing across the front lawn, a guided missile that responded instantly to whatever command he gave. He saw a clutch of mutants converging on the Jeep from the inn's porch to his left and how they flew back, twitching, when Fay fired on them. He saw Delilah's headlights impaling a pair who lunged toward them from the dark and heard the crunch of their bones as the Jeep struck first one and then the other, hurling them off to the side. And he saw the final moment when Delilah swerved violently to the right, bounced up onto the platform, and screeched to a halt inside the truck.

Then there were no more flashes. There were smells—of the soldier's blood on his hands, of the blood spilled outside, of the blood inside of the truck—and there was time, leaping into fast-forward as he and Horn sprang out of the Jeep. While Horn covered Katie's jeep from the back until it was in, Nash got to the front of the truck.

His fists slammed over the locks; he slid behind the wheel. The engine thundered to life, he hit the lever that raised the rear door, and threw the truck into reverse. It lurched into half a dozen mutants, maybe more, knocking them down like bowling pins. Some were dragged under the chassis, and as they died, their screams clawed at the dark, ripping it open.

Bullets sprayed the side of the truck. Nash shouted for Charlie, who scrambled over the seat, lowered the window, and let loose a barrage of return gunfire as mutants swarmed out of the inn like startled termites from a nest. Nash swerved the wheel violently to the right, swinging around so the rear of the truck was to the woods, and flicked on the brights.

There were mutants everywhere—on the ground, the porch, the sidewalk, mutants that were dead, that were twitching, that were groaning, mutants cowering from the lights, and mutants that raced toward them. That macabre keening noise surged around him, through him, electrifying the air. It was a signal of some sort, a magical incantation that empowered them, drove them forward into a collective madness that was as instinctive as a lemming's self-destructive migration to the sea.

Nash jerked the pin from one of the grenades Katie had given him and tossed it into their midst. The explosion burst windows in the inn, rocked the truck, and blew mutants apart like so much debris. He twisted the steering wheel around and took off down the sloping driveway onto Hawthorne Lane.

He didn't think they would make it to the route Horn had planned out for them. He wasn't even sure they would make it off Hawthorne.

2.

Oliver smelled smoke. Firelight flickered against the black sky several blocks away. Now and then he heard shouts, but he couldn't tell where they were coming from or how close they were. The dark absorbed sound like a sponge sucking up water.

He passed more bodies as he reached the sidewalk. Soldiers, townspeople, mutants. Some were alive, crying in pain. Most were dead. He didn't stop. Even though he couldn't run any-more—he didn't have the strength, the cold had numbed his limbs—he moved as rapidly as he could. He hugged the shops to his right and ducked into doorways, alleys, spine pressed to the cold walls, his fear galloping through him, threatening to thrust him into the street, screaming for mercy, redemption.

Please God, let me just get to the station. Where his truck was parked. He didn't think beyond that.

As he neared the center of town, he encountered soldiers in pairs or trios, cowering in breezeways. Some were wounded, some had lost their weapons, all were young and terrified and advised him not to bother with Four Corners. The mutants, they said, had the town. *Had*, as in *possessed*, as in *owned*. They were going to find vehicles and get out, and he'd be smart to do the same.

Oliver moved on. The firelight brightened. The shouts were closer. As he came into Four Corners, a brigade of jeeps roared in, escorting one of the dump trucks that had been in the football field. The back of it was piled high with the unburned cocoons.

Throngs of mutants followed on foot, shouting and hurling torches through the library windows and setting fire to the dry, brittle trees in the town park. As the motorcade headed toward the feeder road that led to the lagoon, the mutants on foot swung right, the light of their torches soldering their bodies into a solid, delirious mass that was going to raze Lagoon to the ground.

Oliver realized they would reach the station before he did. He didn't want to risk exposure by darting across the street toward Kroger's and the army/navy, but if he stayed here, he would die. He sprinted forward, arms pumping, legs screaming for a respite, the subzero cold stabbing at the inside of his nose like a dozen ice picks. He reached the far side of the warehouse and fell against it, chest heaving for air, fear balled in his gut, eyes tearing from the cold.

He wanted to sink to the ground, to curl up into a tiny invisible ball and bounce off into the field of dry weeds in front of him. But the shouts in the streets hurled him away from the warehouse, down the alley.

When the alley ended, he switched to back roads and footpaths until he reached the Brazen Saloon a mile away, on the west side of town. The place looked as if it had been shut down for decades: windows boarded up, street in front empty of cars, wind whining under eaves. Oliver scurried around back and saw Polly's pickup. He pounded at the door, shouting her name. After a few moments, he saw a glimmer of light under the crack. Chains and bolts were disengaged. The door swung open. Polly stood there with her rifle in one hand and a lantern in the other.

"I oughta just shut the door in your goddamn face," she said.

He nodded and blew into his gloved hands; the cold was eating him alive.

"They strung up your pal Fielding on the roof of Prudy's Place and burned him. I saw it happen on my way over here. And the crazies smashed through every barrier the army had. That's where they got the guns. I don't think there's a soldier left in this town."

She paused, waiting for him to say something. But Oliver could hardly remember what Fielding looked like and didn't give a shit what had happened to him, to the soldiers, to any of them. "You were right. Is that what you want to hear?"

"That'll do for starters. Get your ass in here."

It wasn't real warm inside, but at least there was light from a couple of lanterns on the bar. Polly went over to an open suitcase on the pool table, patted the clothes down flat inside, then snapped it shut. A police band radio next to it transmitted nothing but static.

"You reek, Lew. What the hell did you fall in, anyway?"

"A Jiffy John."

"How fitting." She set the suitcase on the floor. "I figure we've got about fifteen minutes before the crazies zoom back through here and burn this side of town. But by then we'll be long gone."

"Gone?" The word curled into the air, as blank as the inside of his head.

She looked up at him. "Yeah, you know. Split. Move out. Depart. L-e-a-v-e."

"And go where?"

"Anywhere. As long as it's away from here."

Leave. Tonight. Now. This instant. *Good-bye, Lagoon, good-bye.* Oh, God, yes, yes. And his head moved up and down, a child's eager agreement to anything, anything at all.

3.

As they approached the end of Hawthorne, Nash spotted headlights glimmering in the trees to his left. A lot of headlights. He guessed they were coming off the feeder road from town; they were definitely headed in this direction.

He told Charlie to warn everyone in back to batten down the hatches, then mashed his foot against the accelerator and shifted into a higher gear. The back end fishtailed, the wheels found purchase, the truck careened forward, engine shrieking like a banshee.

The truck rode so high off the ground that when the first of the headlights turned onto Hawthorne, he felt as if he were seeing them from the lip of a cliff sixty feet above them. They looked like pale, glowing insects traveling in pairs. As they neared, he realized they were jeeps, army issue, identical to the one in the back of the truck, a convoy of them. They were escorting a dump truck stacked high with cocoons, and they weren't driven by soldiers.

"Sweet Christ," Charlie whispered. "More of them. Where in hell are they *coming* from?"

Nash didn't know and didn't care. He jerked the wheel to the left, slammed the heel of his hand against the horn, and kept it there, grinning like a loon as he bore down on the lead jeep.

Wanna play chicken, guy? You know this little game?

"We're gonna hit 'em!" Charlie shouted.

Nash hardly heard him. He was leaning forward, hands clamped to the wheel. He was grinning so hard, he could feel the rush of heat from the vent against his teeth.

Twenty-five feet. Twenty.

The lead jeep wasn't budging. Fine. That was just fine. *Dust to dust, asshole.*

Thirteen feet.

Ten.

Charlie hollered and lunged for the wheel, trying to wrench it to the right. Nash's arm swung out, slammed across his mouth, then shoved him away, and jammed the truck into overdrive.

Eight feet.

Five.

Nash saw the driver's face now, that raised, dark skin pitted with deepening pores, those tiny eyes, insectile eyes. He saw the driver's arm fly up to protect his eyes from the truck's brights.

Two feet.

The jeep swerved, but not quickly enough. The truck's fender struck the edge of its bumper; the jeep tilted onto two wheels and raced toward the trees. It crashed into the woods and, a moment later, exploded.

The other vehicles were now scrambling to get out of his way as fire and debris rained down on them. Then the dump truck suddenly swung in front of them, blocking their exit completely. *"Ram it!"* Charlie shouted. "Ram the goddamn thing!"

Nash slammed the vehicle into a lower gear and bore down on the dump truck. But now mutants were bounding out of jeeps, lighting torches and opening fire as they advanced. Nash slid well below the dash and shouted for Charlie to get down. But he didn't, he kept shooting, and a second later, a hail of bullets tore across the front of the truck, ripped through the windshield, and cut across Charlie's chest. He slumped sideways in the seat, catching most of the glass that showered into the front seat. Shells shredded the seat inches above Nash's head. The cold rushed into the truck. The engine stalled.

He pushed Charlie's bloody corpse to the floor, horror and panic raging through him, his hands wet and sticky with the old man's blood. He grabbed Charlie's fallen weapon and fired through the shattered windshield, buying himself a few seconds as the closest mutants went down. Then he flicked frantically at the key in the ignition and pumped the accelerator. The engine thundered to life and the truck lumbered forward. He hit the lever that opened the panel to the rear of the truck and shouted for Horn, who tumbled into the front seat to take Charlie's place.

Horn jerked the pin from one of the grenades and hurled it into a group of mutants to their right just as Nash swerved and slammed into the rear of the dump truck. The impact knocked some of the cocoons over the side, but the truck still blocked their exit. He jammed the gear into reverse, the engine screeched, the tires spun, caught.

"We're blocked at the back, too!" Horn shouted.

The front, the back, the sides. They were penned in like pigs. But Nash knew if he rammed the dump truck enough times, it would eventually give way. The question was whether any of them would be alive when it happened.

4.

Bud raced through the flickering firelight, the din of gunfire, headed for the dump truck. The stupid bastard who'd blocked the road had intended to sacrifice the cocoons just to get the people from the inn. It couldn't be allowed. As long as some of the cocoons were still alive, everything else became secondary: the girl with the miracle smell, the two cocoons she and the others had, even their escape. He hated to let them go, but the point was to salvage those of his people who had nearly been destroyed.

He threw open the driver's door, his weapon aimed, ready to kill the driver if he had to. But the truck was empty. The keys were still in the ignition, so he scrambled behind the wheel. As the engine cranked up, two of his own appeared, their eyes crazed with blood lust as they yelled, *No, you can't move the truck*, and lunged for him. Bud shot them both, slammed the door, and the truck jerked forward.

5.

Just as Nash gunned the engine to narrow the gap to the dump truck, it pitched forward, opening a space wide enough for them to pass through. He shifted gears, and they flew past it, past the jeeps and the mutants, past the trees, off Hawthorne. He swung the wheel savagely to the right. The rear end fishtailed, the tires spun impotently against the icy asphalt, the truck careened, the trees on his left rushed toward him, a dark, shapeless blur.

Then the tires found purchase and the monster truck rumbled forward. Wind whistled over the jagged edges of the remaining glass in the windshield. His eyes watered from the cold. His cheeks froze.

"We got jeeps on our ass!" Horn bellowed.

Nash saw them in the side mirror, a parade of bright headlights, five, maybe six jeeps in all. "I'll lower the back door. Get rid of them," he shouted over the din of the wind.

Horn vanished.

Nash punched the button that lowered the rear of the truck. Moments later, the lead jeep exploded. He saw it in the side mirror, saw the orange fireball that hurled up, up through the dark like some sort of meteor in reverse. Two of the jeeps behind it swerved out of control and crashed into the woods. The pair behind them kept on coming, side by side, as though they were racing each other. But the next grenade—*The last of the four,* he thought—landed between them and blew them apart.

He hit the lever that closed the truck, that sealed it, then opened the engine all the way and tore down the highway, bound for anywhere at all.

6.

Fay could no longer stand, could barely move her arms, and felt her heartbeat slowing down. She pressed back against the wall of the truck, sucking air in through her teeth. Her gun clattered to the floor. Horn caught her before she fell and eased her down.

"Take it easy, lady," he said gently, holding her elbows. "Just sit there a minute."

She wanted to tell him it wasn't going to pass, it wasn't a wave of dizziness or nausea or fatigue. But she found it difficult to speak. It was simpler to just sit there, looking at him, watching trickles of blood seep from his nostrils and roll from the corners of his eyes like tears. He swiped at them with a handkerchief and held a finger to his lips, asking for her silence.

She squeezed her eyes shut as a pain stabbed at her temple. It wormed its way up over the top of her head; a clump of her hair landed on her arm.

"Aw, Christ," Horn whispered, brushing his cool, callused

hands over her cheeks. "Aw, Fay." He slipped his huge arms around her, cradling her.

She heard the noise of the tires rolling over asphalt and the moan of the wind as the rear door creaked upward again. Her eyes opened; she forced her tongue to form words. "Get Nash, will you, Andy?"

His hands swallowed hers. "Sure thing, honey."

She felt the tug of that other place she explored in the deep sleep, when she was embedded in the web. It called to her, whispered to her. A part of her wanted to surrender to it, but not yet. Please, God, not yet.

Samson nudged her arm with his wet, cool nose, and when she looked down at him, he whimpered and rested his head on her knee. She stroked him, but the movement, small as it was, hurt her hand, and she let her fingers rest against his fur.

Katie lowered herself to the floor beside Fay, her face no longer young. "Is it time?"

"I think so." She wondered if she'd asked Ray the same question and how she knew to even ask at all. "Yes."

Katie nodded and drew her legs up against her. For a time—seconds, minutes, maybe hours, Fay didn't know—she felt as if the girl were extracting something from her and giving it back. Then she realized Katie was not only tracking the scent of her cocooning, but was somehow accompanying her.

"Can I do anything?" she asked.

"Just be there for Nash."

7.

Bud steered the dump truck toward the lagoon.

The cocoons would be safe there, in the black, soundless world two hundred feet under. Perhaps the cold darkness would even preserve them.

He stopped at the edge of the lagoon, stepped down from the truck, and walked out onto the ice. He jumped on it. Pounded it with his fists. It was solid enough to drive on until you approached the center, where the water hadn't frozen. He decided to take the truck out about thirty yards, then put it into neutral and push it to the point where the ice turned brittle. The weight would crack the ice and the truck would sink with the cocoons in the back.

Bud waited for the voice of the web to tell him he should

proceed. But he heard only the murmurs of confusion from his people on Hawthorne.

His hand stuck to the knob when he touched it, and he had trouble getting the door open because of the intense cold. But once he was inside, the truck slipped easily into gear and he pulled out onto the ice. Starlight struck the surface and tipped the trees on the other side of the lagoon. The west side, where he and Betty had lived.

Betty: burned in the first purge.

But he wouldn't think about that. About the dead. These cocoons were what mattered now. Once they were safe, he and the others would move back into the woods on the west shore again and find secure locations for their own cocooning.

Suddenly, the ice beneath him cracked, rumbled, and broke away. The truck's front end dipped and water rushed over the hood, sloshed against the windshield, the windows. Bud grabbed the handle, jerked it up, but the door was frozen shut. He threw himself against it; nothing happened. He lunged for the passenger door, yanked on the handle, slammed his feet against it. The door held fast.

Water had filled the rear of the dump truck and now it tilted back. Panic stampeded through him. He screamed and pounded his fists against the window. A rete of fine lines fissured the glass. He punched at it until his knuckles were bloody and the glass caved in, then swung around on his buttocks and knocked out the rest of it with his feet.

Water poured in through the window, water so cold that even his new skin didn't protect him. It chilled him to the core and just kept coming, coming, closing over his head. He scrambled up, coughing, sputtering, his teeth chattering uncontrollably, and lunged for the window.

But it was too late. The cold, black waters of the lagoon swallowed the truck like a hungry whale.

8.

Polly's pickup tore south on back roads, taking turns on two wheels that left Oliver's head reeling. When they reached the intersection with Route 16, she swerved onto it like she owned the highway, and only then did he look back.

Fire, all he saw was fire and smoke and the end of everything. He slid down low in the seat, hand tight around the .38, and stared straight ahead, the empty road rushing toward him.

9.

Six miles outside of town, Nash saw overturned jeeps and bodies sprawled along the side of the road, the remains of Fielding's quarantine barriers. Fifteen miles out, they passed a couple of burning police cruisers, more abandoned jeeps, more bodies. But Nash didn't begin to slow down until they crossed the Franklin County line, where the air seemed a couple of degrees warmer.

He checked the rearview mirror one last time just to make sure they weren't being followed, then swung onto the shoulder of the road. Horn took over at the wheel and Katie came up front to ride with him while Nash went into the back to be with Fay.

Her hands looked as lifeless as small birds in her lap. But the skin quivered, busy with its own affairs, as threads emerged from her palms, from between her fingers, from her knuckles, from her wrists. It was as if miniature people were inside her, unraveling spools of white, silken fibers, poking the ends through the eyes of invisible needles and shoving the needles up through her skin.

The bones in her face were shifting around: a ridged protrusion at her brow, a caving in at a cheek, the crown of her skull softening. Her beautiful hair fell out in bunches. The bridge of her nose seemed to recede, then snapped into a different position. The pain swept through her in waves, like contractions. When it crested, her mouth formed an O, her eyes rolled back in her head, and she wheezed and clutched blindly at his hand.

Then the pain receded and she was lucid. During those moments, they talked, although later he would be unable to recall specifically what was said. His thoughts had fluttered away from him, and his empty skull filled with other things. He couldn't have said what these things were, except that they were like photographs in a dream, sepia-toned, too hazy to see clearly.

When the fibers began to emerge from the corners of her eyes and mouth, from her nostrils and ears, he collapsed inside. He gathered her in his arms and set her down on one of the sleeping bags. Then he sat there helplessly with Samson, watching as the threads twisted around her body. They bound her arms to her sides, pressed her legs together, molded themselves to her hips and neck.

As the fibers poked through the crown of her head, he wept uncontrollably, his face pressed against the soft threads at her belly, his lips moving, mouthing the same words over and over, that he loved her, that he didn't understand, begging her not to do this, as though she had a choice. He lost himself in a derangement of grief from which he would never fully recover.

Her eyes, nose, and mouth were still free, and she never looked away from him. She whispered something he couldn't hear and he leaned closer.

"Promise me."

I can't: He screamed the words in his mind, but his head bobbed up and down, yes, yes, and he didn't know which was the lie.

Now the threads closed over her mouth, sealing it. Fibers packed her nostrils like gauze and twisted around her eyes, blinding her. In seconds, she was totally encased, except for the crown of her head.

Nash kneeled over her, touching the cocoon, stroking it, shaking his head. Small, frantic sounds popped from his mouth that weren't cries or sobs or even whimpers, but inarticulate expressions of emotions that whipped through him with the power of a raw, terrible wind. He hugged the cocoon, rocking it, gasping, "No, God, no," and felt her inside of it, legs drawing up, head dipping down toward her chest.

He stayed like that for a long time, the cocoon clutched against him as he rocked, rocked, and looked up only when he felt a hand on his shoulder. It was Katie, telling him what he had to do, gently easing the cocoon from his arms.

Together, they lifted the cocoon up toward the ceiling. Fibers shot out of the top of her skull and dug into the metal roof of the truck with the tenacity of roots into soil. The white gradually took on a patina of silver until it matched the cocoons next to it.

When Nash finally let go of it and stepped back, it swayed, a child's empty swing nudged by a breeze.

10.

They lost Horn the next morning. Nash and Katie buried him and Charlie in a six-foot drift deep in a pine forest somewhere in the Great Smoky Mountains.

Afterward, they remained for a few minutes, gazing at the makeshift graves, neither of them speaking. The bright winter sun filtered down through the branches of surrounding pines, creating stark, vivid shadows against the blinding white of the snow. He felt he should say something, a few words of eulogy, words that would comfort both Katie and himself. But he was as empty as a pocket.

"What now?" Katie asked finally.

"I don't know."

He sensed the change would spread with the erratic weather. It would infect other towns, and then it would invade cities, and always there would be the madness that had destroyed Lagoon, the delirium of crazed mutants, of armies, of people who weren't changing pitted against those who were. But the cocoons would proliferate. Some, like the three in the truck, would survive, and perhaps someday they would open into that unimagined future, transformed. Nash just hoped he would be around to see it happen.

He took Katie's hand, and they walked back through the woods and into the world.

About the Author

Alison Drake lives in South Florida. She is the author of TANGO KEY, FEVERED, and BLACK MOON.